MW00639386

ONLY
    HERE,
ONLY
    NOW

ONLY HERE, ONLY NOW

A NOVEL

TOM NEWLANDS

HarperVia

An Imprint of HarperCollinsPublishers

ONLY HERE, ONLY NOW. Copyright © 2024 by Tom Newlands. All rights reserved. Printed in the United States of America. No part of this book may be used or reproduced in any manner whatsoever without written permission except in the case of brief quotations embodied in critical articles and reviews. For information, address HarperCollins Publishers, 195 Broadway, New York, NY 10007.

HarperCollins books may be purchased for educational, business, or sales promotional use. For information, please email the Special Markets Department at SPsales@harpercollins.com.

FIRST HARPERVIA EDITION PUBLISHED 2024

Designed by Yvonne Chan
Photo on p. ii © Mike Goldwater/Alamy Stock Photo
Art © BNMK0819/Adobe Stock

Library of Congress Cataloging-in-Publication Data has been applied for.

ISBN 978-0-06-339345-5

24 25 26 27 28 LBC 5 4 3 2 1

For my mum, dad, and sister

ONLY
HERE,
ONLY
NOW

Part
One

MUIRCROSS,
1994

I t was the second day of the holidays and me and Jo were down the Causeway Field with nothing to do.

The swing park had been cut down when I was nine, so all you saw now was a wee scrap of tarmac with some stumps and a bin and a bench. I was sat there sweltering, picking my knees, squelching my toes inside the Reeboks. All you could hear were the waves and the flies and bees.

I'd had enough of *making the most of it. Getting fresh air.* I wanted to crawl to the Co-op, climb into their lolly freezer and slide the hatch closed over my head. I'd cuddle myself in, go crispy like a mammoth, lie there on the ice lollies until the bees got bored and the school bell rang and all the weekdays had their names again.

The park got used for drinking now and there were cans all over the grass—black cans, goldish cans, crumpled and stamped-on cans with manly names and stupid wee lightning-bolt logos. Saturday nights I'd hear it all from my room—idiots, running mad on the cider, head-locking one another, tonguing their fed-up lassies in the dark. Even with the duvet pulled right over my head I couldn't stop the noise of those Muircross boys.

But it was safer in the daytime, and it was just me and Jo now. I was watching Jo, stood out on the grass kicking blowballs off the dandelions, dog at her feet, arse-revealing hockey shorts on with that big custard-color tracksuit top that was her da's. Two pipe-cleaner legs poking out the bottom, like Big Bird. She must have been baking in that top. Reeking, like me. She had it zipped right the way up to her chin so I knew there were love bites.

That morning Jo and my mam had spoke to each other in that blatant way that told you something was up—they were shite at pretending. *How long will you be at the park, Jo? A good few hours at least, Maggie. Excellent, Jo.* A lot of sensible nodding, a lot of double-checking the wee unimportant things. I knew there had to be plans because my mam never asked my pals anything. And she never used words like *excellent*.

I'd kept my mouth shut because it was Sunday and that usually meant a treat. Never a proper present, like trainers or bangles or a belt, but sometimes a Swiss roll, or a heat-up macaroni, or a film out of Blockbuster with crying in it. My mam was in a wheelchair and that made everything a pain in the arse, so if she was doing me a treat she would need me out the house—*Away and get some fresh air. Stop being fizzy. Away out with Jo.*

Jo was twenty. She had curling tongs and she sometimes paid my bus fare, and growing up she'd had tons of boys in her room. She'd found a syringe once and touched it. When her dog had a phantom pregnancy she didn't cry because she knew that was the circle of life. She'd also got away to college—in Glasgow.

She'd babysat me when I was wee and she'd had her claws in my mam ever since. The pair of them were always scheming and gossiping, calling me a *pee-the-bed*, speaking about me like I didn't exist. My da died when I was four and the boyfriends came and went, and so my mam ended up depending on Jo. Sometimes you knew from Jo's face that she thought she was better than everyone, but my mam never seemed to see.

I sat back on the bench and thought about treats. What would I want the most right now? I don't mean skinnier fingers or a fancy house, just something naughty and stupid, like a cone or a cold Lilt. Chips and juice? Or a boy, maybe.

Not for the squeezing, or the love bites, just someone to sit with me on the hot grass and listen. A wee local boy in Nike or Ellesse with an unscarred face and a heart set on skipping this housing estate and vanishing, like me.

Jo's dog Bam-Bam waddled over and flopped down next to a Blackthorn can, panting, eyeing me sideways from the weeds with that wee bit self-pity and that wee bit suspiciousness that always got me right on edge.

Then Jo came over, fiddling with the leash, and dumped herself down. A minute of heat went by. I couldn't think of anything else, and Jo loved boasting about boys, so I said it.

"You got love bites then, Jo?"

"No," she went.

"Aye, you do."

"No, I don't!"

"Zip the trackie top down then."

She started patting Bam-Bam's knobbly head and telling her she was good. Bam-Bam was doing her sharky smile, slavering, looking all rascally.

Then Jo went, "Fuck off, Cora."

"You must be boiling in that top," I says. I only had shorts and a T-shirt on.

The park had houses round three sides and then the water. A garden radio was going somewhere. Jo stood up and got Bam-Bam on the leash, "Come on. Let's walk."

We started across the grass and I put my sunspecs on. They were lime green and creaky and crap and they were free from Boots and I was ten when I got them. It was a beamer to have to wear them.

Jo's sunspecs were those mad oval white ones with black lenses, like girl singers from the sixties. DKNY on the side, totally smudgeless.

Jo was long and thin and bendy with ginger hair in a center parting. It was chopped straight about chin height and it spread out from her face in two wavy wedges. She always had nice stuff, decent clothes. Jo stood out a mile.

"Don't tell me to fuck off, Jo," was the first thing I said as we walked.

"You're an annoying wee shite. You ask too many questions." She said it in that way that made it sound like you couldn't argue.

We left the park and walked down the steps onto the Causey road. The rubbly ground sloped down then dropped off quick into the Firth. Folk dumped stuff on the side of the road here and we would sometimes throw it over the low fence and into the water, for a laugh.

Today there were burst-open bin bags and a fake leather armchair. Bam-Bam was jerking Jo forward on the leash and flapping her ham tongue at everything spilling out those bags—onion skins, pill packets, coat hangers, own-brand beans tins. The whole heap was baking in the sun.

Jo tied her up. "Let's chuck that chair."

We tipped the sweaty chair up easy and flung it. It scudded off a rock and seagulls went up and then it bounced down and dropped off the cliff at the bottom, smashing into the waves with a faraway splash.

I wiped my hands on my shorts. "So you got a boyfriend now?"

"No. Why?" She untied Bam-Bam and held the leash in one hand.

"The love bites, Jo."

On her free hand she was nibbling her nails—Purple Crush, again. "There's no love bites."

"Zip the top down then."

"I don't want to."

Jo wasn't normally shy like this. I'd heard all her Glasgow stories—blue cocktails, night buses, rashes on her arse from the foam parties. Eating fried rice in graveyards with boys. Boys eating her in graveyards. She had so many stories. There had been so many boys.

We started walking. I went, "Remember Fozzy? You loved Fozzy."
She flicked her curls back. "Fozzy was good to me."

"Fozzy was a creep. He had no lips and his eyes were too close
together."

Jo brought Fozzy to my house once when my mam wasn't there
and it gave me the heebies. He tried to be nice to me but I hated his
bony arse being on my settee. I wanted things to go wrong for Fozzy
and Jo, and Jo had sensed it, and she got weird with me for ages after.
Fozzy did a bolt to Germany last summer and Jo was in bits. I secretly
smiled about it probably most days.

"When you grow up and get a boyfriend then you'll understand.
It's hard to find a decent boy. Even harder to keep them interested,"
she said.

"I'd never want a boy like Fozzy." I was itching and at my absolute
clammiest and I was winding her up on purpose now.

"Fozzy was from Glasgow. He had a motorbike. You'd be doing
well to pull a boy on a pogo stick. Get back to me when you've tongued
a boy."

"Aye, Fozzy had a motorbike but he was probably buying you wee
bits of heart-shaped jewelry, wasn't he? Probably doing smudgy pencil
portraits of Bam-Bam? What a beamer."

She tilted her head down and gawped at me over her sunspecs.
"Cora Mowat, you'd wash the sugar off a doughnut."

"What's that meant to mean?"

"That you're weird and you ruin things."

"I'm not weird!"

"I babysat you for three years. I've seen everything in your room.
I've read your diaries—August 1989, wasn't it? *I want to be a squirrel.*"

"That was a joke, Jo."

One time I told Jo about the sadness I felt when I saw abandoned
microwaves at the side of the road. She was drinking chocolate Yazoo
and she laughed so hard she spat it all down her brand-new crop top—

she wasn't even mad about the staining. After that I tried to be careful with what I was letting out in front of her.

The two of us sat down on the bench at the end of the Causey, by the brambles and the bin. If you looked left from here you could see onto our estate—gray boxy-looking houses that zig-zagged down the slope toward the water, jaggy and squashed like pensioner teeth. You could see the gardens that looked over the Firth, including mine, and the rows of low garages we sunbathed on before the tar and the barbed wire went up.

I'd spent almost every minute of my life here, at the edge of Muircross. It was a manky wee hellhole sat out by itself on a lump of coast the shape of a chicken nugget, surrounded by pylons and filled with moonhowlers and old folk and seagulls the size of ironing boards that shat over everything. Chaos and fighting and shite in your hair, that was Muircross.

There was one long road out. When you went up there on the 127 bus and glanced back from the top deck, the town looked like a handful of gray gravel chucked up the coast. Years back, coal mining had been the thing—*pits this, pits that, pits the next*. An old boy with a red nose and a lamp came to teach us about it in school, but that was at my most difficult time, so I wasn't really listening.

One thing you did learn growing up was the ways out—promises off men, the housing folk, the bingo winnings. Some people in Muircross got famous for their plans—they'd be full of it, bumping their gums about mad schemes and eyeing you like you were the shite on their shoe, until reality gave them a right good slapping. In Fife you saw the same faces over and over. Round here you lived in your town and then you died in your town.

"Sit up straight, Cora. You're giving yourself gigantic rolls of flab hunched over like that."

I didn't move. "See, the Firth makes me sad and dreamy at the same time," I went.

"Here we go."

I looked out over the water. It wasn't the snorkelly, blow-up croc-odile kind of water you saw on telly. You couldn't get into it because most of the land round here came to a stop with shopping trolleys and rubble. And it stank—it wasn't even salty or fishy, it was vile. I wanted to ask Jo if ocean could go out of date.

"I hate living round here," I says.

"People make their own lives."

After a wee minute I went, "Why are you still staying here?"

"Cos living at home is cheaper."

"If I was at college in Glasgow I'd get a flat there. I've seen it on the telly—shops and clubs that never shut. I'd be out enjoying myself, not sat here gawping at the shite-colored water."

"Well why are you still living here, smartarse?"

"Eh, 'cause I'm fourteen?"

"Still begging your maw for a move? Maybe the council's forgotten you." She started rubbing Bam-Bam's chest.

"We're going to Abbotscraig, me and my mam are on the waiting list. We're leaving this place. But I'm not stopping at Abbotscraig."

She cackled and made a face and did my voice. *"I'm not stopping at Abbotscraig."*

"How's that funny?"

"A chunky wee ratbag like you. Having dreams."

Over the water, the big factory, Riggs, was pumping huge clouds of smoke into the sky. I kept my eyes on it and bit my pinky nail and there was silence. Then I asked again because I couldn't not, "Who did that to your neck?"

She pulled the zip up at her chin without thinking. "Shut up, Cora."

"What's the big deal? Is he another wee smoothie like Fozzy?"

"No."

"So there is someone!"

"So what if there is? It's my business," she says, and I saw the sun glisten off her teeth as she said it.

"I'm going home," I went. I'd had that line planned for a while. It would bring out the real reason we were sat around out here. It would flush out my treat.

"You can't go home."

I sat there half in the shade of her. Her trackie top was flapping all huge in the wind. "Why can't I go home?" I says.

Then really quick and casual she goes, "Listen, I wasn't supposed to be telling you, but your maw's got a new man."

There was a clamping round my belly and a wee nettle-sting feeling moving upwards, inside. Everything got urgent so I looked at the ground to try and not give anything away. Slug tracks were sparkling in the sun like strands of fancy fabric. I started using the toe of my Reebok to trace one, dodging the dods of seagull shite, making a game of it.

"I knew there was a surprise!" I says. The words came out all pathetic and thin. "Is that why we're out?"

"He's making a meal for you and your maw. A welcome, for himself."

"Do you think he knows I'm vegetarian?" I goes, keeping the smile glued on.

"I really don't know." She looked so pleased. A groggy bumblebee was doodling in circles behind her. After some silence she went, "Is that all you're going to say?"

All the thoughts were coming at once and my brain couldn't make a sentence. I picked at the side of my thumb. "Liar," I croaked.

"You'll soon see."

Bam-Bam was scratching her eyebrow with her back paw. A gull was screeching. Bits of my hair were tangling themselves on my tongue. I plucked at them. I says, "My mam would have told me."

"She doesn't know how. She's getting him to do it. Haven't you noticed she's changed? She's happier, isn't she?"

I had no idea if my mam was happy or not. All I got off her was hassle—*stop zipping your zip, stop chewing your hair, away and tidy your midden you wee pee-the-bed.* How was I meant to know how happy she was? Was it my job to look out for stuff like this? Maybe if I'd paid attention she wouldn't have needed another man.

Jo's face was glossy with sweat behind the sunspecs. Her hair was the color of Fanta in the sun.

"Go home now if you want. I really don't care," she went, grinning all weaselly, doing a big huffy drama-shrug. "But don't say I didn't warn you! He's in your house. You'll probably catch them at it."

2

Aye, so. I had a job once, at Grahamston's, the yard in the town? You'll be too young to mind it, like. I was seventeen—hell's teeth, I was a raw laddie. Anyway, it was the boss Willy that gave me the name—*Gunner*."

My mam went, "Do you get it, Cora? *Gunner?*"

I looked at them.

Then Gunner went, "Willy used to say it was like I was taking aim, like." He moved his head sideways. His left eye socket was scrunched closed and there was no eyeball in there. "They called me Gunner, as in machine-gunner. The RAF?" He lifted his arms and shot an invisible gun at me.

"Ah, okay. That's really funny," I said, and ate a chip.

I'd come straight home from the park and found the pair of them putting out cutlery, giggling away like the best of pals. The cooking had taken hours so I'd sat up in my room, but we were all round the table now eating this food he'd made. It was one of the latest dinners ever.

He was a gangly-looking thing, head like a conker, hair shaved off, nose like a witch from a crap cartoon. Just the one eye. I wasn't going to stare too much because my mam was looking at me and I didn't want either of them to know that I was bothered.

"Use your knife, Cora. You enjoying it? Tell Gunner you're enjoying the food."

I swapped my fork into my left hand and picked up the knife. We were using the Argos plates. The last meal we ate like this was when Auntie Janine bought us the Singapore noodles after her wedding and my mam chucked it all up. It was before Auntie Janine turned against us—I was nine, I think.

"I'm really enjoying this, Gunner," I says, trying to chew and keep smiling in both their directions at once. I wriggled in my chair. My belly was gurgling. I felt totally full.

"That's cool, lass," he went, beaming.

He was in a cleanish orange T-shirt and looked maybe a teensy bit younger than my mam and there was a tattoo on his scrawny arm—Tweety Pie drinking from a wine bottle with his eyes X-ed out. Growing up I'd learned to keep an eye out for all the wee clues.

"I'm chuffed to meet you, like, Cora," he went. Then he turned to my mam, grinning more. "Your daughter's a wee smasher, Maggie. You've done a right good job, eh."

"Aww, thank you," she went.

They were eating spaghetti mixed in a fancy sauce he'd made from tins of chicken soup. He'd obviously been told I was a vegetarian so he'd done me a baked potato with oven fries. We all had Cresta from a bottle that was sitting in the middle of the table.

"That spaghetti's braw, Gunner. Where'd you get the recipe?" my mam goes, chewing.

"Back of the tin. The soup's concentrated. You just add milk and water, like."

"Amazing," she goes. "And the topping?"

"Crisps, doll. Scrunch them up, fire it under the grill, aye. Magic."

I ate a small, hard oven fry that almost cracked when I forked it.

I was mainly worried in case the men were dangerous. Gunner was a strange one. I could picture him being dragged down off a drainpipe by the police. As he sooked his spaghetti I held my fork in front of my eye so the prongs made little prison bars up and down his face. He looked right at home, but at the same time he'd baked me a potato and oven fries—I was actually eating them—and that was a skill. That was kindness. That meant he was already better than most of the boyfriends my mam had moved into our wee house.

First there was Dunc. Then Grant and his medicine. Then there was Ravey Davey, one minute our hero, the next minute *a scumbag, a rattlesnake, a big baw-faced bastard*. And then Terry. Terry looked like someone that would lock you in the coal bin and force you to eat paint. He drank raw eggs out my plastic Deep Sea World pint cup and had a broken rowing machine that got stored under my bed. His brother owned a timeshare but we never did get to Puerto de la Cruz. Mam had promised that Terry would be the last.

This lot were probably the best that Muircross had to offer—a bunch of kitten stranglers that loved our Trinitron and our family allowance but wouldn't give you the green stuff from under their fingernails.

When the breakups came, I'd put a wash on. I'd sit cross-legged on the lino and watch my pants spin round the glass, hypnotizing myself or maybe hiding in the noise. Sat there like a wee dumpling, maybe I was hoping that one of those men would at least remember I existed—that maybe I'd get a smile, or a head rub, a *good luck, Cora Mowat*, for me.

But I was only there to pick up the pieces—hugging my mam, putting Roy Orbison on, feeding her quiche as she ranted and raved and flung her arms about like the wee guy in the bin off Sesame Street.

"Cora, are you going to finish your baked potato? If you don't eat it now you'll be eating it tomorrow."

"I'm taking my time, mam."

She leaned forward. "You know Gunner's brought a present for you? Eat up and you can get it when you finish." Then she looked up at Gunner like a wee lassie and went, "Could you wheel me out to the phone box please?"

"Aye, no problem, doll," he says, rising up and wheeling her out from the table. She'd always told me she hated being called *doll*.

"Cora, grab me my Santa hat?"

My mam kept all her twenty pences in an old Santa hat left over from Christmas. I got up and found it down the side of the settee and put it in her lap. To be fair to Gunner he didn't look freaked out by any of this—it was like my mam had explained all the wee weirdnesses of our life to him.

When he shut the front door behind them I took the potato remains to the kitchen and binned them, then flopped onto the settee. My mam had gone to the bother of lighting a cherry candle and putting the radio on—it was Phase FM and they had the floor-fillers going. The music made me think of my pal Fiona's mixtapes, and those amazing Fridays when me and her would get a wee dance round the rug, if my mam was at the social and Jo was babysitting.

Sometimes it felt like I was trapped in myself, or like a quicker version of me was stuck in my body, but dancing fixed all that—I loved those nights because it was like my heart and my brain were in time with each other. I sat there on the settee trying to picture all that stupid carry-on happening in the same room where this one-eyed guy had fed me potato.

Then he came back in, alone. I did a grin but I had no idea where to put my hands, and I got that frozen feeling in me, like when you think you have a spider on you but you can't see it. Suddenly I was wondering what he thought of our living room, if it was tidy enough, if it smelled. Working out the smell of your own house is the hardest thing. *Ask Mam about potpourri*, I thought.

"All right, chief?"

"Hi!" I goes. He sat down next to me. Sunk in the cushions you could see how lanky he was—he was built like the men you saw hanging round the pool hall.

Nothing else got said. I was desperate to say it, so I goes, "You know she doesn't need to be wheeled about? It's an act. She can wheel herself."

"Ach, it's nice to be nice. Anyway"—he leaned round to face me—"your mam suggested me and you have a wee blather, explain a few things? She says you like a seat out on the back step, if the weather's all right?"

He stood up and I stood up, then I walked through to the kitchen in silence and he followed. There was mess everywhere from his cooking. I was praying my present wasn't going to be more food.

He stopped by the fridge. "On you go, I'll be out in a sec, eh?"

I switched the outside light on then sat down on the warm step. It was dusky and the sky was darkish-looking. Beyond the Swingball set and the back fence you saw the Firth and the North Sea sparkling in silence. There was an armchair bobbing out there somewhere.

"Right!" Gunner sat down next to me, but on the ground. It made our heads more level. He had an Argos side plate with two damaged doughnuts on it.

"Is this my present?" I took one, grinning.

He laughed. "No, just a wee treat."

I smiled at the doughnut and bit into it like I knew that. I felt like he was watching, so I couldn't chew in my normal way.

"I love doughnuts," he went, wiping sugar off his mouth.

Seeing him close he actually looked all right, even with just the one eye. He had cheekbones, and cute curly lines round his mouth when he smiled. Why wasn't he out doing young man things, dancing, downing cider in cars? What was he wanting with a mam who had a moany wee kid like me?

Right then I got the feeling he must have a few women on the go. For definite. I could picture them—nippy creatures in no-make coats pushing pigletty bairns in prams round the low flats, pouting. Probably calling him G.

He says, "So these phone calls. What's that about?"

"It's stupid. She phones a psychic hotline most days, for advice. This woman Moira tells her when her luck will change. What her destiny is, all that kind of thing."

"Sounds mental. How's she paying for it?"

"Family allowance, I think."

"Right," he went, pushing more doughnut in his mouth. Our voices sounded different outside and I wondered if he heard it too.

I says, "It keeps her happy. She goes out on a Friday to the social, and she gets her hotline most nights. That's about it. We're lucky we've got the phone box in front of the house."

"I suppose." He put the plate in the grass and brushed his hands together. "So how are you getting on at school, darlin'? Do you like the school, eh?"

"No." I stopped and thought of any extra things I could say about it, then I says, "I hate it," with a crinkled nose and a wee crap laugh.

"So what do you see yourself doing in the future, lass?"

Gunner had seen inside our house so he knew the type of folk we were and there was no point acting the wee idiot daydreamer. "I dunno."

He leaned in. "I was the same at your age. What school you at anyway?"

"District. Same as my mam."

"I went to District! Does Argyll still teach English?"

"That's unreal, I have Mr. Argyll! I'm always forgetting stuff. He hates me. *Late again, Mowat! Mowat, calm yourself! Mowat, organize your desk!* Those are his catchphrases."

"Argyll was a cunt," he went. He wasn't sorry for the word in how he said it or how his face was. And he was right. My heart went flimsy. I couldn't gulp.

"Aye," I whispered, wanting to repeat the word back to him, showing him that even though I didn't say it much I still knew it, that we could be pals because of this, but deciding, *Too fast, Cora.*

Then my mam came, wheeling herself round the side path. She had a shoebox on her knee that I just knew was my present so I looked down, because of the awkwardness of presents. There were dots of sugar and doughnut crumbles stuck in the laces of my Reeboks.

"Hello, Maggie doll," he went.

"That's me done on the phone. I'm going in to do Ceefax, but here, this is for you, Cora, from Gunner."

I stood up and took the box off her and then sat back down.

"Only a wee thing," Gunner says.

I flipped the lid back and scrumpled the tissue away—pink Asics. Soon as I saw them some of my nerves went—brand new, rubbery-smelling, spotless, with tags. They hadn't belonged to anyone else. I couldn't wait to see Jo's face.

"Oh wow! I love them!" I went straight over and gave my mam a hug.

"Go and hug Gunner. It was all his stupid idea!"

Gunner was sat with his arms out. I told myself it was okay and put the shoebox down in the grass. Then I walked over and leaned down and hugged him. He smelled like a stranger. His shoulders felt solid, like a tree, or the monkey bars.

"See you pair soon," my mam went, disappearing round the side of the house.

After a wee minute he goes, "So, your mam gave me the size. Do you like the color?"

I hated the idea of pink, but I nodded yes. Then I sat down again. There was a silence so I says, "Where is it you live?"

He looked at me funny. "I've been staying with a friend. Big Ally. In his garage. Just temporary, like."

"Do you not have a house?"

Then suddenly he goes, "Shh, listen." He was pointing at the sky.

I sat on my hands and looked up. It was getting near total black and there was nothing there—no moon, no patterns of stars. Then there was a noise—the weird soft noise of a bird saying something.

"What is that?"

"A hoolet. Hoolet's the Scottish word for *owl*."

"How can you tell without seeing?"

"My da taught me."

The trainer tissue hissed in the wind. I looked at him. Did people with shaved heads really know birds? I went, "So do you know other bird names as well?"

"Aye—paitrick, hern, cushat. There's loads," he goes. "My da was a miner, but he was a poacher too. We used to walk a lot, before he did a bolt."

"That sounds cool."

There was a pause. Then he goes, "You really like them?"

"Owls?" I went, trying to be funny.

"Trainers!" He rubbed his neck. "Like, it's no easy. You—I've never—there's never been a kid involved, eh."

Right away I just says, "What's that like then? Me being here?"

"Hopefully we can be pals, lass. Would you maybe want to go for a walk or something, sometime?"

I looked at him. I knew I wanted to go in—I was tired from the sun and the worrying, and the amount of potato. "Maybe," I says.

Then he put his hand on my shoulder. I felt like a big lump of nervousness underneath it, like I was sat there waiting to be crushed up like a cracker.

I was dying to wriggle but I grinned more instead. Was this all right? Was this him trying to be a da? Jo would know. Fiona might. When Fiona got back off holiday I'd be telling her the lot.

"It's been nice speaking to you, darlin'," he went, squeezing harder.

The owl had stopped. My calves were crampy from sitting the same way too long. I nodded. "Thanks for the doughnut and the potatoes. And for the trainers. And for telling me about the hoolet."

All I wanted was to put those Asics on—inside, alone in my room, where I could sit and think and look down calmly at myself and be myself in silence. Then after, me and my mam would sit up late with a big bowl of Space Raiders in front of the telly—we'd be wearing our jammies, breathing normal, not having to smile and pretend. And I'd still have the trainers on.

Gunner had spoke to me like he was my pal. He had used one of the worst swear words in front of me. He had made me feel like it was all right to speak, so without going over it too much I just says, "What time do you think you'll be heading home?"

Then he went, "This is my home."

3

Fiona was the year below me at District and me and her had met in the corridor—I'd be getting sent out of German for being me, and she'd be getting sent out of French for being her.

The two of us would sit by the vending machine at the top of the stair, blocking the coin slot with chewed-up jotter paper, doing Chinese burns, singing that song she loved, about the parrots. Classes were just pure shame for me, and who needed German anyway? Fozzy maybe. And Hitler.

Her family always went away the first week of the school holidays, but she was back the Monday after Gunner's move and I met her at the top of her road. She was stood in her roller skates eating a banana, wearing a crumpled neon tracksuit with her fringe stuck to her forehead in a row of oily upside-down question marks. Eye shadow on, again. Blue stuff. I did wonder who was letting her out like this.

There was a whole week of Gunner in the house to tell her about. The night of the potatoes I'd gone straight upstair and got my Always and my razor and my Salon Selectives out the bathroom and hid it all under my desk. Then I put the new Asics in the middle of my rug and lay on my bed sideways just gaping at them. It was like the more I thought about everything the more the newness and the pinkness seemed to be draining away.

I was already exhausted from grinning but I knew there was more to come—more potato, more rubbishy jokes, more wee chats with his hand on my shoulder calling me *darlin'* or *lassie* or *doll*. I was kind of an expert at dealing with these things—guessing men's moods, learning their footsteps, keeping myself calm when it was just me and him on the settee. But having another big guy stooping round the place made our wee house feel half the size it used to be.

Fiona was pale as a custard cream. I goes, "Was the holiday all right then?"

"The caravan smelled like school steak pie." She pushed off and started rolling. "Greenock's a shiteheap."

"It must be better than here?" I was jogging after, kind of clomping the Asics on the pavement, trying to make her see.

She zoomed ahead then she birled round and goes, "So, Cora! This latest da of yours, does he look like he sniffs the swing-seats then?"

"Fiona!"

"Am I not supposed to know? It was Jo that says. You know what she's like."

"A muntery wee gossip hound."

We crossed the road and started up the brae. At the top the air was pure and coolish and there were night puddles still. You saw glimpses of the Firth all round, stuck flat behind the houses like a bit of brown tape.

Fiona was clacking up behind me. I was panting, "Listen. First off, he's not my *da*. Second, no he doesn't look like he sniffs the fucking swing-seats. That's typical Jo. I wanted to tell you about him myself." I stopped and rocked on my feet, tensed my thighs a bit. "Anyway. Look what he got me."

She put her skates at angles and stopped. Streets away you heard workies clanking and mopeds going down the coast. "Jesus! He must be rolling in it."

"Brand new."

Fiona used words off telly like *asswipe* and *wicked* and when her cat Stevie was ill she gave him a saucer of Calpol. She even wore wool tights outside of the school once. I was best pals with the lassie but I wondered sometimes why I cared about her opinion.

Over the week I'd walked the Asics up the high flats and twice round the newsagent, and on Wednesday night me and some third-year girls had gone up the old Miner's Welfare and danced in the car park, then dropped half a paving slab through a skylight. The only damage was a single dot of bean-juice on the left laces, from last Friday's dinner. They looked amazing still. It was just hard to know how to feel about having them.

I'd worn them out again because me and Fiona had agreed I'd be asking Gary Grieve to the park. I'd asked five different boys for a date since starting at District and I'd got five different *nos*. Everyone knew. I couldn't wait to start fresh somewhere else—I'd speak slower, stand straighter, smile. I'd get my words out in order and I'd concentrate. There'd be different boys. Better boys. A way more fanciable me.

But Fiona had told me to keep trying and today was mainly her idea. *A good wee project*, that's what she called Gary Grieve, and I kind of got it. He worked in the Co-op and he had one of those hunky JCB chins, but he owned an anorak with a removeable hood and his head was shaped like a lightbulb. Plus, he took himself way too serious—I saw him practicing his own signature once in detention.

"You don't think my mam's new boyfriend buttering me up with trainers is weird?"

"What is it you're even wanting? All men turn out to be ratty eventually."

"Maybe someone decent?"

One of the wheels on her skate started chirping like a wee mad bird. "Cora, they're worth thirty-five quid at least. He must be loaded. Looks like your mam'll not need her place in Abbotscraig!"

"We're on the list, she's desperate for that downstairs toilet. Anyway, he's taken me for chips, twice. Without my mam. And she seems happy. If my mam's happy then maybe we can make a wee go of it."

She ate a bit of banana and chucked the peel in the hedge, then rolled away and shouted back, "Do you think this one will make you wash his quad bike, like Ravey Davey?"

"He doesn't have a quad bike, actually. He cooks. He makes us meals. He sometimes calls me *chief*."

"That's cute. Anyway, you nervous about Gary Grieve?"

"I think so."

"You'll be amazing. Be bolshy! Imagine someone's tied a skipping rope round your chest and is pulling you—it makes you walk confident. And show him those shoes. You always think the boy has the power, but he'll be shiting it too. Look at you, you wee fucking stunner. What boy's going to say no?"

We turned onto the path by the low flats. At the junction a man was drilling the pavement. The beeps went and we crossed.

"So was the move-in okay?"

"Gunner brought his stuff round the Tuesday night. His mate Jack helped. They used my mam's stairlift to get it all upstair. I had to help shove it all into my mam's wardrobe, in the drawers under her bed. Loads of it, in carrier bags. My mam ended up moving some into my room."

"Presents, maybe?"

I pictured the manky bags and boxes. "Could be. Anyway, his mate Jack has a car, and he picked us up and we moved all these boxes from Jack's house into a shed on another estate. Then after, Jack got us all pizza crunch suppers and we sat listening to his handheld radio. You tune in and listen to the police on it."

"What kind of car?"

"An Astra."

"Holy moly."

"It felt a wee bit weird, like. Moving bags about in the dark."

She winked at me. "Wait till he goes out. Then rake through it all in your own time."

The pavements in town were packed with old folk and druggies and lassies with prams, and you could smell all different types of frying from the cafés and pubs. The sun was out and it was roasting.

Yonks back, men fought battles over Muircross. There were olden buildings and a thing called the Muir Cross—where the maidens hung about—and that's why it got called Muircross now. Mr. Macfarlane taught us how the harbor was important four hundred years ago. It was crusted in sea-crap now and when the water went out you sometimes saw bald guys in anoraks measuring stuff down in the slime. Muircross boys dropped a shopping trolley on them once.

We crossed the road and stood outside the Co-op where the window at the front had a blown-up image of a lasagna covering it. Fiona tried a wee moonwalk in her skates while I moved around a bit, checking my reflection in the dark bits where the cheese had burnt. I was five-foot-nothing and glossy like a chicken breast.

I was never going to grow into one of those babes you saw stroking Porsches on the telly—I was a wide-hipped girl with crumbs in her bed. Did I make up for that with an arse-licking personality and a push-up bra? Not really, no, but standing there thinking about it was only going to make everything worse.

I strolled through the sliding door into the cool shop picturing the skipping rope round me. It was a tiny crappy Co-op with only a couple of staff, but I'd never seen the boy behind the counter before.

Fiona rolled next to me, whispering, "That's not Gary Grieve!"

"Gary always works a Monday in the holidays," I says.

"Maybe he's ill?"

I felt like I wanted to bolt. Then the tall boy went, "Can I help you lassies?"

Fiona leaned forward onto the counter and started flapping her eyelashes. "What's your name then?"

"Dennis."

"That's a luscious name," she goes, all squeaky.

It felt like the noise of my breathing was getting played over the shop Tannoy. Then she suddenly says, "Dennis, do you want to go to the park with my pal Cora Mowat?"

I felt like someone had shot an arrow in me, but not in the romance way. I swiveled quick on one tiptoe, firming up the flab in my thigh, posing the Asics a bit, trying to seem clean and female and normal and wantable through the racks of Juicy Fruit and Tic Tacs.

My right eyelid was spasming. I needed a pee. He looked into me. "I dunno. How old are you?"

"She's sixteen!" Fiona was giggling.

Dennis says, "Just me and you, Cora, aye?"

I tilted my head down and looked up at him through my eyelashes, like sixteen-year-olds do, and felt my chin-flab doubling. "Think so," I went, foxy as I could.

He flicked his fringe out of his eyes and went, "Aye okay, I suppose." *Aye okay, I suppose.* It sounded amazing. "How about Friday night? I've got my provisional, I'll pick you up?"

Fiona's eyes went like bin lids. I took a huge breath. "Aye? Okay, brill! I'll be at the bus shelter! Top of Viewpark Terrace. Maybe?"

"Fine. Eight o'clock?"

"Aye."

"Amazing!" Fiona goes, dragging me through the sliding doors. "Wicked!"

Outside, buses were hissing through the heat. Fiona put her hand up and we high-fived—that was the kind of thing Fiona loved to do.

"Easy-peasy."

"Fiona! Who the fuck is he?"

"He's got a car!"

We sat on the bench by the postbox. Over the big square harbor seagulls were floating like kites against the grim drifty clouds from Riggs. "You said I was sixteen?!"

"Well he's seventeen."

"You've set me up with a stranger and he's three years older than me!"

"His mum's a teacher. My big sister got her in P7. The family's loaded."

My brain started doing that usual thing of jumping ten chapters ahead at a million miles an hour, but for a change it was positive. Me and this Dennis, driving the road out of Muircross in his car, proba- bly a big sporty one, removable roof, "Insanity" by Oceanic giving the cows the heebies. Gary Grieve was a looker, aye, but there was no way Gary Grieve had a car—Gary Grieve had velcro trainers.

"He seemed so tall. I'll see his proper clothes on Friday. I'm guess- ing he won't turn up in the Co-op polo."

Then she went, "We gonna go back in and get a drink?"

I was about to say we should go down the Savoy plaza when a voice, calmer and older, went, "Hello, Cora."

I looked up. It was Samantha the school nurse. She was standing in a yellow flamingo-pattern dress, with her boyfriend, Jay. The pair of them looked so clean and healthy, like they'd been snipped out the Freemans catalogue and sellotaped down in the wrong town.

"Oh hiya," I went.

"Cora, you're purple, pet, are you okay?"

"Just a bit warm."

"So how are you getting on? Weather's amazing, isn't it?"

No, I thought. "Aye," I says. "Me and Fiona were going to go to the Savoy, for juice."

Jay tapped Samantha's arm and nodded at the Co-op, then went off toward the shop. Jay had flame tattoos and a tree-trunk neck—he was famous in Muircross for smashing melons with his head on *Record Breakers*.

"Jay and I are off to Glasgow, to the cinema," Samantha said. "You ever been to the big Odeon in Glasgow, Cora? Renfield Street?"

"Never been to Glasgow, no."

Then she leaned in with her cute sharp bob swishing forward, and I smelled a lipsticky smell off her, and she went, "Listen, did your mum manage to make that appointment for you? The thing we chatted about on the printouts, before the holiday? We've not got a number for you at the school."

I couldn't move. I wanted to complain about how she'd said it. How loud she'd said it. How she'd said it outside the fucking Co-op. It was just classic Muircross. Round here you dropped your Mr. Whippy and the whole fucking estate found out before the ants had even tasted the flake.

I did a chuckle. "Aye, she did. Thanks."

Then Jay walked back over with a carrier bag of cans and crisps, rubbing his face with his palm like he was sick of kids. A tatty seagull started prancing round the postbox, one bent wing going like a window wiper.

It was like my lie was floating there between us in a speech bubble. I shuffled my damp arse, then Samantha said something else, and before I worked out who was going where, or what had really been said, they were gone.

There was tingling round my skull. Techno in my ribcage. My pits were fucking reeking. I wanted to fly up like one of those brightly colored pricks in a comic and punch that sun square in the fucking face.

I closed my eyes. I breathed. I could picture it—me, in a grown-up life, away from this shite. On my own two feet, with stuff to do, and a job. And a man. On a motorbike maybe? Or maybe a motorbike of my own?

A life in a place where nobody knew my name, or read my diary, or came up with explanations and printouts about me. No psychics, no boyfriends, no council waiting lists. No *how you getting on, pet?* No big plug-licking bastard of a stepda leaving his pubes on the soap and feeding me potato and lies.

Fiona goes, "They bought a shitload of crisps!"

I looked at her sideways. She says, "Sometimes I open two packets in the kitchen, in secret, then I pour one into the other so my mam thinks I'm only having one. It's wicked!"

"Amazing, Fiona." I shut my eyes so tight the sparkles were starting. "Absolutely wicked."

4

My mam was on her seventeenth twenty pence—I was counting. She goes, "But do you see any cash on my horizon, Moira?"

We were sat out in the phone box together. The rain was bucketing. It had started after me and Fiona got to the Savoy and had basically kept on all night—we were supposed to be having a summer but the sky outside was the color of slush.

I was chasing the droplets down the plastic window with my pinky, tracing them round the old graffiti—scratchy-looking cocks and balls and jaggy hearts and names from my mam's day like *RAB* and *YODSY*. "There are opportunities ahead," I heard Moira saying. Her words were thin and crackly in the handset and they mixed with the rain sounds outside.

The Amazing Moira was my mam's favorite psychic. My mam asked her the same old questions—about men, money, the future, her cholesterol. It made me feel sad to think, but sometimes I did wonder what it would be like to just have a normal mam.

There were good bits. Unlike most Muircross mams she was pretty—her skin was pale with no plooks or scars, and she had cheekbones. She had the same ski-slope nose that I had, but maybe age ten I realized a lot of my features probably came from the side we never spoke about.

My mam couldn't reverse her chair properly into the phone box, so when it rained I would sit on her knee and hold an umbrella to cover her legs. I was too old to be sitting on her knee but it let me help her with something. And it gave me time to think. I was never sure if that was a good or a bad thing.

I'd only said about five words to Samantha but I couldn't stop replaying them. She'd helped a lot of folk in school—my classes were filled with lassies and boys who couldn't shut up and toe the line and she didn't want me getting expelled like them. She'd been a help to me too, but it annoyed me sometimes because she spoke about my life like I could just choose different.

I wanted to say to her, *My name's not* Melody *or* Beth. *My mam never kept cereal in plastic tubs. None of my clothes were OshKosh anything. In winter I took the shower gel to bed to warm it up for morning.* Round here the options for lassies like me were school or a baby, shelf-stacking or shoplifting, gin on the Shreddies or tongue in the socket. I wanted my own proper future, but I wasn't choosing it the way other folk could.

Samantha saw I was sometimes struggling. She says to me I should be getting checked for anxiety, and for being hyper. Samantha never had a life like mine but when I read the printouts she gave me it was like she knew me inside out. It was just a couple of photocopied sheets stapled together but reading it I felt like maybe everything wasn't my fault after all.

I was supposed to ask my mam to make an appointment for after the holidays, but my mam's life was already full of shite that when I grew up I would never do—ringing helplines and going on waiting lists. Opening envelopes. Crying. I didn't want to give her more hassle. I didn't want to be sounding like a *wee pee-the-bed*.

"Thank you, Moira. So will my aura improve if I buy these supplements you're talking about?" She did the hand movement so I held up the Santa hat. She grabbed a couple of coins and shoved them quickly in the slot.

"I'm hungry," I says.

She did the angry *shush* face at me and put a finger in her open ear. The phone box was one of the things my mam had been obsessed with—it had taken her two years to get the council to lower the phone so she could dial it easier.

"And do you think a different diet might bring more success?" She nodded along with Moira all smiley then said thank you quickly twice and then hung up. Then she did a moody face.

"I'm starving," I went. "Do we have soup?"

"Look, Miss Fizzy, don't you speak to me when I'm on with Moira. It's a waste of money if I can't hear the advice, pet."

"I've had no breakfast. My knees are soaked. I'm starving."

"Let's go inside."

I ran ahead with the umbrella as she wheeled herself through the swish of the rain, then I bumped her up the steps. Our house had a gray face and sneaky eyes and our front door was black. The only colors were the crap red concrete toadstools that Terry had bought and painted for her, on one of his good weeks.

The house was dim inside. In the kitchen, through the back door glass, the Firth was all wild and the Causey was blank and the rain was two types at once. I stared out and thought about Dennis. I'd spoken to him only for maybe a minute but he was already helping me escape.

"There's no soup," my mam said from the doorway. "But put some noodles on. Top cupboard. I'm sticking the telly on."

My mam was mainly good at frying eggs or doing crisp sandwiches. Her other meals were honestly rank—Auntie Janine used to say that even wasps wouldn't land on my mam's cooking.

"I can't make noodles, Mam."

She closed her eyes in that careful way, "Cora, shush! Moira is sending me wavelengths."

I stood and watched her, wondering if this kind of stuff went on in other houses. I says it again, "I can't make noodles, Mam."

She opened her eyes and flung her head back, sighing. "You are some lassie, Cora Mowat. Get the noodles down. Find the smallest pan."

I did what she asked as she wheeled herself up to the cooker.

"Right, boil the kettle," she went. I filled it and clicked the button and we looked at each other while it started rumbling. I hated doing tasks while other folk watched—it was a different-feeling pressure to anything else, like when magnets won't touch.

"Where's Gunner?" I asked.

"Out earning. He's got business. In Edinburgh."

"What sort of business?"

"All you need to know is that he's looking after us. He's getting me some things in the next few weeks. Things that the council turned us down for."

"Like an electric tin opener?"

"Be a smart aleck if you like. I've needed one for years."

The kettle was growling now, drowning out the pecking of the rain on the window. "What does he do?"

"He's an independent trader. Now put the ring on. Number six."

I thought about the bags and boxes in my mam's room as she held up the packet of instant noodles. "Now, these are not the best. These are the Panda ones. The best ones have the Dragon holding a wok on them. But these are braw all the same."

"Chicken?"

"Flavoring, Cora. They'll not start clucking. First, take the brick of noodles and the powder sachet out, then chuck the packet away."

I flipped the bin lid up and chucked it in. "Do you think Gunner could fix our shower curtain?"

"Not a clue. Now pay attention, the ring is hot. Put the empty pan on the ring for a minute, it will heat up and the water will boil quicker when you put it in." She put the pan on the ring, raising herself up to see what was happening from down in her chair. She started grinning. "Aw, Cora, I'm hunky-dory with these. I love them. I'll tell you what, they're beezers for a rainy day like this."

"You're easily pleased."

"Listen, enough of your cheek. Now, look at the state of this place. When I'm at the social on Friday night I want you tidying this kitchen."

"I'm busy on Friday night!"

"Busy?! Throwing shite off the Causey? Cora, what did I say to you? The three of us are to be a team. Everyone's to turn over a new leaf. You're cleaning this kitchen on Friday, madam."

I did my moodiest mouth. "Right."

"Look, pour the water in." She wheeled herself back while I poured it in. The water started gargling as it hit the hot pan. "Brilliant. Now empty the powder in the water and grab a fork and stir, then lay the noodles flat in there."

I did what she said, then took a step back and started fiddling with the alphabet magnets on the fridge.

"Now, they should sit for two minutes, then you turn them. Soften each side, you see? I hope you're remembering all this. When you get your own place you'll be able to make these for yourself!"

"I am, Mam." We both stared into the noodle steam like it was hypnotizing us. I spelled out FLAPS on the fridge. I says, "So when's Gunner back?"

"I'm not sure."

"He seems nice," I went, to keep her speaking.

"He is nice." She said it quiet, and didn't look up from the pan. "He's going to start taking you on walks. Regular."

"To the chippy again?" I did BALLS with the letters.

"No, proper walks. Just you and him. You'll have to ask him where." Behind my mam, along the top edge of the flaky window frame some wee droplets were shimmying, ready to drip. She goes, "The pair of you seem to get along."

"The Asics are cool. He seems all right."

She reached over and shook the noodle pan. "I sense a *but* coming."

"I want him to get to know me. Like, I'm fourteen now, I've got my own ideas. I was younger before with Terry and stuff. I don't want you telling Gunner all my beamer stories."

She laughed. "*My own ideas.* And what do you mean *beamer stories*?"

"Don't ruin it telling him stuff about me when I was wee. Making fun of me. And don't tell him I have a diary."

"What stuff?"

"How I used to be afraid of Miss Piggy. The time I found the bottle of lemonade in the hedge. When I tried breakdancing. The fizziness. All the usual stories."

"You were a good wee breakdancer."

"Mam."

"Cora, are you worrying again? I'm not going to bring a man in here who isn't nice. I know you were upset in the past, with what happened with Dunc and Terry. But Gunner is a way better man than that pair. I guarantee that, pet."

"I see that," I says. I wasn't lying. I looked at the pan. "Can I turn the noodle brick?"

"Aye."

I flipped it. "Does it look all right?"

"Softening up nicely," she went. "Anyway, don't you worry about Gunner. He's my problem. And listen, this time you need to make more effort too. You're older now. Open up a bit." Then there was a silence where I was supposed to respond but the rain spoke instead. Then she went, "You don't see Jo as much these days. You pair not going on the buses anymore? She's always good for a gossip."

"Gossip gets boring."

"Maybe you should find some different pals then? Listen, at your age I was out all day and all night. By the time I was sixteen I'd been to gigs in Paisley and all sorts! I'll never forget, right"—she moved round to face me—"1980, Altered Images, in Edinburgh. Oh, Cora, I was braw. I had this dusty-blue Crimplene blouse, and my hair cut short and styled up like wee Clare."

"Who's wee Clare?"

"Clare Grogan! Altered Images. Tanya always says I looked like her. What a magic night that was, I had the time of my life—me, Tanya and Saskia. Of course, two weeks later I met your da. And that was my life over."

"It was easy for you. You were pretty and popular. You never loved bread the way I do."

"*Easy?* In a wheelchair? In the eighties? It's not about how popular you are, not when you can't get on a train. Not when you're getting called a cabbage and a spaz in the street. You're a right idiot sometimes, Cora Mowat. Pass me that tea towel."

I handed it to her. I says, "Jo goes to foam parties," just to change the subject. "At college. It sounds amazing!"

"Foam parties?"

"A normal disco but they pump foam in, like Matey or whatever. Jo met Fozzy at a foam party. Jo meets all the boys there. Do you think you get wet at a foam party?"

"I'll need to speak to Gunner. See if me and him can go to one."

"You're thirty!"

"Your mam's still got moves." She started rocking herself back and forward, shimmying left and right with the tea towel in her lap. "Now come here!" She pulled me round and I wheeled her back and forth a bit over the lumpy lino while she waved her arms and wiggled in the chair.

My mam always tried to drag me into dancing and it was a right beamer, but it was nice too because those were the times she smiled. I squeezed round next to her, watching how she closed her eyes as she sang whatever tune she was singing to herself.

Then she blinked them open. "Ah, but keep stirring! Fuck sake, you'll burn the arse out of them, you stupid lassie!"

I grabbed the fork and poked the noodles. The straggly top layer was fine but underneath they had gone burnt and brown and wouldn't come off the bottom of the pan.

"Fuck sake," she whispered, all scowly. She grabbed the pan and took a bowl out and used the fork to scrape the noodles into it. "My last packet of the Panda brand. Why can't you do anything without getting fizzy? Pay attention, lassie! These aren't cheap!"

The first thing I thought was, *Yes they are*. Watching her tutting and huffing I started to wonder what was happening inside her head. I hated her, sometimes.

Was it wrong to imagine rolling my mam into the sea? I looked through the wet window at the Firth. I'd pictured it so many times it never even felt like a fantasy—she'd drop off the edge of the Causey and I'd wait for the plop, then I'd walk back and use all her twenty pences to order an eighteen-inch margherita from Fusco's, extra cheese. I'd make a den up on the settee and get Phase FM on and I wouldn't wash my hair for a fortnight. And then I'd change the locks and there'd be no more men.

She shoved the bowl at me—a wee slop of noodles the color of highlighter pen with burnt bits squiggling through. "Finish those," she went, sighing off into the living room.

"Thanks!" I went, all cheery.

"You being sarcastic, you cheeky wee shite? On Friday you can practice making them again by yourself, after you've cleaned the kitchen. What kind of fourteen-year-old girl can't make food for herself? You really need to start pulling your weight."

When it got like this between us I knew her music always helped her calm down. I walked through after her. "Can we put a record on, Mam?"

"I'm putting the snooker on."

"'Tracks of My Tears'?" I went. "Or 'Raglan Road'?" I tasted a fork-ful of the salty noodles.

"You can put Lena on," she went, pulling herself onto the settee.

I forked up all the remaining noodles and chewed them down. My mam only had about fifteen records, and Lena Zavaroni was always near the front. She was obsessed with her.

"Nice and loud," she goes.

I pulled the record out. Lena looked up at me from the dusty carpet with her naughty-boy bowl cut. The album crackled and the house was dim. I saw the silhouette of the artificial ferns in the window, the telly, the doilies, the ornaments. Everything in exactly the place it had been for years.

I got up and put my bowl in the kitchen sink. In the living room my mam was singing along, then shouting through over the top of wee Lena, she goes, "Cora, there's a new Spot the Ball slip in the bread bin, bring it through and we can have a go while we're listening."

Out the window the rain had gone soft and a wimpy wee rainbow was stretching over the Causey. It looked like it had been scribbled across the gray with dried-out felt tips—all the colors were in it, like the puddles at the petrol station.

"Cora Mowat, you're a funny one, but I do love you, pet. Gunner tells me that business is on the up—so don't be worrying, eh? It's all falling into place—"

I stuck my leg out behind me and kicked the kitchen door shut because I'd heard it all before. *"This is our year,"* I whispered. "This is our year!" she shouted, muffled by the door and by Lena and by the last gray swishes of rain.

5

Before me and Gunner left on our first walk my mam says all
the usual—*behave yourself, stay calm, keep your hair out your
mouth*—but she'd also sat me down and explained how she
wanted me to speak and share things.

I suppose she wanted us to try and be wee walking pals and it made
sense—if we were going to make an actual family me and him would
have to have something in common that wasn't her.

We were silent at first. The weirdest thing was going from seeing
him squeezing round the house to being outside in the open with him,
alone in the air and daylight. We weren't just dodging to the chippy at
teatime or out in Jack's car—you got a proper look at how he walked,
like a big gawkit Pink Panther with a rod up its arse.

We went up through the town and out past the bus depot, then
over the footpath that took you round the old posh houses with the
gravel. Soon we were passing the sign with the pellet-holes that wel-
comed you to Muircross—it was the furthest I had ever been on foot.
My belly was going but it felt like the further away we got the easier it
was for me to speak to him.

I says, "So did your da take you walking like this?"

"Eh?" He shrugged the rucksack up his back, then looked down at
me. I could tell he'd been in a different thought, and I had broken it.

"Aye, he taught me loads when I was wee, but I never really knew my da growing up. He put me in care. When I was eight, like."

"In care?"

Gunner did a half-smile. "My da drank a lot. He slapped me and he slapped my maw. In the end my maw walked out and my da couldn't cope, so he put me in a children's home. It was different then. You got dropped on the doorstep."

"That's terrible."

"Ach, I was out by age twelve. Making my own way."

We walked again for maybe five minutes of silence. The land was starting to fold out around us, all sunny and green. "Why did your da slap your mam?"

"Who knows? He'd been in prison. Never spoke about it—you called it *doing your number* back then, you didn't advertise. That's just how he was, eh."

"Maybe there's two sides to everybody?"

He laughed. "Maybe."

I smiled, trying to hide my nerves. He pointed off toward some dark bushes that were going up over the hill, where the land went down into the water. "Anyway, look. I'll teach you a wee bit. What's that over there?"

"A hedge."

"It's called broom. April to June that will be bright yellow. We're in July now so the yellow's off the broom." Then he was walking quick again.

I looked out over the fields, over the water, trying to make sense of how bright and empty everything was. I was still expecting to hear a voice or a bottle breaking, then to turn and see in the distance some topless idiots all stumbly from the cider and sun, lighting fires and leathering fuck out one another. But the land was huge and there was only me and him in it.

It felt exciting when he spoke to me. I was wearing the Asics. Now he was going on about teaching me things. Me and him had already spent more time together than I had with my mam's other boyfriends and it did feel sometimes like we could be pals. Maybe mam was right, maybe I could open up more. Maybe I could even tell him about Dennis.

"Love comes in all different ways and you can't choose your family," I goes. It was something Jo had said to me. I could feel my face going pink but he was beaming so I kept going. "Are we going to be a family?"

"Aye, as long as you're helping your mam, like. That's the main thing."

"I'm cleaning the kitchen tomorrow night."

He turned and looked at me. "Your mam gets stressed dead easy, you know. She loves you a lot, Cora, but she's struggling right now, like."

I wondered how he knew all this and what I was supposed to do about it. "It's not easy between the two of us, sometimes. But I'll help more."

We breathed for a minute together. Through the haziness the town looked tiny in front of the electrical pylons and all the manky smoke spreading up from the chimneys at Riggs. My mam was in that wee scrabble of gray houses somewhere, maybe on her third or fourth coffee, maybe listening to Lena, or Clare. I could see it clear, almost like I was looking through a telescope. I didn't want her to be struggling.

"Can you maybe fix our shower curtain?"

"Aye."

"That would be amazing." I smiled, then after a wee second I went, "So before you were eight your da taught you stuff. Then after, did you never want to do anything else?"

He laughed. "I grew up on the streets. School wasn't for me. The home wasn't for me either, eh."

He started walking ahead again, faster now. I could feel my heart work more as I tried to keep up. After maybe twenty minutes we were high up at the edge of the woods. I was panting like Bam-Bam.

One time in primary school Mrs. McMillan had let the whole class go on top of the Portakabins to watch the Red Arrows flying over from Leuchars, for the Queen. I was shiting myself to climb up but my pal Lesley helped. I wasn't bothered about planes but from up there you could see all round Fife—the whole brown, glittery Firth and the big red bridge. Mrs. McMillan pointed out Culross, Kincardine, Bo'ness, the castle at Blackness. I'd seen these woods as a big, dark, faraway shape, and now I was almost in them.

We stood by the fence. Behind us was a big stretch of railway line, like a string curving round the coast. Soft clicking started and there was a train—crawling all slow with the sun flashing on it. We were close enough to see the faces of the passengers, all thinking about their own wee things. Some were reading, some were chatting, one or two were looking out at us.

"Gie them a wave, chief," Gunner says.

I waved a bit at first, and then jumped up and down, flapping my arms. Gunner joined in, grinning like a big idiot. The train folk seemed too grumpy to wave back.

"Cunts," I went, as the train disappeared.

He was grinning. "Cunts."

He turned and stood on the wooden fence step. He got one foot over, straddling the wires with his gangly legs, then put a hand out for me.

There were some things I still didn't understand about Gunner, but I knew his hands were good. They were big and simple, and scratchy and soft at the same time, like ancient towels. You could see the power in them from just the three or four bones that bulged through the back, hard like pebbles, and white when he held your hand.

He hopped down into the longer grass of the brand-new field, then pulled me up over the fence and guided me down beside him. It wasn't a proper lift, but I couldn't think of a time an adult had got me off the ground like that. I was way too old for getting picked up, but he didn't know that—he'd never tried to act the da before.

We crossed the corner of the field, then walked further up a grassy track. There was a gigantic flat bit of long grass with a view of the dark water through two big patches of trees. "Let's get our lunch here," he goes, and we both sat down.

He got the food my mam packed out of his rucksack—a packet of dry roasted peanuts, a baguette, a Curly Wurly and four cans of Lilt. He broke the baguette in two in his hands and gave me half and it was warm from the sun.

We were still a wee bit away from the actual forest but you could already feel the different air that was blowing out, all cool and damp. The noise of the birds seemed different—squeaks and beeping and longer, angry scrawing noises.

"How's the legs?"

"A wee bit achy, but I'm okay."

"We'll get you up to speed."

Big marshmallowy-looking clouds were unfolding at the faraway edge of the Firth and moving slowly in. A mega gust came here and there that would make the grass flat, or comb it about. My hair was flapping but it was amazing to eat out under the sun, to be sat on grass I didn't know. No cans, no broken bottles, no shouting.

"Listen. What's that?" he went. "No looking!"

"A seagull."

"Brilliant. But we call it—"

"A pewl."

He put his hand up for a sideways high five and I slapped it, hard-as. It wasn't pathetic like when Fiona did it. He went, "*Pewl.* Don't let those arsehole teachers tell you different."

He opened the Curly Wurly and folded it a few times until the caramel came apart in long melty strings. As I sat there with my Lilt I was calmer than I thought I'd ever be with a stranger. Like my heart was on holiday. Like I wasn't with a stranger at all.

"I had a dream about you, Gunner."

"Oh aye?"

"Well, not only you. The three of us. We were on a cruise ship. I'm not sure where but it was warm and the sea was blue. My mam was enjoying it. The ship had ramps and she was getting around fine, and there was even a ramp to the pool area. Mam spent the whole cruise at the side of the pool, drinking cocktails, while me and you explored the ship together."

"What did we find?"

"Nothing much! We went round and round looking at every part of it while you explained how things worked. Our settee was there, in our room. We didn't really do much. Then I woke up. What does that mean?"

"Well, I can't read dreams, lass. Maybe you should get on the phone to Moira?"

He was smiling. It was weird hearing someone talk about the things that just me and my mam knew. He stood up and brushed himself off so I did the same. Then he turned and crouched in front of me. "Jump on."

"Eh?"

"I'll give you a piggyback for a wee bit, like. You take the rucksack."

I slipped the warm rucksack on. He grabbed both my legs under the knee and took my weight as I cuddled my arms round his neck. On the back of his head I saw pale wee lightning bolts where healed-over scabs had stopped his hair from growing.

"I think my dream was about the fact my mam doesn't have ramps at home. She's always angry at the council."

"I'm fixing that."

"That's one of the reasons my mam wants a house in Abbotscraig."

He shunted me comfy on his wide shoulders. "Abbotscraig?" The wind was cool and all the usual feelings of wanting to be in someone else's life were gone.

"My mam's got us on the council list. The house there has got ramps and a downstairs loo."

"But you don't want to go?"

I looked around. Everything seemed new—the wide land, the waves pushing in, the big gangly pylons striding up over the hill. It was like I could say whatever I was thinking. "You asked before about seeing myself in the future. It's like—I don't dream of living in Abbotscraig, but it must be better than here? There's things to do, at least. That's what I want, things to do. Decent shops. Opportunities!"

"For what?"

"I speak to the school nurse sometimes. She's always saying take things step by step. Maybe if I could get to somewhere like Abbotscraig, then I can think of a next step. Maybe like, Glasgow? Pals and a job, in a big place like that! And fun, parties and stuff, without all these wee Muircross beasties ruining your life."

"You don't want much!" He stopped and crouched down, and then he took my wrist and guided me off and round onto the ground in front of him. "That council are a shower of useless fucking bastards. But I'll fix the house for your mam."

I goes, "Her heart's set on that house in Abbotscraig." It wasn't totally true, but it was true enough. The grass whipped back and forth again and the strange-sounding birds were going mental in the tallness of the woods. I tried to breathe like I was breathing before.

"Cora, I know your mam. She understands reality. Me and you and your mam, if we're going to try and be a wee team, or make a proper family, well—someone's going to need to pay the bills, eh. My business is in Muircross—my reputation's here, my customers are here. Aye, I'm out and about but this is where the deals get done. You know your mam's benefits have changed."

"Have they?"

"Aye. Look, you'll get your job and your parties and all that, but you're just a wee lassie now. You're not really sure what you want. But listen, there's no chance we're moving anywhere. Not now. Specially not Abbotscraig, eh."

I looked up at the birds that were floating in circles. Did these seagulls never get a fucking rest? "How come?" I says.

He laughed. "You never heard of the Gillespies? They run the place. I can't show my face in Abbotscraig."

I'd never heard of the Gillespies, but I didn't care. I took a big breath and looked him right in the eye. "What is your business, anyway?"

He laughed, louder this time. "You're a right nosey wee thing, aren't you, darlin'?" Then he turned and started walking, kicking the weeds, taking the path that curled up and away from the coast.

6

I hardly slept because my legs were aching from the walk, but also because of the big grimy feeling of hopelessness that was thumping in me like a toothache.

I knew Gunner and my mam had been speaking about me next morning. My mam was all cheery, asking for help with her nails for the social that night. Doing my mam's nails meant one thing—*sit still in front of me while I tell you some difficult shite you don't want to hear.*

"You'll trip over that lip of yours if you're not careful."

"I'm fine."

We were sat down the bottom of the garden. I'd helped her out of her chair and onto the rug and we were facing the water.

"Cora Mowat, I know you inside out. I've not seen a lip on you like that since the day with oh, what was the lassie's name again, Jane McEwan's daughter?"

I sighed. "Rhiannon?"

"Rhiannon McEwan!" She already couldn't talk for giggling. "Rhiannon McEwan had said to you, this was primary four I think, you were only wee. She had said to you, *Cora, there's a new girl started in primary five, her name's Iona Dick. Go and ask if anyone knows her.*"

"So funny."

"I can't believe you don't remember this. And you went round the playground going, *Does anyone know Iona Dick?*"

She choked a bit with the laughing and I had to actually pat her back. The adult world was just a bubble where grown-ups sat being smug and laughing down at you—they knew all the beamer stories in your childhood and they knew best about everything and they loved reminding you. When you tried to answer back you got called a *ratbag* or a *pee-the-bed*.

"You've told this story a hundred times, Mam. I don't remember it and it isn't funny anyway."

"Even when you came home that afternoon and told me about it, I still don't think you got the joke. Your face looked so innocent, until I explained it!"

As I unscrewed my mam's red nail polish, seagulls fired up off the Causey and there were faraway shouts. I looked over—wee hotheads out in the baking air with their bags of cans, skelping one another. It gave me a wee exciting shiver to think I was going out on an actual Friday night.

My mam had really beautiful feet, but then she never used them much. I held her big toe straight. "Gunner knows about birds. He was teaching me."

"You enjoyed your walk then? You and him will be doing that regular. Get some air in those lungs. Tire you out a wee bit."

I stopped painting and looked at her. "What does Gunner do, Mam?"

She laughed and flung her head back. "Ah, Cora."

"He's saying we can't move away from Muircross."

"He mentioned this had come up! It's not that we can't ever move away, it's just that things are tricky at the moment. Gunner's going to help us, but it'll take a wee bit time. We should concentrate on being a team first. And you need to pull your weight, miss."

"Mam, if we're going to be a team then treat me like a grown-up and tell me the truth."

"That is the truth!"

"What about the new house? It's all you ever went on about!"

She wiggled her toe, looking down at the nail I'd done. "Well, I've applied for the move but I've not heard back, so even if we wanted to go we'd still have to get word from the council. The house will still be there in a year or two. And if it isn't, we'll get somewhere else. Cora, we've all had dreams. The main thing now is for you to apply yourself at school."

I leaned right into her foot with the wee paintbrush. Sometimes in the moments when I could concentrate really hard it felt like nothing existed but here and now. "Tell me about the house."

"Only if you tell me about the school."

"Mam. There's nothing to tell."

"I know when something's not right." I blew on her nails, then moved to the other foot. "Right, well, this Abbotscraig house. It's a newer house, with a big living room that has beautiful picture windows. It has a downstairs bathroom with a glass shower screen! It's not a wheel-in shower but it will be better for me anyway. The bedrooms are all bigger than our rooms here. And there's double glazing! And a proper immerser. It'll be so cozy for us at Christmas."

"And ramps, aye?"

"Big ramp at the front door. And main thing, the rent is going to be much cheaper. I'll have a wee bit extra left over every month, once my payments are back to normal. Cora, I had no idea you wanted to move to Abbotscraig so badly!"

"It's not Abbotscraig, it's anywhere."

My mam laughed. "You ever been?"

"Been through it going to that careers day in Falkirk."

"Oh it's a braw place, Cora. Way bigger than here. There's an Our Price and a Schuh! There's a swimming bath with big flumes. There's this restaurant, La Cantina, they do this amazing Tex Mex platter, it's like a Scottish slant on Tex Mex. Janine and I went there once. Since I'll have a bit extra money we'll maybe be able to eat out now and again?"

I looked up at her. "Are you still in charge of things, Mam?"

"What do you mean? This is our wee house, of course I am."

I held her little toe. "It feels different having another person here again, that's all." I finished up on her foot. There were voices coming off the neighbors' tellies now. Thin wee traffic sounds from the main roads and motorways. "Mam, I don't say it much, but I do love you."

"Cora Mowat!" She started laughing again. "What's got into you? You're so cute and serious sometimes, honestly. Hey, do you think your old mam's stupid, eh?" She jabbed me in the side. "You're changing the subject so you don't have to talk about the school."

"Shut up."

"Well go on, then."

I sat round so we were more side by side. "I was looking again at the printouts. Those ones the school nurse gave us. I bumped into her."

"Oh, come on! How can a lassie that sits on her arse as much as you be hyper? Honestly, the stuff that school comes out with."

"Mam, it's not just school, it's everything. I just want to get away from here. It's full of crackpots."

"Full of crackpots?"

I rolled and lay on my front and stared at the nail polish bottle. The color name was Burnin' Love. "Ugly wee clowns in Helly Hansen jackets. Druggies. Tramps everywhere. Like that man outside the Savoy with the harmonica and the bottle of brown Sprite that shouts at you."

"That's big Eustie Neill! He used to be the foreman in the pit. He's a harmless old fella."

"I hate it, Mam. It's all stress."

"Cora, you've got a roof over your head and a loving mother. There's plenty worse off than you."

"Who exactly?"

"Don't speak to me in that tone. Listen, Gunner told me you were full of beans about moving to Glasgow! Maybe you should learn to hand your homework in on time and fold your clothes before you start gallivanting."

I knew that winding her up was probably the easiest way to get the truth, so I did my wee smile and just said it. "Are you pair in love then? You and Gunner getting married one day?"

"Jesus, Cora."

"And do you promise he's not my da?"

"Cora! Good god, lassie. I don't know where you got that imagination of yours. You've seen your da's grave. You were nine, you wouldn't shut up about it. We had ice lollies on the bus?"

"I remember."

"Well, stop being ridiculous then! Gunner's not perfect, love. But one thing about Gunner, and this is what sets him apart from Terry and your da, is that Gunner is going to help us. Look, I get it, when you're wee everything has to be a big fairy story! I've never been married but I'll tell you two things about love right now for free—there's not much of it out there. And it doesn't pay the bills." She leaned right in. "It's hard enough just keeping your head above water, but you'll learn all that when you're grown up yourself."

"Mam, stop making out I'm wee." She threw her head back again and laughed, then ruffled my hair. I could feel the tickly grass through my hot socks, my heart thumping against the ground. "I'm going inside," I says.

"It's karaoke at the social tonight. You don't want to sit out here and help your old mam practice?"

I stood up and brushed the grass off. "No, I don't."

"Well thanks for doing my toes, you've made a nice job of that!"

In the doorway I stopped and looked back down the garden at her, framed by the water and the silvery-white clouds from Riggs. I watched one big gust of wind quietly moving her hair. Then I went upstair.

I shuffled myself cross-legged on the floor of my mam's room, by the drawers under her bed. If they weren't going to treat me grown-up and tell me about Gunner's work and Gunner's plans and everything else then I'd just do it Fiona's way.

I pulled the drawer out all smooth and silent and heavy. It was stuffed full of Gunner's crispy, worn-out carrier bags. I lifted out a white one and unwrapped it and peeked in.

Five bottles of Obsession by Calvin Klein. Boxed, sealed. Boots labels on.

As if I didn't know. As if I didn't fucking know.

I wrapped up the white carrier and lifted out the next one—an ancient Sweater Shop bag. Brand-new CDs—Simply Red. Mariah. Sting. M People, maybe five copies of that. All with the prices on. Two radio alarm clocks underneath. Four jars of Kenco at the bottom. I wrapped it up and put it all back.

A big thieving, shapeshifting bastard. A liar and a creep.

If I was being honest then I had to admit I did want to find something—something exciting, or something that pointed to some proof of a plan, but a nice plan. I wanted something that would bring us together. Give us a future. Not stolen stuff. Not Sting.

One more, I says to myself, just to see. Hope was an absolute arsehole.

The Tesco bag was heavy and folded round. I unwrapped it carefully and looked in.

Porno mags. I felt like I had air in my brain. I spread them out on the stoory carpet. Every single one was about food—*Jam Parade*, *Cakesitting*, *Hot Tart*. *Marmalade Fever*. Two copies of something called *Foot Pie*. I wanted to cry. I wanted to boak. I wanted to find a snooker ball and put it in a sock then beat Gunner to a pulp with it.

Fiona was right—lift the lid and all men were ratty. I started flicking through. I couldn't help it. The headlines went by in a daze. *Mindy's Mixer. Tanya and Natalie butter their scones. Randy Ray's Porridge Gun. Debbi Decorates—Eight pages of the stickiest oven-ready snaps from our favorite Brighton Babe—in full color.*

There was a woman in a zig-zag pattern leotard sitting on a wedding cake. A girl pouring Coke down herself in a paddling pool. There were perms and half ponytails. Crimped ponytails. Sport socks. Sprinkles. Viennetta in cleavages, arses in milk. Butter, Marmite, cream of chicken soup. Tits and snatches everywhere.

It was fucking disgusting. How was I going to eat anything again? I loved eating scones, but not how they were eating them here.

This was Gunner's business. Trading in thefted goods. This is what he was obviously known for in Muircross—if it wasn't bolted to the floor and guarded by dogs then Gunner would thieve it for you.

I knew there had been something up with those Asics. That they were brand new. That he was giving them to me. The whole thing seemed too good to be true because it was. I'd throw them on the train tracks. I'd frazzle and melt them in the microwave. I'd never wear them again as long as I lived.

I wrapped the bags up and put them back, then slid the drawer shut soft as I could. I'd probably get the blame for finding it because that's the way it usually worked with adults—shite the bed, then blame the quilt.

As if I was cleaning her kitchen now. Cora Mowat, turning down a date with Dennis to stand like a sap on a Friday night sweeping noodle-dust off the lino like a Kwik Save Cinderella in her stolen Asics with the ceiling above creaking under the weight of her fake-da's thefted porno mags, while the whole time her mam is out guzzling Malibu and Coke, murdering "Cracklin' Rosie" in that rancid Dorothy Perkins blouse with the fake gold buttons. As if I was joining their wee arsehole team now. As if I was getting on their same page. The only place my weight was getting pulled was out that fucking front door.

I put on my cream striped Tammy top, my tight white jeans and my spangly red belt, and I was back in the Reeboks. I'd Tipp-exed the toes and swapped the laces and they'd do for now.

I had the big hoops in and my hair tight in a bun. Black eyeliner, Peach Pit lip gloss, six big skooshes of Impulse. It was a Friday night and Dennis was seventeen and I wasn't going out looking like Polly fucking Pocket.

Everything was getting shiter in my life but there was no way I was missing my date. My mam would be at the social till eleven at least. Gunner was out doing god knows. All I wanted was to work out what an actual tall boy from a nice house with a real job would make of a lassie like me.

He was parked by the bus stop at Viewpark Terrace. I waved, then as I crossed the road it was like I suddenly remembered everything that was wrong with me—my brain was going like one of those sparkling game show wheels. I breathed my belly in. Sucked in my mouth to make cheekbones. Pictured the skipping rope.

He was wearing a black T-shirt, baggy black jeans with a chain, a spiked belt. Earrings, a nose hoop, actual eyeliner—black like mine, but neater. Amazing, really, you had to admit. I sat down in the car.

Before me and him had even said a word I was already picturing my mam telling this story to other folk. Maybe I could keep him secret? Or could I just bolt now? I says to myself, *Be brave, Cora, it's just a goth*.

I adjusted my top. I didn't know anything about goths except they loved being in the woods. "You're looking a wee bit different from the Co-op!"

"I wasn't going to come on a date in my work shirt, was I?"

I couldn't stop seeing Jo's cackling face. "Sorry I'm late," I says. "My mam says lateness is my middle name!" I did a horrible gulping giggle and wanted to die.

"I didn't mind waiting." He looked right in my eyes. He had a really nice fringe. Could he tell I'd seen a man with a beard slurping beans out a woman's cleavage a few hours before? I'd had two showers soon as my mam left for the social and I still felt it on me. "You look lovely," he says, starting the engine.

As the car got going I says, "Who's that on your T-shirt then?" Fiona had said to speak first and ask him a question to show how confident I was. I sat on my hands to stop myself picking my fingers.

"It's Charles Manson. Probably best known for overseeing the ritual slaying of Sharon Tate." He laughed. "He's in prison now."

I nodded to show my interest. "That sounds cool. Where exactly are we heading?"

"We could drive over to the new McDonald's and get some food?"

"Oh, I'm a vegetarian, Dennis."

"Do you like fries?"

We drove out of my estate and up through the town. It wasn't even dark yet, but I had to admit it was exciting and romantic to be out in the night with a boy. You could count on one hand the amount of times I had been in a car.

There were churches and trees and roofless buildings and crappy flickering disco lights coloring the windows of pubs. Men smoking in doorways and lassies with their legs out, arm in arm. Big bright chippies I'd never eaten out of before. Everything seemed alive.

Further out, the pavements rolled by, bringing crews of wee eager-faced boys swilling in huddles with their shining eyes and their crumpled two-liters and their spotless trackie bottoms. There were heaps of them round every bus stop or phone box in town.

Without even thinking I goes, "Do you not get hassle for your clothes? Coming out on a Friday night?"

"I don't go out much. I have a TV in my room." His face was lit all ghostly green by the dashboard. He pressed the central locking down.

"I sit bickering with my mam, eating Space Raiders. Watching people win caravans on game shows."

The McDonald's was part of a new half-finished retail park out in the country behind the town. We spoke about wee things on the way. The Co-op, the Causey, the school. Dennis had a flick-knife collection, he did tricks with them. He lived in the new Barratt houses—his family had two rowboats, two Great Danes and a gazebo in the garden where Dennis did his homework. As far as I knew, Jo or my mam had never been in a gazebo.

I told him about me, about Jo and my mam and Fiona. I didn't mention Gunner. Dennis nodded and smiled at the right times and told some jokes. They weren't really funny but he said them in a way that made you wish they were. Facially he was nobody you would climb out your window for, but he was a nice boy, and even with all the spikes and the eyeliner he definitely wasn't dangerous.

He indicated left at a junction. "I'm going to be a chartered accountant," he says. "I'm planning on uni in Edinburgh, and then London for work. I'll take a year off somewhere. Do Costa Rica. How about you?"

"I dunno. School's shite."

"You must have a plan?"

"I want to get away from here. I don't care where. I want to prove to my mam that I'm not just, you know. A wee ratbag!" I laughed. "I want decent money for my own place. I'm going to get nice carpets and a stereo. And I'll live on my own. I want the opposite of what I've got. Maybe even a car like this?"

"This is my sister's car. Rosemarie. She's at the police college at the moment, up at Tulliallan. So I get to drive it."

"So she's going into the police?"

He moved into a higher gear. "Yeah, she went down to uni in Leicester and got her degree, and now she's got a flat in Kincardine."

"You see, that sounds amazing."

"Her tapes are in the glovebox there."

I reached and took one of the cassettes out. The label said "NEW BEAT—BELGIUM," in bouncy red ballpoint. I put it in the slot.

Spooky keyboards started, then a big clicky pumping beat that seemed to go in time with the speed of us. I turned it up. We drove up onto the back road under the leaning trees and the feeling of moving under the smudgy blue evening sky made me feel so calm. "Her taste is a wee bit different to mine," Dennis shouted over it, laughing.

A careers woman had come to District last year. They had redecorated the library with big boards that had faded photos of the old Muircross mines on one side and then on the other side computers and rainbows and a smiley-looking dolphin all in color.

The multiple-choice questions were stupid. The woman tapped my answers into a computer then the printer screeched out my future—top of the list was deep sea diver. Fiona got dog groomer. Wee Alanna Khan with her neon-green Salomon ski jacket was going to be a glassblower.

The boys got told to look for a job at Riggs, and Riggs had a weird short man in a suit there to sign them up on a clipboard. Stacey Gilchrist, who has cerebral palsy, got told she would be a ladies netball coach. The boys all laughed about it in front of her and it upset me for a week.

The McDonald's car park was packed. Under the huge yellow M the Muircross boys stood round in groups and sat on their car hoods laughing and drinking while their girlfriends jumped round them like yappy dogs. The air was mental with big revving engines and techno. Dennis steered us over to the drive-thru but there was a chain across the entrance.

He turned the New Beat down a bit. "I'll have to park up and go in for the food."

I looked out my window at the gangs of boys with their bottles and cans—they were already pointing and nudging one another. I was no lip reader but you knew when someone was saying *sweaty bastard* and *moshing cunt*. "You gonna be okay?"

"I've got my wallet chain. Fries, aye?"

"And a Coke."

I clicked the locks down as soon as he left. He walked up the middle of the car park lit by other headlights in the dusk as gherkins and fries and bits of gravel flew toward him. Something in me was melting a bit. I couldn't believe his bravery.

He dressed a bit different, but so what? When you grew up getting singled out yourself your heart always went out to anyone you saw getting picked on. And plus, what if you kissed a random cool-looking boy then later you found a Bible or a Games Workshop carrier bag in his room? At least with Dennis the bad stuff was out in the open—he was wearing it.

He reappeared ten minutes later. He had a brown bag of food, and barbecue sauce in his hair and he was wheezing. I helped him wipe it out with some napkins then we locked the doors and started eating. He had a nugget meal with Fanta, and I had three large fries and a Coke.

I ate a handful of hot fries. "I never knew any of the shops were open here."

"They're building a Comet over there. And a B&Q. It'll all join up when it's completed."

"It's weird how the place is changing."

"They're planning a museum too. A heritage center. About the mines. Hey, we could come back and see it in the daytime? I could show you where Comet's going to be. Or, I dunno. Maybe your mum and dad can take you?"

"Ah, I've only got a mam. She's in a wheelchair. So we can't just go places. It takes a lot of planning."

"Sorry."

It had all come out at once. I kept looking into my fries. "It's fine."

He bit into a nugget. "Can I ask what happened?"

"She got shaken and hit when she was a baby but she's never really spoken about it. My Auntie Janine told me when she was drunk. Something happened to my mam's spine. She's had the chair forever."

"God, I'm sorry."

"Don't be too sorry. She's a pain in the arse. I've never met my grandparents. Alkies apparently. My mam's not had an easy life, like. My Auntie Janine used to say that all she had to show for it was me!"

I had a long slurp on my icy Coke because my face was burning. It was when you spoke things out loud that you realized how much you said only to yourself.

Then Dennis goes, "But that's okay." He cleared his throat and sipped his Fanta with a cute pout. "I mean, you're really pretty. She must be proud of you."

Nobody had said I was pretty before, except my mam, and Fiona, and that old man with the breath that smelled like hamster bedding who hugged me outside the swimming baths when I was six. I wanted the words to sit there forever.

"Oh," I says, "thanks." But I was already replaying the whole conversation. How had I ended up speaking so much? I wanted to climb out the car window and bolt.

I says, "Sorry, Dennis. I dunno—there's something about being out here that's making me say all this stupid crap."

"That's okay. I love your outfit."

I went to speak when shouting started, over by the cars. Then suddenly a big, world-ending thud. I felt a shock right through my veins, and I shrank down in the seat and suddenly everything around us went bright white. For a wee split second I wondered if we were maybe already in heaven. Then Dennis put the wipers on and I realized it was liquid over the windscreen—we'd been hit. I could smell it in the vents. A large vanilla milkshake.

"*Goth cunt!*" someone screamed. "*Moshing bastard!*" Then fries and nuggets over the window as well. A half-eaten Filet-O-Fish smashed down and exploded on the bonnet.

"Drive please, Dennis," I said. He flicked his fringe amazingly then reversed out and swung the car round and as he did my Coke flew out of my hands and sloshed all over my jeans. "Just drive!" I goes, with the hysterics starting, thinking of the lassies in the magazines. Praying with everything I had that Dennis wasn't into all that.

As we flew off I could see in the mirror some big mad tracksuited Terminator bastard running after, roaring something about my fanny and tits. I tried to breathe to stop the laughing as I mopped myself up with napkins. Then as we went off into the black distance you saw in the mirror other headlights turning out of the car park onto the road under the big yellow M, speeding up, doing *Wacky Races* maneuvers, following us.

"They're coming, I know. Sit tight," Dennis goes.

I turned the stereo up to make it more like a film.

We swung off the road onto dark lanes. He did long swerves and quick swerves and little sudden slownesses where he braked and the world braked and my belly did a little hop and the tops of my thighs got soft and goosebumped despite the Coke because I knew he was looking after me. He was saving me.

Then he'd speed up again, and I saw the hedges and fences go runny through the glass, and I'd hate it, and I'd love it, and I'd have that mental sexy terror all over that told me I was alive and there had been an actual night—one night I could remember later, when I was a cleaner, or a summer waitress, or homeless in Glasgow, or actually dead.

Then the rain came on, lashing, washing milkshake and chips and shredded lettuce down the windscreen. We tilted round the bend at the top of the hill, wipers going, and all the dark trees flew to one side like a curtain going back, and for a couple of seconds, as we came out of the woods, I saw the whole shitey town—dark-window houses, long street-light roads snaking down to the Firth, motorways twinkling in the faraway black, like lines of glitter glue on a crap pasta collage. I breathed in the smell of fries and nuggets and rainfall. The moon looked like a giant Pringle. I could feel New Beat in my chest, cold Coke in my arsecrack. Muircross seemed like the maddest cheese dream.

"It's amazing to think of all this life going on!"

"While we're sat in our rooms." Dennis shook his head.

"It's like a nightmare." I looked back. There was nobody following us now. We drove down the brae and through the weird estates on the edge of town. The rain had scattered all the moonhowlers home, and the roads looked clear and wet and shiny black like the Deep Sea World eels. I couldn't describe the feeling in me. It was like for a few precious minutes the world had been going the same speed as I was.

"Could you drop me at the end of my street? I'll need to go in. Get out of these jeans."

He pulled in at the top of my road. He took his seatbelt off and leaned into the back of the car, then he handed me a black umbrella. "Use this. I'm sorry about everything. Maybe we can try again another time?"

"I'd like to."

He looked off into the distance for a wee minute and I knew a question was coming. Then he goes, "Cora, how old are you really?"

I put the umbrella on my knee and tucked my loose hair behind my ears then did the skipping rope again. I wasn't going to be that stupid naive wee Cora at the back of the queue. "Sixteen," I goes. "Did Fiona not say?"

Then he reached in his jeans pocket and handed me a napkin. It was warm and damp and when I unfolded it, it said *DENNIS WONG (CO-OP GUY)*. And his number. "In case you need to get hold of me," he says. I knew from his voice that he was nervous and it made my heart go suddenly hot.

I had to sound like a lassie who was smart and up for things but who also couldn't care less. Jo used to say that she always left Fozzy wanting more. I opened the car door, then I blew him a kiss. "'Night, Dennis!"

"'Night, Cora."

I slipped the napkin in my bra as I crossed the road in the rain. I'd keep it in my diary forever, it was like I'd passed an exam—proof that a boy with a car and a gazebo was mine, once, for a night.

I went down the dark side path then I clicked the back door open gently and then I stopped. I knew me and my mam's wee house and I could tell when the air was different in there.

I had a clear view straight down through the gloomy kitchen and into the yellowy-lit living room. He must have been laid out on his back on the settee because I could only see the one hand of his reaching up. His fist was gripping her hair, it was curling out from between his fingers like the frayed ends of some horrible ginger rope.

It was Jo, and she was on top of him, and they were shagging. Gunner had raised his head and was kissing her. Her eyes were shut and she was making a face like the lassie with the Viennetta from his rancid magazine.

That custard-yellow trackie top had been covering love bites. Now he was in me and my mam's house chewing her neck all over again. My knees were going. I couldn't breathe. I felt like I was learning some obvious thing that I had always needed to learn, but that it was all coming far too late.

Jo let out a big vile moan. I stood there under Dennis's umbrella, just a pathetic wee smear in the rain, chewing my cheeks, crying. There was a hot, hard pressing in my face and it felt like all the major bits inside me were ungluing themselves. I was coming apart in my own back garden like a cheap figurine off the market.

I calmly shut the door. I blinked and breathed slowly. From nowhere I remembered the printouts—*In moments of high stress you can avoid a meltdown by retreating to a quiet, safe place.* I walked to the bottom of our garden in a trance. I sat in the wet grass under the umbrella with the drizzle and the wind around me like TV fuzz, my cold feet trembling in the rain-ruined Reeboks, the moon sprinkling glitter on the Firth, the sound of Gunner and Jo still at it all tiny behind our closed back door.

8

In the morning I took my white jeans to the bathroom and sat there with the nail brush like a granny, scrubbing Coke out the thighs and the crotch.

I was dying to hear some door bangs and smashes and *fuck-yous* from downstairs—I wanted my mam to go mental, like she did with Ravey Davey and the rest. I wanted her shouting *Scumbag. Rattlesnake. Big cyclops bastard.*

He must have let Jo out before my mam came home because I heard my mam getting dropped off and when she went in there was no screaming or shouting at all. I'd given them time to get to bed and then I'd gone in myself and sneaked up to my room about half eleven, soaked to the skin.

I was laughing, sat there on the edge of the bath. He'd put up a brand-new rail and got us a silky-looking shower curtain with the Eiffel Tower on. When I'd come in the night before I could see he'd cleaned the kitchen for me too.

All these wee efforts, everything he'd done since he'd come, it was all so he could keep the peace and get his sleazy way with Jo. I'd always had some doubts about Gunner, but fair play to him, he had broke the record for quickest boyfriend transformation—weird, weird-but-decent, maybe decent, defo decent, cunt.

All you heard now from down the stair was horrible normality—my mam's laughter, his doofy comments, distant plonky music off the morning telly. I probably knew my mam's wee tone of voice better than anything else in the whole world, I could tell her exact mood from one word—and she was fine. She hadn't seen a thing.

It was my life that was changing—there was a nervousness on me already, opening doors and moving round, listening out. Waking up I'd do heavy footprints on the floorboards, even in my socks, to give Gunner a warning I was awake. I didn't want to be walking in on things, finding stuff, by mistake. Every drawer or cupboard I opened felt like a test.

It was a big rancid pantomime that I knew would end one shitey day with me in tears and telling her I'd seen Jo riding her boyfriend. It would break my mam's heart—I'd break my mam's heart—but she'd find out one way or another. There were no secrets on this estate.

The Tuesday after, the sky out my bedroom window was the same old bright blue. Outside you could hear the seagulls arguing, bus horns, power tools—sounds of another hot and beautiful day that I'd be wasting. Then my mam shouts up that Gunner wanted to speak.

"Do I have to?"

Her voice went moany. "Cora Mowat, get your arse down here now."

I changed into my shorts and vest, then stomped down into the living room. My mam was watching a game show with a lanky presenter. Stood there I got the heebies right through me because I knew something big was going to be said.

"Gunner's out front," she goes, without looking away from the flashing circle that the man on the telly was pointing at.

Outside, I shielded my eyes. Gunner was topless in the front garden in scuffed trainers and vile red swimming shorts and nothing else. You saw how muscular he was, thin and stringy, but probably heftier in the shoulders than even Samantha's boyfriend. The sun and the work had put a sheen of sweat right over him—I felt the boak rise just looking.

I says, "What is it?" He had a load of chopped-up wood lying round the grass, screws and wee bags and boxes everywhere, and a big yellow drill in his hand.

He stood up straight and had one hand on his hip as he spoke. "Building your mam's ramp. Like we spoke about. You want to give me a hand, eh?"

"I've not got shoes on."

He put the drill down. "What's your problem, miss?" I felt the nerves jangle up but I wasn't going to make things all nice with a smiley face or a cute wee question like normal.

"I've not got a problem." All I wanted was to go inside and blab to my mam about him and Jo, then get down and hide behind her while she tore the arse off him and flung him out into the gutter.

He stepped toward me. "You've not been right the past few days. Your mam's noticed it too."

I could smell the tangy sweat off him and it was giving me the heave. I shrugged. "What was it you wanted me for?"

"Those two boxes there." He pointed toward the smallish cardboard boxes by the gate. "Jack's dropped them off. You remember Jack? Bought you a pizza crunch. So grab them please and take them up to your room."

"My room?"

He tilted his head and started talking to me like a wee kid. "You know your mam's room is already full. We need you to store the boxes for a couple of days, love, eh."

Love. I wanted to leap right forward like a snake and bite his arm. "Fine."

I walked to the boxes in my bare feet and lifted them, dodging the screws and the cubes of sawn-up wood in the grass. There was no trace of shame in him, or a single bit of fear that I might know. It was as if being an adult let you do whatever you want.

"Stick them under your bed, good lass, eh."

I went inside and heeled the door shut behind me, loud enough so my mam would look. She glanced at me, then went back to her program. A car was moving in circles round the stage. A woman with Tic-Tac teeth was on the bonnet in a swimsuit. I started up the stair.

Then as I got near the top the front door opened again. I looked down and he was in the doorway, wiping sweat off himself with a T-shirt. "Cora, come and sit down." Then he put on that big smarmy voice. "Maggie, maybe now's the time to tell Cora about our plans, eh?"

I felt my belly go. My mam switched the telly off with the remote. I heard some seagulls outside laughing.

Gunner crouched beside her whispering, giving her a big rub and hug round the shoulders, like she was a Labrador at a fireworks display. It was weird to see them touching. I closed my eyes. My mam goes, "Cora, come down and get a seat, love."

There was still only normalness in her voice. I dropped the boxes on the stair and went down and slumped in the armchair facing them. I pressed down my emotions. Clamped my jaw shut tight.

"Now you are to sit and listen, miss. I know Gunner cleaned the kitchen for you. And I know you were out till all hours. It's fair enough that it's the school holidays, and you're fourteen. I don't mind you having your wee bit fun. But the housework comes first, okay?"

I looked at her. Was I actually going to have to sit through this?

What I wanted to say was, *Mam, Gunner was rattling Jo on the cushion you're sat on right now. That's why the kitchen never got done by me. Oh and by the way there's a heap of crispy magazines hidden upstair with lassies in the buff wiping their arses with Swiss rolls, and they all belong to Gunner. Oh and he's a big dopey criminal bastard and I want to put his other eye out with a fork.*

I goes, "Okay. Sorry, Mam."

Then Gunner started. "What me and your mam were thinking is we'd start having a regular family meeting. Maybe a way of everyone checking in."

"It was Gunner's idea." My mam was grinning. "We're going to treat it proper, maybe go and get a seat somewhere and a cup of tea or some food. We can get a wee housework rota going, and talk about that, and we can discuss all the other issues in the house as well. Make sure everyone's pulling together."

I felt like someone was inside of me, hoovering. *Discuss all the other issues in the house.* I looked down into the pattern on the carpet. My mam's toenails were looking chipped already in her sandals.

I wanted to tell her, but I could still hear the happiness in her voice just from him being there. And he was building her a free ramp too. If I told her about Jo I'd ruin her life and I'd ruin her chances of getting in the front door. I says, "Okay."

"And listen, Gunner and me are here to support you."

Her face was clear and beautiful. It was dim inside but it seemed like her eyes were sparkling, somehow. I had a heartbroken feeling in me, but not only in my heart. "The meeting sounds good. Can I go up the stair now?"

"Aye," my mam goes. Then, "Oh, and Cora—"

I looked through the slats of the banister and down at the pair of them.

"I've asked Jo to come round on Thursday. Pair of you can do a bit of sunbathing or whatever. Now, before you say it, I know you're fourteen. She's not looking after you."

"Mam—"

"Me and Gunner are going for a day out to Edinburgh and I think it would be better to have somebody here with you. Keep you occupied, okay?"

When I spoke it was gravelly and pathetic and almost not there at all. "Mam, it's fine. I know what you think of me."

"Cora—"

"A wee fucking pee-the-bed!" I was shouting now, I couldn't stop myself.

"Cora Mowat!"

"A wee fucking pee-the-bed that needs a babysitter at age four-teen!" The *teen* bit of *fourteen* came out like a squeal and I wanted to die. I grabbed the boxes and stomped up the stairs and kicked my mam's stairlift on the way and I heard her say *leave her* to Gunner before I slammed my bedroom door.

I dumped the boxes in the middle of the room then I knelt down and tore the lid off the first one in a crappy wee frenzy.

A vacuum-packed leg of lamb.

I ripped open the second—another, the same. Stolen, no doubt.

I poked it. It was squishy. Warm like my own leg. I sat back against my bed, used my feet to kick both boxes into the corner of the room. I could feel the tears coming.

I jumped up and pulled the Asics out from the bottom of my ward-robe and I flung the left one at my wall, and then the right one at my door. It bounced back and hit me on the side of the head, then landed on my bed.

One way or another the end was coming. I knew that. Whether I told her, or he told her, or Jo told her, someone had to. And then he had to go. He had to.

I rubbed my head. Eating meat was grim, but thieving it seemed even grimmer. It was classic Muircross—warm secondhand meat, from under a bed. Imagine buying your kids' Sunday dinner round the back of the bookies. Surely no mam would ever allow that? The whole thing seemed like something dreamt up by men.

I chucked myself on my bed. Mam had the game shows and Gunner and the social and Lena Zavaroni and the Amazing Moira. What did I have? *Why can't you apply yourself, Cora? Could you stop singing in class, Miss Mowat? How is it possible for an intelligent girl to forget so much?*

This was my future—bus stops, bobbled V-necks, pencil shavings, second bell. Teachers thinking I'm a lazy moo. Seagull shite on the Reeboks. Chucking chairs in the sea. Brown envelopes, waiting lists, months of my mam's disappointments and rage. Emptying torn-up bingo cards out the bathroom bin. Feeling ashamed. And when Gunner went, different men in the house at night, again.

And then eventually I suppose I'd have to be sixteen—failed exams and coupons and crumbs and broken immersers. Saving up for a carpet. A job in Halfords, if I applied myself. Maybe a wee clean-cut shitebag boyfriend with a Lego haircut, and an overweight Wagon Wheel gobbling toddler called Tony. Ginger, maybe? Jesus.

I hated that creepy thieving topless gremlin Gunner—his clothes, his shoulders, his stolen lamb. A thefting, care home scumbag. I buried my face in the pillow.

I hated my pillow. I hated my clothes. I hated my armpits. I hated the Asics. I hated the sun and the sky and I hated my mam. I hated not being free. I hated sunbathing because I could never lie still and I could never relax and I always ended up crispy like a rasher. I hated plans and agreements and having to do things with people you never even liked. Most of all I hated the future—anything could happen there.

9

When I was nine I stood on a slug with my naked foot at Burntisland and Auntie Janine had to scrape it off with her Dorothy Perkins account card. I was screaming but it was really the slug I felt sorry for. I liked all wee living things but sometimes I felt different about people.

Especially Jo. Watching her come up the garden path that Thursday I wanted to stomp her. I wished she had a shell so I could crush it or wings so I could pull them off. I wanted to body-slam her to the ground then tell her exactly what I thought of her as she lay there blubbing.

I opened the door before she knocked. "Hey, Jo."

"Like my new togs?" She started doing poses. "Oh cheer up for fuck's sake, Cora, your face is tripping you!"

She was wearing a denim jumpsuit with a wide white belt made of pencil case plastic that had her Walkman clipped on. When she took the headphones off I could hear "More Than Words" by Extreme. She was planning an Extreme tattoo for her Christmas. She already had *Live for Tomorrow* in Chinese above her arsecrack.

"You look amazing, Jo."

My mam had been nothing but decent to her and she goes and does what she did. She was scum. Lower than frogspawn. But at the same time I felt pathetic and bad because my mam relied on Jo and my mam was always saying Jo had been good to me. It wasn't really true but it probably seemed true to her.

I went to the fridge to get myself a drink and when I came back to the living room Jo was half out of her denim. She had a bikini on. I looked at my feet because I just couldn't deal with more love bites. "We sunbathing?" She held up her expensive-looking zebra-print towel. I wanted her away from my living room, away from my settee. Out of my house completely.

"You head out. I'll be out in a sec."

She walked past with the towel and out through the kitchen. "Wear something decent, eh?"

Outside it was roasting. I spread out my towel on the grass and lay down and peeked over at Jo. Her legs were like two strips of squirted-out toothpaste and her hair was like flames in the sun. She had new sunspecs on, silver reflecting wraparound ones, like the guy with the greased perm off WWF.

She tilted her head up at me. "A vest and shorts?"

"I don't want to get burnt."

"Whatever. Oh, guess what? I was out this morning, getting Alka-Seltzer." She looked up into the blue, shielding her eyes from the sun with one flat hand.

"Oh?"

"Could you show some interest please? Anyway. You'll never guess where I got it?"

I went up on my elbows. "Tell me?"

"All right, sad sack, if you're not playing. It was the Co-op."

I knew right away she was starting on me because I felt it in my tummy. Jo was in one of her moods. I tried to do my cheery voice. "The Co-op's miles from you?"

"Yes, but a certain someone works there and I wanted the goss! Don't try and be a mystery, Miss Butter-wouldn't-melt. Everyone knows."

I flopped back and felt the hot towel scorching my shoulders. I could picture myself melting and vanishing, draining down through the grass like old paddling pool water, the kind with flies and crumpled buttercups in. "Why did you have to speak to him?"

"A little birdy called Fiona was telling me about your comment. *A muntery wee gossip hound*, was that what you called me?"

I looked at her. "You are a gossip."

She rolled toward me and pulled her sunspecs down her freckled nose. "Say it to my face in future." Then she rolled away again.

I looked round at our back garden and remembered other times Jo and me had out here. On the Swingball set. The night we camped in sleeping bags. When Terry got us a barbecue and he used to bake those bananas with melted chocolate in. Jo loved Terry. Was she shagging him too? Was that how his rowing machine broke? I could picture it.

There used to be a shed right at the bottom of our garden. Jo would take me in there when I was wee and tell me stories, like how she lost her virginity to a panel beater from Tillicoultry called Enzo. She said Enzo was a bit Halloweeny face-wise but his wage was decent and he bought her Laura Biagiotti and he had a caravanette with a bed in it that him and his cousin converted. Jo had been on two dates with Enzo. She thought he was the one.

Enzo had his caravanette parked on the waste ground behind Allied Carpets and Jo had turned up expecting petals and foily balloons, but Enzo was already on the floor all covered in masking tape, wanking in the dark. He made her dress up in bin bags and pour Babycham on his balls and there was a wasp in the caravanette and Enzo kept shouting at it, even when they were shagging.

She didn't tell me every detail but I still remember crying after. I was so sorry for what happened to her but I was disgusted too. I was probably nine when she told me and I still didn't like thinking about it. All the weird, horrible stuff she went on about stayed in my head and I wondered why she'd even said it. Then I was thirteen when it dawned on me that Jo maybe had no real pals to speak to about things except me.

I adjusted my specs, then my shorts. "What did you say to Dennis, Jo?"

"Nothing bad. Forget it."

"Look, whatever it is you've done or said, whatever it is you want to wind me up about, just fucking get on with it."

She rolled over again. "Don't be like that, I'm only excited for you! What can I say? Mr. Dennis Wong and I had a great chat. I can't believe I had to wait on Fiona to fill me in about your naughty little piece of stuff. You should have been telling me everything!"

Other times I'd sunbathed with Jo she'd compared my body to a hot dog bun or an unbaked scone. She called me Pakora Mowat once. She compared my feet to an ewok's and when I wore a T-shirt once over my bikini she said I looked like a seal in a pillowcase. It hurt at first but I'd got used to how Jo was.

This time was different because this was Dennis, and Dennis was really decent. Jo had ruined things for Gunner and my mam, and now she had her wee snout in about Dennis too.

"Not speaking?" she went.

"Me and Dennis is none of your business."

"Dennis is an animal lover. How cute is that? He told me about his Great Danes. I said, *Oh how super-sweet! I know Cora loves animals too.* You do, don't you?"

"Whatever."

"He told me he liked walking the dogs up in Laburnum Wood. Off the lead. Usually they were well-behaved, he said, but sometimes they chased the squirrels. And then it just popped into my head—I said, *Did you know Cora wanted to be a squirrel once?*"

"Fuck off, Jo." I don't know where the strength came to say it, but I said it.

"Cora Marie Mowat!"

"Seriously, Joanne, fuck right off. I was nine. You shouldn't have been reading my diaries. Why are you saying that to him?"

"I was only excited for you, Cora." I looked over at her. She was swishing her head about. "Do you know why I reckon you get nowhere with boys? Your clothes aren't tight enough. I really sense that Dennis is hot for you, he's waiting. Boys hate to wait. Give him a signal."

She wasn't to know I knew her filthy dirty ratty wee secret. My mouth started going. "That's your specialty, eh, Jo? Signals? Lure them in. Jump on them. Bounce all over them like a fucking space hopper."

"So what if I do? Maybe you need to get in touch with your body, Cora. Let's face it, you've got a bit of heft about you, so advertise it— bit of *strategic cleavage*."

I scrunched the hot towel fabric up under my toes. "Don't call me hefty or chunky again," I goes. "And I don't need your advice, Jo."

"You're always going on about how you're moving, Abbotscraig this, Glasgow that." She started pointing at me. "You're always on about college and how I made it there. About the boys I know and all my parties. I can't help if I've been a role model to you, but don't turn round and tell me you don't want my advice." Her face went all moody. "Stay here if you like! Hiding in the library at school. Hanging round the Co-op in your bright-pink pavement slappers. Down the Causey, waiting for some slobber-tongued virgin to finger you on a swing. They cut the swings down! That's how bad it is! The truth is a good man is your only ticket out. You'll end up shacked with some mouthbreather who spends his weekend snoring in the armchair while you peel tatties and watch the light moving through your musty net curtains."

"They aren't pavement slappers."

"If you think Gunner bought those you must be even more deluded than I thought." Every nerve in me was twitching to jump up and bolt. But it was like I was paralyzed. Tongueless. Heartless. Stuck down. "Poor wee cow in her stolen poverty clogs. You must hate them, really."

"You jealous? 'Cause I got something nice for once?"

"Cora, love. Half of Muircross is ordering off Big G. He heads to the city and brings it all back. Where do you think I got these sunglasses? But don't worry, it's good news for you. He'll get you looking half decent in no time."

Sparks were going across my brain. "It's really no secret, Jo." She wasn't to know I'd worked out the story of my trainers, that I'd found the bags of Obsession and Sting. The M People. She wasn't to know I had meat in my room.

She lay back and wiggled herself comfy. "He'll get you some decent gear."

"You're a skid-mark. The biggest arsehole in Muircross."

She did a wee chuckle out of her nostrils then went, "What? It's true."

"Not every girl needs fancy gear. I don't need Moschino or Tommy Hilfinger stuff like you do. And me and my mam are happy, it doesn't matter what Gunner does."

She let out a yelp of a laugh. "Did you say Tommy *HILFINGER*?"

"Oh whatever. Honestly. You gigantic streak of pish."

She scrambled up and sat cross-legged with the venom going. I could see my own wee body like a silver sausage in the mirror of her wrestler specs. "Listen, chunk. There was a wee untruth earlier."

"Oh aye?"

"Aye—when I told you I didn't say anything else to Dennis. You see, Fiona told me you'd actually gone in there looking for Gary Grieve. That's deceitful, Cora!" She pinged a dead bumblebee out of the grass. "So I told Dennis that. It didn't feel good, but then I thought about the way you've spoken about Fozzy over the years. You've never shown me any respect, so why should I care? And he deserved to know. Nobody likes being second best."

The only thing I could think was that bumblebees deserve respect, even when they're dead. Leave it alone. Let it have some dignity in its wee bed in the grass. Then the Gary Grieve thing sunk in. And the anger came.

"Why do you always act like a cunt?"

"What was I supposed to do? I thought, *Why has Cora told Fiona and not me?* So I thought I'd go and see him with my own eyes. Conversation unfolded, naturally." She looked down over her silver specs at me again, fluttering her eyes.

I closed my eyes and pictured punching her, one big moment of private revenge that wouldn't ruin everything in my mam's house. I pictured a big manky crack in the earth appearing, the sky going peach. The garden would split like a dry digestive, the pylons would fall, the bit with Jo on would slide slowly out of sight. I'd be smiling.

Bye-bye, clarty Jo and your blue cocktails, your limited-edition Filofax, your Lenny Kravitz mixtapes. She would be screaming, scrabbling as she slid off the edge of Scotland. I'd go inside and I'd get the Yellow Pages and start arranging a proper loving home for poor wee Bam-Bam. Jo's poison bones would be halfway to Antarctica by then.

I looked over at her, she was on her back again, smiling, bopping her head left and right to some tune she was humming herself, pink as a foam shrimp from a sweet shop. One thing I'd learned living in Muircross was that there had to be blame. I thought, *I am never letting you near me again.* My brain kept repeating it so loud I was worried it might start coming out my mouth. *From now until the final hour of my life, I will never trust you again, Joanne Chantal Buchanan.*

loved early mornings when the moon was still about. It was a wee wet loo-roll moon up there, hardly seeable—like a finger-smear on glass. You just wanted to reach up and squeak-squeak it away with your jumper cuff like, *It's daytime now!*

I was sat on my front garden wall gawping up, praying that Dennis would come. When Jo had gone home I went out to the phone box and rang Dennis's number off the napkin. I was too scared to bring up Jo, so I just did my best hamster voice and asked if he'd come round next morning and help me with something. He said he would see what he could do.

After that I'd gone in and I'd lain on my bed and started crying. I knew the tears would have to come at some point, and that there would be liters, so I'd got myself ready. I lay back and had two bits of loo roll scrunched up and stuffed round my ears. You could never let go and do the proper wailing if you had those wee arsehole teardrops dangling off your earlobes tickling you, driving you mad.

"Hey, Cora."

I looked up. Then I stood up and smiled. "Dennis!"

He had a black bandanna on, blue eyeliner, black jeans and a T-shirt that said *Cannibal Corpse*. It was eight a.m. but he had turned up and he was happy. I wanted to cry from every emotion tangling in me at once, just from seeing the boy. I'd never been a mushy-hearted lassie but my heart was going mushy now.

"Your mate Jo seems like a right idiot," he says.

I closed my eyes and breathed in the words. He was like a mind reader. "Dennis, I'm so sorry. I can explain about her. She's a cow and a bully. The things she said—about Gary Grieve, it's not—"

"Is this what I'm helping with?" He pointed to the two boxes sitting by my mam's half-finished ramp. I'd taped them back together and used the stairlift to get them downstairs without waking her or Gunner.

"Aye."

He took one step forward and put his handsome hand on my forearm. It felt all warm in the morning freshness. "Don't explain. I'm not really into gossip."

"Dennis—"

"That jumpsuit though? The denim thing."

"Oh god. Horrendous! I mean half the time she looks like she died two weeks ago and forgot to lie down, it's—"

"Let's not be nasty."

"Sorry! Sometimes—sometimes when I'm nervous, well, and all the time really, I can't stop talking. Things come out."

He was already up the path lifting the boxes. "It's sweet. You lead the way, Cora."

We headed up the brae and turned onto the path toward the Causey. As we walked I felt all smooth and sugary inside, like after downing room-temperature Yazoo. Was this how love felt? It gave me heebies even thinking about it. "So did you bring it, like we said?"

"I did. I was going to point out on the phone, they're called butterfly knives, not flick knives."

There was still an urge in me to ask. Not about his knife collection— about what Jo had said. If it hurt him, if he really didn't care about

Gary Grieve. "Okay, Dennis," I went, smiling. Thinking, *Leave it, Cora. Don't ruin everything with nosiness.*

"I can do a trick with it for you? A Zen Rollover or a Horizontal Chaplin? My Chaplin is a bit rusty but I'd still like to show you."

"Maybe once we open the boxes?"

On the Causey we walked the length of the tarmac path and then he dumped the boxes and we both let ourselves drop onto the bench by the brambles.

He brought out his knife and opened it with a spin in a show-offy way that I had to admit gave me a wee feeling. Then he crouched down and sliced the tape open carefully along each join while cutely biting his bottom lip.

"Meat?"

"Lamb."

"I thought you were a vegetarian?"

"It's complicated. I've got a new—stepda?" I rubbed my forehead. "There is basically a man in my house called Gunner."

"Gunner?"

I felt a surprising wee feeling like relief when he said it. I sat up straight. "Aye, Gunner."

"So how's that been?"

I looked at the water. "Not easy. Anyway, that's his meat."

"He's a chef?"

"He buys and sells things. Sometimes meat."

"What else?" Dennis sat back beside me on the bench and flicked his fringe beautifully.

I pictured the Kenco, the pornos, the Calvin Klein. I looked down at my Reeboks and watched my toes doing wiggly worms inside the leather. "Kind of a variety of things."

"Well, he sounds cool."

"He's done some awful stuff too."

"Like what?"

"Can we just put the meat in the sea please?"

"Okay. Can I ask though—"

"In the sea, Dennis." The way it came out I sounded like Mr. Argyll. I did a giggle. "Please?"

He slid off the bench and knelt back down in the grass. I drew the line at explaining to Dennis that this was revenge, my chance to put a screwdriver in the spokes of my mam and Gunner's plans.

Throwing stolen meat in the sea seemed even sadder than stealing it in the first place. Just like sending a message to your fake da that you knew he was a lowlife was sad. Sadness, right the way through, like a cold sausage roll.

"Make sure all the packaging is off. I don't want anything saved."

"Should we not stop and think calmly about this?"

"Have you met me, Dennis?" As he fiddled at the meat with his knife I stood up with my arms folded. "I realize this must be weird for you, like, early morning, and meat and that, but afterward? I do want for us to do date things. I enjoyed our drive." I thought hard to myself and then I says, "Things won't always be weird with me."

"I want it to be a date too." He looked round toward me. "A second date. I was going to say earlier on. You look really nice today."

I felt heat behind my eyes. "Thanks. The date starts when the lamb is floating."

He nodded, then lifted the first leg, carrying it like a fireman with a guinea pig. He crossed to the low fence then chucked it. It hit the rubbly slope with a damp thud and scraped very slowly all the way down, then dropped off the edge and into the brown water.

"One to go!" I did a thumbs-up.

The second one landed a bit different. He made the same chucking movements and released it the same way, but this one landed with a slap and stuff got stuck to it, and it didn't trundle anywhere at all. One seagull flapped down to inspect the thing.

Dennis rubbed his slimy hands together. "Let's get cleaned up."

"It will have to go in the water." He looked at me. "It has to go in the water. I'm sorry. I can't explain it. It's weird. I'm weird. It needs to be gone."

"It's dangerous."

"I'll go." I waited for him to tell me not to be silly.

"Okay."

I looked at the rusty wire fence. I'd thrown tons of stuff over there but I'd never stepped across it myself. I closed my eyes and louped over on pure instinct, putting my Reeboks down on the slope with my hair flapping everywhere. The loudness of the sea seemed to double right away and I saw how foamy the water was. I felt closer to the crabs and the starfish than I did to Muircross.

My body had gone all heavy, like my muscles had turned to mashed tattie. The ground was all types of rock and gravel and seagull shite and litter. I slowly got down on all fours, facing up toward Dennis. Co-ordination and bravery weren't my strong points but I knew it would be easier if I wasn't able to stare down into my smelly brown grave.

Dennis was standing on the other side of the fence. "You're doing amazing. You need to move back maybe about three and a half feet? Then kick out. Backward. With your right leg."

"What's three and a half feet?"

"Shuffle yourself back. Careful. I'll tell you when."

I crawled slowly backward, trying to ignore the pain of the grit and gravel in my palms and my kneecaps.

"Right, stop! Now stretch your right leg out low to the ground and kick."

I was wobbling everywhere and my hair was in a wee tornado above my head. After a shaky few seconds searching with my outstretched Reebok I felt it touch the lamb.

I kicked out at it and saw it slide a bit. Then I started sliding a bit too.

Dennis shouted something but I was screaming so loud I couldn't make it out. At each side right along the coast big gangs of seagulls flapped up, terrified of this sweaty new species in the mangled trainers that was slipping backward down their wee crumbly cliff. The only prayer I could think of was that my mam would burn my diary.

Then after a second or two, like a miracle, I came up against a rusty exercise bike that had got stuck on a rock, and I stopped.

"Climb, Cora, quick!" Dennis shouted. I looked up at him. I couldn't help wondering if he'd still fancy me after all this.

I scrambled. I ran like Bam-Bam would, waddling awkward on all fours, trying to dodge all the rubbish like I was in an arcade game—condoms, a toaster, a stapler, a broken pint glass.

I got up onto the Causey and stood in front of him panting. I was wishing for a hug, a forehead kiss, for him to carefully rub my stinging kneecaps until all the grit was gone and then for him to tell me I was beautiful again, that I was brave. That everything was okay. Then he'd jog to the Co-op and get me a Lilt, on discount.

"This was such a reckless idea," he went.

"Dennis," I croaked.

He took off his bandanna and unfolded it, then he began to wipe down my sweaty arms. In a voice that was probably wobbly I goes, "I want to say thanks. Don't ask why, because I don't want to tell you, but that was something I had to do. I couldn't have ever done it without you."

He smiled at me, then he sat down on the bench. I sat down beside him and licked my thumb and tried to get some of the dirt off my Reeboks. Then I felt his arm across my back. When I looked up he was leaning right in toward me.

He closed his eyes. I could see the teensy individual gleams of sweat sitting in the pores of his nose and making his top lip glitter.

He put his hand on my damp thigh in a really careful way and suddenly there was acid in my chest and sugar all through me—he was going to kiss me.

I'd only been on land a few minutes and I was aching all over and panting still so I was hardly prepared for it, but I said to myself, *Now or never, Cora. Get the fucking love bites.*

His face came closer and got bigger, like an asteroid in a film.

Yes, I'd found him. Yes, I was normal. Yes, this was going to be it.

Everything looked hazy and my only thought was *aim for my neck*. For that wee second it felt like I could hardly take everything in—the future, the past, the present. The lamb. The Asics. Gunner. Everything rolled into one big emotion-ball weighing on top of me, like all the crap I had lived through had led me to this weird-feeling moment by the water. Then my legs weren't there at all. I was floating, weightless. From nowhere I pictured myself up in the air, like a seagull, or maybe a goldfish from the showies, dangling in a clear plastic bag.

One time Jo and Fozzy took me to the showies. They bought me candy floss but I knew they didn't want me there—Fozzy couldn't keep his hands off Jo's arse. Fozzy won a goldfish after hitting a bell with a hammer but Jo turned her nose up at it. Fozzy asked if I wanted him. Dunc was with my mam at that point and it would have been great to have a fish to speak to in my room, but when I saw him in the bag I knew he was sad about his life and so I said no. I went home alone, and Jo and Fozzy went down the Causey to grope each other in the weeds. Later on Jo told me Fozzy had flung the goldfish in the Firth, without even letting him out his bag.

Before I could even start to ask why my brain was making me think all this I began to greet.

My lip was doing trembles. Sniffling started. Everything I saw looked woozy and soggy and rained-on. Dennis opened his eyes. I tried my best to not do one of those skelped-arse elasticated crybaby faces but it was useless—the floodgates were going. It was a beamer to be crying about whatever this was—my mam probably. Unfairness. Muircross. Jo. Being poor. Samantha. Men. Gary Grieve. Fucked-up hyperactive me and my excessive talking and my fucked-up future and my unbitten neck. The loneliness of a chucked-away goldfish who died two summers ago and who lived in a sandwich bag and never even knew he was alive.

Dennis moved his hand from my thigh to my shoulder but I shrugged it off. I couldn't shut the floodgates. I was bawling.

"Oh god sorry," he went, looking terrified. "I thought it might be nice."

"Dennis, it's not you." Sobs were revving my shoulders. Everything was ruined. I wanted to crawl into a hedge and eat muck till I choked.

It was the touch, I thought. That wee touch on my leg had set this all off. There was a feeling in it, like a tingliness, but not just on the surface. It did something deeper, in my limbs and my chest, in the places where I felt stuff. Everything I'd wanted was in that touch, but I couldn't take the feeling when it came. I wasn't brave. I couldn't handle getting what I thought I wanted the most.

11

Gunner ate a long bendy chip from his paper bundle. "Things are going to change for us, Cora. The three of us."

I watched steam from the chip coming out his mouth as he smiled. It had been two days since the lamb went swimming and my mam and him had never even mentioned it.

We were doing our first family meeting, outside, down on the faded red seats in the Savoy plaza. The old Muir Cross got moved here in the 1980s but someone spray-painted balls on it so they put it in storage in Kincardine. All you saw now was the big concrete 50p-shaped base. The council had bolted red plastic seats to it.

Me and Gunner were sat on them, with my mam wheeled in close beside us looking all smart and serious. A wee pavement tornado was going with a Twix wrapper and a burger box and pages from a newspaper in it. A dog was taking itself for a walk.

There'd been no anger or chaos, no massive fight, no mam raging in my face about my fucking fizziness and the price of lamb and cleaning the kitchen. I thought they must be saving it for the family meeting. I ate a chip. Maybe not?

Gunner goes, "I'm going to train myself up. Get some real money coming in the house, aye? Make it stable. Me and your mam have been planning it all, for ages."

I kept my head down because looking at him made me think of

topless Jo and lamb with gravel in it and men's beards dripping in soup and beans. It would put me off my chips. "Train yourself up as what?" I went, dreading the reply but knowing that this whole big production relied on me sitting asking wee-lassie questions.

"Well, like I say, after discussing it with your mam I've signed up for a training scheme. The job center puts you in a profession, like. I'm going to train in a bakery, in Cardenden. Become a cake decorator."

My mam wheeled herself to face me. She was in a brand-new pretty dress. "It's stability for us, Cora. Gunner's making a change."

Gunner's grin reminded me of Bam-Bam. "It's part of a community thing, like, funded by the government. They're going to pay me to ice cakes. Might even be able to bring some home, eh?"

I looked down at the oily lump of chips in the newspaper on my knee. I grabbed five at once and forced them into my mouth, all firm and slimy and boiling hot. There was no way I'd be able to talk for at least a minute.

"Are you all right, pet?" my mam went.

I did a chewy smile. There was no sign in either of them that this was a wind-up.

Between the sadness and the anger and all the potato in my system and his big grinning head, I felt like I might boak. Was it not illegal to have a food-porn enthusiast icing cakes for a living? Around wee lassies, probably? With those big repulsive hands? Didn't they know where they'd been? He'd soon get his way. I'd seen page 24—*Debbi Gets a Dusting*. Sometimes I wondered why I had the best memory in the world for things I didn't want to remember.

I had tried to run away once, when I was ten. Me and my mam had an argument about how often I should wash my hair, and all the usual stuff about me getting too fizzy. The night of that argument was the first time I'd ever told her to fuck off out loud. It just came out. She went tomato color with rage.

Next morning I put my vest and shorts on then packed my Umbro jumper and my sunspecs. I took every twenty pence from my mam's Santa hat, and one bit of stoory plastic fern from the front window to remember her by. I had £12.20. First thing I did was go to the Co-op and buy custard creams for my journey. I had so much energy.

I walked out along the sea wall, then went and sat in the train station car park to build up my bravery. I ate some of the warm custard creams and thought about buying a ticket. Seagulls started noising me up so I chucked some biscuits round the tarmac. One of them was a wee injured waddling thing—I knew it was a girl in my head and called her Nina.

After forty minutes no bravery had come. When you saw people run away on telly they were happy and they looked free. I wasn't smiling and there was no massive feeling of relief, only a million tiny fears—where would I get money? Where would I sleep? Who would heat me up my spaghetti hoops? What would happen to my mam?

Moody clouds moved in and the birds got angry, and it felt like all those tiny fears were growing and joining together—it started seeming like the worst idea probably ever. I stood up all shaky. I was in the Muircross Station car park. Nobody was making me leave except my own stupid brain. I started walking. I'd been an idiot again. My mam loved me and I had a home.

As I left the car park the gulls followed me, shouting and dive-bombing down all sinister for biscuits. I tried to explain calmly that I was sorry but I'd eaten them all and that I was a growing lassie. They wouldn't stop so I ended up shouting at them. One of them swooped and pressed his flappy foot on my head to launch himself away again. Tears nearly came and I ran all the way home. I will never forget how muscular a seagull leg feels.

My mam was sat in the kitchen frying eggs for herself, crying by the cooker. She wasn't angry, all she wanted was to have me home. We hugged for twenty minutes then made a deal and I started washing my hair on a Wednesday and a Saturday and she even bought me my own Salon Selectives. I said to myself then that, however bad things got, my mam loved me and she was doing her best and I had to start growing up.

So now I was trying to stay calm. I went, "Is there anything else? I mean, thanks for the chips, but do I need to listen to any more of this?"

"Cora, Moira told me family meetings are a way forward and I want to do them regular, like we spoke about? Gunner's getting a job. That's brilliant, is it not?"

There was nothing in her beautiful wee face but hope. I felt chewed-up chips swimming in my belly. I went, "Aye, brilliant."

There was no way she knew about the magazines. No way she knew about Jo. He was fooling her. And recruiting her to try and fool me. For definite. It was up to me to tell her everything.

"I hope you've listened to your mam, Cora—we've both thought long and hard about this, like," Gunner said. He had one hand on the padded shoulder of her dress. It was the exact thing he did to me the night he gave me the thefted Asics. "I'll leave you two alone, eh?" He stood up and did an awkward nod, then walked off toward the window of Ferguson's, the army shop.

My mam started grinning. "Remember when I used to bring you up here, when you were a bairn, we'd have a roll and corned beef for our packed lunch?"

"I do actually, Mam."

"Those were the days, eh? Corned beef was your favorite. That was before you got into that vegetarianism."

"Those were happy days when it was only the two of us, aye."

"You were a braw wee lassie back then, Cora. A well-behaved lassie."

I tucked my hands under my legs. "I'm a big lassie now."

"Whatever happens at the school you'll always be my braw wee lassie." She leaned forward and did a hopeful face. "We'll have those days again. There are only good times here, for the three of us."

"I want out of here, Mam. I want to get away, me and you, somewhere happier. I want to live in Glasgow."

"Oh, Cora, not this again. Where's all these mad ideas about going to Glasgow come from all of a sudden? Glasgow's a huge place. Full of dodgy people."

"Will we go to Abbotscraig then?"

"Gunner's getting a role that will pay him, love. He can develop skills. Do you know how rare that is round here, since they shut the pits? Why would we need Abbotscraig? You've still got me. There's plenty for you here."

"Right." I felt dark inside. My emotions and my blood were blootering round me. I stood up. Everything got urgent and I wanted to bolt.

"We'll get you sorted out at the school." She was beaming up at me and it was hard to see. "Gunner understands what you're like. We know about the lamb, we've spoken about it. He saw you messing about with it out the kitchen window, but it's all forgotten. We'll get you sorted! And, hey, listen! You never know, Abbotscraig will still be there in a year or two. You know that teacher? The one with the waistcoat? He says to me once, *Cora can be anything she wants if she'd only make an effort!* I know it will come good for you, love. With effort. Everyone pulling together."

"Do you know why he wants to become a cake decorator?"

"He was chosen." She ate the last few of her chips, the wee crispy ones.

I sat back down. "Mam, Gunner's a big weirdo. He's done all sorts of weird stuff."

"Look, love, I don't know what stories you've heard, but you have to believe me that Gunner has a heart of gold. He's here to help me *and* you. Has Jo been feeding you gossip? Jo can be a right midden at times."

"Mam, I never want to hear about Jo again."

"Cora, I don't know what's got into you these days, but look, all I'm asking for is your help." She put her hand on my knee. "I know I'm a nag, but it's only because I want to see you get better than I got. That school will pump your head full of all sorts but they never tell you how hard things get. We need to stick together and I need you on board. It's all I'm asking. You're my own flesh and blood, Cora."

I looked over at Gunner, crouched down at the air rifles now, in Ferguson's window. My mam didn't know a single thing.

"I've tried, Mam," I went, and I stood up. For a wee second the words about him and Jo were right on the tip of my tongue, but I turned. Then I walked off across the plaza toward Fusco's. I heard her shout my name a couple of times, not angry, not enough to make a scene, just surprised. Maybe Moira hadn't predicted this for her.

"I'm getting fresh air," I shouted, without looking.

I walked up the grassy mound behind the shops and sat up on the wall that gave you a view over the top of the Savoy then down the main street toward the harbor. You could see all the backs of the shops— someone had spray-painted YOUNG MUIRCROSS CREW over the old Poll Tax graffiti on the back of Foodland.

It felt like everything good in the world was happening somewhere else to somebody else. Samantha and Jay, Dunc, Ravey Davey, Dennis, Dennis's big sister. Auntie Janine. Fozzy and his motorbike, in Dusseldorf, or wherever. That reptile Jo Buchanan. These people were all on their way. They were all from Muircross like me but they hadn't let that stop them. What was stopping me? Why couldn't I push myself? Organize things? Why couldn't a lassie like me have a gazebo, or a motorbike? A love bite?

I stood up on the wall so I could see over the shops and down onto the Savoy plaza. Gunner was sat on one of the plastic seats on the slab now. He was leaned right in to my mam with both of his arms stretched out around her and he was rubbing her back with those grotty hands. She had her head down and she was crying. I couldn't see her face but I knew the movements—her head shaking left and right, the quick, jerky shrugging shoulders.

The Firth looked flat and shiny like the film on a heat-up macaroni.

Blobs of cloud-shadow were sliding in over the plaza. On one of the red plastic seats our three scrunched-up chip papers were trembling in the wind.

I turned and I ran. I had so much energy in me that it felt like I could either stand still and explode or bolt until it stopped—bolt until the sun went in, bolt until I was lost. Bolt until my face went shiny and my batteries died.

At the big gravelly roundabout I crossed and ran up the road toward the leisure center. My heart felt spongy and I had a kind of crumpled tinfoil feeling in my lungs but I just kept going, because the further and faster I went the better I felt. The better my plans got.

I'd run all the way to McDonald's. I had no money but I'd lie on the grass there and relive my night with Dennis and then there'd be a noise and I'd look up and he'd be pulling in. We'd kiss and I'd get in his sister's car and I'd explain and then he'd buy me fries and drive me away. Glasgow, Edinburgh, Dundee, Perth, I didn't care.

At the brae by the leisure center I felt like I might be about to die so I went and sat on the small bit of waste ground next to it. I waited in the warm chlorine smell just trying to breathe, then the minute I was able I got up and started again. I walked the whole length of the Old Market Road then did a loop around the edge of the town twice, and when I got bored of that I started out toward Sycamore Park.

I had no idea what time it was when I got to the park, but I wasn't worried. There was a triangle of boys with bikes and bags playing football but apart from that it was deserted. I walked past the dented slide and the tire swing with no tire, and up through the trees past the wee gang of hardnut crows who stole Fiona's hairband that time she pinged it at them to make them go away. I suddenly felt exhausted in the shade.

It was cooler up there, near where the woods began, and I sat down next to one of the infoboard maps that showed you all the walks you could do around the old abandoned holes. I lay down in the long twiggy grass and spread myself out and made an angel. Up through the trees I watched the clouds move. I closed my eyes and listened to the sound of the dry nettles swishing in the wind.

I must have fallen asleep, because when I blinked again and rolled to the side the sun was still up but the sky was grimier. My skin felt tight and there was chilliness in the air that I could feel inside my knees and my elbows. The grass was tickling my neck and my mouth tasted like the smell of that white school glue.

I headed out of the park all creaky then back over the roundabout and toward the old streets of the town. I went back across the center, keeping my head low. I'd left the two of them at the Savoy at one and now the clock on the big stony building said ten past five. I knew I was in lorry-loads of shit.

On the estate I turned into my road and saw a car parked outside our house, by the phone box. I walked down the hill and as I got closer I could see it was the police.

I turned into the garden and kept my eyes on the toadstools as I walked past the half-finished ramp to the door. Then a voice from behind, all friendly, says, "Are you Cora Mowat? Margaret Mowat's daughter?"

I birled round. I hadn't heard my mam called Margaret since the council fixed the phone box. And nobody ever used my full name except my mam. A policeman, with the window down and his arm leaning out. Someone was getting lifted, for definite. "I'm Cora Mowat, aye."

"How are you doing, Cora?"

"If this is about Gunner's magazines and the other stuff I can take you in and show you it all? He's sorry about all that. Honestly."

"Magazines? Listen, is there another adult around? An uncle or an auntie? My name's PC Lennox and this is PC Drummond." The beardy policeman waved at me from the car. "We've been out looking for you. Gunner's at the police station. We're needing a little chat."

The sky was deciding about rain. I went, "Listen, Gunner's not my da, my da died when I was wee. But you know, we are trying to make a go of it here. Like a family."

"Cora—"

"Has Jo phoned you? He takes me on walks but he's not fiddling me. You can't go listening to gossip off of Jo."

He got out of the car, stood at the gate with his thumbs in his belt. He had a face you wanted to put your foot through. "Cora, we need to speak to you about your mum."

"My mam?"

"Yes."

His voice had went sensible and straight away I couldn't move. Not even my toes. I stared down at his bandy-legged shadow stretching out across the pavement. The wind was restyling my hair. I says, "I was just with her. What's my mam done?"

"Your mum's not done anything. Listen, it would be better if we sat down."

"Is she coming home?"

He leaned down so he was more level, then from nowhere he did a smile that said *I am feeling so sorry for you.* My heart was roller-coastering and all I could do was in-breaths. Then he put his hand on my shoulder and he went, "Cora, I'm sorry to have to tell you—"

"To tell me what?"

"To tell you that there's been an accident."

12

A couple of years back my mam got me *Beauty and the Beast* pajamas for Christmas and I hated them. I'd wanted rollerblades. The pajamas were yellow and when you wore them you looked like you were dressed like Belle from the cartoon. It was an absolute beamer to think I'd ever wear something like that.

I went up to my room and spent Christmas Day on my bed in a silent huff eating my entire selection box, even the Topic and the Bounty. All I could think was how much I hated my mam, how she didn't know me at all, how I wanted a different family and a different house and grown-up pajamas and to never be born.

In my dreams now I go downstairs. Her and Terry are on the settee watching *The Snowman* and the Christmas tree is blinking away. I stand there and tell her I hate her, I tell her she doesn't know me, I tell her I want a different family and a different house. She's crying and crying and Terry is laughing and I can't stop myself. Then she disappears and I am stuck in Christmas 1992 with Terry. Then I wake up and I want to die.

In the weeks after my mam went Dennis came round all the time, asking for me. I'd lie at the top of the stair dehydrated from crying, and listen as he handed over wee presents for me—Rainbow Drops from the Co-op, the shells off hermit crabs from the harbor, the New Beat cassettes from his sister's car. Gunner stacked them all on the table by the front door. It was Gunner that eventually told him not to come back. It was Gunner that told him *Cora's not going to be seeing anyone for a while.*

I missed her. From the first second I missed her. I never thought I would ever miss her but I did. I just wanted to say one or two more things to her—I was sorry, I would wash my hair, I would calm myself, I would do anything. I was sorry and I was ready to listen, if she wanted to speak again. She'd spent her whole life trying to teach me about growing up and I'd never ever listened. I was listening now.

My mam had been wound up, Gunner said. There'd been arguing and more arguing. He didn't say about what. I never asked about what because I knew it was me.

He said he'd done everything he could to calm her down but in the end when she wheeled herself away from the Savoy he thought it would be best to let her go off and have some space. To think over things and calm herself down.

"She'd got like this before," was the thing he repeated over and over. I was just thinking *when can I see her* because I didn't know then the answer was *never again.*

He said she'd stormed off wheeling herself and he'd followed behind her anyway, at a distance, kind of secretly, in case she had needed help, with the pavements, with the steps. When the accident happened he was a bit behind her, at the triangle park, by the fountain with the road cones in it.

She'd crossed over by the fire station without looking and a man in a Range Rover had swung round the corner and hit her. Gunner never said anything after that, just that she was gone. He never talked any more about outside the fire station. She was safe now, is all he kept saying. She hadn't suffered at all.

I felt like she'd be home any minute. It was like someone had made a copy of my wee world and put every single thing in it the exact same, apart from my mam. And I was supposed to be living there now. Sometimes I'd feel panicky about getting back to the place I used to live, other times it felt easier—I told myself I'd have to wait. Something would happen. It would have to. I would go back—awake, with a blink, in the old world, in the real world, happy, with my mam again.

It was maybe three weeks after the funeral that I managed to drag myself out of bed and get downstairs for my Coco Pops. A Friday morning. Gunner was sleeping still.

The light in the kitchen was amazing. The sun was long and yellow on the lino, big mad sunbeams like aliens or Jesus was landing in the garden. I sometimes got the feeling my mam was with me, but that Friday morning, seeing that light, I really felt she was there.

Then I saw—all the magnet letters off the fridge were scattered across the floor. I felt the floodgates coming—the way the light was shining, the way my heart felt. I knelt straight down in my pajamas and started looking for any words spelled out, like it was maybe my mam in the sky doing a message for me.

It was all a scrambled heap and even when I moved round to opposite angles it didn't make sense. Was it all in code or a different language? Was my mam in another country's heaven? My mam had watched every episode of *Eldorado* but she never learned the words.

Then when I went to get the milk I saw there was a massive dent in the fridge door. Gunner had punched it. It was obvious from how it had caved in. He'd smashed it up and knocked the letters off everywhere.

Aye there had been tears, of course there had, there was more rage and sadness in me than I could ever get out, like my crying dials were jammed at ten, but I was stopping it.

I was choking and blubbing but the only thought I could ever really manage was *keep it in, Cora*. Maybe I was afraid that if I let go I wouldn't be able to stop. I'd explode, like a bag of Skips—you're pulling and pulling and it won't open then all of a sudden it splits and your crisps are in the road.

I ran round in my bare feet scooping the letters off the floor and then I binned them. I took my Coco Pops to the settee and sat there in the dimness looking down into them, trying not to see her records, or her Santa hat, or all the other things still lying about. Then Gunner came down the stair.

"Morning, lass."

I nodded.

He sat next to me in his dressing gown and put his arm around me. It felt thin and heavy, and hot from bed. "Good to see you up and eating. I told you it would come back, eh."

"Aye." I did a wee side look. His knuckles were scraped and bruised.

He went to say something else but there was a metal clacking noise—post dropping through the front door. He jumped up and got it. I pressed some dry Coco Pops down into the milk with my spoon and heard them muttering.

"Right," he goes, walking toward the kitchen with an envelope. You knew from the voice he had found something out in the letter he had opened. "How about a cup of tea?"

I sat for a wee minute, then I went through and put my bowl by the other dirty dishes. The sun was lighting up the kitchen again. I wasn't into poltergeists and stuff but then I'd never known someone that had died. Now I had a dead person in my life maybe I would have to learn these signs and teach myself how to communicate. At the funeral I'd kept my face in Gunner's coat nearly the whole time, and about half-way through a wee demented-looking ladybird had landed next to his pocket. I had said hello to it right away. I hated myself for thinking it, but I knew that was my mam.

Out the back he was sat on the step leaning forward, resting his head on his knees with his stripey dressing gown flapping in the wind. All the grass looked fresh and the Firth was glinting and I was wishing I could tell it to stop.

"Sit down, chief," he goes. His face was serious as he handed me my tea and I sat down. He'd used an old white mug from the back of the cupboard that my mam hadn't touched in years.

"Did you sleep at all?"

I watched the top of my tea wobble as I did wee swilling movements on the mug. "Not much."

He rubbed my head and put his fingers through my hair and I let him. "It'll take time."

I nodded. I think he realized I wasn't saying anything else—ever since the funeral it had felt like one little wrong word and the unstoppable flood would start.

"Listen, Cora-doll, there's something I need to tell you—well, it's difficult."

I looked down at the concrete step. Was he going to start confessing about Jo? I felt my body clamping up closed from top to bottom like a robot transforming on the telly.

When your mam gets hit by a car and dies, and you sit in a hospital corridor watching police try and untangle her broken wheelchair, and everything's whispers—in the police car, in the station, in the hospital, in the taxis, at the house, in the phone box after—when it's all whispered, behind your back, as if you're not the one who knew your mam best, as if you're not the one who deserves most to know what's happening, as if everything's out of your control now. Well.

The feeling of that—it makes every other problem or feeling or bad thing or good thing in your life disappear. Everything gets replaced by heaviness and pain. I couldn't have given two fucks about Jo. Jo had vanished down to nothing. Finished. Taped up in a box in the attic. Drowned in a sack. I was too busy breathing in and out. Trying to put Coco Pops in my mouth. Looking forward to the day when I brushed my hair.

"Honestly—"

"Cora, first I need to say that I'm not a da. Not yours, not anybody's. We can agree on that, eh?"

I looked him in the eye. He still wasn't smiling. I sipped the burny tea and says, "What's this about?"

"Let's—I dunno." He gulped his whole tea down and put the mug on the step, nearly lined up in my mam's old spill-circles. I listened for my insides and for my heartbeat in my ears but the panic and fear couldn't budge the numbness.

"Tell me."

He looked out over the Firth. "One of the first things I got asked to do by the police and those arsehole social workers—I've filled some forms out, darlin', about us. I had to put your next of kin down and all the rest of it. Your next of kin is your closest relative."

"How did you know my next of kin?"

"Your mam explained things, before. And the social workers helped. There's records."

"Me and you are not related, are we?"

"I'm not your da. I know that for sure."

"My da got electrocuted in 1984. He was trying to steal copper out a mining tunnel."

"Aye."

"My mam said he was an arsepiece anyway." Over on the Causey there were men from the council strimming weeds in white helmets. I focused on the one nearest the water. "My mam seemed to end up with the wrong folk over and over."

"It wasn't easy for your mam. But there were good times, Cora. She loved you more than anything."

"So what does this letter say?"

He pulled it folded from his dressing gown pocket. The sun was glowing his lugs pinky-orange. "It's confirming your next of kin, eh."

"Auntie Janine. I've not seen her since I was about ten."

"That makes sense because, well—the letter says she's—*Janine Mowat is ruling herself out.* Of looking after you."

I laughed. "I wouldn't go near her if you paid me."

ONLY HERE, ONLY NOW   101

He looked down at me, totally blank and empty. "The letter's saying there's two options. You stay here with me or you're going in care.
A children's home."

I breathed and waited for a feeling but nothing came. "When do
we have to choose by?"

He did a big gulp of air and straightened his back. "You're not going in a home."

I looked at my knees and then at him. The paper was shaking in his
hand now. "What then?"

"Well, until everything's sorted, it's me and you." He shook his
head. "Like, it's not ideal. And it can't be forever. I—I dunno, I'm not
a da. But I'm not leaving you on a doorstep."

"I don't even know your second name."

"McCallum. Michael McCallum."

I sipped my tea. "That's a boring name."

"It's no *Cora Mowat*, eh."

I smiled a wee bit. There was a pause. Then I don't know what it
was—maybe just the stupidness of hearing him say my name, or thinking about him having to look after me, or picturing my mam's face if
she could hear all this—but I started crying.

It was another big tangle—relief, hate, fear, sadness, guilt. Everything all at once. I started bawling. Wailing so loud the wee man with
the strimmer on the Causey could probably hear. Right away I knew I
had one of those screwed-up jellyfish faces that you saw other lassies
make when they were blubbing their eyes out on buses about boys, but
I didn't care.

Gunner shunted close and put his arms right round me and squeezed.
He smelled of cucumbery deodorant and teabags. For maybe only the
second or third time in my life I let my brain relax and my body go limp
because for a wee minute it felt like the only place on earth I had.

And then my brain started the usual, rerunning everything he'd
said and making it worse and worse. Here was this total stranger talking

about my future like I was just some lost wee lassie with scraped knees. What right did he have to be in me and my mam's house? Using her mugs? Deciding things? Touching me?

I pulled away from him and sooked up a string of slavers and tried to stop the blubbing. My face was roasty and damp.

"It'll be okay," he whispered, looking at me through my matted hair. But I'd heard that before and I never believed it. All adults ever did was tell you bad news or lies or make you eat things at a certain speed.

I was trying to think of something to do or say that would maybe put the feelings from the whole horrible past behind me. I thought for maybe five seconds before something else took over.

I jumped at him with every bit of strength I had and punched him right in the face, and I punched again and again with both fists and I scratched and clawed and screamed like an animal until he clamped my arms down in a hug and wrestled me flat on the grass.

Then he scrambled away and stood gawping down as I lay there all shaky like something that escaped from the zoo and got shot by a dart. Then slowly he sat back down, apart from me, and then he leaned in and reached over, and he took my hand, and he pulled me into him, trembling.

"Oh, lass," he went, and when I heard his voice crack I started crying again. It felt this time like there was no holding back. It felt this time as if the crying would maybe never stop.

Part Two

ABBOTSCRAIG, 1996

13

The first thing I felt was cold clean air in one nostril. My brain saying, *Cora, you've been woken.* I blinked—thin light and washing lines, fences, a shed.

My own back garden, and me outside in it.

"Cora!" It was a female voice. "It's morning. Are you okay, pet?"

I pulled my hair off my face and checked my earrings and blinked more to separate my lashes. Our neighbor Donna was leaning over the fence smiling down at me, all respectable in her nurse's uniform with the upside-down watch.

"I'm okay! Sorry." I sat up, tugging down at my dress. I got onto my knees and gathered my tangled parka and hair pins out of the grass. My face was going burny from the disgrace.

Our gray house was joined to another gray house, like a mirror of ours, and Donna lived there by herself. Donna and Gunner spoke sometimes and he told me that she was thirty-two and Abbotscraig born and bred.

When we first moved in she'd just said *hiya* but as months passed she started leaning over the fence every two minutes lending us utensils and sponge cake. She had brown hair and she was slim and tall and she had eyes like Beth off *Neighbours*. I didn't like her—whenever she appeared I just sat there silent like a chunky wee scowler.

"You've not been out all night, have you? It's bloody October! Have you forgot your keys, pet?"

"I came back a while ago. He's locked the doors." I tried to do an easygoing grin on my hands and knees. "Morning, Donna." It was way too shameful to say the truth—that I'd come back drunk and slept the whole night in the grass.

"Gunner's on nightshift tonight, Cora. But he gave me a spare key?" She smiled. "He did say something like this might happen!"

"Oh did he?" I stood up, started picking dead grass and leaf crumbs off of my tights. The cold hard muck had made my bones go achy and strange. I felt like I had dropped out of the sky.

"Do you want to come in and warm up, love? I'm off to work shortly but I could make you a hot chocolate?"

"It's okay. That key would be good though?" She disappeared and came back a second later with keys on a hoop. I unlocked our door and handed them back to her. She had weird pale forearms with hardly any hair.

She goes, "Were you out last night? Oh god, what's that place in town? Halo Lounge?"

"No, it was quiet, really. Me and my pal Vicki. I'm kind of penniless."

"You look so grown up in that dress. It's like you're sprouting every day!"

I tried to smile. The vodka was reversing through me. "Thanks. I'm going to go in. I've got loads to do."

"Take care then, pet." She waited an awkward second then went inside.

"Donna?" I says. Her head popped back out. I was picking at my thumb. "Please don't tell him."

"Ach, Cora. I was young once too. My lips are sealed."

The cooker clock was telling me eight twenty and I'd not done a single job from the night before. Gunner's nightshift finished at eight and he was always home by eight forty-five.

I scraped cold chips and dry beans off our plates, then I took the bin out. I wiped down the benches and did the dishes and mopped the floor, then I downed three mugs of water. When I stood still and stopped to think my head kept going, *Cora, you're a useless wee shite*.

In the bathroom I took my makeup off and did a pish. I flushed once then knelt down and stared into the circle of water, waiting. I boaked full force into the bowl four times. I blew the vom out my nostrils and flushed, then I opened the window and skooshed Glade everywhere and ran up the stair giggling.

My mam used to call the puddles of boak you'd see on the Causey on a Sunday morning the Muircross omelets—*If you land in one of those Muircross omelets don't expect me to hose you down!* Even the worst stuff like throwing up my guts in secret still managed to remind me of her.

My house keys were sat on my bed where I'd left them before I went out. I dumped the cold parka then whipped the shoes, dress and tights off and chucked them in the bottom of my wardrobe. I shut my curtains and put the hair pins in the bedside drawer with the keys.

My brand-new double bed had seashell-pattern covers. I got in and huddled myself round and waited for the sound of the front door. On my alarm clock Minnie Mouse's bendy arms were pointing to eight forty-two. Most mornings I wanted to punch fuck out of her smarmy rodent face. Every present Gunner got me was practical.

Sometimes me and him felt like two bashed tatties circling round a microwave that would never go *ping*. Every wee thing that happened in the house—a blocked hoover tube or a burnt fish finger or a night sleeping in the grass—just turned the heat up and up and up.

Looking back, the year and a half together in Muircross had actually been easier—numbness got me through the funeral and the worst weeks, and her death was the focus of everything. Eventually, Gunner and me got back to our walks and we stuck together because the pain was like glue. There was no room back then to be worrying about wee things, but now the normalness of Abbotscraig life was showing us how different we were.

I must have fallen back asleep because next thing he's home and the kitchen radio's on and I can hear Spice Girls mingling with manly pish noises rumbling in the toilet bowl downstair. Then the voice— *Cora. Cora, lass. Cora!* I knew if I ignored it he'd come up the stair and give me toast.

The letter from the council had arrived about five months after the one about my Auntie Janine. They'd processed my mam's application. "Are we leaving Muircross?" I goes, when he'd finished explaining how it worked, because he hadn't actually said for definite. He nodded slowly aye and I burst out with the floodgates again.

He handed me the letter. It said *60 Weavers Row, Abbotscraig* at the top. My mam's name wasn't on it. Because of the forms he'd done, everything said Michael McCallum now. There was a glossy snapshot of the house stapled to the front—a gray cube with empty black windows sitting under a thundercloud. It looked nothing like how my mam had explained it. Big letters said, *If you choose not to accept the accommodation detailed below you will be moved to the bottom of the waiting list.*

He said it was me and him, now or never. He had put in for a job as a caretaker at the hospital and we were accepting the council's offer and we were escaping to Abbotscraig. There was no mention of the Gillespies or his business, it was like everything was going to change and there would be a new plan.

We sat down and done more forms about my mam and I helped him with the spelling and told him my middle name and then we sent them off. There were meetings and panels and folk in the house and I thought we would sort everything out between us once they were done, but we never did.

We both knew there was too much of my mam in Muircross. It felt like every tree and branch and cushion and plate and chair reminded me of her. I'd tried with everything I had to live next to those things—

the phone box and the sound of the Firth and the way the sun sent a big stripe through our window and onto wee Lena Zavaroni most afternoons. But I failed. It was December 1995 when we left. I felt guilty thinking it but I was glad to go.

Gunner hired a big van but in the end we left a lot of things behind—things that were ancient, things that were broken, things that were too difficult to hold. I remember the last thing I saw as we drove away was our old fridge freezer, standing all punched-in and lonely in the sleety rain. As we rolled off I couldn't help waving bye-bye to that fridge because it had known me for years.

The house turned out way worse than the photo. There was a wheelchair ramp at the front door to remind you of her every day. Inside there were echoes and mold and stoor-balls and the skeletons of dried-out spiders everywhere. The taps coughed and the doors moaned and it smelled like a bus station waiting room. When I was by myself in the bathroom I sometimes whispered *sorry* to my mam. I was glad though, that she never had to see it.

On our first week, during the big clean, I was looking in the cupboard under the kitchen sink for a bucket so I could help. All that was in there was mouse poo and a crinkled *Sunday Sport* from 11 April 1993. There was a blond-haired woman on the front called *Tracey-Anne, 24, Coventry*. Her bra was down and she was holding her bits. All my brain kept telling me over and over was *Your mam was alive that Sunday*.

Later that day, after we'd cleaned the kitchen, I took the crinkled *Sunday Sport* out the back and Gunner lit a fire in the rusted wheelbarrow we'd found in the shed and we burned it. When the flames got going I went up to my room and dug stuff out—report cards and jotters, notes from Dennis, old rave flyers Jo gave me. Samantha's printouts and that ancient issue of *Mizz* that explained boys' moods.

I chucked most of it in. The printouts were last. I held them, thinking how sometimes they'd felt like magic to me, the way they had described things. I stood there in the frosty grass watching the flames and tears came. I folded the printouts away in my jeans pocket and said to myself that things would have to get better.

About eleven months ago, that day—shivering in Gunner's plum-color decorating fleece and my old bobble hat, seeing fluttery scraps of English homework and *Mizz* and *Tracey-Anne, 24, Coventry* burn and loop and crumble up in the air in front of us—was the last time I cried about things. The last time I cried about my mam.

I kept my eyes squeezed shut as Gunner came in my room. I could smell the melted butter. "Cora. Up you get." I rolled round and did a big panto yawn. He handed me the plate. "Thanks for putting my mug out. Have you been up?"

"Only for the loo."

"Our appointment is in forty minutes. Get that in you then get showered. You stink."

I sat round and pulled the duvet to my chin while he opened my curtains. I bit the toast and looked at the cartoon shape my teeth had made, then I yawned again and said it. "I'm not going anymore."

He sat on the end of my bed. "Cora—"

"Like, I wanted to say before. It's stupid to keep seeing a counselor when it's not doing anything. Sorry. I'm fine." A dog was barking over in the park. Brightness from my window was punishing my brain. The room was baltic as usual.

He leaned on his elbow near my feet. "You're sixteen. If you don't feel it's working then I'm not going to force you, like."

"My mam died over two years ago."

"Yep."

I was amazed how easy he gave in. Going into every discussion I would always worry about getting my own way, but the one big thing I had was that I knew about him and Jo.

There was so much stuff my mam never found out about, and it made me sad to carry it round, but at the same time it was a bit like having a weapon in your sock. I didn't know if it would be a tiny blade or a big fuck-off chib but I knew the Jo thing would do some kind of damage when I eventually pulled it out and used it. I gulped my toast quick so I could speak before he started on again. "How was work?"

"The usual. I need my bed."

"Is that a beard you're trying to grow? A cat would lick that off."

"Eh? Oh, I've not had a chance to sort it. My mind's on other things, eh."

"Like what?"

"Life."

I smiled. "Jeez! All right, sad sack."

"What time did you get in last night?"

"Oh, maybe nine? Vicki had a bottle of vodka. But it was just a few drinks."

"On a Thursday?" I nodded while chewing. A year ago, I would probably have started tearing up because he didn't remember that 24 October was my mam's birthday. "Could you not sit in here and have a drink?"

I looked at him. "With you creeping round the door to make sure we're okay?"

He lay right back on my bed and crossed his arms over his chest. It felt like we'd done every single type of discussion so I knew like magic when something serious was coming. "If you're not going to talk to the counselor then you better find someone to speak with. Because I know it's all fun right now, going out and drinking and all the rest, but it's no future."

I finished the last bit of toast and felt something through me. What was I meant to say? Sometimes the truth that was in me just sounded too weird to say out into the world.

I didn't talk to the counselor because he wore shirts patterned like the floor of the amusement arcade and he was called Dan and he acted like he was me and my mam's best pal. *What's made you sad this week, Cora?* I dunno, bin smells? Knicker labels? Losing my favorite spoon?

Getting told off for slouching? He asked the same shite every week and he talked about grief like it was a thing—like it was a dangerous frog off a documentary that you could smack dead with a stick.

His favorite was Grief Mountain. *You're both at the top. Every bone in your body is broken. You and Gunner cannot help each other down—you must find your own route, alone.* Then that wee shite-slurping posho grin of his. The whole time I'm nibbling my pinky nails and picturing him tied to a sledge, me shoeing him right off the side of Grief Mountain into the sea. When he spoke like he knew my mam I wanted to hit him until my hands broke apart.

Dan gave Gunner leaflets for me about the workings of the brain, and a key ring with a cartoon banana saying a speech bubble about the five rules for grieving. There was a card for my purse with the number of a charity in England. Gunner bought a brand-new phone for the house, to save me walking to the box. Soon it was the main way me and him referred to my mam—leaflets. *Have you looked at your leaflets? Let me know if you want to go over the leaflets tonight? Have you rang that number on that pamphlet yet, Cora?*

"I talk to lassies at school about it. To Vicki."

"Come on."

"Talking's not magic."

"Well it's a big year for you, eh, with exams. You'll be getting a wee job soon. You'll have weeks and months that are going to shape your future and you can't be going out hammering cider and hoping all this goes away."

"Vodka." There was silence. I focused on the duvet cover. "I know all this. You're boring me."

"You think you do. Anyway, gimme that plate."

He sounded nearly too tired to speak. I handed him the toast plate and he stood up. "Listen, you want to tackle the shed soon? This week-end or next? There's a few boxes still unopened, like. Bits and bobs from the old house."

"I've got plans. With Vicki."

"If we sort through those last boxes that's us properly moved in. It's only taken us ten bloody months, eh!"

"I'll see. Now you going to get out so I can get ready or do I need to ring ChildLine and tell them you're perving?" He turned and walked out the door. "Gunner?"

He stepped back in. Stood in the doorway he looked all gangly and gentle-seeming with one arm angled out against the wall. "Aye?"

I did my wee arse-licker smile. "Since I'm off school this morning anyway could I not just maybe take—"

"They gave you time off for counseling, not sleeping off hangovers. You're going to school." It was that sitcom da voice he'd perfected.

"Were you never young once?"

He rubbed his nostrils twice quickly and snorted like my words had gone right up there and irritated his brain. "There will be serious trouble if you are not at that school within the hour."

He walked out, then put his head back round the door. "By the way, you dropped this." He chucked my purse onto the bed. Coins tinkled and boinged out over the seashells on the duvet. "If you're lurking round the garden in the dark you better tidy up after yourself, love." I pictured Donna and her sponge cake and her giant gob and her gallons of tea. "And brush the grass out your hair?"

"Gunner—"

"I'll be up at the usual time, make sure the dinner's ready and the hoovering's done."

"Gunner!"

He walked out the door. "I'm going to bed, so keep the noise down. I've been awake since this time yesterday."

14

In the kitchen I glugged some water out my Maltesers mug and ate four slices of dry bread. Then I slipped a tenner out his wallet.

I always kept my eyes closed because he kept a photo of my mam from 1992 in the wee plastic window. I knew she wouldn't mind me giving the big goon a taste of his own medicine but I still didn't feel like looking her in the eye while I did it.

Cash was motivation, mainly. The thought of a sausage supper and Lilt on lunch would drag me to the school. Rainbow Drops or Softmints for my blazer pocket to try and fast-forward the afternoon. Mini Rolls after, maybe.

In all the stress and crying the first thing that went was my vegetarianism. Gunner had tried his best—beans with tattie, beans on toast, beans in a bowl—but I told him it was fine. There just wasn't room to care about things like I used to.

I shoved on my high-heel Kickers and pulled the parka over my uniform. He was snoring like a moped up the stair. I grabbed my bag, then slipped out like a burglar and locked the front door.

The first thing I saw was the wee prowler down at my front gate, loitering under a big fuck-off crispy-blue sky—Vicki Conroy, uniform on, ponytail up, big bottle of cream soda hanging out her coat pocket.

She did that smile. "No appointment after all?"

"I says, *My mam died two years ago,* and that was that! He's too tired from work to fight me now." I looked up at his bedroom curtains as I zipped my parka.

She started laughing. "I'm heading into town."

On dry afternoons, and sometimes when it rained, me and Vicki would just forget the school—we'd drift round Abbotscraig with chips or Pringles or limeade, tightroping the curbs and gossiping, fingering the parking meter change slots to look for fifty pences that the rich folk missed. It was freedom.

I creaked the flaky gate shut and walked ahead. "I can't. Honestly. He's said I've to go in. I could tell by the face he's serious."

"He's asleep for fuck's sake!"

"He's tired now but when he wakes up he'll be raring to go, trust me."

"Well my cousin Pauline's got a job interview and I'm going with. Come and meet her! She's twenty-four. You'll love her."

There was something about these wide bright days that wasn't good for a lassie like me. I was all over any wee bit of newness or excitement like a crow dismantling a hamburger. "All right. But let's get out my street," I whispered. "It always feels like he can hear."

Vicki was in my year at St. Therese and we'd been paired up to help me settle. She lived five streets away in a grayer house than mine and she loved explaining all the shortcuts and local loyalties.

Abbotscraig was basically new bottle same old pish. There were flumes at the baths and a café in the Tesco and a gleamy shopping center with plastic plants and a Schuh and an Our Price, just like my mam had said. But the outer parts where me and Vicki stayed were a big Muircrossy jumble of drainpipes and police tape and aerials.

The town was famous for a train crash and a sex-pest footballer who hung himself with a hosepipe in his wife's knickers the year I was born. The place was chocka with loonies and mutants and I had to giggle—it was mental to think a shithole like this would sort me out. Abbotscraig was basically Muircross on stilts.

We turned left out of my street and crossed to the entrance of the

Backy Park. Pigeons were out, being stupid in piles of leaves. Vicki took a huge swig of her cream soda and passed me the bottle. "So I was in first thing. I walked to school with that cousin-fucker Kira Coathanger this morning."

"No way! Was she wearing the jumper?" I glugged then passed it back to her.

"Under her cagoule. *Performance Sport.* Chip-shop menu lettering. No-make tramp."

There were three groups at the school—normal Twix-eating girls like Vicki and me. Then the wee alicebands called Stephie and Gail who ate nectarines on break and lived in the Barratt homes and probably had gazebos like Dennis. And then Kira-Louise Cantwell, in her own wee group of one.

She'd enrolled at St. Therese in March, three months after me, and was still getting switched between classes and taking time off and you knew it wasn't just mumps or a dying gran. Folk were nasty to her, but her newness took the heat off me, so I wasn't losing sleep. Someone called her Kira Coathanger and it was random so it stuck.

"She was waiting on the top path, right." Vicki turned and walked backward, facing me. Her eyes were gleaming from cream soda nose-fizz and mischief. "Wee bin-dipper looks like she won her clothes in a fucking tombola! Anyway, I pass her, I'm keeping my head down, then I hear, *Hiyaa, Victoooria!*"

We left the park. "So what did she want?"

"She asked me to go rollerblading. No small talk, just *d'ya want to come rollerblading, Victoooria?* She goes rollerblading up the Mill Loan. My jaw was hanging. I says I've got no interest in your fucking rollerblading because I haven't been eleven for years!" She took a big swig. "Anyway, halfway to the school she pulls a roll and corned beef from the jacket pocket! No foil, no bag, no nothing. What kind of tramp eats rolls and corned beef?!"

"Horrible wee cow."

"Pauline's staying with my other cousin. It's number forty-one, up here."

Vicki's big cousin's doorbell did "Oh When the Saints." Pauline came out with her back to us and as she shut the door you could smell that smell of ironing from the house.

For the whole time we'd been at Abbotscraig, Gunner was like *get back in touch with Fiona, what about that goth boy you were courting?* He never realized I was a different lassie to the Fiona days, that Dennis was sweet but I was over sweet. And Gunner didn't know how many cool people I met just from being pals with Vicki.

Pauline had on a gold crushed-velvet smock dress with a man's longish black leather coat. White tights and black patent brogues. Dark brown hair in a bowl cut, hoop earrings like me. And a neck tattoo. I was thinking that it must be fake but she was looking right at me so I couldn't really investigate.

She goes, "These early sunsets are ruining my life."

"It's no even lunchtime, Pauline," Vicki says.

Pauline came down off the step, grinning. Her eyes were the color of puddle water and she had wee kissy-bow lips like off an advert. "Aye but I can feel it coming! Can you not feel it coming?"

I smiled because the way she said it you didn't know if she actually wanted an answer.

"This is Cora," Vicki goes. "She's only moved here last Christmas, from Muircross. She's sound though."

"Pauline Sclater," she goes, and stuck her hand out.

I stood as cool as I could then I shook it. "Cora Mowat."

We turned out of Pauline's garden. She goes, "Muircross, eh?" then made a wee finger-cross at me, like you did at a vampire. "So you up near Vicki now?"

"Weavers Row."

We crossed the road at the big ugly spaceship church. "Ooh, *Hell-meadow.*"

The Abbotscraig estates had nicknames—Greyskull, Toaty Bronx, the Deathy, Beirut. Our estate got called Hellmeadow after the Well-meadow Road, the main road that looped round the park and the golf course and joined onto our street.

"Cora, two things you'll need to learn quick round here," Pauline goes. "One, how to spot which boys are the nutters."

Vicki says, "Clue—it's all of them."

I laughed, then Pauline turned to us. "They'll feed you the usual shite about the cosmos but the minute they get your tights down? You wait and see!"

Vicki says, "A survey found that one in three Abbotscraig boys . . . are just as mental as the other two." The pair of them burst out in the exact same cackle.

"So what's number two?"

Pauline goes, "How to look after yourself, physically, like. The two are linked, chick. It'll be worse for you, you're a brand-new dish round here. A spicy meatball. You must be batting them off already with that figure."

I looked down at my scuffed-up Kickers because I knew how compliments made my face do stuff. I laughed.

"So what you making of *here*?"

"Maybe I built it up in my head a bit."

"How the fuck did you manage that?" Vicki says.

At the row of shops we stopped so Vicki could get the money back off her glass cream soda bottle. She bought us two bags of 10p crisps to share.

"So you've got an interview?" I goes.

"It's a Job Center scheme, a photocopying job. Doesn't start till after Christmas. It's in Glasgow."

"Amazing."

"I'm out of here when I get it." She chucked a handful of crisps in her mouth and wiped the crisp dust down the front of her dress.

We stopped outside Littlewoods in town, right at the start of the pedestrian high street, next to the bank. The streets were buzzing. There were gothy circus folk juggling opposite Superdrug and a man playing a Guns N' Roses song on an accordion. Two old boys were in the fountain getting coins out, for drink probably.

Pauline says to me and Vicki to wait outside and Vicki nodded and seemed to know what was going on. Pauline went inside.

"What's she doing?" I says, after a wee minute.

"Getting an outfit. She won't be long."

I leaned against the wall of the doorway. "Is her tattoo real?"

"Ask to see Frank. That's what she calls it."

Just then Pauline shot out the double doors, speedwalking, hands in pockets, all stiff and upright. As she passed us she says, "Run!" in a whisper then started sprinting. Vicki ran after her. Then I ran too.

We raced down the New Road and across the heart-shaped flower beds that sat in front of the town hall, going so fast there were mad jolts going up my legs and a jellyish feeling in my head from the breathlessness.

At the side of the town hall we louped the wall, then took the alley to the back of the public toilets by the adventure playground. I was panting when I caught them up and was getting the armpit smell even through my shirt and blazer and parka.

Pauline was standing up on the verge, in the sunshine. She pulled a black jumper from the inside pocket of her coat and held it up by the shoulders. "Cashmere turtleneck. Tell me an easier way to get yourself respectable?"

She took the coat off and handed it to Vicki, then pulled the turtleneck on over her dress—it made it into a gold skirt. The whole thing worked even with the shiny brogues and crisp dust.

"Covers Frank too," I goes, when I could breathe.

"They'll probably only be looking at me waist up. Fuck anybody that doesn't like white tights anyway, Cora."

"Can I see the tattoo?" I says.

She leaned into me then pulled the neck of the jumper down, and I smelled her perfume—like fields of clean washing under rabbit-shaped clouds. Frank was a cute blurry scorpion wearing boxing gloves and a baseball cap, about two inches below her ear.

"That's—I dunno. That's insane," I goes.

She went into the loos to check her makeup then after a big hug with Vicki and an agreement to meet by the cinema she stomped off by herself to the job center while we looked after her leather jacket.

Vicki and me walked up and over the brae. We sat with our school-bags on the broken brick wall that ran the length of the cinema car park, peeling off moss, bouncing our heels. We were kneeling by the bins a bit later, trying to speak to a cat with a manky face, when Pauline reappeared. She was sprinting at us so fast her hair got pushed back like a boy's.

"I fucking got it!" She birled on the spot and Vicki ran to hug her. After a wee awkward minute I did too. When we'd stopped hopping round in a circle Pauline squeals, "Let's get blootered!"

Her favorite pub was called the Keg. It smelled like wet wood and there were four puggies and my stool was warm from someone else's arse. I took Gunner's tenner out of my blazer and gave it to Pauline for drinks, but Vicki goes, "You look about twenty-six, Cora," and then the pair of them made me go up and get them myself.

I walked up picturing Fiona's skipping rope. The barman had Pantene hair and a black T-shirt with a skull on it, but he served me the three pints of cider fine. I picked them up in a triangle and managed to get them back to the table with only four or five splashes down the front of my school shirt. Like all the biggest moments of my life it was over in fifteen seconds.

"Lovely," Pauline goes, taking her pint.

Vicki says, "I'm going to the loo before we start." She walked off up the side of the bar and there was awkwardness. I sipped the cider and Pauline did too. The pints made a noise when you lifted them because of the stickiness of the table.

"Vicki filled you in about wee Frank, did she?"

"I spied it right away."

"My granda Frank was a champion boxer. My da's da. He got called *the Scorpion*. The tattoo's for him."

"That's so cool."

"What else was she telling you?"

"Not much."

"She'll have done the spoonburner routine, aye?" She took three big gulps so I matched her. She wiped her mouth. "Vicki just loves warning folk in advance about me."

"Spoonburner?" I says, burping nearly silently.

"Being funny is how she deals with it. Spoonburners—it's what they call heroin users, chick, round here. All that's behind me now but she still loves announcing it to people. It's exciting for her." She looked across the pub and out the window. "This job's gonna take me out of this sewer. For good."

"I thought heroin lassies had obvious lip liner and scabs on their tits?" She burst out laughing, spurting a half mouthful of cider back into her glass. "Like, are you not meant to be a walking skeleton?"

"Well, I love my mashed tattie. And you've never seen my tits."

"I'm going off your immaculate face."

"Rookie mistake."

Vicki sat back down and undid her ponytail. "Here's to Pauline, in Glasgow," and we all cheersed our pints. She took some big swigs to catch up. "What are you pair giggling about?"

"That barman's T-shirt," I goes.

Pauline leaned over to me. "So, Bonfire Night. Me and Vicki are planning a bevvy if you want to come?"

"Next Tuesday?" I says.

"Aye. Up in the grounds of the old infirmary there's a wee abandoned community hall, on the hill. You can get on the roof dead easy and the view's incred. And it'll be deserted. Just us three. Watch the fireworks."

"I'll need to get a story together."

"Her stepda is always on her back," Vicki goes.

Pauline finished her pint. "Parents are fucking cold custard, aren't they?"

I says, "Cold custard?"

"Rubbishy. *Cold custard*—vile and abysmal. Deeply suss. Useless. Shite."

We ended up in the Keg for nearly two hours. Pauline wanted to stay for more and Vicki agreed, but I couldn't stop thinking about the hassle I'd get for not doing the housework, so I waved them bye before five and wobbled out alone.

Evening had started and fog had appeared, and I'd hardly made it five steps from the pub door when the tiny ball of panic inside me started unscrunching itself. I was kind of ready for it. From the moment that policeman had opened his mouth to tell me the news there was a feeling like being underwater, and it got ten times worse when I was alone.

I started running, because moving always helped. I took the dual carriageway that curved up away from the town then cut through the churchyard and over the back by Safeway. Street lights flickered on and lit the cracked pavement.

The Backy Park was blurry and darkish and nearly empty. Boys were huddled at the bottom of the skateboard bowl trying to fire rockets in the fog. I climbed the fence at the far side behind Easyprice and went through the gap in the hedge to the row of glowing phone boxes. The inside smelled like fag ash and melted plastic. I stood for a minute sobering myself up then I took the change from the tenner out and put some twenty pences in my palm. Did Moira know my mam was dead?

My head kept telling me not to do it, but if I needed to hear that she once existed, who else was I going to ring? I had to sleep in a house that she dreamed of but never saw and live a life she'd never know, and I was just to tuck my laces in and grin about it. But I didn't want lessons and key rings and *a core of serenity*. I wanted to hear a voice from outside our shitey gray house say the word *Maggie* out loud. I lifted the freezing handset and pressed it to my ear.

Then I put the change back in my parka and pushed the handset to my mouth and whispered straight to her, over the tone, for free, "Gunner's going to go apeshit, Mam." My breathing had gone quick and I just wanted to shrink myself down to a frozen pea from how stupid I felt but I kept on speaking anyway. "I've been in my first pub. I bought pints for me and my pals! It was amazing, Mam, but I'm late. I'm steaming drunk. Gunner's going to go fucking apeshit."

15

walked our estate. Through big front windows you saw other families lit by blueish telly light, and by the front gates you smelled dinners the mams were making—grill pans and Bisto and broccoli water, and that dry bakey fish finger breadcrumb smell.

Fog was still rubbing out the roofs in our street but I could see from over the road that Gunner's curtains were dark. Downstair our living room looked hollow through the gaps in the long slat blinds. I didn't want to go in but at the same time I couldn't stay out.

I used my key and crept inside with no clicks, like the wee expert I was. I slipped off the Kickers and used every bit of calmness to snuggle them by the Reeboks with their toes cutely kissing on the mat. I hung up my parka and blazer and zipped on Gunner's old fleece.

In the living room I closed the blinds and put the light on. I punched the cushions then chucked round some Shake n' Vac and tiptoed the hoover across it with my eyes softly swimming. We had a roll hoover so it was easy to use without waking him up. Waking him up was one of the main ways to fuck things.

The kitchen smelled like old burgers and fresh paint. I boiled the kettle and measured out spaghetti, then got a tin of chicken soup out. The cooker clock said five twenty. I put the ring on and the pan on top with no water in, just to heat it up.

He worked all the time and put a brave face on things but we were skint. We had a coin-operated Daewoo telly and we used tea-bags twice and wore fleeces all the time. He brought home green paper towels and individual foily butter portions from the hospital. He was obsessed about wasting food.

The water sputtered everywhere when I poured it in. I could see my mam smiling. Moira would probably have told me some useless shite about wearing red, or acting carefully around a woman called Alice. One day I'd ring up with real questions. How come a cunt in a Range Rover can run someone over and get off free? Did my dead da ever have trouble concentrating? Was there an actual name for the sadness that nearly stopped you breathing?

I dropped the spaghetti in and set the timer. When I turned to get the crisps from the bread bin I glanced out into the darkness and got a shallow feeling in my chest.

He'd hung the sheets out. Without unfolding them—his usual way. They were swaying all damp, sagging the line down so their bottom edges were nearly brushing the grass.

I went and got my Reeboks and when I switched the back light on I saw the shed door open and shadows moving inside. Our stuff was scattered round the grass. He was up, sorting through boxes.

I opened the back door. "Thief!" I shouted, pulling the shoes on, smiling. He came to the doorway of the shed with the moody mouth on. I walked out and started unpegging the sheets one by one, opening them properly. For a wee minute all I heard was the rustley cotton and my feet in the grass. "Not speaking?" I goes.

"Too busy sorting through your shite. Those sheets are drying fine by the way."

"Aye, lovely October night for the drying, isn't it?" I giggled and gulped down a hiccup but he didn't respond. "Why you even awake?"

"School phoned."

I froze with a wet duvet cover twisted in my arms. Blood started going toward my toes. "Oh. Sorry. Vicki and me and—"

"I'm sick of *sorry*. It's meaningless, eh."

I started with the pegs again. "Fine."

"Mrs. McClair wants to get you an appointment with the school psychologist. They think you're stressed. Your absences have triggered an intervention."

"You need to open out these sheets."

"She says to me you're struggling. With grief."

"You can't dry wet washing in fog."

"Can you listen?"

I pegged the last one out and walked to the back step. "Spaghetti's on."

"Look." He pointed a wee puddle of torchlight round the gloomy grass—the cushions off the Muircross settee, our old hall mirror, Dennis's sister's tapes. My mam's Santa hat. The pink Asics lying sideways, sad and spider-invaded. It was all damp and out of order, miles from the life it belonged to. "We need to make a decision about this."

"Throw it out." I stepped back into the kitchen.

"Cora."

I turned back with the anger starting. I reached and grabbed the Asics by their laces, then I stomped to the wheelie bin, lifted the lid and slam-dunked them in. "Like that. Now the rest of it. Please."

In the kitchen I wiped a hole in the steamy glass and watched him gangling about through the gaps in the sheets as they flapped and bulged. I pulled the blind down.

We had a wee wood dining table for two with a red plastic tablecloth that was already rubbing white where our elbows went almost every night. He came back in as I was straggling the chicken soup spaghetti into bowls. I twiddled the grill off and thumped the bowls down.

He washed his hands and sat down opposite. "Crisps are perfect this time, chief. And thanks for fixing the washing." I nodded. He started twirling his fork in the bowl. "Look. You'd give ibuprofen a headache,

Cora, but you're a good lassie, really. And y'know, you've got—god knows—all sorts of hormones flying round that body of yours and—"

"Gunner."

He laughed. "Sorry."

I didn't look away from my food. "You've lightened up."

"Seeing that stuff from the house puts things in perspective." He ate a big forkful. "But there's things of your mam's out there. Your own stuff too. Those poor trainers. You can't just bin things you don't want to remember."

"The Asics are naff. They're a beamer now."

After the silence, he leaned in a bit. "Hey, Donna was telling me she's getting a wee rabbit."

"Good for Donna."

He mixed his spaghetti round. "You never fancied a pet?"

"My mam got me a hamster when I was eight." I finished chewing. "Oswald, my first best pal. He loved popcorn but he had to get his leg amputated. It cost my mam eighty quid. His leg was about the size of a bit of rice. I never heard the end of it. *That fucking gammy hamster of yours. I could have got myself an electric tin opener.*"

"I shouldn't laugh."

"I always wanted a goldfish, for speaking to." I sooked a bit of spaghetti up. "I did nearly have one, for about two minutes. From the Muircross showies. A boy called Fozzy won it. Jo's old boyfriend."

He looked up at me. It was like suddenly you could hear the sheets sighing on the line and the threads of miles-away teatime traffic. Sometimes the thoughts went so quick that I couldn't remember not to remember. Not this time. I'd pulled it out my sock.

"Goldfish are braw!" he says, with a wee grin that wasn't really hiding what he wanted to hide. He scrubbed his palm all over his stubbly head and it made a sound like teeth getting brushed but softer. It was so interesting to watch his face.

The weak way he said it switched something in me. It had been one of those blustery days where the air feels pure and the leaves are crunchy and your mates are giggling your sadness away and it just seems totally fine to let things go. "You remember Jo?"

He put his fork down first, and then his knife. "What about her?"

I still knew the bit from the printouts by heart—*Being argumentative or saying hurtful things can come from an inability to step back and recognize the way others are reacting.* I didn't care this time. The buzz off the cider was fading but other feelings weren't. "You must remember shagging her?"

I took a bite of spaghetti and heard the fork do a single tiny *ting-ting* on my teeth because of the nerves fucking up my hand. My heart needed air. I knew I must be doing the frog nostrils.

His face crinkled up like the sole of a foot. "How the fuck do you know about that, what—?"

"Was it the ginger hair that got you going? Maybe the wraparound shades?"

"What did you see?"

"Everything. I was stood at the back door. In the pouring rain."

"Whatever you saw it's none of your fucking business. It's nothing you should be speaking about, and even if it was, you'd do well to keep your trap shut because you don't know the facts."

I ate more spaghetti. "How many times?"

"You really want to go looking for more upset?"

"We're upset about something *I* do nearly every single day in here. Maybe you don't always get to choose what we get upset about."

"Cora, do you even realize the sacrifices I make day in, day out for you? All the things I—"

"Oh shut up, you got a fucking house out of it."

I knew I'd said it too loud. He stared at me. I could see his Adam's apple going up and down. "Maybe if you were less emotional, if you'd had relationships of your own, maybe I could explain the past—"

"I don't want explanations!"

"Will you stop shouting, eh?"

There was a feeling in my throat like when you've not chewed the bon-bon small enough. "I don't want piles of rubble and shite and lies to tiptoe round. I want it out on the table, where we can see it, like—that!" I chucked my fork in my bowl and it bounced back out.

"This fucking Jo thing—ach, y'know what, if it means I can speak to you about me and your mam—I've tried to say it god knows how many—"

"I'm not an idiot." My legs started doing their own beat under the table. "Don't try using my mam to give yourself a bigger role in my life. You knew her five fucking minutes."

"Maybe if you faced up to things we could talk about her. We could go and visit her for once. Maybe then you'd calm down and stop blubbing."

"Fuck off. I haven't cried about it in ages."

"Cora, this is it. There's no man with a clipboard coming to take you to a Barratt house full of rugs and plants. We done the forms. We passed the visits, the interviews, the panel. Now we get on with it, at least until you're eighteen. Then you've got your own life."

"I've got my own life. Out there!"

He laughed. "Been to the zoo once and think you're a tiger."

"What's that supposed to mean?"

"That you wouldn't last two minutes in the real world." He went forward on his elbows, grinning suddenly. "I remember. Our walks. Our chats. Training courses, uni, moving to Glasgow. Jobs and pals and parties. What happened to all that? I know you think you can charm the pigeons out the bins with that smile and pretend everything inside's okay, but I know you, Cora."

I jumped up and my chair fell back. "Away and do one, you big cyclops bastard!" I ran straight through to the hall.

"Sit back down here. Now."

I stopped at the bottom of the stair. He hadn't shouted but it was like his voice had frozen me right in that horrible wee split-second gap between making everything hell again or running back and sorrying and crying and eating our puddings in peace.

I walked back with amazing ragey little steps, then picked the chair up and chucked myself down side-on to him. I wiped the tear-streaks from round my jaw with my fleece cuff and looked into the pleats of my skirt.

"All this fighting. It's my fault. I know I've been hardly any use. I wasn't really built for paying bills or tying ties or working out what temperature you wash the pillowcases on, eh. Never mind understanding what's going on in there." He leaned across the table and tried to tap the side of my head, but I moved away. "I am trying though. I just wish I had more useful stuff to teach you."

"Teach me to fight."

"Eh?"

"Show me how you punch someone. Properly."

He chuckled. "Away."

I wiped my nose on the fleece. "Scared I might turn on you?"

"You already did that." I laughed through the snot and he stood up and got me a green paper towel, then he leaned against the bench watching me fix my damp face. "Are you getting in bother?"

"No, but if you'd been out round here—folk are into all sorts. It's worse than Muircross. And like, it's been years now, me sat in my room crying and eating bread while everyone else is out in cars and at parties learning how to exist. I've missed out on fucking everything."

"You're only sixteen!"

"St. Therese—turn your back and there's some creepy wee first-year mutant jumping about like a fucking ninja turtle filling your bag with soil or pinging your knickers or pelting you with double-A batteries. You need to send a message about who you are. Just the once. Lassies have already told me."

"See when I was your age—"

"Oh did you *grow up on the streets*? Were you *in care*? You never ever mention it!"

He laughed. "How am I going to teach a wee drink-of-water like you to knuckle up?"

The back light was still on and the air was chilly and there were combed-down shapes in the grass where the past had been scattered an hour before. I had the laces of my Reeboks loose and my cheeks were still achy from shouting.

"I'm sorry for calling you a cyclops bastard."

"I've had worse."

I stepped down from the doorway. "Stuff just comes out."

The fog had gone thin. We stood facing one another between the sheets and the fence, and he set himself with his legs apart, like a proper fighter. So I did the same. "My uncle taught me this. I was thirteen. Remember the Maywood Estate?"

"Before the big houses where Dennis stayed?"

"There was a gang up there. Young Valley. Causing problems for our lot, the Muiry Toll. They were all the sharp-dressed cunts with no respect, we were just shirts off, blades out, eh. It was all fucking nonsense looking back, but I went to my uncle's one night with my head dinged-in and he took me out the back and showed me the moves, eh. It's not much of a lesson. There's only one thing to know."

I put my legs wide as the skirt would let me and rolled my shoulders. "Aye?"

He laughed. "The first and only rule of punching fuck out of somebody—don't aim for the face because you'll ease off before hitting them. Aim for the ground behind them. If your fist is heading for the ground, where does it need to go to get there?"

"Through the face!"

He held his hand out flat to his side. "Punch right through them. That's the universal language."

I pulled my arm back and swung a punch at his hand full force, aiming at the grass behind. It made a slapping noise and I stumbled. "Again."

He held his hand out again and I punched it, smacking him hard. There was throbbing under my knuckles.

"Better. Are you not still angry though? Let's feel it. How about we make that appointment with the school psychologist?"

I thumped his hand and he opened his mouth all wide and silent. "Jesus, lassie. Okay, good. Again."

I punched his hand as hard as I could.

"I had an amazing day. I got told I look twenty-six today."

I punched again.

"You're still a wee short-arse. A wee girlypuncher."

I punched harder. "Vicki's cousin's moving to Glasgow. And I'm going out for Bonfire Night. Vicki and me. Drinking."

"You think so?" He held his hand out again, and I went to punch it full force, aiming at the grass, picturing him, picturing Jo, picturing Mrs. McClair. Then he swiped it up out the way.

I went flying forward toward the shed and landed shoulder-first in the grass. My hair was over my face and it smelled like grilled crisps. My hip started throbbing. He was bent over laughing.

"The ground's rock-hard, you big fucking dunce," I says, trying to rub some feeling back. "I'm ringing ChildLine."

"You need some new patter." He walked over and lifted me back to my feet with those hands.

"Again," I says, leaning sideways, trying to hook my hair back out my earrings.

"That's enough."

I put my legs apart. "Again, you big—cunt."

He put his hand out flat. I looked him in the eye to make sure, then I punched at his hand as hard as I could, and just as I did he lifted it again, and in a blink I'd stumbled back down into the cold grass. I lay there with my head tilted back, trying to make it look like I was enjoying the pain.

Above the chimneys, lit-up clouds were moving over the moon. The upside-down houses were dark except for the light in our kitchen, and the light in Donna's kitchen too. She was at her sink and we made eye contact for a wee weird second before she ducked back and pretended not to see me, down in the grass again. Gunner put his hands in his pockets. "I'm going in to get a bath then I'm heading to work. You're grounded this weekend. School first thing Monday. No excuses." I sat round and watched him loping up the back step. "Now get the dishes done. And remember tell ChildLine I'm training you up, for free."

16

onday I had biology first two periods, nine a.m. My teacher
was called Solsgirth. He wore linty chinos and had skin on
his forehead that looked like picked-off glue. I called it ath-
lete's face once and wee Shona Blevin behind me nearly choked on
her Chewit.

In most subjects, information went in my brain like drizzle going
through a cobweb, but when I was actually interested it was different.
I liked biology because I was quite good at it. I remembered stuff. The
only issue was that big baldy dour dickhead of a teacher.

"Yes, these were living creatures, class, but they are *not living now*.
If anyone feels they are not able to attempt a dissection, please make
it known and we can have it out in front of everyone. Any takers?"
Nobody said a word. "Okay good," he went.

The science lab was brand new and beige like a hospital and all you
could smell was the plasticky floor—like we were sat suffocating inside
a beach ball.

We were set out two to a bench, but because I was new I had been
dumped at the last free work station alone. This was one of the only
classes where I didn't have Vicki and there was always a dread about
who might end up on that stool.

I kept at it in my jotter with a clumsy-looking clown face then did
an eyeball with wings, then a big long mesmerizing squiggle like a

piglet's tail. The more days in a row I came to school the more the dread built and the harder it got to sit completely still. Doodling was movement and any movement helped.

There was a nervous tap-tap on the griddy glass window in the classroom door and everyone's head shot up. Solsgirth clomped over and opened it and there's Kira Coathanger.

She walked in and stood looking poor and strange in her own clothes with her feet pointing outward but not in the cute way. Then without any words Solsgirth points her with his Hitlery palm toward that empty stool right next to me. Her manky Hi-Tecs squelched across the rubber floor. I was getting heebies from all the people watching.

She screeched the stool out. The zips off her rucksack clacked on everything and air came out her as she plonked herself down. "Hello," she goes, in a too-loud whisper.

"Oh, hey," I whispered, blanking my face.

She'd been booted out her last school and nobody knew why. I dogged the odd day here and there but it was nothing compared to Kira Coathanger's absences. Even when she did turn up she was in and out of classes like a yo-yo.

"Looks like we're cutting something up?"

I shrugged.

Solsgirth was asking more questions, but I had already missed them. I sat up straight, looked alert, like I was listening—like I'd learned to. I'd pretended all through District so it was easy to pretend at St. Therese.

"Okay good!" he went. He lurched back over to the door and swung it open again, then leaned out into the corridor. A lanky bare-shouldered sixth-year girl walked in pulling a tall metal trolley.

Then from beside me, out of nowhere, "I'm Kira-Louise Cantwell."

I turned. I wanted to tell her there was no need for introductions—the whole entire year was talking about her. "Cora Mowat," I goes.

Seeing her close up you had to admit the rumors were a load

of shite. Everything about her was more weird and sudden than it needed to be, but she definitely washed herself. There were no plooks like Jelly Tots or pishy smell like they said.

Solsgirth started with the arsehole voice. "When I instruct you, walk to the trolley and take a tray. One tray between two, no japery, no facetiousness—understood?" He stuck his hand toward us like a karate chop. "Front row please."

Kira-Louise got straight up and I watched her walk to the trolley— the neat broken robot steps, the nervy carefulness, the way nothing really moved above her waist. You could tell how closed-up she was.

It reminded me of me, during the last months in Muircross— trudging to school alone, down the Causey alone, up the stair to my room, in tears, alone. Then when things got better, or worse, or different at least, the gloomy baltic hours in the welfare car park with Fiona, Fiona's big sister, her big sister's boyfriend and his mates. Drinking for the first time—the feeling it gave.

I went back to District but I wasn't really there. I tiptoed from class to class like Kira-Louise, like any unexpected word or movement might shake something loose inside. School had always been a cunt but I was so on edge now. And then Becci Devine that Tuesday afternoon in physics standing up and going, in front of everyone, *Cora, just because you don't have a mam, that doesn't give you the right to behave any way you want.*

The fight was so mental Gunner had to come in for a meeting, in his baggy BHS suit. I was ready to talk about everything—my lateness, my forgetfulness, my fizziness, my anger—but Samantha never showed up. It was the first time I saw Gunner trying to act like my da though—he wouldn't back down from the teachers, and that day probably became the first wee thing we had.

I remember after, showing him the clump of fringe I'd ripped out of Becci Devine's head. I had kept it in a crisp packet. He high-fived me, in stitches. Then we hugged.

Kira-Louise came back with the tray. She was wearing a red T-shirt and a cardigan with buttons made of wood. A black mini tube skirt and white fake-mohair knee socks. Two chunks of bare thigh the color of boiled egg peeking between.

It was the fact that teachers were allowing her to turn up like this that told you something was really wrong—even the dole families made sure their kids were in black and purple and white and a clean-ish pair of Kickers.

"Before we begin," Solsgirth goes, looming over his desk, "I will read out the names of our top performers in last month's multiple choice on crop protection. In no particular order—Ian McKinnon, Carrie Dudgeon, David Muirhead, Cora Mowat, Gail Templeton. You five can all breathe a sigh of relief in the run-up to parents' evening."

I froze then I grinned because I thought people might be looking. "Amazing," Kira-Louise whispered at me, as she sat down.

"Let me congratulate Mr. Muirhead—ninety-six percent—exceptional. Miss Mowat"—I kind of ducked automatically—"let us just say that we're all glad to see you here, aren't we, class?" There was mumbling from folk and I wanted to die. "Now, I would love to say that these five are what the rest of you should be modeling your-self on, but—let's just say four of them are setting a brilliant example for you all." There were sniggers and tutting. I was roasting. It was like his words were in my hair, itching me like nits.

He brought his specs down. "Now. There is a specimen in front of you. A rat. *Rattus*, of the rodent family. Some of you will have black rats, others will have white." He started striding. "With reference to your worksheet I want you to open up the rat and check off each part of the anatomy listed. You are to *find and identify*."

Our rat was a wee chunky white thing, pinned down, out for the count on his back. He had teensy buck teeth and a sneer stuck on. I wanted to say, *Chin up, wee Rattus, it could be worse—being alive is a fucking nightmare.*

There were pen lines on his belly where we were supposed to be slicing. I tried to breathe through my nose. I looked at Kira-Louise thinking we could decide who did what. "I love your hair," she goes. "My hair never does what I want it to."

"Thanks." My hair was back in a scrunchie and I hadn't washed it for four days.

"I've just had mine cut." She swished. It was thin and sleep-crumpled and black.

Solsgirth kept on, "You shouldn't require my input. You have all been trained to safely use a scalpel. You may speak quietly to one another at your benches, only. Now get on with it." He sat down and pulled his hearing aids out and laid them on his desk, like a dare to us.

There were blue gloves, plastic tweezers, a knife, a lollipop stick and a green paper towel on the tray. We put our gloves on. I was hot still and I'd already half-forgotten the instructions. Before I could speak Kira-Louise had picked up the scalpel and was carving at the belly.

You never wanted to be first. I got the usual dread of failing and getting mixed up and blamed so I sat up straight and looked out the window like it wasn't my problem.

It was a boring dampish morning. I was praying as usual for some excitement—like at primary when I'd stare out the window and wish for a dog in the playground, or a burst water pipe. A fire alarm. Lightning from the sky.

The minute I sat down in class and wanted to concentrate there was suddenly a wee rebel in my body that wanted to jump up and leave. A rebel that needed the sluggishness of the world to speed right up until it matched what was happening inside her.

"Cora, tick off the heart."

I turned. The rat's wee glisteny purple heart was in her palm, twisted-looking, like a bit of chewed-up Hubba Bubba. He was open now with a hatch and she'd been ploutering round the innards with her lollipop stick.

"I don't think we're supposed to be pulling stuff out," I whispered. "Everyone else is taking their time."

She didn't look up. "I've done this before. In my last school."

I ticked off the heart. "Where was your last school, anyway?" She shushed me. My hands were going gluey with sweat inside the gloves. I looked outside at the blustery playground, then back at her. "Where do you live?"

"Abbotscraig. Top end."

"You do rollerblading?"

"Yep." She put the stick down and looked at me. Her eyes were paleish gray dotted with brown bits like leaf-crumbs. She had some freckles. There was a prettiness about her that nobody ever mentioned. "I go up the Mill Loan."

The Mill Loan was the name of the big straight road that went through the countryside and connected the back of Hellmeadow to the tall flats at the Deathy. "Aren't there a lot of cars up there?"

"Only me. Me and the cows under starlight."

I wanted to laugh but wasn't sure if I was meant to. "At night? Are you not a bit old to be rollerblading?"

"I enjoy the speed and the dark. And being out gets me away from my maw and da." She put the lollipop stick down and picked up the tweezers. "Are your maw and da sound?"

I looked round for anyone watching but they were all working away. It was a weird thing to be speaking about but I didn't want her shutting up. "I've just got a stepda," I goes, whispery. "He's all right. He wants me in all the time. By myself."

"Like a bird in a shoebox."

I laughed a bit too loud. Solsgirth had his feet up reading a metal detecting magazine.

Then she says, "You did amazing in the test."

"Remembering this stuff is easy." I looked back out at the clear sky to calm my nerves. "And I'm good at filling in blanks."

Then she says, "Look."

I looked down.

She'd plucked a string of fat beads the color of watery grape juice out of the rat's belly. It looked like art-teacher jewelry. "That's its babies," she went.

Our wee guy was a she. I was feeling the boak now. "The stuff they make you do in school."

She started filling in details about the pregnancy on our worksheet. "Having to turn up is bad enough."

"Cold custard, this place," I goes.

She put the lollipop stick and the tweezers down and says, "Do you want to come rollerblading?"

She said it so clear and breezy and as she did she began to pick the end of her finger through the glove, on autopilot. I watched the movement, six or seven times, agitated, with her thumb. Like me. I nearly forgot to answer.

"Oh, no. No! Thanks though."

Then Solsgirth started up. "Attention, please." He was sat still, looking over the top of his magazine. "Since you are applying yourself so *expertly* and so *quietly* to today's task, when you are finished you may take the rest of this period as revision time. Understood?" One or two people nodded. "Okay good. All the worksheets must be placed on my desk after you have put your trays back."

"What's revision time?"

"Basically we sit and read through our textbooks."

"Sounds fun," Kira-Louise said, going back to the worksheet.

"So how's St. Therese treating you then?"

She didn't look up. "I'm going through the process of seeing where I fit in. I'm used to it. I know it takes time." She sounded like a teacher or a doctor. "Are you going to the dance?"

Gunner had already brought it up—did I have pals to go with, who was I taking? *Don't be stressed. You'll feel better about everything if you go.* I had been trying not to think about it, but you had to go if you wanted to fit in at St. Therese. "Oh right. So you're going to the Christmas dance?!"

"What's that supposed to mean?"

"It's not supposed to mean anything. You should go. Why wouldn't you go? Everyone is going." I smiled. "I am," I went, suddenly sure. "You got an outfit?"

"Yep." She slipped off the stool and stood up with the tray then walked over to the trolley. The back of her cardigan had a wigwam embroidered on it. I opened my jotter at the back and made it look like I was working.

Then I felt a jab. It was Gary Cowan on the bench behind and to the left, poking my shoulder with a ruler. He held out a note and I took it.

I unfolded it in the shadow of the bench. *CORA COATHANGER 4 KIRA COATHANGER* in his wee goblin handwriting. Then under *FANNY FIDDLERS 4 EVA.*

I'd said maybe nineteen words to her but that was Abbotscraig. I crumpled it, then put my arm behind my back and gave him the middle finger. I dropped the note on the floor and started the spirals in my jotter again.

Kira-Louise came back and we sat side by side in silence. Then the bare-shouldered girl arrived and took the trolley of opened rats away. Outside, some clouds had come and the sun was just a wee chilly-looking disc.

The bell went and over the rumbling of stools Solsgirth told us something about how he'd mark our work, but as each word went by I was listening less and less. As we walked out together past his desk he goes, over the specs, "Kira-Louise, that skirt of yours is not at all suitable. Rectify please."

What you looking at her skirt for? I thought.

"What are you looking at my skirt for?" she says.

I looked at him. Then I looked at her until I couldn't. And then I looked down at the creamy swirls on the new floor and smiled as she started speedwalking ahead with those neat steps and inside me something changed.

In the hot corridor I ran through the bodies. "Kira-Louise," I goes. I tapped her shoulder as other groups of threes and fours went by giving us the evils.

She jumped slightly. I pulled her behind the brick pillar by the English staircase. I says, "Sorry, I will come. Rollerblading. I want to."

Nobody could see us. I felt somehow like I was full of cold air. I seemed to always be moving toward those things that would give me noisier dreams.

"Oh. Amazing!" She smiled, showing off her cute side-fangs. "I'm grounded all this week but what about next Tuesday? We could watch the fireworks?"

"I can't next Tuesday." I pictured Gunner's face, then I says it anyway. "Next Thursday though?"

"Okay. I'll bring you blades. I've got a few pairs."

"I'm a size six."

She had started walking away. "I'm a seven, but we can stuff them out with loo roll!"

I moved quick behind her and walked with her through a rush of boys—stuck to her shoulder, watching her movements, noting every filthy look she got. Then I spun back with a smile and as I slowed my feet I looked to my side and saw that Kira-Louise had gone.

17

Pauline and Vicki and me were sat round on the roof of the abandoned community hall in the grounds of the old infirmary. It was only the two floors up but the feeling was totally secret, like you were huddled in your own wee private room full of fireworks and sky.

We were already mad on the schnapps and the cider—giggling over nothing, breathing in time as the drink hit and the sky tilted over our heads. Rockets shot up and over us from the playparks and dark back gardens and curtains glowed all over the town. It felt like our wee circle was the center of everything.

I was sat cross-legged in Gunner's plum fleece, gawping at Pauline. I'd been asking her all about it—I'd never in my whole existence met anyone who had done something actually exciting.

She lifted the cider. "Aye, so basically I died. That's how I stopped in the end. I was OD-ing on the settee. I could feel it slipping away. Life, I mean."

"Jeez," I goes. She passed me the crumpled bottle. There was a boom in the sky that you felt in your chest, then a sweetie-packet crackle.

"Then *Gladiators* comes on telly. The music's pumping. I remember thinking—this can't be it. I'm not dying in front of Ulrika Jonsson. *Pauline Sclater, 21, junkie, died watching Saracen's tight arse wiggling in the Atlasphere.* Imagine your primary school teachers reading that."

"Did you turn over to *Brookside*?"

"I rolled onto the floor and crawled like a snake on my belly to the TV and switched Ulrika off. Then I lay down for all eternity with my face against the cold fireplace tiles."

Vicki took the bottle. "You're talking to a ghost, Cora."

"Was only a few minutes, the doctor said. But I was so fucked-up, then. I'd been drinking too. See this wasn't long after my mam died."

"What's dying even like?" I says, making it sound jokey.

"Stops you worrying about stuff. Nothing's important since that day."

Down in the town a gigantic rocket squealed up from the playing fields, spinning quick shadows round the chimneys and X-raying the trees before sizzling into mental red rain. I couldn't stop saying in my head that her mam was dead.

"There'll be a few melted kids the night," Vicki goes, burping.

Pauline says, "Don't forget the hedgehogs."

I went to speak but suddenly from somewhere near there was liveliness—trainers in gravel, bottle caps bouncing. I zipped the fleece and slid over to the edge and Vicki followed. We lay flat on our fronts shoulder to shoulder, looking down over the long grass and through the far line of trees.

Life, over in the hospital car park—a circle of mainly shaven-headed boys in bright designer anoraks, a big gang of them, drinking at the concrete ramp.

I'd made an effort to learn the faces at school, but I wasn't much use. Vicki started her teachery bit. "That's Brian Inglis. Tony Gow. Steussie, maybe. Cosh from physics next to him, the tall guy's called Pliers. The two guys in the T-shirts are Thomas Sneddon's cousins, Bin-Lid and Pudge. It's mainly Greyskull boys." Then she leans in and says, "See the one in the orange Helly Hansen, that's Fulton. He ambulanced my uncle Rab's best mate, summer before last."

We stayed low, listening. One boy would step in and add their bit, then they'd all rock back doing big doofy laughs. Now and again there was a shoulder-punch or a kiddy-on headlock. In the middle of the circle you could see five fat blue carrier bags stretched all thin from tins and bottles—hours more alcohol. The sky was flashing above them like a telly with the leads loose.

Pauline fixed her lipstick. "Where were we?"

"*My journey to heaven and back* by Pauline Sclater," Vicki goes, rolling her eyes.

"Did you never do actual rehab then, Pauline?" I zipped my zip. Took the biggest fizzy glug. A buzz was starting up my legs, from the drink.

"'Course." She took the bottle off me. "*Eat kiwis to sleep better.*"

I laughed. "Do you get kiwis in Abbotscraig?"

"Top-end Co-op, probably, but that's not the point," Vicki says.

"The men get knowing shoulder-nudges and chit-chat about the football or the *wife* and spoke to like a human, the women get told *be strong* and that's that. Fuck 'em."

"Tell Cora about the beach."

Pauline took a swig. "Aye, mad pointless excursions. It's all printouts and KitKats and tea. Minibuses. Group of us picking crab parts and bits of hairy rope off the beach and sellotaping them to colored card. Writing haikus about fishing nets. I'm twenty-one here, remember. Some bearded skidmark in a catalogue cagoule is telling me to enjoy the fresh air and *recenter myself*. Fresh air! I wanted to leather the bastard."

I says, "What's wrong with fresh air?"

"Chick, what's breathing going to do when you've had something that put the sun inside you?"

Just then a big rocket whistled over, doing a toothpastey-white corkscrew, turning everything bright. We sat watching as more came and over Vicki's shoulder I saw a tiny sparkle out toward the coast. The clouds from Riggs glowing against the black sky. Up on the hill next to it four fancy glass pyramids lit up—the new Muircross Heritage Center. There was a feeling, seeing the place from miles off, but I never said a thing. The past mainly meant questions and sadness.

It was getting awkward so I goes, "Hey," shuffling in a bit to get the feeling back in my thighs, "Kira Coathanger's going to the Christmas dance!"

"Who's this?" Pauline goes.

Vicki says, "Weirdo in our year. The school tramp." She burped. "How do you know she's going?"

"Boy in biology told me."

"Wonder if we'll see *Performance Sport*?" Vicki took a drink. "Ugly toad. Bet she's drier than a prison cannelloni."

Pauline screwed up her face and burst out laughing through it. "Vicki, you always go too far. Poor lassie."

"Trust me. Haunted fanny, that one. If you'd seen her you'd know."

And then there were noises, from right down on the ground. We ducked our heads again and scrambled round on our bums.

Fulton—tramping through the grass.

Next thing he's right below us, side-on with his belt undone and his pish drumming the dry leaves. A feeling came—the night was taking a turn and there was no rewinding it.

The three of us got down flat, shushing each other, doing panto-faces. Vicki's eyes were beaming with pure drunken trouble. I already knew I loved the lassie—I would probably choose her to burn my diaries if I died—but she was just a wee bit unpredictable with cider in her belly.

Right down into the darkness she roars, "Put your dick away, ya clown!"

She looked so chuffed with herself. I breathed in, then out, then Fulton shouts, "Who's up there?"

She took a sideways swig. "Who's down there?"

"Come down and find out," Fulton goes.

Vicki jumped up and tiptoed to the edge, then turned and started climbing down backward. You heard her and Fulton chit-chatting for a wee minute, then suddenly she's running off over the grass toward the big group of boys. When she got excited she ran like she was on a trampoline.

Pauline was smiling. "She'll not be coming back. That's her ex, Brian Inglis, over there."

"Dirty moo."

"Brian broke her heart."

The pair of us shuffled back and sat up. "More for us two then." I took a swig.

She took the bottle off me and hooked her choppy fringe to one side with her pinky. "That *Gladiators* thing. I don't go round telling it to everyone."

"I realize. Does stuff like that not just leave you thinking *why me?*"

"I don't waste time wondering why things happen." She handed me the bottle and I took a drink. "Life is capable of being a complete cunt without any encouragement from you or me."

"I wish it was easy."

"Cora, you've always got that look like you're puzzled at yourself. Do you need to speak about anything, chick?"

"I'm all right."

Suddenly layers of shimmery fireworks were bursting in the air above us. I was gulping hard, but I kept as calm as I had it in me to be.

Pauline pulled her sheepskin coat shut and looked at me, her face flickering like a mirror of the sky. "Did you know sharks have to keep moving or they croak it? That's me and you, Cora!"

Then as the rockets died off a voice faded up.

"Fulton's shouting on you!" Pauline goes, giggling. "Fucking hell! Bet you Vicki's told him all about you."

"Fuck sake," I whispered, but I could already feel something in my tummy.

She nodded me closer then reached in her bag and went, "Close your eyes." I felt a cold mist on my face and I smelled that clean-washing perfume again.

"What is that?"

"White Musk. Take it."

I was down on the ground before I could think anything through, stood there in the grass with my breath held, trying to make my drunken heart behave.

"Hiya, Fulton," I goes, sweet as I could, brushing roof-moss off of my jeans.

"Cora, aye?" He said my name like something weird off a foreign menu. "Vicki says you might be up for speaking."

He had one of those pill-dealer faces but I wasn't really caring if I was getting a tingly or not—the more folk I could get around me the less I'd be alone. "Cora Mowat, aye." I stood up straight, thinking how Donna said I'd sprouted.

"What you lassies doin' up there in the dark?"

"Drinking. Talking." I couldn't stop shrugging my shoulders.

"Lassies can't climb," he says.

His circle of boys were yelping and shouting on the other side of the trees, a menace to everything. I could hear Vicki's giggling a mile off. "Aye they can."

He started swaying. "Do you like my new Timberlands?" I looked down. The orange suede was freckled in pish drops and I wasn't sure if he knew. "C'mere," he goes.

He swaggered off, flattening the grass with his big boots, hands in his bum pockets, elbows out. His hair was short and dark and fuzzy and from behind his head was round as a gobstopper. The boom from a rocket opened above us as we walked, like a big invisible umbrella.

He was a heart-squasher for sure, but I wasn't caring. I'd been picked for something at last. Dennis had said to me once, *Believe in yourself and you'll be unstoppable*, so I skooshed myself in Pauline's perfume again and kept on into the grass.

We stopped at a big concrete slab and sat down in front of it. Fulton stared into me for maybe five seconds then he cleared his throat and went, "So what you into?"

I thought, *Lilt. Dancing. Leggings with pockets. Speaking to insects. Eating bread. Crying in private. Rain.*

"Just hanging about," I said, staring down at my deformed Reeboks. The air was thin and it smelled like nothing and you knew that autumn was gone.

He shuffled his arse closer. "You're a wee stunner. How come I've no seen you round?"

To me it didn't seem true you could be a wee stunner dressed in a plum-color fleece with house paint up the sleeve.

"I moved here not long ago," I went. "I'm totally new."

"What school?"

"St. Therese." I looked up and saw smoke break apart as it rose from the incinerator chimney. It reminded me of Riggs. Sometimes it felt like every time I stopped moving I started to think of my mam.

"Me too," he goes. "Till I got kicked out. Hey, you enjoying these rockets? We were supposed to be letting our own off but I forgot to bring them."

I felt my face lighting up for the first time. "How do you forget fireworks on Bonfire Night?" It sounded to me like something I would do.

He smiled all cute then after a few big pops in the sky he looked at his pishy boots and says, "I really fancy you."

His drunken brain had maybe judged that this would be enough to get me surrendering in the weeds. I breathed a big breath in and looked back at the rooftop, but Pauline was either hiding, or gone. I knew she'd be pleased for me. I didn't want to walk home alone.

His tongue was like a wet marshmallow in my cidery mouth. It was hard to think thoughts but more than anything I was just wishing for a chair. Wooden and sensible, like my mam's old dining table chairs. It would have helped with my pins and needles, at least.

"Oh, Fulton," I went when we stopped to breathe, because I had to say something. There was honey on my brain. Chains in my belly. My nerves were flickering like cheap tinsel.

He went in on my neck and I prayed there would be a mark. My bladder was jangling. His shoulder smelled like Lenor. All my effort went on keeping my nose-breath quiet and trying not to pee on his hand.

There was kissing and touching, but not much more, and it was all over within a half hour of hearing him pish in the trees. But I was changed. I was bulletproof, ginormous-feeling, puny, fragile, free.

After, we picked the leaves off one another. I wasn't floating or fainting, or thinking about the cosmos—I did a huge drunk pee behind a grit bin, then he took my hand.

We crossed the dual carriageway and he told me about his catapult and his motorbike and his granda, who he loved. When he goes, "Would you want to come and meet him, one day?" I tried to play it cool just nodding with my trap shut. There'd been no boys after Dennis, because I'd mainly been in my room crying and counting my toes. Now I couldn't believe what I was hearing.

We chatted the whole way then stopped round the back of the shops at the edge of the Hellmeadow. The takeaways were closed but the air still smelled like pizza crust.

He handed me a melted-looking Double Decker from his anorak pocket. "I'm this way, babe," he goes, nodding up to the Greyskull flats, stretching the Helly Hansen down with his fists in the front pocket, "You wanna stay at mine? I've got disco biscuits and ice cream."

"I can't."

"The old man?"

I thought of words I could explain it with and then I just said, "Kinda."

I used my pinky nail to scrape my number in the grease under the kebab shop extractor fan, then I stood there and made him read it five times. Nerves suddenly came and my head started up with the usual stuff—*Why are you doing this, you're mental, Cora, what's he wanting with a naive wee lassie like you?*

He looked at me like he'd heard it and then squidged a lukewarm kiss onto my forehead. I just stood there nearly dying from the feeling it gave. Then he squeezed me so hard in a hug and whispered my number then we walked an awkward bit and then he left me tingling under a security light at the loading bay ramp behind Safeway.

I watched him turn into a dot as he crossed the main road and went up the hill. It felt like a scene from a film, so I stood up straight in my fleece. I felt like I should be shouting something, but there was nothing I could think of to shout.

I walked home under the last of the big booms. Gunner was working and the house was dead and the thudding inside me meant I was never going to sleep, so I forced the Reeboks off then danced alone to Phase FM while drunkenly scrubbing the grill pan.

Upstair I put the Double Decker in my bedside drawer, with my Dan pamphlets and my pads and that wee nugget of coral that Dennis brought me back from the Seychelles in September 1994.When I got under my covers and saw my own skin I realized it was the closest I'd been to another human being since my mam died.

18

Fulton rang me the next night and soon as Gunner was sleeping I met him at the Easyprice and we went up the woods.

He had a bag with cans in it and a bottle of Mad Dog 20/20 that we started with, hoods up on the bench by the TV transmitter, tonguing under the bone-bare trees. When the Mad Dog and the kissing was done he put his hand on my thigh and over the noise of the sullen hoolets went, "You know you're beautiful, aye?"

Looking back, I realized that you got ideas about yourself gradually and you held them all—it took years, like a big wheelie bin filling up with rain. You were supposed to live for the attention of boys but never told what to do with that attention when it landed on you like a slab. What were you even meant to do with words? Say *cheers*? Do a backflip? Wear them like a prefect's badge? Who believes they're beautiful anyway?

I touched his stubbly face and tried out my voice in the moonlight. "I dunno if I deserve you, Fulton."

He asked what that meant, but a feeling had started in me, a wee spoilsport feeling small as a blazer button. I knew there was no way of explaining stuff without crying over everything, so we started on the cans instead.

He told me he was working cash-in-hand for his uncle now, digging irrigation ditches. He loved his uncle, idolized his granda. And he had plans for me and him already. Between kisses I sat on my hands and listened while he spoke about money and the future. I didn't even know this boy but the world sounded solid when he explained things.

That night he walked me halfway home again and at the Safeway loading bay—our loading bay—he gave me a present. A black choker from Littlewoods with a diamante daisy stitched at the front. "To cover the bites," he goes. The night was dark and shivery but I didn't want to leave this world. I hated going back to the bickering and Shake n' Vac and beige-color overcooked food that tasted of being penniless.

I clipped the choker on in front of him and it itched my throat and he told me I looked hot to trot. Standing there wearing it, watching him walk off up the hill, it felt like proof. I wore it to bed then I took it to school the day after folded up in my top blazer pocket. I even put it on that night to meet Kira-Louise.

She was sat at the smashed-in bus stop, cuddling two big pairs of plasticky neon rollerblades. Glass was diamonded all round the pavement, cubey and small like McDonald's burger onion.

She looked up with her cartoony grin and nodded *hiya* then started window-wipering her legs, scraping rainbow shapes in the gritty glass with her Hi-Tecs. "You wanna walk down a bit?"

We crossed the road in silence and turned down the hill where the Mill Loan dipped away from the edge of the estate into creepy dark tunnels of hedges and trees. When I went to speak my lips felt elasticky, like I'd never used them before. "Kira-Louise. This—I dunno." I laughed. "It's a bit weird, isn't it?"

She looked at me. "No need for *Louise*." She had a black hairband and leaf-shaped ear studs and barmaid eye shadow that twinkled in the dark. Her coat was one of those dark wool ones with tartan in the hood like Paddington or tramps wore.

I wanted to say that it was nice to see her, to be away from the stress of the names and the screwed-up faces and the show-offs in school. "Is it not weird?" I goes.

"You don't have to kid on you've not heard things about me. I saw how you were when I sat down on that empty stool." I could feel my face heating. "But that's okay! We're here."

She went ahead, crossing to the low wall over the other side of the road, at the top of a dip. I had a kind of feeling that if I listened to her properly everything would be explained. "I always wanted rollerblades when I was wee. My pal Fiona had a pair."

She clattered them down. "I've stuffed yours out. Come and see if they fit."

We tied our trainers by the laces and put them round our necks, then shoved the rollerblades on. It took me five minutes just to get up off my knees and stand up straight.

"We'll go down here past the back fields. There's a turn-off into where the carpet factory used to be. We can spin round the old car park. When you get good on these blades it feels amazing."

I looked at her. I was a bit thinner these days but she wasn't to know I was never really a PE lassie. "Amazing how?"

"Like there's nothing to worry about. Anyway"—she clacked toward me, and birled me round by the shoulders—"look up there. Stars and shit."

I was about to say there were no stars but then her hands were on my hips. She shoved me full force down the brae.

The wind went loud and my sight turned wet and smeary. My arms and legs were rigid like that tin can man off the film with the arsehole lion. I was too scared to scream. I was too scared to do anything in case my feet disappeared.

"Keep calm and stand up straight! You're doing brilliant!" She was shouting through giggles, rolling next to me now, gliding all smooth with perfect push-off leg movements. "Say something!"

"Can't."

She started twirling in circles in front of me, laughing. I didn't mind because it made me smile to see her being natural. Then she turned and rolled backward. "Well, do you like bees?"

It was November. I could barely remember what a bee looked like. I managed to stand straighter without sticking my arse out. "I've got socks with bees on."

"Think of all the stuff you get bees on—pencil cases, curtains, cakes. Paintings of them. They will never know! That's sad." She was striding ahead. "You're doing great."

We started pushing on a bit faster, side by side. "My stepda told me on a walk once that before bumblebees they got called humble bees but I never believed it."

For a minute all you heard was our wheels together on the road making the noise of a tiny river. Then, in a new voice she says, "What's the stepdad like then?"

I could feel words rising, too many, too quick, but for once I didn't try and keep them in. "It was weird at first but it's normal now. Arguing, doing dishes."

"Is he sound with housework?"

"'Suppose." There was something about speaking at night—it didn't leave you as naked-feeling as it did in the day. "We stripped the bathroom lino together, papered the hall. Our house was a kind of nightmare but we're sorting it slowly."

"It's hard for me to start tasks sometimes."

"Me too. My mam really loved her cleaning products—*kind to skin, cuts through grease, deep cushiony softness.*" I was pushing forward now on different feet, copying what she did. "All that kind of stuff makes me feel she's near. Maybe I should have done more stuff like that with her when she was alive." I looked to see if she'd say anything. Then I went, "She died, my mam. I don't visit her grave. But I think about her in the house. She was in a wheelchair. We have a wheelchair ramp still and I walk up and down it every day." There was a silence. "What's your mam and da like, anyway?"

"They fight loads. About me, mainly."

"Maybe you should stop being a wee nightmare."

"Takes one to know one!" She shrugged at her coat. "My da claims he had a work injury when he was underground and that fucked his heart or something, but really he drinks too much." She glided closer to me and held my arm as we turned a tight corner. She spoke while I was still thinking of a reply. "So what you wearing? To the dance?"

"Oh, dunno."

"I'm not buying anything new."

"Same, probably. Do you think the teachers will be there?"

"Oh yeah."

I slowed myself. "Do they help you much?"

"It was hard when I started but my mum sorted them all out. Same as my last school. I do what I can manage. Then I go home."

"They give you time off?"

"Aye."

"McClair wants me to speak to the school psychologist. About grief."

She turned to me and pulled her hairband off. "Oh, Adele? She's amazing."

"Adele?"

"The psychologist. She's really friendly. There's a telly in her office." She fixed the hairband back on, rolling still without messing up her stride. "She's given me loads of photocopies, to help me organize myself. My mam bought me a couple of trays for my room. I lay out everything I need on it for the next day. I just find it a stress to remember what to take with you. Laying it out helps."

I went, "Things will settle down at school." I thought to go on more but then I stopped and looked down at my rollerblades wobbling still.

"It'll get better, it'll settle down, it'll even itself out. It never works that way."

We swerved into the wide-open car park and after a few seconds rolling in the shadow of the ruined factory these big beam headlights came on, like a giant waking up in the corner. The car was small and red and you knew it was driven by boys.

Both of us birled round calmly as we could on our skates, me stumbling a bit, and then we started back toward the road because even though both of us were new to Abbotscraig we weren't new to boys at night in cars.

"Quick," she goes, doing wee hurry-steps. As we moved, a single vodka bottle came sailing over and exploded on the weedy tarmac in front of us with a big shardy splash. "I've never seen anyone else down here ever."

"Everything gets ruined."

We clacked over the gravelly ground toward the road, then right on cue you heard the Abbotscraigy gargoyle voices giving it the usual *c'mere, babe, get it pumped, show's yer fannies, tits out, Coathanger.* I couldn't tell if *Coathanger* meant the both of us now and I couldn't help hoping that it just meant her, and I hated that, and I felt so much anger at everything.

I clomped round and put my arms out, then roared right into the blinding wall of headlight. "Why don't you get your wee baldy ball bags out instead, eh? Show us, you shitebags! Fucking dunce bastards!" I bent down and nearly did the splits but I managed to pick up the neck of the broken vodka bottle and chuck it pathetically back at them.

I was wiping vodka from between my fingers when the engine revved right up and the car roared toward us. Kira yelped, I screamed, probably the loudest scream I'd done since the day that man followed me and Fiona home and we thought we were going to get beheaded by some mad flasher but he was actually returning my rucksack because I'd left it on a hedge outside the newsagent.

The car skidded to a stop on the gravel about two feet in front of us. I scrambled away and nearly fell. Kira flew ahead all smooth while I did awkward slidey clown steps, then right there magically in the dark the big ball of fear in me meant I could all of a sudden rollerblade. The pair of us swerved back out of the car park, fast, and onto the wide silvery-black road where you could see the moon above us up ahead, and she went off ahead on her own.

When I caught up she goes, "You should never have shouted back at them."

"You can't just take all that?"

"You learn that ignoring it works best."

She wanted to go home. I could tell she was panicking, but I says to her that we could go and get a drink at the service station, that it was quiet. She said no but I was already halfway over the wall and I knew she'd follow. We sat in the grass and changed into our trainers again then tramped together through a field of sleepy cows, then up over the big empty bright-lit roundabout. We ducked through a line of trees at the edge of the motorway, then up over the verge.

There was a hotel and petrol pumps and a crappy café built so truck drivers could wank in the car park and families could shut their babies up with chips on wee breaks away in their Renaults. It was mental expensive but I scraped up 68p from between my parka pockets, which was enough for a skoosh-gun coke in a paper cup with two straws to share.

We sat together on the edge of the raised concrete drain at the side of the café. Kira put her chin on her knees and started speaking. "Carly Hutcheson tried to cut my hair from behind in physics, right. I basically spend the whole class leaning forward because she just sits behind me making snip noises with these big steel scissors that she stole out of art. It's all a laugh to everyone else."

"Carly Hutcheson is a wee dog."

"Aye but what am I meant to do? I like my hair."

"Blow the fucking school up."

"Carly threw my skirt on the science block roof, after PE. My da went berserk at me because it cost him eight quid."

"Fuck sake," I says. There was a silence. What could you say to her about things without sounding like a wee groveler or it all coming out stupid and wrong?

I wanted to say we were both new, that it was okay she was struggling, that maybe I was struggling too? That most of the rest of the school had had their whole lives in Abbotscraig, and we hadn't, and it was really fine and normal to feel the way we did. Thinking words sometimes made me emotional because I knew deep in me they were good but I never trusted myself to say them right.

She looked at me and like some mad Moira telepathy goes, "How you finding here?"

"Well, I came from Muircross, so? I mean—where did you come from?"

"A mining village, near Stirling. It's where my da worked."

"Shite here, isn't it?"

"I tell myself, *Kira, the future's got to start somewhere.*" She had a sideways look at me. You knew it had come off some waffly printout. "You get sick of the running. Bigger towns. Different kitchens. Brand-new strangers. I need to make friends now. I need to approach people and start living, Adele says. Now. Not in the next place."

"Moving's not the worst. Folk get stuck."

"Oh I know! And one minute you're laughing at them then the next you're an assistant in MFI with an arse the size of a house. Permanent heartburn from chicken balls out of Golden Garden. You're old."

"Imagine being old. Saying *okey-doke.* Liking porridge."

She laughed and I saw her cute fangs. "Getting heartburn off of everything."

"Gasping for a Buscopan but nobody to bring you it."

"A decent man is your only hope."

I goes, "A big chunky local moaner with ingrown toenails, allergic to everything."

"Allergic to being tall and handsome."

I was giggling. "Argos pool table in the spare room."

"Golf clubs in every room."

There was a pause and the only sound was trucks zooming behind trees and our tiny, crisp laughter. I says, "And a 140-pound pit bull with a head like a housebrick."

"And a budgie that hates his guts."

"He'll help you squeeze out a freckly skitter-caked whooping-cough baby with a huge face."

She sat up straighter, grinning, chewing her finger. Her nails were Tipp-exed and had little blood marks in the folds from biting. "You'll get type 2 diabetes and a hairdressing job."

"And married in a pebbledash church."

"He'll get money off his maw to take you to Faliraki."

"He'll call you Poppet and emulsion the bathroom, if you beg."

"With paint from his work."

"Oh aye," I says, "a decorator. Or a semi-skilled laborer!"

"Coming home smelling of reheated meat pies and turpentine."

"Emulsion in his arsecrack."

"Emulsion in your arsecrack."

I was in harder hysterics than I could remember, the hardest maybe since probably 1994, and my chest felt spongey, and our shoulders touched, and then she looked at me suddenly all serious and says, "I'm going to have a wee go on these now," and dangled her big blades up by the mucky laces.

I wanted to say, *Do you have to?* It wasn't like me and her were going to be big pals, it was just sometimes our words came out in a jumble and a mess but somehow they fitted. And out here we were unshushable.

I wanted to say just sit here and speak to me more, but I saw that she needed to move. Then I huddled my knees tighter in the light from the café window, sat close to her sad and stinky-looking Hi-Tecs and crunched ice cubes out the cup as I watched her loop the car park alone, flying, arms out and eyes shut, hair flashing behind her like flickering black flame.

19

It was December before I got to go and meet Fulton's granda, Jackie. He lived up near me and Gunner, by the edge of the golf course, and I skipped double history so Fulton could take me to say *hiya*.

Apparently Jackie never got up before eleven so Fulton and me were stood in the phone box opposite his house, scraping hearts in the frost patterns, killing time. Fulton had his Helly Hansen on and I had my parka but we were freezing, still. He was going to be showing me a trick.

"You dial the operator, first. Give them a random number." He waited on the line. Then he whispered to me with his hand over the handset, "The operator rings the number. Then connects. You tell the operator there's been an emergency and ask to reverse the charges to that number, aye?" I nodded. He started panting. "It's . . . Christopher! There's been a pure mental accident . . . can the charges be reversed?"

He tilted the handset and I heard the operator talking to the other line—"*I have a Christopher, with a medical emergency. He's asking to reverse the charges, do you accept?*"

There was a pause, then an older woman said, "*I suppose. What's this about? I don't know any Christopher?*" There was an Edinburgh arseyness in her voice that made me feel all right about doing this.

The operator spoke to us, "The charge has been accepted—

connecting you now." Fulton kissed my forehead and did one of his big dafty smiles.

Then, "Who *is this*?" I heard the arsey woman saying.

Right away Fulton started screaming a big heap of words into the handset—*wanker, cunt, prick, arsehole, slag*—I joined in. When he slammed the handset down my jaw was fucked from roaring and my face felt tight with joy. He kissed me on the mouth.

"Right, come on," he goes, wedging the door open, letting the icier air in. "Y'know, you can burst open the money box on these phones pure easy. With a car jack. I'll show you sometime."

I pulled my parka tight round my uniform and we crossed the road, scuffing stripes in the frost with our soles.

"If he says anything weird just smile," Fulton goes, squeezing my hand, setting me up for something that might happen in that way he liked to do. "He's old but he's lively, still. It's the tablets they fed him years back, in the jail."

To me there were mainly two types of granda. The decent, round-faced granda with fluffy white hair and a neat white beard that wore jumpers and gave you cake and praise. He was predictable, he smelled fine, he reminded you of Santa.

Then other more menacing grandas. They were scrawny with stale hair and they lived in doorways. They would call you adult nicknames, give you banknotes and drink, press their chests against yours with every single hug.

We stopped at Jackie's gate. Beyond the back fences you could see peeks of the huge frosty golf course, looking like a big empty kingdom of mint ice cream. "Do I call him granda, or what?"

"Jackie's best."

I took the White Musk out my pocket and skooshed myself. There were icicles hanging like wee glass snotters from the door frame. Fulton knocked and I was picking my pinky when Jackie appeared.

"Hiya, Jackie!" I went, right away, doing my confidence voice.

Jackie turned back into the dark all stiff without a word. Fulton gave me a serious nod. I followed first and we got led through to the living room.

Jackie's hair was glossy and yellow like Stork and he had it slicked back all shiny like a singer off the fifties. He was wearing a vest with a cloud of sparkly white chest hair sticking out the top, like the blowball off a dandelion. He was the thinnest old man I had ever seen.

His living room was colder than outside. Three armchairs and a table, sat round a dark three-bar fire with stoory plastic coal in it. No telly, no carpet. The walls had been half-stripped like in a crime scene on telly. I was clamping my jaw to stop the chatters.

We all sat down. "Before I forget," Fulton went, bringing notes out of his coat pocket and counting some into his granda's hands. I didn't ask and I didn't look. Then they started talking all energized about Dundee United and what they had done to the league.

I looked around. There was a heap of brownish clothes under the window. A toothbrush on the fireplace. Jesus being eerie in an old framed print. I knew that Fulton really loved his granda but it was hard to think nice thoughts about the person that lived here.

Jackie jumped up. "Do youse pair want a couple a cans?" I could see all the veins in his biceps—he was a wee bit see-through, like the bag off a hot sausage roll. I tensed my arse-muscles in sequence on the seat to release some nerves.

"Aye please, Jackie," Fulton says. Jackie disappeared into the kitchen and Fulton gave me a serious nod. It said, *well done, thanks, I'm proud, I'm sorry*.

I could tell he was stressed—I was learning really quick that when Fulton wasn't out at midnight headlocking his pals and setting fire to road cones he was a boy who got stressed quite easy about things he cared about. I was seeing that boy from time to time.

Jackie came creaking back with three cans of the Sweetheart Stout.

He handed me mine without looking at me and we opened them nearly together with three flat clicks.

"This is the bird, Fulton, is it?" Jackie sucked foam out his tin. "Plucked yersel' a right dolly bird. Well done, son." I did a tiny pout and hoovered stout from the rim of my can. My heart was going like a cartoon frog.

"Aye, this is Cora." Fulton grinned at me.

I smiled. "Aw thanks. Thanks for the drink." I cheersed the can toward Jackie and felt a kind of queasiness but in my veins.

"Are youse hungry at all? Can I heat youse up a pie?"

"We've had some food on the way up," Fulton says.

"Hey, did I tell you the news, son—I might be moving to Barrhead?"

"No, you never."

"Aye, waiting to hear back from the council about a swap. Barrhead's a cracking place," Jackie goes. "It's aw business for me now, here. The factory's gone and the boys I've worked with are aw deid." Fulton did his best adult nod. "But listen, son—don't you be thinking on it, the move's an age away, and you'll still be able to visit. There'll be a foldout sofa. Bring the bird!"

"Aye that would be amazing, Jackie," Fulton goes. I crossed my legs tight, smoothed my school skirt down, fiddled with the ring pull on my can.

"Anyway," Jackie goes suddenly, "let's hear about you, lassie. You're on Weavers Row? Gunner's lassie, that right?"

I tried to keep my body doing wee normal-person movements but inside I wanted to get up and go out and run round the block. "Yes," I goes, all proper, then for some reason, "But he's not my dad."

"Stepda?"

I sat straight and gulped more stout. "No."

"It's a bit weird," Fulton says.

"It's not that weird! Basically, Jackie, I grew up just me and my mam. Then she died. Hit by a car! And so it's me and Gunner. Gunner was her boyfriend."

It felt mental to be saying these things out loud into a room. I thought of how every new place I went to now she would never know. Then I wondered how I'd ever explain my life to folk when I didn't understand it myself. I took another big slurp.

"So he's just agreed to be your da, nae issues there?"

"It's not easy to explain. But I think he likes me!" I did a single pathetic gulped-down chuckle. "He's not my da though."

"He must be right sound, this Gunner, taking on a teenager. You pair must be ay close"—he smiled—"a great wee team."

I chugged the rest of my stout and felt my tummy clench. A bit of boak came up. I felt guilty about tasting vom when Gunner was being talked about.

Were we a team? We existed side by side and never really spoke about what it was. I was still mainly trying to work out how he managed to put up with me. I used my pinky to wipe some mascara-scum from the corner of my eye then I went, "He pisses me off, but he's a good guy. Fulton's coming to meet him. Aren't you, Fulton?"

"We're going to La Cantina after Cora's parents' night. Three of us."

"And you and this Gunner came frae Muircross, Fulton tells me?"

"I grew up in Muircross."

"Fuck me! A daughter of the cross!" Jackie's face went into a big cheeky grin. His teeth were like bits of sweetcorn. "Oh you poor thing. You must be a right hard bitch, eh?"

"Muircross isn't the worst!" I went.

"Aye it is! They ripped the fucking arse oot that place. When the pits went they'd have been as well dynamiting the whole heap. I had a pal there in the seventies, Peter Togneri, gravedigger, good lad. Me and him used to do a bit of roving in his old camper van. Muircross was decent then, tidy place, honest folk. There's a museum aboot it all now, ha! Tell you one thing, the only reason you'd go there today's for the smack. Top notch, apparently. Dinghy-loads, straight up the Firth frae Rotterdam. Heroin Heights they call it."

"Do they?"

"See! You'll no read that in a fancy glass museum!"

"No."

"Listen, love, you and Fulton are looking the part, that's what counts. You'll no be bored with Fulton—always got a deal on the go." I was about to reply when Jackie turned to Fulton. "Listen, son, speaking of deals"—he stood up—"the pair of youse come through to the kitchen till I show youse something."

"Actually, I'll need to go to the loo," I said.

"Nae problem, lass. Straight up the stair." He pointed one milky arm at the ceiling. The skin was hanging off it like an old pajama top.

It was so cold in the bathroom that clouds of steam came up off my pish—when I opened my legs it was like the bit in *Stars in Their Eyes* when the contestant appears. I washed my hands and dried them on my skirt then I tiptoed over the hallway floorboards and had a nosey in the end bedroom.

The floor was lined with crispy newspaper. In the middle was a weightlifting bench surrounded by mounds of tins and scrunched-up Strongbow bottles. There were clowns and rainbows on the wallpaper and a tree outside was growing right up against the window, blocking out most of the light.

I was thinking, *Who the fuck is this guy to slag off Muircross?*

Then as I walked back toward the stairs I heard a noise from the other room. Softly as I could, not able to stop myself, I stepped toward the doorway and stuck my head round.

It smelled dry and biscuity in there. This room was bare too, but in the middle was a double bed and lying on the bare mattress were two yellow-haired men about Jackie's age, out for the count, one in brown clothes, one in an *A-Team* sleeping bag. Their snores were making clouds, like little cartoon dragons.

Back downstair Jackie and Fulton were at the kitchen table with a bottle of advocaat and a black nylon satchel between them. The cooker clock blinked with four red zeros.

"Here she is!" Jackie goes, grinning.

There was no feeling from him that I might have seen something upstair. I thought two things at once—that maybe I was lucky I had never met my grandparents, and that Fulton better be living differently when he was a granda too.

After ten minutes of drinking and chatting Fulton got up with the satchel and we said goodbye. I nodded, smiled, did the eyebrows then wedged myself halfway out the back door behind Fulton, to avoid the hug. Out the back the grass was waist high and full of crisp packets and rusted shite. Then Jackie appeared from nowhere, ahead of us, like a special effect. "Actually, c'mere, lass."

At the back of the garden by the tall fence was a big wavy metal garage. Jackie jingled the big chain about then swung the doors open. Inside, a strip light started blinking and everything was grotty. There were heaps of tools and machines on benches at the back and then maybe about eight manky-looking motorbikes all crammed together, lined up, a wee bit tilted.

I was thinking I had to be enthusiastic to get this over with. "Wow! Motorbikes!"

"Scramblers," Jackie whispered.

"He raced them, back in the seventies!" Fulton was grinning, "Sources them now. Fixes them." It was the most excited I'd ever heard him.

"I've never ridden a scrambler. I'm jealous!" I says.

Jackie started squeezing between the bikes, maneuvering his wee ancient arse, looking. "Now let me see. A Kawasaki." He kicked the side of one and rolled it out into the wintry daylight. "I say Kawasaki, but a lot of this I've salvaged myself. It's a custom. A wee beauty, for another wee beauty—for you, Cora."

"What?! Oh Jesus no," I went, before I could think. I made a big screwy face like *what the fuck* then quickly covered it with a grin. "Really?" I looked at Fulton hoping it was a joke. Suddenly all I could picture was Fozzy.

Jackie goes, "You're a Gillespie now, and this is oor business! One strand of it, anyway. Fulton'll make you a rider. Won't you, son?"

Fulton nodded, grinning at me. The bike was white and green and caked in shite and had the number 27 painted on it in a circle. Its headlight was like a big miserable eye and I was already feeling sorry for it.

I giggled all cute despite the nightmare of everything. I goes, "Thanks, Jackie. Wow! My own scrambler."

I took the handlebars and Jackie started locking up the shed. I wiggled the bike back and forth a bit and it seemed quite easy to roll. I kept hold of the handlegrips so Jackie couldn't get in to hug me near my boobs.

"Right then," he goes, and came up behind me and gave me a big squeezy bear hug. "Fulton, son. Keep this dirty minx oot o trouble!"

"That's my job!" Fulton goes, laughing.

I rolled the bike. "Thank you again, Jackie. I'm going to learn all about scrambling." Out on the path behind the house Fulton grabbed the handlebars and started wheeling it away all moody. I closed Jackie's gate then shielded my eyes from the wintry sun. "What the fuck?" I goes.

"I can't believe he's given you that today."

"I didn't fucking want it!" He kept huffing and puffing ahead. "Where we going? What's in that bag?"

"Pornos. Rare ones."

"Why's your granda giving you pornos, Fulton?"

He looked at me. His eyes had gone from brown to honeyish red in the brightness. "He's finished with them."

"Did you know he's got people asleep upstair in that house? One of them's in a sleeping bag with B. A. Baracus on it!"

"It's probably big Yogi. It's his pals. It's his business."

"Where we going?"

"Stashing these scudbooks. Where no cunt will find them."

We went through a gap in the stone wall and trudged together into the middle of the deserted minty golf course. The satchel of magazines was bouncing heavy on his hip while the bike flattened dark lines in the grass. My high-heel Kickers were wet and wobbling.

Fulton explained how he could sell the pornos round the building sites. He would hide them now and come back in future when he needed them. He couldn't take them home because his da might find them. I wasn't sure if he meant that his da would punish him, or that his da would sell them, or that his da would use them himself.

We reached an island of bushes and trees in the middle of the course. The clearing inside smelled of pish and pineyness, like the PE toilets. There were tins and torn up bin bags scattered round, a half-melted road cone, a wooden pallet covered in moldy carpet offcuts. He stood the bike up. All around us the wind in the bushes was hissing.

"Hold this," Fulton went, and passed me the satchel of pornos. He got down on one knee and tucked his trackie bottoms into his socks.

"What the hell am I supposed to do with that bike, Fulton?"

"Take it home."

I lifted the flap of the bag and saw the edges of twenty or thirty buckled-looking pornos. You could make out little peachy patches and glisteny bits of veins and hair, but as far as I could see no cake. No beans anywhere.

"You upset Jackie's going to Barrhead?" I says. I knew he was, I just wanted to see what he'd say. He seemed to be getting wound up and I wasn't sure how to calm him down.

"Nope! He's getting out of here." He tugged his laces tight. "Fuck Abbotscraig. Fuck St. Therese. Fuck the whole fucking place, man."

I looked up at the trees all trembly in the wind. My face hurt. The feeling of stout in my belly was making me ill.

He sprang to his feet and did a little hop to make himself ready. His face looked damp and drunk. "Right," he says. I handed him the heavy satchel. He put the strap round his neck so the bag hung down his back—it was cutting right into his throat.

He leaped at the trunk and in three rapid moves was already right off the ground. Clumps of the tree shivered as he moved and you couldn't help but be a wee bit impressed. I picked at my finger. As I looked up, needles and seeds dropped down out of the branches and into my face and hair. Then in a wee minute he jumped down too.

He was brushing himself off, looking happier. He put his hand round onto my bum and kissed my forehead. "Sorry for being a moody cunt."

"Barrhead's not that far," I said. I had no real idea where Barrhead was.

"Aye well," he goes, adjusting his jacket, looking round shifty. He made that face I knew. "Listen, do you want to?"

"What? Oh, aye, 'course. Help me get the bike home first?"

"Here." The word made a cloud when he said it.

"Fulton."

"You said you would. Vicki done it with Brian up at the fireworks. And you said you would."

Vicki had never mentioned that but I managed to keep my eyebrows still. "It's baltic, Fulton. And we're inside a hedge."

He kissed my nose. "It'll just be quick. Keep your jacket on. And use mine if you want?" He took his Helly Hansen off and laid it on the ground. "I'll pull out, babe. And once we've done it then that's us serious."

I folded my arms. "Serious as in I'd be your girlfriend?"

"Yep."

I looked out through the gaps in the trees. There really was nobody for miles and I couldn't believe this was going to be it. I put my parka down too. "This is mental. I've got a brand-new double bed in my room!"

"You said you'd feel pure guilty there." He stepped onto the wood pallet and pulled his Timberlands off, then tugged his trackie bottoms and boxers off, then put the boots back on. He was wearing just his jumper and Timberlands and winter had turned his willy into a lilac dolly mixture.

He sat down on his Helly Hansen and started wanking. The bike stood still like it was perving on us. I squatted down.

We started tonguing and his hand gripped my shoulder. He tipped me back flat and then he tried his hand up my skirt, and I let him.

He kissed me so hard it made my heart feel thin and dirty and when he rolled on top and his weight pressed me into the earth, in my sixteen years of breathing I'd never wanted anything more.

Our eyes met. His knuckles were cold on the inside flab of my thigh. He fumbled for a second, then a pressure, then a pain. Then a feeling somewhere in me like untangling.

I looked up, I says *breathe, Cora*, to the trees. They were thrashing now and the sounds made me think of the Firth. I closed my eyes and there was Jo.

One time she told me how you could shag a guy then wake up before him in the morning and steal food out his freezer—burgers and waffles, big sacks of value sausages. *Keep you going for a week*, she said. She used to sneak out and run home and make herself a big breakfast fry-up, like a reward.

When I'd said that was weird and wrong she called me a fat fuck and a munter and said I'd never ever get a man to touch me as long as I lived. *Not unless you grow a tail and enter Crufts*, that was the words. I had no idea what Crufts was then, but I learned.

It wasn't perfect, but here I was—leaves on the ground, frost on the leaves, sun in the sky like a wee pickled onion. I blinked her away and squished my mouth onto Fulton's jaw again and again and again.

I was trying to get comfy because I think I was lying on a tree root and I didn't want to rip his Helly Hansen, but just as I moved he made a grunting noise and then he rolled off me and away.

I stayed still on the ground. I moved onto my elbow and he tugged his jacket from under me and shook the twigs off. His cum had slimed an Australia-shaped stain onto the lining. He kicked the boots off again and got properly dressed.

"Cheers," he goes, all growly. He sounded like the Cookie Monster.

I looked at him. His eyes were wild and his face had gone a Wham bar color. His ears looked raw like rashers. I wondered how I looked. There was icy-damp wind on the sole of my foot because one of my shoes was off.

Then I remembered to smile. *Mizz* had explained about shyness and the summery thunder feeling, but all I wanted was soup and heels of bread in front of the *Rugrats* or *Doug*.

"Thanks," I goes. Pauline had told me I should look forward to the second time not the first. Fulton was still scraping big glops of cum off his jacket with a bit of bark, so at least I wasn't going to be pregnant.

He went over and started fiddling with the bike, annoyed again. "Let's get going. C'mere and I'll show you how to start it."

He talked me through the controls while I tugged my laddery tights back round and finger-combed the tree-crap out my hair. He got on and started the scrambler roaring then patted the seat behind him.

"Do I not need a helmet?" I shouted, but he couldn't hear. I clamped my arms tight round his body and we zoomed out over the course. The bike tires gouged a big mucky squiggle behind us in the frosted grass.

20

What was it about parents' evening that made you feel like you were four again, having your fish fingers chopped into fifteen bits and airplaned into your mouth on a plastic spoon while getting told you're amazing and brave?

McClair hated me and I hated her but here we were stood grinning at one another like the absolute best of pals. She handed me my school photos.

"Thanks so much for filling me in on Cora's progress, Janet," Gunner goes, in his best High Court voice. I gripped the brown envelope and kept the smile on in that way I was expert at now.

McClair straightened the collar of her tasseled suede waistcoat. "Honestly, it was my pleasure."

The minute we stepped outside Gunner dropped the easygoing act and went back to being all shruggy. He'd been in a rage for a whole week because of the scrambler. First he was telling me to give it back, then he wanted me to sell it, then he was ranting about how he'd scrap it himself. Eventually I won. We had to wheel it up the ramp and into the hall and put it on bin bags, because the shed was still full of my Muircross crap.

I couldn't have cared less about it really but when I saw how wound-up Gunner was getting I decided I'd keep it. I put tinsel round the handlebars for a laugh but he tore it all off in a mood and called me a *disrespectful wee shite*. I told him it was my hall too. I reminded him we were standing in a house that my mam had applied for, for her and me.

In the end I promised him I'd clear the shed out if he came with me and Fulton to the Tex Mex, La Cantina—he'd get to meet Fulton, and there'd be room in the shed for the scrambler. Everyone would be happy.

I slipped the photos out for a peek on the school front steps, in the snow. There was a big one, in an oval cardboard frame, then a sheet of smaller versions. I looked repulsive—hunch back, slug's neck, cider-jowls. Stringy hair, sky-blue shirt, a face like a just-hatched bird.

"You finished admiring yourself?" He was at the bottom of the steps.

Vicki ran past with her parents and said bye to me, and then Carrie and Ishbel, and I was trying to nod and smile to them all while at the same time hiding my photo and also pretending not to know this one-eyed man in the flappy suit.

Gunner pulled his fleece over the suit and zipped it up. "I'm sure you're looking gorgeous, doll, but are we not in a hurry?"

I ran down the steps and stomped ahead. "Bus stop's that way."

"We're walking."

"It's snowing!" I goes, shrugging my rucksack. "My shins are numb. Can we maybe not worry about a few fucking pennies for once?"

"I want to speak to you."

I stood there with my heart deflating and snow tickling my nose. Then I started walking. He ran beside me and put his long arm round my shoulders. I couldn't remember the last time he'd done that. He goes, "Lass, I care about you. Do you think I'd put a fucking suit on otherwise? But I can't listen to what those teachers said and just do nothing, eh."

"It's the same shite I've had in every parents' evening going right back to primary."

"Like what?"

"*Lazy and overemotional. Talks too much. Born late. Distracted in her own world of wasted potential.* I'm sick of hearing it."

"Are they lying then?"

I shrugged his arm off. "They think I'm doing it on purpose! I'm not. I try and hide it but it's who I am."

I stopped and looked at him as the snow scribbled down all Disneyish around us. I wanted to speak and to tell him and to explain everything right back to Samantha, but I was tired. All I wanted now was to get through to Christmas without any more tears or fights or discussions about me and what a problem I was. I went to speak then turned and started walking again instead.

"Janet says you get distracted a lot. She thinks you're struggling with grief."

"How am I struggling? Honestly, in case you haven't noticed I'm grown-up now. Did you not hear my biology grades? The comments on my essays?" I started walking faster. "And can you stop calling her Janet? It's McClair. She locked me in the stationery cupboard once for talking too much and she's an absolute cunt."

He burst out laughing. "Right, what was it that Mr. Abbasi says? *She retains information very easily despite giving off the impression she isn't listening.* Now that second bit I recognize!"

"Can you shut up?"

"Ach, Cora. My heart was bursting in there, honestly." I stopped, his face was rough-looking under the street lamp. "*She's a quick thinker, a wee perfectionist!* Listen, I'm not caring too much about the bad bits, because I know you're still processing everything. If you're distracted, maybe thinking about your mam, how about we visit her and—"

"I just need time," I goes, "with the grief." It wasn't even true but it would shut him up.

"Well, Cora, speak to me, eh?"

"There's not much more to say."

Gunner had dragged me round the gym hall and we'd seen all the teachers—Big Scary, Big Pishy, Diplodocus, Solsgirth, Gorilla Mitts and that sex-pest English supply teacher who ate sweets with icing sugar on them and blew on them before putting them in his mouth. Almost every one of them had mentioned grief, like they'd all agreed about it beforehand.

Nobody said, *What do* you *think's wrong, Cora? How do you feel?* My mam going made me feel like I wanted to die myself, but all these school problems had been the same when she was alive. There was nobody around that knew that now, but how did you explain something so personal that you hardly understood to this man who wasn't even your da?

He touched my shoulder. "Let's have a proper meeting at the school."

"Look, thank you for not mentioning the psychologist in front of McClair. But that's where this is going. More meetings, more waiting lists, more appointments, more men like Dan to speak to. No thanks." I goes, "Can we stop talking now? I'm going to greet. And I spent forty-five minutes this morning doing this makeup for our meal. And we're nearly there. And Fulton's waiting."

He put his arm around my shoulder again, tighter. "You're looking braw, Cora."

La Cantina was empty and you could hear kitchen radio and fridge noises. We peeked through from the foyer bit—Fulton was sat up the back at a big round table doing a napkin wigwam. I told Gunner to wait there while I went in the loo to do deep breaths and get ready.

Fulton had taken me into Debenhams the week before to choose something decent for the Christmas dance—a Lurex silver swing minidress and a pair of black velour leggings to go under. He'd got me shoes out of Littlewoods—silver-color Sacha London high-heel loafers that were £44.99. I stood next to him at the counter and watched him pay for everything with his own money and I couldn't make sense of how special I felt. I couldn't think how I'd repay him.

The cubicle was freezing. I balled my uniform up into my bag, wiggled the Lurex dress down and smoothed the leggings nice. I put my head under the hand dryer then wobbled back into the restaurant with Fiona's skipping rope round me and the biggest smile I could manage.

As me and Gunner walked toward the table I whispered, "No wee stories about me, please."

"Not even the one where I have to climb over a fucking motorbike to do a shite in my own toilet?" He started grinning down toward the table. "So you're Fulton, aye?"

Fulton stood up. His dark brown hair was only about a centimeter long but he had forced it into a middle parting with wax. He was wearing his navy-blue Henri-Lloyd jumper. He winked at me. He looked so smart. "Hello. All right? Can I get you a drink Mr. McCallum?"

Gunner looked at me. "Will we sit down first?"

I could see Fulton was wondering about Gunner's eye, and the fleece in his hand that I'd been wearing at the fireworks. Then a moody waiter appeared, a goth who had been made to take his piercings out. I couldn't help thinking about Dennis. He goes, "Drinks then, guys?"

Fulton says, "Pint of Tennent's please. Mr. McCallum, will you have a pint?"

"Tap water please," Gunner goes, into the tablecloth.

I breathed in slowly. I looked at the menu. "Bonnie Prince Charlie Colada please!"

The waiter nodded and left. You could hear Take That on the kitchen radio. Gunner sat back and scratched his jaw casually with his thumbnail. "So, you're how old?"

"Sixteen, Mr. McCallum, same as Cora."

There was a pause. I kept grinning. Then before I could speak he goes, "Listen, son, save the *yes sir, no sir* shite. Are you off your fucking nut, giving my daughter a motorbike?"

I went all woozy-headed, like the time on the chairoplane at Burntisland with Auntie Janine. *Daughter?* I started picking at my thumb. "Gunner—"

"My Granda Jackie done it, Mr. McCallum, not me. Scramblers are his—"

"My Granda Jackie done it and ran away?"

"Look!" I says, loud as I dared to.

The pair of them looked at me. They were suddenly sat all sad-shouldered with their hands under the table like a pair of bad dogs.

I breathed and wiggled in my chair and fixed my straps so my dress was sitting perfect, then I tucked my hair calmly behind my ears and stared at the wee cactus in the kilt and Santa hat in the middle of our table. "My mam told me all about this place years ago, when I was a wee lassie in Muircross. I was always wondering about it when she told me it was a Scottish Tex Mex idea! And here we are. So please, let's have a nice night?"

The torn-faced goth came back and plopped the three drinks down in front of us. I picked up my cocktail. "Here's to my mam. Happy Christmas, Mam, when it comes."

"To your mam," Fulton went.

"To Maggie," Gunner goes.

When the waitress appeared I asked for the Tex Mex platter that my mam had told me about in the garden that day but it had been discontinued in 1995. We ordered other stuff instead—Fulton had the Buffalo Balmoral Chicken, Gunner had the Haggis Tacos, and I had the Braveheart Burrito.

The food came and we ate it. We sat and I told the pair of them stories from school and Fulton barely said a thing and Gunner didn't even bother to do his usual chuckle and half-smile when I'd finished talking. We'd been silently munching for about five minutes when Gunner suddenly goes, "So you'll be taking Cora to the Christmas dance then I take it?"

"He's coming along, aye, but, Gunner, I told you, Fulton's not at the school anymore."

"Ah, sorry. What is he *at* then, like?" You could hear cars honking on the road outside.

"I'm a laborer, Mr. McCallum."

I put my cutlery down and sat back. "Honest work!" Gunner didn't flinch.

Fulton started speaking. "I didn't mind the school, really. But they never liked me much. And I wasn't sitting in a classroom on a sunny day, not when there was money to be made. I've got to work ten times harder than other folk, like, because I've got a point to prove. I never got a start, you know. Never learned to write or read or anything like that. I'm just a worker. A hard fucking worker, though."

Gunner took a drink. "You want a medal?"

I ate a forkful and thought of Vicki. When Vicki was with you, even if you knew times were bad or shit stuff had happened, even if she was on the verge of nearly crying, you still knew she'd put a smile on it. She'd have some comment, a joke to make, a voice to do. It was like she had her own wee world she went in, to cope, and it helped you cope as well. More than anything I wanted Vicki with me.

"I'm just explaining," Fulton goes, through his chewing. "I've got plans for the future and for me and Cora."

"Good for you, son," Gunner went, like he was reading out the phone book.

There was a minute more chewing, then Fulton put his cutlery down and looked at his plate. "I'm going to the loo." He honked his chair out and walked off.

Gunner kept eating. "Can you not be nice to him, for me?" I goes. "Please? Speak to him properly. Take an interest, ask him his star sign or his surname or his favorite color or something, fuck sake."

"What's his full name?"

"Fulton Gillespie."

Gunner's forehead went into a shape I'd never seen, like someone had shat in his tacos. He started itching behind his ear like his brain hurt. "You better be fucking having me on."

"What?"

"The Gillespies! Him and his family are up to all sorts."

I felt a cramp in my chest. "Give him a chance."

"Your wee Romeo and his crooked da and his demented granda are the reason I'm having to work my arse off sweeping the hospital corridors at midnight."

I kept my face straight over my hammering heart. "Oh boohoo. You can't get out thieving your M People CDs and your Calvin Klein."

"The Gillespies think they own this place. Drugs, weapons, house-breaking, all sorts."

"So you're the police now? Hilarious."

"Do you think I took it lightly, packing in the lifting?"

I saw Fulton ducking back through from the toilet. "Here he comes. You can thank him for putting you on the straight and narrow."

"Things were tight and I did what I had to. Reality, chief. Ever been there?"

I smiled at Fulton as he sat. "Gunner was just asking about your plans for the flat."

"Oh aye? I'm thinking of getting a flat soon. Going to be a right smart place." He put his napkin back on. "Cora can come over and stay."

"I'll tell the jokes," Gunner went, under his breath.

"My mate Sluggo's got decks and a smoke machine."

Gunner kept his face flat the entire time Fulton spoke, but I didn't care. The future with Fulton would at least be free of the memories hanging over me like shite-filled balloons that floated up every time I had to sit and rake round the past with Gunner. I'd never need to speak about Muircross again. Diaries. Dennis. Nettles and warm rain. Bleach and off milk and seagull shite. I'd never tell Fulton about Jo, bread, stairlifts. Lena Zavaroni. He'd never ever see me crying.

For pudding we shared the lime and whisky sauce cheesecake. I moved round so I could sit closer to Fulton, then Gunner got up and paid for the meal and then said he'd wait across the road for me at the bus stop.

Fulton relaxed as soon as the door swooshed shut behind Gunner. I kissed the side of his forehead. There was a wee bit of hair wax he'd missed, white and blobby, like glue. It was so cute all the effort he had made. I rubbed it in with my finger for him.

I says, "I'm sorry about him."

He didn't look up. "It's all right."

"You okay? It doesn't matter what he thinks, he can't control me."

He chucked his napkin on the table. "My boys were saying they saw you."

"Eh?"

"Roller-skating with that mongo lassie. You not a wee bit old for all that?"

"I'm—"

"Parked down the old factory." I pictured the vodka bottle. Heard my own words screamed back at me. "It's no a big deal, babe, but maybe just better watch who you're seen with. Since you're my bird. Folk are calling you Cora Coathanger."

"What? Oh." I smiled. "Oh, who cares, really?"

He took a sip and looked up through the empty restaurant. "Me."

At the bus stop opposite I did the nod. I had said to Fulton that maybe he could come to ours for a drink and he could see my room, but if things weren't going well I would do a nod to let him know.

"I better be heading then," Fulton goes. I winked at him. I hadn't let my smile drop.

"Toodle-pip, son," Gunner goes.

"See ya." Fulton stood there and thought about trying to shake Gunner's hand then zipped his Helly Hansen up and walked off. The snow was settling and the disappointing Abbotscraig Christmas lights were sagging above our heads.

"A living fucking nightmare," I goes.

"Am I supposed to sit there and let you have your life ruined by some wee slithering waster?"

"As opposed to some big slithering waster?"

"Who puts a roof over your head? You really need to have a think to yourself."

"You've made me look like a fucking idiot," I went. "I told him all about you and us. You could have been nice at least."

"Is that my job, is it? Sit there and shut up and be nice? I'm trying to protect you, lass. But, Cora, I'm tired. I don't know how to sit and be the adult and be the peacemaker and act like it's all a happy fantasy. I don't know how to be a da. But I'll tell you, one thing I do know is how to get the measure of folk. It's an instinct. You can laugh if you want, but I grew up amongst it and I'm rarely wrong when it comes to spotting bother—and I'll tell you now, you're headed for bother with him."

I was trying to keep the breaths going normal. I shrugged. "Maybe bother's what I want."

He looked at his feet then started shuffling off through the snow. "You've not got the first clue what you want."

21

said it out into the cold air of the kitchen. "That's me leaving for the dance, then."

He was out the back huddling round a mug of tea with Donna. The washing machine was bumping away and the door was closed and there was no way he could hear me, but I'd come down and told him I was going, like he'd asked.

The week had been starey meals and three-word sentences, him feeding coins in the telly and the two of us sat curled apart on the settee watching crap while I silently stressed about the dance and the tree lights blinked over the both of us in sleepy wee heartbeat sequences.

All he'd said was *don't go on an empty stomach*. It was one of those comments where you knew he wasn't bothered about me actually starving or dying, he was just putting down a marker that he could prove himself right with later.

In the living room I lifted his wallet off the mantelpiece.

I'd wanted to get Vicki over so we could get ready together but with Gunner so huffy I decided not to push it. In the end I'd sat in my room by myself listening to Phase FM, combing glitter spray through my ponytail and trembling liner round my lips with a cold pencil while I drank flat Lilt out a mug and felt eleven again.

I crouched down behind the armchair and flipped the wallet open.

Right away my eyes were woozing in and out. It was me there—the wee just-hatched bird in a sky-blue school shirt, snipped out and stuck shoulder to shoulder with my mam behind the plastic window. Her about 1992, me four weeks ago. The shapes of our hairlines were identical now and our noses were even more the same.

I could feel the tears coming. Then a painful chuckle escaped, because the way we were both staring out all vacant it looked like me and her were in a huff together, about the exact same thing. Gunner, maybe? Then something too-big and achy rose up the center of me, like it always did before the floodgates opened.

I flipped his wallet closed and pushed every feeling down. I got my parka in the hall and went over my hair once in the mirror there. I squeezed past the scrambler and gave it a quick pat on the headlight to keep it cheery then I headed out the door.

Vicki was sat on a swing in her fake fur coat, knee-length boots, blondish hair fountaining up behind a tiny heart-shaped tiara. I tiptoed down the crispy path in my bunched-up parka with my thighs on fire, trying to keep upright and learn how not to stomp in my brand-new shoes.

She swung herself, jumped off, hugged me. "About time, hen." Her perfume smelled like lawnmowing. "I was thinking your motorbike must have broke down?"

As we crossed the main road and walked into the Deathy you saw other folk from school leaving their houses—wee flashes of silk and sequin at the hems and collars of coats, the odd tiara. You saw the trees all still, the size of the moon, the breath of your mate as she's giving you her theory about how your stepda is probably jealous of your boyfriend.

"Fulton knows he's barred, aye? This is amazing. Solsgirth will go mental!"

"Him and his pals are coming but they're not going in. They're doing their own thing."

She laughed. "This is going to be so funny."

We took the path round the back of the estate by the church and then climbed the steps up to the side of the dual carriageway. The whole night was looming and there was nothing in my head but bundles of nerves and we were halfway down the road before I zoned back in. "I love those silver shoes," Vicki goes. Cars were ripping past. She was gawping at me through her thick lashes.

"Oh, aye. Forty-four ninety-nine." I stopped and straightened them together all pretty on the churned-up slush. "So what drink did you bring? Let's make a start, eh?"

"I've not actually brought any."

"Serious?"

"Can we move a bit further up and get a seat?"

I followed her on the path up the verge and she patted the wet bench and I folded my parka up under my legs and sat next to her, shivering.

"It's all a bit weird, really," she goes.

I looked at her and she looked at her cold pink hands. "Can it be quick? We're already late."

"Remember I said about Brian? Things were going good between us again? Well—things." She laughed loud and her eyes went unfocused. Vicki was my best pal so I knew from just a few wee movements that something was up. "It's nothing big. Just me and him are getting more serious." She tucked her arms round herself tight as they would go. "He's asked me to put some stuff behind me. The drinking. Living on street corners and rooftops."

"So what, you're giving up booze?" I laughed. "What's this really about?"

"I'm having a baby, Cora." She wobbled her head and did an eye-roll like she was talking about something mortifying she'd seen someone doing on telly. "I didn't want to say it on the phone. But there's no point fucking about."

I wanted to hug her then slap her then get her away from me forever. "Nothing big, eh? Your life is over. You're such a fucking idiot, lassie."

"Fuck off."

"No, you fuck off." After a sad second of breathing I goes, "You'll have to get rid of it."

"My mam's going to help."

"Do you not want to go to college? Have a life?"

"This will be a life." I laughed because I didn't know what else to do. And then she stood up in front of me. "Something funny?"

"Sit down, you stupid cow," I goes, laughing a bit more to make things calmer but already thinking *aim for the pavement behind her*, in case.

"Just 'cause you've never done it. Just 'cause your boyfriend would rather chase people about with baseball bats and blow stuff up than actually touch you!"

"I have done it, actually."

"Makes sense."

I stood up. "You slept with Brian and never even told me. I had to hear it off Fulton!"

She started stomping off down the dual carriageway, her ponytail springing left and right all shiny gold as headlights scanned over it in the darkness. I shouted, "So I'm going to the dance myself, am I? What about Jackie's party?"

She turned with the wind ruffling the fur of her coat. "Your wee hero Pauline will be at the party, don't you worry," she started screaming. "You pair away and have a great time!"

I clomped toward her. "Vicki, come on."

"Fuck off, Cora. Go and find your wee pal."

I tried to hug her but she shoved me off. "Have you told Pauline you're pregnant?"

She started walking. "Pauline's running for her life. That's what Glasgow is!"

I stopped and I stood and as I watched Vicki turn into a dot I wondered what had happened between the two of them. Then a big black feeling started in me because I knew things were changing in all parts of my life and I had no idea what I could do to stop it.

Up at St. Therese, snow was softly dropping and groups of stragglers were shuffling in. Fulton was sat up on the fence with a big gang of Greyskull boys milling behind. I knew a few of the names now—Steussie, Hambo, Pliers, Cosh. They had a fancy black cassette-deck planted in the snow pumping out happy hardcore.

I stepped off to the side of the wall and put the choker on, then the smile, then walked over. We had a big relieving kiss in the cold. He tasted like Kestrel Super. "Vicki's off in a mood," I went.

He went straight into his white trackie top and pulled out notes and counted thirty quid. "If you can't find me later take a taxi to Jackie's house. Bring drink. Bring whoever."

"Aw thanks." I slipped the money straight in my bra then I kissed him again. "You're looking fit as fuck by the way," I goes, posing slightly, clacking the shoes.

"That dress looks pure amazing on you, babes."

The Greyskull boys behind him had turned the stereo up and were raving on the ruined grass now, trampling mud-circles in the snow. He goes, "I'm gonna show these cunts."

"Show what cunts?"

"This school, man. These teachers. Pure arseholes and poshos. Get a look at this." He ran over to the boys and came back dragging a pensioner's wheelie bag. He opened the lid—boxes of the fireworks from Bonfire Night, and cans of spray paint.

"I like you with two arms, babe. Don't fuck up our night, eh?"

He took a can of spray paint and flipped it like a cocktail-maker then put it in his pocket. "We'll have a good night. Later on. Telling you, Jackie's got all sorts."

"Teachers are gonna be on the lookout."

"Fuck them."

I felt something rising in me, and at the same time pressing on me. "All right. Aim one at Solsgirth for me?"

"He's getting a Thunderwolf up his trouser leg!" He kissed me again with big warm tongues until there were sweet waves round my middle, then I pushed him off and waved *bye*. As soon as I turned from him the safety-feeling went and tension was squeezing my body again.

Inside the gym hall the tall windows were dripping and all you could smell was fresh sweat and Juicy Fruit. A banner was hanging up high in the gloominess—*Happy Christmas. St. Therese, Abbotscraig—1996*. There were five sets of lights and a disco ball, cheap plastic cups, black plastic bins, tinsel taped up and hanging off of everything.

Through the movement of feet and legs you saw the dance floor already shimmering while little groups jumped and shuffled through it, all rosy-elbowed and damp, doing frisky bits, bopping away without thinking at all. Here and there I picked out eyes and smiles—Lourdes from geography, Kashvi Jodhawat, Roslyn Boles, Davie Thornton. No Vicki anywhere.

I touched my earlobes, checked the hem of my dress, flattened my hair down carefully twice then watched the glitter twinkle and shift around my pale palms. The choker was itching.

Sometimes it was hard to think, or to speak, or even to move in the middle of sound. I took the White Musk out my parka pocket and held my coat open and clouded myself, rehearsing *hellos* and *all rights* and *no, I'm not sure where she is* as I tried to move all invisible round the side of the hall to the cloakroom. Speaking to myself helped. My brain felt forty, sometimes.

I flung off my coat and then right away wee Amanda McNicol appears with a plastic cup of the school punch, handing me it with a wink to tell me she'd been mixing. After a big hug she vanished back through the double doors to the dance floor and I shouted that I'd follow soon.

It was nonalcoholic Tixylix-tasting school stuff but you felt the vodka watering your eyes before the cup even touched your lips. When Vicki had come out with the baby bombshell, for a split second I'd pictured myself sober all night to help her feel normal, but fuck that. I gulped the entire cup and crushed it.

As I got moving I shook off the weird robotic nervous feeling and danced with whoever would dance, with whoever was stood in front of me, and amazing Amanda kept bringing us cups. Then James and Roslyn Boles and a boy with a waistcoat nudging and bumping into the middle, using his fingers to pinch four big sloshy cups of vodka-punch together at a time, and me grabbing one and drinking the lot again.

I watched Morgan Lambie, up by the stage, preening like a parrot around her boyfriend. He had a joke-shop Christmas suit on, he looked like a lion tamer. Vicki told me once that she'd heard Morgan Lambie eating crisps while doing a shit in the PE toilets. When I heard Vicki's laugh in my head I wanted her next to me more than anything.

It was hard to tell time in there but I danced for ten songs, easy, and things got blurry quick. Next thing after that I've bumped onto the wet floor and I can see the high tinselly ceiling and my bum and my thighs are aching and I'm wet, and there are all sized arms reaching down to help me up and then an arm locked round my shoulders leading me out of the hall and into the corridor.

My head was mainly hanging down and watching my lank hair straggling and the floor pass under me slowly, and before I knew it there was a toilet bowl and I was roaring down into it.

"Fulton," I gurgled, rubbing my own neck.

Then someone was behind me, next to me, and a hand was holding back the loose hair. Waves of the sweet cut-grass perfume made me feel more sick but it was okay because I knew it was Vicki.

"You're like that owl we saw on the school trip. The one regurgitating the mouse at Sunnybrook Farm."

"I want Fulton! Chips and egg. Cheeseburgers."

Vicki was her usual brave self, right down in the smell with me, distracting me with stories. Bass was coming up the floor and rattling my guts. I chucked up again.

She kept on, "Me and my sister, on a Friday night, right, we'd set up a kind of stage and backdrop. My sister would get her Crayolas out and do a big sign like *Victoria and Daisy's Show*, with rainbows round it. Daisy would go to the shop and get loads of cans of juice and bags of 10p crisps, Space Raiders, Tangy Toms. Tangy Toms are my favorite."

I spat over and over into the toilet. The knobbly floor tiles were making my knees ache. "Don't talk to me about fucking Tangy Toms. I am boaking my arsehole up here."

"Yeah so we'd put Eurythmics on, and do a dance routine. It was the same dance routine every time! At the end we'd get a pound each. That's quite a lot looking back, don't you think?"

I was blinking repeatedly to make sure my eyes worked.

Vicki goes, "I think you're done. Come on, let's get you up and sorted."

"Why isn't Fulton here? Where's Dennis?"

"Fuck sake." She hauled me up under my armpits and struggled me to the sink. "Fulton doesn't go to school anymore, remember? Fuck Fulton. And who's Dennis?"

She started cupping cold water and splashing it on my face. My makeup was fucked, my face was a smudge in the mirror. "So—have you got—a name for it yet?"

She was smiling. "For what?"

I stroked her cheek with my palm. "The baby!"

"Let's get some air."

Outside the gym-hall door there was a crowd of folk jeering. Solsgirth was stood at the front all flustered in his chinos, tuning in his hearing aid, Mr. Abbasi and Gorilla Mitts by his side. Fulton was stood opposite, boys behind him. Snow was dotting down everywhere. Vicki led me round to the edge of the crowd and Katie from my form class leaned right over. "Fulton had Solsgirth in a headlock, it was amazing."

I focused my eyes and looked at Fulton. He was manic, shaking a beer bottle and spraying it at the teachers. Other Greyskull boys were letting off fireworks. There were screams every time a rocket went off, and with each one I felt my insides tighten. I could still taste boak in my mouth. My heels hurt.

"Don't let Fulton see me." Vicki moved to stand in front, with her back to me. I put an arm round her belly and my chin on her shoulder. "I'm not getting involved. I'm not talking him out of it." I smelled my own tangy breath between my face and her soft, furry neck.

"Shall I call the police?" Gorilla Mitts shouts. "You are leaving us no option, Mr. Gillespie!" I couldn't help laughing. More rockets screamed off toward the roof of the gym. I wondered what a Thunderwolf actually looked like.

"I'm sorry for being a cunt," Vicki went, whispery. "I'm scared."

"I'm sorry too."

"Ram your criminal records! Fuck your school!" Fulton shouted. One or two lads cheered.

A wee fourth-year aliceband in a satin blouse leaned forward and squealed, "Fulton you are an absolute banger, man!"

Solsgirth made a big thing of loudly telling Gorilla Mitts he was going inside to phone the police. I'd done what Gunner said, I'd made the effort and here I was, and this was it. I hugged Vicki closer. "Being scared's okay."

Over the road one of the Greyskull boys had spray-painted *ROCK ON, DOLE C'MON* on the side of a house. He was crouching, spraying a big penis on next to it. Gorilla Mitts shouts, "Fulton, you and your family are barred from school property. Last chance—remove yourself and your associates."

Fulton flung his beer bottle in the air and it exploded on the snowy tarmac with a sad crump. He started ranting, "Tell Solsgirth I'm suing him. I'm pure suing that old sex pest!"

People were moving back inside the hall now, bored. I squeezed Vicki even tighter. She was soft, like she'd been raised on a diet of candy floss and Flumps. "You know when we sat up on the bench on the Yellow Hill, that windy day on lunch?" I goes.

"When we shared the Cresta?"

"Aye. And remember how I said that all I wanted was to have some excitement enter this crappy wee existence of ours? To have times we could look back on ten years from now when we were chunky and bored, sat watching lottery balls and ringing game shows to try and win a fireplace?"

"Aye," she said. A big firework like a sonic boom went off, almost sucking the air out of my throat.

"I think maybe this isn't it." I squeezed her until she made a cartoon strangulation noise. "When I was twelve all I wanted was to be sixteen. Now look."

"Sometimes with boys it feels like you're wasting your time."

"And your heart."

Back in the hall it seemed like the teachers had managed to get Fulton and his mates out of the grounds. Through the window you still saw flashes in the sky, but the bangs and wooshes were way out over the park now.

That big ginger was on the sound system, singing about how he don't believe in many things except you. I wasn't sure what to do now that the alcohol was out of me so I grabbed another cup of punch and stood in the corner sipping carefully. Most folk had come back in, and couples were shuffling in the middle, but nothing seemed the same as before.

I actually thought about leaving. Then from the edge of a small group at the side of the stage there's Kira-Louise.

Her hair was looser. Her arms were bare. She was wearing DMs, sport socks, a charity-shop dress with strawberries on it—like something my Auntie Janine would have cut about in, back in 1989.

She slid through the crowd, stopping here and there at a random boy, saying just a few words, her hair swishing in that way I knew, her eyes wide and metallic-looking in the dim distance. The disco ball was spraying glinty dots over everything. I wanted to hide. There was no air anywhere.

As she moved between the groups her chin was out, her chest was out, her body seemed open and different. It scared me a bit that there was no sign of wanting to hide from all the people who hated her guts. By the side of the big speaker she waited for a minute with the lazy disco-bulbs pulsing over her, green to red, red to yellow, yellow to blue. My mind fast-forwarded to the *hiya*, to the giggles, the evils, the whispering. I felt like boaking again.

I shuffled sideways in my new heavy shoes, back into the shadow, away from the crowd. Then she was on her mission again, dodging in and out of the bodies, leaning in, whispering at boys all secret-like, all alone in the middle of everyone under the loops of scrappy tinsel.

I saw Christopher Jacks shake his head and mouth really clearly to her, *No.*

Davie Nowak, *No.*

Was she asking if they'd seen someone? What was it she had lost?

And then as she birled round and spoke to a dark-haired boy I saw her face, dewy and pale and bold under the blinking light. Her gentle wee mouth made the shapes of certain words. "Mr. Vain" was drowning them out but I could see now for definite that she was asking these boys to dance.

I couldn't deny that my heart was beginning to burst for her. Gary

Cowan told her no with a swatting movement of the left hand. Then Hairy Andrew, no, with a laugh. A tall boy with Lego hair in a Hugo Boss jumper, no, but nicer at least. It was hard to look away.

She stood still again, probably right on the spot where McClair had sat on parents' evening, fiddling her waistcoat buttons, whining on about *Cora knows the answers, but she won't sit still long enough to write them down!* Gunner chuckling and ruffling my hair. Everyone grinning like the best of pals.

Louder music started. Arms were moving. Gorilla Mitts walked over and opened the double doors for air, and snow started coming in, each wee lit-up survivor flake twirling through the hot dark gym like a star that had come down to dance.

Kira-Louise walked toward Mr. Abbasi, who was leaning with one elbow on the stage, nodding along, his forehead half-shiny with hair gel. She leaned into him for a second, smiling sweetly.

I was aware of my heart again and what was happening to it—the pressure feeling. Abbasi chuckled, did his normal cocky head shake, made a long *noooo* shape with his mouth.

I was breathless. I straightened my silver straps, pulled the dress up at my chest. Felt for my earrings and counted them slowly, one by one.

I watched her twirl away, darker and quicker this time, and slink round the edges of the hall. As she moved under one of the big spotlights I saw for a second how her face had blanked and I knew what she was feeling.

Then she was doing a big dash for the open doors.

I thought about how baltic it was. About rolls and corned beef. Babies and families. Rollerblading. Fulton and his boys. About my own weird face in Gunner's wallet, next to my mam. About Carly Hutcheson and golf courses and *FANNY FIDDLERS 4 EVA*. About Abbotscraig.

Then I thought about my mam at her own dance, all young and pretty with the life in her, like how I saw her in dreams, and I couldn't take that feeling. *Life is capable of being a complete cunt without any encouragement from you or me.* Pauline seemed to be right about everything.

I chucked the sticky punch cup I'd been chewing in the bin and ran right at her.

"Kira," then louder, "Kira-Louise."

I grabbed her wrist almost without meaning to. The line from Samantha's printouts that was saying itself was the one that went, *Your behavior might be neatly defined as action without foresight.*

I dragged her by the arm toward the middle of the hall with the eyes around us starting to work out what the fuss was. My throat was pulsing. My heart was nearly not able to cooperate.

Then in a moment almost too good to be true Mariah comes on, doing that mad squealy song about getting hectic inside. We squished together through the elbows and shoulders and out onto the greasy floor and without breathing or thinking to breathe I grabbed both of Kira's wrists and swung her arms up.

We came closer and I noticed her skin again, her white shins, saw how she had done her legs and the way her glittery blue bootlaces had been knotted tightly, twice.

"Cora!" She looked so taken aback, so happy that it made me ashamed.

"We're dancing, Kira!"

We locked our palms, arched arms, leaned in till our noses were near kissing, then pushed each other away, then did it over and over without ever letting our fingers unhook. I glanced up here and there and saw the sniggering and craning and—*when asked why you are doing what you are doing you may not have an answer.*

I closed my eyes and felt her rawness round me like a spell, and as Mariah went hysterical we spun and wriggled and made the shapes of the words with our mouths, and when I looked up I saw Fulton's rockets sparkle and fade through the big fuck-off misted gymnasium windows and I remembered—*in periods of heightened stress you will often act first then process your actions later.*

As we jumped together doing our wonky moves, and being our steaming and young and useless selves, I felt in tune with the world, and in tune with her, and I knew she was the same because she was soggy, purple nearly, smiling now like I'd never seen—smiling like no minute or hour or day had ever passed her by.

22

The back door was open and out in the garden three naked boys in wellies were flinging snowballs at one another. An Alsatian with a star-shaped bauble taped to its tail was chasing them round in the blizzard, yowling.

Jackie's mate Yogi from the *A-Team* sleeping bag was sat between the kitchen door and the cooker in a red Pringle jumper and flat cap guarding the drink table. There was all sorts—Miller, Metz, Mad Dog. Sweetheart Stout everywhere.

I turned back inside. "Can I take some more?"

"Take whatever you want, my wee pal."

Yogi had let me in earlier and he'd asked about my accent and we'd spoken a bit. It was good I knew one person at least to talk to, because no one from the dance was there and I'd hardly seen Fulton at all.

I took another Metz off the top of the cooker and swigged. The beats got crisper and the air got hot as I moved back into Jackie's living room. It smelled of roll-up smoke and cider-burps and the walls were shiny in there.

It was maybe seventy–thirty young folk to old, young folk in the middle dancing, Jackie's mates stood round smoking and watching. I pulled my dress down, smoothed the silvery folds around my tummy, hitched the leggings right up at my thighs, where my golf course bruises had nearly cleared. I wanted Fulton.

My mam had dressed me up in rah-rah skirts for parties and whatever, but feeling that shiny silver fabric it made me realize she'd never seen me in something actually special. Other lassies got to ask their mams about outfits. Nothing seemed to matter more than what your mam thought.

I dropped the empty bottle on the wet floor and jiggled awkwardly round the edge of the room, smelling different Christmassy aftershaves, doing festive-looking robot nods to Jackie's pals. Then I felt a pinch on my arse cheek. I swung right round with my punching hand up and there's Pauline, stood squished between two old boys, grinning in her Santa's Little Helper dress.

She clamped me in a hug and stuck a five-second kiss right on my lips, then rocked us side to side. I could feel her heart in her wrist against my neck and I couldn't help picturing her blood bubbling round. I wanted to take her to a silent room and sit on a sunken sofa under a blanket and tell her all about Fulton and Kira and Jackie and life. Ask her about Vicki. Look in her soft eyes and ask her everything. I shouted, "Nice seeing you too!"

She turned and dragged me by the arm through the damp dancing figures and out into Jackie's stale hallway. It was just me and her. She hugged me again. "We smell the same," she shouted.

I laughed. "We do."

"Amazing to see you, chick. My mates have fucked off." She downed the rest of her hooch then chucked the empty bottle against the front door, smashing it all over the carpet.

"You better watch, Pauline!"

"Fuck the Gillespies!" She turned and shouted into the living room, "They can come and catch me in Glasgow!"

"Oh aye?"

"All signed."

"Wow," I goes, and as the beat rose behind her and the living room crowd went mental, our eyes met for a weird second. "Have you seen Fulton?" I says.

"Honestly, Cora. Don't let anyone dilute your juice!"

"Have you seen him though?"

"Nope!" She shrugged her body back against the wall and I looked at the floor. "It's all fucking geriatrics in here!"

"He's kind of disappeared."

"An absolute toolbelt, that boy." She slumped forward onto me in a hug and I felt her breath in my ear. "Will we dance, chick?" She moved into the doorway with the party behind her.

"I'm waiting here," I shouted. "Too much noise!"

"Come on, I've hardly seen you." She started hauling me by the arm in a tug-of-war.

"No!" I went and when I wriggled free she stumbled. She straightened herself and turned into the crowd and I watched her pick up the beat of the music as if I'd never been there at all.

Then from nowhere the music stopped. There was soft booing and a few wee growly shouts in the quiet as someone mucked about with the tapes. In the little chunk of calm I heard Jackie's voice, on the landing upstair.

My drunken nosiness clicked on. He had piled three living room chairs across the bottom of the stair to keep the party from spreading but I felt like I was allowed to climb over, since I was a Gillespie now.

Jackie was up on the landing barking at Fulton, "Don't make me pull the powercaird oot, son!" He was dressed like someone from Texas off the telly, but with Hi-Tec Silver Shadows instead of crocodile boots.

A ladder was laid into the hatch of the attic and folk were up there. Fulton was doing the solemn act. "They'll no go up there again. I don't even know the boys."

I felt a movement in me. "Fulton's really sorry," I went. Then Fulton noticed me and did the drunken shut-it face and I really wanted to kiss him hello but I nodded to agree that I should shut it, aye.

Jackie calmly says to Fulton, "Tell Eldo to put my merchandise down and get oot ma fucking attic, or the powercaird comes oot and the party's over." Fulton looked over at me, like I might go up and sort it. I shook my head absolutely fucking not. Jackie glared at Fulton. "Up you go, son, or yer forever known round here as the cunt that fucked Christmas."

Then a wee hard-faced guy pops out of the hatch. "Listen, you old cunt!" You knew right away that this Eldo was just one of those classic deranged Abbotscraig zoomers that invited himself to parties and attics and god knows what else. Him and his pals seemed to be up there raiding Jackie's stuff.

Jackie goes, *"Old cunt?"*

Eldo started clanging down in his jeans. Fulton jumped out of the way. "I'll put you in the ground!" Eldo says.

Then Jackie grabbed Eldo by his silky hair and dragged him off the ladder. "Listen, you middle-shed cunt, I may be sixty-two years old but for fifty of they years I've been using the likes of you as arsepaper. I'll no be switching to Andrex anytime soon." Jackie flung Eldo against the wall like a dishcloth. "Now stand up straight till I split that chin of yours fair and square."

Fulton quickly moved to Jackie's side. "Jackie. Honestly. I'll deal with him." Then he turned to Eldo. "You lot. Out."

Jackie did a big mad laugh then cuffed Eldo full force on the side of the head. "Yer lucky I've had my mince pie, pal."

My gums were prickly with the anxiousness but I kept still and did my best authority nod as Eldo stumbled past, fixing his center parting. Two other rat-looking boys came down out of the attic and ran down the stairs after him.

Fulton was nervous, twitching his shoulders. "Done," he went, into his chin, then rumbled down the stair.

Then it was just me and Jackie. He went up the ladder to slide the hatch closed. I says to him all cutely, "What's up there then?"

He stopped halfway down. The arse of his brown trousers was shiny—a kind of curtain material. "I'll tell you one thing, hen, for free. The ones that mind their business live the longest."

I burped into my mouth. "Thanks for all the drink," I says, but he put the ladder away, then switched the landing light off and went down the stairs like I didn't exist.

Right away my brain couldn't think of anything else—I wanted to look in that *A-Team* room again. I waited till the stairs stopped squeaking then I tiptoed across and opened the door.

It was empty—no old boys, no sleeping bags. I clicked the door behind me, sat down on the double bed, then swung my legs up on the silky bare mattress.

It was freezing but it still felt amazing to get off my feet. The heat from the downstairs dancing had misted the windows, and the foggy glass was glowing orange from a street lamp outside. I lay back and watched the weird light moving across my liquidy-silver dress.

Then as a downstairs song faded I heard scrabbling and bumping noises from the cupboard in the wall opposite where I was lying.

I thought about that mad Alsatian with the taped-up tail. I took one of my silver shoes off and held it heel out.

"Sit?" I shouted. What words did dogs know? "Relax!"

Then the cupboard door swung open.

It was Yogi. He crawled out the cupboard on his hands and knees then stood up and brushed himself and put his specs on. His cap was off and his hair was like spiderwebs on top. I squeezed my shoe back on.

"Oh, hey, wee pal!" he goes.

I felt like someone had laid a cold cloth on my face. I scrambled up straight and swung my legs off the bed. "What you doing in there?"

"Just getting a sleep."

"You can't sleep in there!" I giggled, twice. "Why don't you go home? It's late."

He laughed, loud. "There's sleeping bags!" He walked over and sat next to me on the bed and took a yellow pencil case out his coat pocket. It had Mr. Blobby on the side. I was doing gulps, trying to make slavers. Mentally checking my choker, my leggings, my boobs, my bum. Praying for my parka.

He zipped the pencil case open and shook it toward me. I held my hair back, leaned in, looked—ecstasy tablets. Pink and freckly with logos and hearts and smiles.

"Wire in, wee pal," he goes, putting the case on the bed next to me, then rolling a fag on his knee.

"I'm all right, Yogi."

"Mitsubishis in there!" He lit his fag and blew smoke that lit up as it spread toward the window.

"Honestly, no."

"It's mad this, in't it?"

"What?" I folded my arms.

"This room, man. This light." He motioned at the window with his fag then took another long draw.

"It's a great house," I went, cheery as I could. "Jackie's a star."

"Hey, how's about some drink? I've got grappa?"

"What's grappa?"

"Lassies love the grappa!" He put the fag in his mouth and started cleaning his specs on his jumper. They were thick binocular specs and when he took them off his eyes were wee and black, like two olives picked off a pizza. He walked to the cupboard and came back with a liter glass bottle that didn't have a label. "Take a swally."

I wiped the mouth of it then sipped, to keep him happy. It tasted like my house keys. I kept smiling as my throat closed. "Are you having me on, Yogi? Lassies don't love this."

"Have a bigger swally."

I leaned over and put the bottle on the bedside table. Then before I even knew it I was turned, flattened-down. He was gripping me, strangling my body, squeezing like a snake in a film. My hair in my eyes, him panting, the smell off his clothes—stale towels, roll-up smoke. Then the fat blunt tips of his fingers crushing into my left boob. Then his other hand sawing between my legs.

I screamed, then screamed again.

He grunted the words out like he was tasting them. "You're a sexy wee thing, aren't you?"

There was a rippling sick feeling in my flesh that made me want to die, or to kill. I wriggled and wrestled with my elbows until I got just an inch away and could turn, and I pushed him back with my forearm and sat up. Then I looked at the floorboards behind his fat head and I aimed, like I'd been taught. Then I smashed through his face with my fist.

I leaped without looking or listening, and I was out of the room, across the landing, clacking down the stairs before I could breathe. I scrambled over the chairs and stood looking into the sweltering living room. "Champagne Supernova" was going.

I moved round the side of the room again, head up, heart going, scanning for Fulton through the waving arms, rubbing at my hand which felt three times the size and was bleeding a bit from where I crunched Yogi's specs into his face.

Through into the kitchen and there he was at the back door, with Jackie and another of Jackie's yellow-eyeballed mates I didn't know, an old guy on crutches.

I reminded myself to breathe. "Fulton."

"Babe, where you been?" He had a mini Super Soaker in his hand. Him and Crutch Man and Jackie were squirting something into the mouths of two tall girls who were out in the garden. He held it up. "Want a skoosh?"

Then Jackie shouts, "Ah! Here she is, wee Cora Coathanger."

I shoved Fulton to one side. "Yogi's tried to give me pills. He grabbed me!"

"Probly eccies," Jackie went, leaning in.

"Generous fella, old Yogi," Crutch Man goes, cackling.

"He touched me too!" My guts were rolling, like my feet weren't on the floor. "I punched the cunt. He was feeling me up, Fulton! It's fucking disgusting."

Fulton screwed his face up. "Yogi's sound. He taught me how to cast a fishing rod, Cora. Don't be giving me a red face for fuck's sake— it's Christmas."

Then Jackie put his shoulders back and says into the garden, "Ungrateful hoor! That's all she is, son."

Fulton waved the Super Soaker at me. "You're doing my brain in. Take a skoosh of grappa, chill out for fuck sake."

It felt like my bones were gone. "I don't want your rancid fucking grappa!"

Just then Fulton's pal Steussie appeared, whispering something into Jackie's ear. His eyes went wide. Steussie ran back toward the front door and Jackie followed. "Fulton!" he goes. Then Fulton ran with him.

I went to the kitchen cupboard and grabbed my parka.

Out the front snow was falling still, gentle and different-sized and nearly silver, like scratch card scratchings. Over by the phone box, Jackie and Fulton and a couple of his mates had Eldo on the ground— his parting was ruined and they were leathering him.

I walked down the street a bit then ducked into one of the alleys between the houses and watched from behind a fence as Fulton and his mate Pliers dragged Eldo up and threw him into the phone box over the road. Pliers and Jackie leaned up against the door to keep it shut, then Fulton reappeared with his tray of his fireworks.

Fulton's mate lit a match then dropped it into the tray of rockets, then Fulton crouched and slid the fizzing tray through the gap under the door of the phone box. Eldo was on his feet in there now with his stewed-fruit face, bumping at the door, kicking all frantic at the big tray of fireworks to try and get them back out.

Then the first rocket went off—a big boom of smoke and light and frazzling noises all contained in there with him. Over the popping you could hear Eldo's gurgles as he shoulder-bumped round the blinding white box like a Reebok in the washing machine. Jackie started staggering backward in hysterics with his hair dangling down like a corpse that's climbed out the ground in a film.

I was already sick from the feeling—not a throbbing, not a bruise. Itchy and faint, like ants. Ants on the skin, where that cunt's fingers had been. Then anger at everything right through me, like the colors twisted in a marble.

Waves of shadow moved over Fulton and his mates as big air-sucking thuds kept going, then ravey flashes, war sounds, smoke drifting out under the door. A dark streak started down the frosted pavement at the front of the box where Eldo's pish was rivering out. There was a smell in the air like matches and popcorn. Pliers held the door shut still. I felt like I was in a trance.

Then a rocket wriggled out under the gap in the door like a mad snake, and shot past me down the road, bending up and loop-the-looping over the houses and then divebombing into the distance, exploding somewhere, lighting the playing fields tinfoily white, outlining the Hellmeadow rooftops for a quick fading second.

"For fuck sake help him!" I screamed, because I couldn't not.

Jackie stood up straight. "Hambo, Hambo," he shouts toward Fulton's mate, pointing at me. "Grab that bitch."

I turned and sprinted up the alley into the dark. I ran by the darkened newsagents, the cemetery, slid across the Backy Park, took the shortcut between the hedges at Easyprice in total fear. Even the snow looked like it was shiting it now, going sideways in places, some of it swooping and floating up like all it wanted was to go back toward the moon.

My toes felt like stones but my whole body was burning. As I came over the brow of the hill at the top of Weavers Row the snow got harder, and as I looked down at our house I had to screw my eyes up twice, three times—a figure in a dark coat. Hood up. Waiting by my front gate.

I moved across the pavement to the wall, trying to crouch carefully but I ended up falling to my knees. The cold burning snow on my shins felt so right that I clamped my eyes closed, and when I opened them, I could focus, just for a wee minute, right down the street—long coat, hood up. Hambo? Yogi? Big boots. Rollerblades—it was Kira-Louise.

I scrambled to my feet, swaying, my brain going a few seconds behind from the pull of the drink. Then something horrible woke up in me and I started to run.

"What the fuck are you doing?"

She smiled, pulled her hood back. "I came to look for you."

"You better not have been to my door." I was pointing in her face. "It's probably fucking five a.m.!"

She looked away. Snow was speckling her hair, melting. "No, I was only waiting. I couldn't sleep. The dancing was amazing, I couldn't—"

"I've had the worst fucking night of my life and I need you to disappear."

"Cora—"

"How do you even know where I live?"

She straightened quickly, no Bambiness in the legs, no wobbling at all on her wheels. "I knew the street. And that you had a ramp. For your mam. I thought we could maybe—"

"Maybe what? At fucking five a.m.? In the snow?"

"It's an amazing morning, look at the moon."

The blood was licking right round me. The booze. My head hurt. My face stung. "Fuck the moon. Really, off you fuck, Coathanger."

She turned without speaking or moving to speak and pushed off and zipped away. I watched her plough slowly on her blades to the end of my slushy street then turn left and disappear with a swoop of speed behind the row of darkened houses.

I ripped the choker off and chucked it in the road, then I sat down in the cold snow at my own front gate. I closed my eyes and breathed in through my nose—grappa, roll-ups, Sweetheart Stout. I looked at my still and silent house, and thought of the man who was in there now. The only thing I really had. And then I looked up at his open curtains and remembered it was a nightshift night again.

23

"You get lost on your motorbike?"

"So original." We were stood outside the Safeway. I'd walked over and waited—I knew if I hung about on the corner steps I'd catch him coming home.

"Bit early to see you up and about."

"I've not slept."

There was an awkward minute where I saw him realize I was serious, then he says, "You love that old fleece of mine, don't you?"

I pushed my hands deep in the front pockets and scuffed the Reeboks on the spot. I couldn't stand still because of the freezingness and the feelings and how tight my thighs still were from the dancing. I knew in my head the first thing I wanted to say and I had enough drink in me still to say it. "You know you can, like, hug me, aye? Properly. If you ever wanted to? Like a squeeze." The words sounded crisp in the snow.

He looked at me and I looked up, woozy. The sky was a transparent bluey-black with the teensiest smudges of daylight coming through. Nighttime felt like years ago but I was still so fucking nervy inside. He grabbed me into a big tight hug. "You're turning me soft, Cora."

I stood there for a wee minute, face buried in his shoulder, head slightly sailing, heart in pain. As something sank down through me I wanted more than anything to be able to tell him how much I needed him but all I could manage was, "I won't ring ChildLine."

"You smell like a petrol station."

I pushed him off fake-huffily. "Hey, check this." I held my hand out. The back was podgy purple marshmallow and there were little hot pink scrapes all round. "I aimed for the floor," I goes, smiling, reliving it.

"Was it a dance or a boxing match?"

"Maybe I'm not a wee drink-of-water after all?"

"So did you go to Fulton's granda's?"

"No! No." I smiled. Sometimes he still amazed you with how he sniffed things out. "Too much hassle."

"Listen, what is it you're wanting?"

"Food? I'll pay. I need hot food. And a seat. With you." I walked up the crackly steps to the entrance and he followed, going careful on the slippy bits. Lights were coming on in the café. "Can we get them to let us in?"

Our table was halfway back, underneath a wall-mounted telly with tinsel round it. The table and chairs were all connected like a picnic bench and the red molded plastic was freezing to touch. Steam was rising from over behind the counter. We were the only ones in.

The woman came over with a pad. Before he could order the cheapest option like I knew he would, I said, "Two full fried breakfasts, extra square sausage. Two rounds of white toast, and a pot of tea please."

"Cora-doll," he whispered.

"I'm treating you. It's nearly Christmas!"

He looked at the woman like, *What's this lassie like?* The woman looked back at him and I could tell she was wondering about his eye. She wrote in her pad and walked off.

"Do you ever want to say to folk, *You can ask if you want to*?"

"I should hang a sign round my neck."

"Or get some shades?" I pulled the thirty quid Fulton had given me out of the fleece pocket. "Take this and pay for the breakfast. Keep the rest."

He smiled. "If you're trying to pay me back then say so, like."

"For what?"

He ran his palm back over his stubbly head. "Lass, remember that wee chat? The week we moved in the house? *You're not my da and I don't want your fucking pocket money?*"

"Yeah, so?"

"Do you think I leave my wallet lying about for the good of my health?" I felt my tummy lurch a few steps ahead of me. "If you weren't going to take cash off of me then I dread to think where you'd end up getting it, eh. It's my job to make you feel like you're being independent. I saw it on a telly thing, about parenting."

"Fuck off."

He burst out laughing. "Okay, that last bit's a lie. But I'm not taking your money, doll."

"It's Fulton's money. Take it." The toast came and I started spreading from the squishy foil butter. It was the same make we had at home.

"Well, that'll do the electric." He took a big crunch of toast.

The waitress came back with our two plates of breakfast and I ate a bit of bacon. I wanted to tell him about the night, one detail after the other, from start to finish.

"Look at this." He was poking about at his fried egg with his knife, scraping the uncooked slime off the top. "What do you call that?"

"Egg white. It doesn't kill you."

"I'm still not eating it." He was blobbing it all at the side of the plate. "It's called snot, love. Never make me a snotty egg. Your mam must have told you what makes a good fried egg?"

"My mam taught me how to make noodles but that was about it."

"Oh, if I was making your mam egg and chips the eggs would have to be perfect. *Gunner, you better not be giving me snotty eggs!* She was right though."

"She was fussy."

He slurped his tea. "Aye, and she loved the kitchen. She never shut up about that electric tin opener."

"She didn't really need one," I went.

"I never found one anyway."

I crunched my toast. "You were usually good at finding."

He told me about his shift as we ate and I was glad for once just to listen to him going into detail about little pointless things from a place I couldn't picture. Outside the sky was navy and cars were going now, and buses too, but it was still only us in the café.

I hadn't slept but I wasn't tired. Like I always did when I was stressed I'd sat in my room picturing how I'd explain to Vicki about the party, listening to her give her imaginary opinions—*Classic Abbotscraig, that's just what happens round here, go with it, Cora.* I couldn't forget the stale towel smell, the feel of Yogi's fingers, the sound of muffled rockets, Eldo melting. And then every single thing I thought and felt was clouded by Vicki's news and what it meant for me and her and everyone.

"So the main excitement of the dance, other than Gorilla Mitts's trousers"—I stopped and looked down at the six beans on my fork, then I ate them. Gunner was really the only person I had to tell it to— "turns out Vicki's pregnant."

"Eh? She's not got her head straight. Never heard of a lassie drinking so much." He squished his mouth left then right. "How are you feeling about it?"

"Shite." The telly was showing an advert with planes taking off and landing.

He nodded at my hand. "It wasn't you and her fighting?"

I straightened it out and looked at it. "Oh, no."

"Was Fulton not there then?"

"Aye, but it's different to how it is with my pals." Gunner held his mug out in front of his face, watching the steam curling off it, waiting on me saying more. I did think sometimes in wee moments about how he coped, but all we ever spoke about was me. "I dunno. Not everything is about him."

"I thought he was getting a flat and all sorts? Is that not what you wanted?"

I looked at the ceiling. "I want my own money in future. My own place. I've seen how his granda lives. His granda is what people become round here. I want nice stuff, cute things around the place, for the windowsill. Not tins and sleeping bags and bare floorboards. Eating Double Deckers for breakfast."

"Ornaments?!"

"I never said ornaments!" I opened the teapot and ploutered the teabags about with the spoon. "All this shite at school, it's not easy but it doesn't mean I don't want a future. A job. College. I dunno. Fulton's got plans. And he's earning already. It's stability, isn't it?"

"Cora, you're sixteen, love. You don't need to be worrying about stability. Have your fun, as long as you're being safe."

"Gunner."

"I know what boys are like."

"All the boys at St. Therese are out eating bowls of drugs and drinking glo-sticks. Wee moon units. Anyway"—I poured steamy tea out between us—"do you think I ruined things for my mam?"

He sat forward. "Eh? What do you mean? No!"

"Like, with men. You know, I realize now that that's what she wanted too, I suppose—stability. Me and her, it wasn't much of a deal. I mean"—we looked at each other—"I mean, you're here, obviously. I dunno, maybe I scared the other ones away?"

"Well I'm not going anywhere."

"Why, though?"

He looked down like he'd lost something in his mug. "Well, I care. About you, about your mam. It's a lot to explain, this early."

"You don't have to."

"You know, you look a bit like her now, with all that makeup on," he goes.

"It's all fucked up from puking and crying!"

"You know what I mean, having all that darkness round the eyes makes you look more grown up."

"She will be spinning right now at you saying that!"

"Shall we give her a visit soon?" He goes, cheery and quick, like he'd been waiting for the moment.

I watched the woman behind the counter pick out change into a young lassie's hand, then after waiting as long as I could I went, "Soon. It's not that I don't want to. I'm settling in, still, here. I need my own life. She'd think the same."

He rolled his lips and stared off out into the street. "Okay."

"The easier it gets to think about her the more the other bad stuff comes back. Like, it's her house. That's the house we dreamed of and it's not easy to forget when I'm sleeping in there. Her going just filled up every thought for yonks but now there's room for other stuff, and sometimes I'm going over it. I mean, her, you. Her, you and Jo. You and me."

He rolled his sleeves up and I saw the fuzzy Tweety Pie on his forearm. "Try and keep speaking about it, like. Dan always said that was the main thing."

There were two presenters on the telly now. We sat in silence for a bit and I waited for some emotion to build in me but nothing did. I was so drained I could barely make myself angry. Then Gunner goes, "I was going to make you a meal last night. You left."

"You were out speaking to Donna."

"She's having trouble with her wee rabbit. It's eating everything in sight, bin bags, teabags, Sellotape."

"Has it got a name yet?"

"Jumpy."

I shut my eyes and let the giggles take over until I couldn't think to speak. And I thought they would never stop. And then I thought I might cry, so I opened my eyes and downed the last of my tea. "Amazing."

He gulped the last of his tea. "It's a cute wee thing."

He went to the counter and paid while I went to the loo. Outside the light was totally up and the world had started. Gunner wanted to use the Fulton money to get the bus back home but I told him he had to walk with me to help my hangover.

We headed out past the shops and through the snow then onto the dual carriageway. I looked across from the other side of the road and saw the spot where Vicki had told me, hours ago, before everything else. We headed up the long concrete path past the church and onto the estate, seeing all the different tinsel in the windows, thinking how so much had changed.

Over the Backy Park the sky was gray like a bedsheet. You could just hear the birds going and a tiny mutter of traffic. The hedges and the grass and even the weeds were glittering, and all last night's cans and bottles had frost on them already. We kept our arms linked and took careful steps on the tarmac.

"So what do you want for your Christmas? If I'm working long empty nights in long empty corridors then the money's getting spent on something special."

I looked at him. "*Spent?*"

"Cora, whatever I get you I'll pay for. Come on."

"You can hardly blame me for saying!"

"As if I'm going to risk getting caught by a lassie like you twice. I haven't forgotten what you did to my lamb!"

"I don't want trouble brought to our door."

"Or parked up in our front hall?" He was grinning.

"I'm not asking for stuff because it's weird and a beamer and it's memories of being wee."

"Like what?"

"Asking for perfume and a Mr. Frosty and getting sweeties and a Spirograph. Like, I loved my mam, but it's hard for a child to think fairly about stuff like that. When you get told time after time that you're growing out of your shoes too fast you don't forget it. I don't like presents."

"But Santa knows how good you've been this year."

"There's two weeks still to go."

At home I put the immersion heater on. I did the dishes looking out over our perfect white garden, then got my mam's records out. I put her favorite T. Rex song on then got a load of Gunner's work shirts out of the basket and started the ironing in the middle of the living room.

After doing all six shirts I was tying up the bin in the kitchen when the phone went. I jogged into the hall to get it before Gunner woke up. It was Fulton.

"What do you want?" I said in a low voice, resting the bag on the seat of the scrambler to keep it off the floor.

"Checking you made it home, babe."

"I did. I needed my bed." I squeezed past the scrambler and opened the front door and chucked the bin bag over the ramp and into the wheelie bin at the side of the steps. I stood for a second feeling my skin go tight from the cold, looking at me and Gunner's footsteps, at the rollerblade patterns still carved in the snow at the end of our front path.

"So who did you go home with?"

"I walked home myself."

There was a pause and I could hear random chanting in the background, girls giggling, fun. "So how you doing?"

"Fulton, I'm really not in the mood right now."

"Is this about Eldo?"

"It's about everything."

"What happened to him, babe, you can't let someone like that walk over you. That's how it is, here. It's like Jackie's wee song, *See a nail sticking up, with a hammer in your hand—*"

"I'm going."

"Cora!"

"What?"

"Speak soon, eh?" A glass got dropped somewhere in the room behind him.

"Have a Happy Christmas, Fulton."

24

Fulton came round to my door two nights later, on the Monday after school. He handed me a foily helium heart balloon and a Christmas present wrapped in a blue Easyprice carrier bag. He was wasted.

"Don't open that now, but it's limited edition." He was swaying. I took the bag, eyeing him. He squinted at me. "I love you," he goes, leaning in to my ear. He tried his palm on the flab of my left hip so I shifted back, just a wee inch. I kept my arms folded because Gunner was showering for work and I had cutlery soaking and I wanted this over quick.

He took a step back onto the ramp then his face went suddenly rubbery and he started to greet. "Please don't go out with any of my pals," he says. I did long spaced-out blinks to stop the giggles. I'd never seen a boy blub like that.

"Fulton," I goes, calm as I could, "I need some time by myself, that's all. You're steaming. Go home."

He wiped his nose with his wrist. "Listen, Cora, you're my bird, and if I knew what that fucking Yogi done to you I would have smashed him, if that dirty fucking—"

"I did tell you. And you did nothing. Now away and give me some peace, eh?" I tugged the balloon in and closed the front door.

I squeezed past the scrambler then moved through the silence to the kitchen, dragging Fulton's heart after me by the ribbon. When I let it go it bumbled itself all flat on the ceiling. *YOU ARE MY WORLD*, it said, staring down at me. It was the same exact writing as *Performance Sport*.

I cleaned the cutlery, then sat down at the kitchen table and tipped the carrier bag out. He'd got me a brand-new Adidas tracksuit, the top and the bottoms, matching. Green with the three white stripes. The tag did say *limited edition*—it was the kind of thing I would have died for twice, growing up.

I took it and ran up the stair to try it on, and I was twirling in the mirror when Gunner knocks on the door. "You decent?"

"Aye." He walked in in his uniform, rubbing round his ear with a towel. You smelled the Imperial Leather off him. I did a pose in amongst all the mess. "Ta-da! It's my Christmas present."

"I saw the balloon. You and him back on track then, eh?"

"He told me he loved me."

He laughed. "What is it now, six weeks?"

"Five."

Gunner looked down at his boots. "Do you want to sit with me on the bed a wee minute? The school just rang." I could hear dogs arguing over in the park. Then he says, "The Christmas service at the school's been canceled. Emergency assembly tomorrow morning instead, in the gym hall. Parents are to come too. I think that means me." He sat down looking serious and patted next to him on the duvet.

I sat on my bed. I knew from his voice that things were going wrong again. "Assembly about what?"

"Were you pals with Callum Cantwell's daughter?"

I had the heebies right away. "Who?" I goes, but I knew fine well who.

"Kira-Louise Cantwell? She wouldn't have been in today."

"She never is."

"Something's happened." He put his hand on my leg. "She's died, like. Unfortunately."

I wanted to look at him and crumple my eyebrows and say, *Why are you even telling me this?* But I felt ice going up the backs of my fingers before I could get my lips to move. "Kira-Louise?"

"It's upsetting." There was a big, wide slab of pressure in my chest that I knew from before. "The school will probably speak to you about it." Then silence, a car, the dogs in the park again. "They're getting counselors in for tomorrow."

"Everyone hated her."

"Eh?"

"I don't know why they're bothering with counselors because everyone hated her fucking guts."

"I'm sure that's not true."

"I didn't know her," I goes, picking my pinky, drawing triangles on the carpet with my cold big toe. Fear was tightening a belt round my skull and there was already a feeling that I'd become someone different to who I was two minutes before.

Then in a rush I pictured him bringing up evidence—how I'd sat next to her, danced with her, stumbled through a field of cows in the pitch black with her. How I giggled at the names. How I called her things too. Maybe he would ask about what was wrong with her. Maybe there would be leaflets. Maybe he'd bring everything back to my mam.

"Okay. Well. I'm already late, so I'm heading. Make sure the dishes are done and I want both beds stripped and washed." Then he walked out without shutting the door.

I was roasting in the tracksuit as I came down the stair. Breathless, like something was filling the bits where air should go. I stood in the doorway to the kitchen watching the Christmas tree blink, the slats of street light striping the rug, wondering how much more misery and guilt a lassie could fit inside her body.

I turned into the kitchen and got bread out. I took the multipack crisps from the cupboard and opened some prawn cocktail. I started arranging the crisps on a bit of the bread, carefully overlapping around the edges, then in the middle, neatly, like my mam would. Then I put another slice on top and crunched it all flat with my palm. Then I felt the boak rising and threw the whole lot in the bin.

I had the total crybaby feeling. I went in the hall and sat and dialed Vicki because there wasn't a single other thing I could think to do.

"Hello?"

"Hello," I says, nice and low.

Her voice went normal. "Hiya, Cora."

"Do you know what happened?"

"Hanging," she went, in a normal voice, like she'd been waiting on me ringing. "I knew the teachers were acting funny today! I was trying to signal to you in physics but you never looked round. Amanda McNicol rang me twenty minutes ago. She told me the lot."

"Like what?"

"She washed her hair, cleaned the house, put her favorite dress on, then locked all the doors." She chuckled after the favorite dress part. "Done it with her dressing gown belt." My body started closing in on itself. "She went out at night rollerblading because she didn't like being in the house with her da. Callum, the old smackhead. Fiddling her probably."

"Favorite dress?" I says.

"Cora, don't get weepy! She's rollerblading through heaven right now! White silk angel outfit. Corned beef roll in the pocket."

"What do you think was wrong with her? I mean, why would you do something like that?"

"Do you reckon those angel outfits have pockets?"

"Vicki, someone's died. It's a wee bit serious."

"Why? She wasn't my pal."

"What's that meant to mean?"

"You were her wee dancing partner."

"I was steaming."

"Davie says you kissed her."

"Fuck off. Wisen up with your fucking nonsense."

"Well, did you?"

I clacked the handset down and then I was alone. I stood up and turned to go upstair, then as I saw the scrambler it was like everything else around me vanished down to a dot.

There was a magnet in me, a wee rebel again, and I couldn't stop the urge even if I wanted to, and I thought to myself, *Get on it and leave*, and the words were sweet and crystal clear amongst the grimness. Fulton had rode it over the course. Fulton had showed me.

I gripped the cold handlegrips and felt the hair prickling on the backs of my fingers. It felt like I could drive out of my life on it. The speed and the windy dark would rinse every burning thing out of my heart and my head. Like the car to McDonald's with Dennis. Like the rollerblades. Like the chairoplane when I was wee. I had no idea where I'd go, all I knew was that I was tired of here.

I climbed back off and fumbled my freezing Reeboks on then opened the front door to the cold, kicked the bike stand and rolled it all heavy and sleepy off the bin bags and out onto the slushy ramp, then down the path and into the road. Words and thoughts started, uncatchable and nightmarey, like spiders.

The whole snowy closed-curtained street looked still. I climbed on and started the thing and a dial lit up and it roared slightly and I was nearly boaking at the loudness. All I wanted was a hand to land on my shoulder and someone to say the word *Cora*. Snow was feathering down and making dark dots on the green of my tracksuit.

I tried and tried to make myself stop thinking, then I just says *fuck it* down into my chest. I squeezed the handlegrip with all my strength and I twisted it back like the worst Chinese burn.

For four beautiful seconds I was flying. My head jerked back and the sky was a blur and all of the neglected and wasted past slipped by in the corners of my eyes, and the future vanished too—gym halls and counselors and Christmas and Kira, gone. Vicki, Dan, Gunner, Pauline, Jackie, Fulton—gone. I was alone and happy and leaving this existence.

Then the sky got pulled to one side, the houses tilted, there was a sound like hair mousse getting skooshed out the tin. Everything went into a mad skidding spin and I saw the parked cars and hedges and the street lamps spiral like I was being sucked down a plughole, and then in one huge roar of the engine and crunch of custom Kawasaki I saw a sideways freeze-frame of slushy snow and graveliness and numbers painted on wheelie bins. The dark skyline was upside down. I blinked once. The bike was screaming. A pain like being pummeled was setting my arm and my thigh on fire.

I tried to greet but everything in me was focused on the pain. I kicked and crawled myself onto the pavement then lay there soaked from snow, numb and wailing and starting to greet under the rumble of the scrambler that was spasming round on the spot like a crap breakdancer in the middle of the road, shooting its headlight round the houses, basically telling every cunt to come out quick and see this wee arsehole lassie in the snow.

"Fucking hell! Cora!" I twisted my head round. It was Donna, charging up the road toward me. I could actually see her front gate. I'd managed to ride the bike about ten meters. "Are you all right, pet?!"

I breathed in then shouted over the sound of engine, "I'm on the ground again, Donna."

She crouched and put her palm on my cheek, shouting, "Why the hell are you riding a motorbike, pet?"

"It's called a scrambler."

"Can you move okay? Let's get you inside."

Donna's living room was calm and she sat me down on her squishy leather sofa. I was breathing quick to try and deal with the pain. My fingers felt numb and hot and freezing and sore.

She put all three bars of the fire on and then the telly and then peeled the soggy torn tracksuit off me. My belly had a big stinging scrape like I'd been grated with that weird side of the grater nobody uses. Some parts of my legs and arm were bright pink just from the stinging snow, other parts looked ripped and bloody where the tracksuit had come away. Veins were scribbling everywhere, all ballpoint blue.

I kicked away the Reeboks. Donna had an ice cream tub with pads and bottles and plasters in it and she wiped the blood from my arm and thigh and belly and put ointment on me and told me I was brave and it was mainly grazes.

She disappeared, then came back and dressed me in her pajamas and a dressing gown. Then she tied a pink towel round my wet hair and said we were going to the hospital. I lay back in a fake faint and pretended not to hear her. Then she said it again and I started begging no.

"Cora, you are lucky not to have been more seriously injured!" I kept my head down and picked at my thumb to avoid the words. "You've come flying off a moving motorbike. You need to be checked."

"I wasn't going fast."

"You're probably in shock. When the adrenaline subsides you'll be in even more pain."

I started blubbing, like a baby. "Fulton bought me a tracksuit," was all that came out, through snottery noise.

Donna went behind one of the armchairs and got a fuzzy blanket then laid it over me. "It's in the bin, sorry." She handed me a box of tissues off the sideboard. You knew you were in a nice house when they didn't just have loo roll in the living room.

"Everything's ruined. I can't go to a hospital." I wiped my face. "If anything hurts tomorrow I promise to go. Honestly. Not tonight."

"What would Gunner say if he found out I hadn't had you properly checked out?"

"It's my decision."

She looked away at the telly and then back at me. "Well, sit tight here. I'm going to go and see Andy at fifty-two and see if he can give me a hand to move the bike out of the road. Will you be okay? Don't move and I'll be back in five."

When the front door clicked shut I flopped sideways onto the cold leather. Her living room was all newish and clean, like something from the Littlewoods catalogue where you have those gawkit families sat round pointing and grinning at a shelving unit.

Two leather armchairs, a big telly and a VCR in a fancy wooden cabinet with glass doors. A bigger tree than ours, with colored icicle lights. There was a white furry rug with a coffee table on it in the middle and she had magazines laid out across it. The mantelpiece was covered in photos and knick-knacks.

I could hear a soft scraping noise from the kitchen. I creaked myself up onto my feet just from nosiness, then wrapped the blanket tight round me like a tramp and limped through for a look.

Donna's kitchen was like a mirror of ours but it was warm and it smelled like Fairy liquid and scones. Her lino was flat and perfect and you couldn't hear her fridge and you knew the cupboards were probably full of spotty teapots. I wanted to rake through those cupboards right away but I says to myself, *Cora, you're seriously injured, no.*

On the far wall she had a corkboard covered in lists and photos— her with other nurses in a pub, her on the beach, teenage her in a pink bikini top with pigtailed hair and a whistle in her mouth, raving. Over the kitchen table there was a fancy poster in a frame showing diagrams of every type of pasta shape.

The noise was the rabbit. He was in a wooden hutch that sat on some newspaper by the back door. "You must be Jumpy," I says, hearing my voice new for the first time alone in someone else's kitchen.

I pulled a chair up and leaned in. The rabbit was fluffy and pitch-black and hunched up like it hated everything.

I goes, "I ate Sellotape once, Jumpy." No response. "A wee square. First year. Fiona dared me. I wandered about all day panicking that my intestines might be stuck together forever. Fiona was a pal of mine." There was no movement or answer at all. Outside, snow was falling into all the gardens. My insides wouldn't calm down. "You probably don't even worry about that. Do rabbits have intestines? You probably don't worry about anything."

There was scrabbling from inside the hutch. I opened the door and straight away Jumpy fumbled backward, gawping sideways at me with his nose going mental, almost invisible apart from his wet marble eye.

It smelled sleepy in there with a hint of something tangy that was probably pish. There was a carrot that Donna must have given him on the floor. It was old and bendy so I snapped it in two and moved it nearer to him. Then I closed the door again.

"You don't do much, do you, Jumpy? Sit on your fat arse sweating all day, in your fur coat. No need to choose an outfit. No need to worry about whether it looks right. Just laze around wetting yourself and eating Sellotape."

He was wheezing slowly up and down in fear. I got down on the floor and sat cross-legged so I could lean right in, feeling a huge seizing pain in my left hip. It was funny picturing what Jumpy must have seen, a big pink gurning face floating outside his front door. I spoke through the wire. "I'm speaking too much, as usual. That's probably why you're pretending to be asleep. They call it *excessive talking*."

Then in the same voice, a bit louder, I goes, "You know people, Jumpy? When they start getting on your nerves, that's it. But he's not a bad boy. He's not a bad boy at all. It's a different type of life. I'd get used to it. Maybe I will get used to it. He has money and a family. He loves me. I'm a wee stunner. I'm his bird. Hearing stories about getting your neck sucked and having teeth marks on your tongue and all that sounded mega exciting growing up, but really boys are just a weird kind of insanity. I do like tracksuits though. I'm sad about that. I could have shown you it. I could tell you about school and scramblers. Abbotscraig. About the vegetable aisle at Easyprice and the cute way that Kira-Louise pronounced *roundabout*. About *Heartbreak High*. About my idiot pal, my idiot pregnant pal."

I heard the front door going. The rabbit had barely moved. I did my smallest whisper. "All they want is for me to talk about my mam but what does talking do anyway, Jumpy?"

Donna's voice came through from the living room. "Cora?"

As soon as she came in the kitchen I said it, like I had to get it out of me. "I think I want to dump my boyfriend, Donna. I think that's what's stressing me. Like, tonight. All this."

She smiled. "You've met Jumpy then? Listen, Andy has taken the bike out of the road, it's in his drive. We can sort it all out tomorrow."

I pulled my chair back round to the table. "Have you dumped boys before, Donna?"

She laughed. "Of course."

"Tell me about one. Please."

"Well." She sat down opposite me. She had her house keys looped on her finger and they clacked on the table. "Darren Longmuir."

"Was he an arsehole? That's an arsehole name."

"Grade A," she goes. I laughed and the side of my tummy hurt. "But he had a car. First person I knew with a car. So we'd go up the playing fields and do doughnuts on the grass in his old Renault, or drink Buckie on the verge behind the Main Street car park with lassies he knew from the caravans. We walked a lot, listening to the sound of the birds and the bottling plant. He wasn't a talker."

"That sounds all right."

"The Renault was convertible, but there was a tear in the roof. He'd patched it up with silver tape but it still whistled when he went over forty miles an hour. You live and learn, Cora."

"Where is he now?"

"Glasgow. Listen, how are you feeling?"

"What's the main thing you remember about Darren? Apart from his car."

"He was always covered in cat hair?" She burst out laughing and I did too and the pain in my middle and down into my hip nearly made me want to greet.

"That's going to be you now, but with rabbit fluff!"

"Ah, see, I tape it off."

I undid the pink towel and started rubbing my hair properly dry. "Is that where he gets the Sellotape to eat?"

She laughed. "I used to leave it lying around. Being in a rush in the morning. I don't let him out round the floor anymore."

"What do you think I should do, about my boyfriend? If I want to dump him?"

She put her keys to one side then took my hand in hers. "I think you should rest and get better and not even think about making a decision tonight, pet. Listen, do you want a hot chocolate? Your hands are still freezing. Why don't you go back through in front of the fire?"

Then the doorbell went. "Who's that going to be?"

Donna scraped her chair out and stood up. "It's probably Gunner."

"Gunner's at work."

"I rang him, pet. Andy let me use his phone. I had to. He's your— well, he's your guardian."

"Please don't let him in. Please."

"If he's angry it's because he cares about you, pet."

The doorbell rang again, four times, quick. "Please."

"Okay, look. Are you staying here tonight?"

"Yes."

"I'll tell him that's what's happening. But tomorrow, you're to speak to him. And if you need the hospital or if you feel anything different you are to tell me and we're to go right there, no nonsense. Promise?"

"I promise, Donna."

"Wait here."

I could hear Gunner's deep voice going up and down with annoyance as Donna explained everything to him. It seemed to go on and on. I stood up and sneaked into Donna's living room so I could hear what they were saying. I heard her say I was staying the night. I could hear her say *Cora's feeling a bit emotional. A bit battered and scraped but she'll be fine.* I heard her say *all Cora needs right now is a wee bit of space* and I tried to nod aye to no one through tears that were starting to come.

25

Because of the pain I hardly slept but in the morning there were Coco Pops. Donna was up and ready in her blue uniform with the brown tights and the upside-down watch and she had the table all set for me and her, special.

More snow had lain during the night and the ceiling and the walls and all of the kitchen was bright with light from the blanketed back garden. Her house was warm in every room and I still had her pajamas on. Both knees and my left hip hurt. I felt like I'd been fired out a cannon.

"Do you want a cup of tea?" she says. The radio was playing "2 Become 1" and it was making me smile.

"Please." I did a huge yawn. "Donna, I'm so sorry. I made a total fool of myself last night. On the bike. In your living room. Things are just stressful for me. My pal's got pregnant, school—"

"Get some Coco Pops." She started filling the kettle. Then in that playschool voice everyone does when they're trying to stop someone moping, "Gunner was telling me a certain someone bought you a balloon?"

"Aye, and the tracksuit that's in your bin over there."

"Oh right." She was laughing, leaning down the side of her fridge. "Gunner was back round after you went to bed." She put a fat carrier bag down on the floor next to me. "He dropped off more clothes."

I put my spoon down and looked in the bag. He'd taken a pile of useless clothes out of my wardrobe and rolled them in a ball with my parka, then chucked my toothbrush and Minnie Mouse alarm clock on top. You knew he had been too scared to go near my underwear.

"Are you and him having a bit of a rough time of it?"

I shrugged.

She leaned back against the bench. Her hair was in a claw clip and it was the prettiest I'd seen her. "Can I say something to you?"

"'Suppose."

"He thinks the world of you, Cora, but it's hard for him. He's not from a background that lets him express himself the way you maybe need him to."

I kept crunching. "He expresses himself plenty."

She laughed. "He speaks about you all the time." The kettle rumbled then stopped. She started pouring. "The days you and him used to go walking in Muircross. Said you were always buzzing with all your plans."

I shrugged.

"He said you were a bright lassie, different from the other Muircross folk. He says he doesn't hear that stuff anymore."

I ate a spoon of cereal. "We don't go walking now."

Donna put a polka-dot mug down in front of me. The radio started "Un-Break My Heart" and I was trying to zone it out. "How are you feeling? Do we need to get you to the hospital?"

"I'm too achy for school. But I don't think I need the hospital."

I looked at her and she was giggling. Then in a quick movement she sat down opposite me with her mug of tea. Her eyes were bigger and even more alive than normal and I could tell she was rushing to speak to me about stuff before she went to work. "It must be so hard when one of your classmates passes away."

I kind of smiled at the word *classmates*. It made St. Therese sound like a proper school. Like we were a gang of pigtailed sisters with our knees out in some crap Sunday film. "They're having an assembly for her today."

Donna blew on her tea. "Did you know her well?"

"Kind of. But no."

"Do you think it might be bringing back feelings of when your mam passed away?"

I looked at her. "I had a dream last night. I always have them." Donna sipped her tea and looked at me like, *go on*. "I have the same two dreams over and over. Have you ever been to Muircross?"

"I haven't."

I looked down at the circle of brownish milk. "Near my old house in Muircross there was a park called the Causeway Field. It's where everyone went. When I dream, sometimes I'm stood in the sun there. There's no clouds and planes are going over and there's a dry summer smell right across the estate. It's just a hot morning and time's rewound and I've got another chance. All I have to do is walk home and say hi to her and behave. Make things different. Then life will be normal. But I can't move."

"Oh, pet."

"That's one dream. The other is about her funeral."

"Well, I think it's normal that you might still dream about that. It must have been so difficult at such a young age."

"Thing is, I never saw anything that day. I could hear it, though. The wind off the Firth, everyone's words. Feet on gravel, feet on grass. Other folk crying. I had my face in Gunner's coat. Even when my legs went, and he carried me over his shoulder, I put my face in his collar. I didn't feel like hugging him, but I had to." I tipped the bowl up to my face and drank the chocolate milk. "It's still fresh now, I think because all I can remember is the sound. I don't even know what my mam's gravestone looks like. I've never visited. I'm sorry this has all come out now," I goes. "That's what happens."

She smiled at me. "Do you need me to stay here with you today?"

"No. I'm fine. These dreams, I think one of the worst things I always think is that me and my mam spent our whole life in one place. In Muircross."

"Well, I grew up in Abbotscraig. I've never lived anywhere else."

"It's like, it all came back because me and Gunner got this counselor, Dan. I had to do homework for him!"

"Homework!"

"Aye! He gave me a sheet like, write out five times when you and your mam were happy, five times when you and your mam shared something special, five positive words to describe you and your mam's relationship. I couldn't do it, it's like getting asked for memories I don't have."

"I'll say one thing. Your memories are important. But that was the past. It doesn't have to be your future."

I looked at her, then into my bowl. "Thanks for these. I'm sad still, but I'm not starving."

"Progress." When she stood up she looked tall and beautiful. "Right, I need to be off. Sometimes I wish I could pack it all in, but there are bills to pay."

"Donna, see before you go, you don't have any change you could lend me? Twenty pences maybe? I can pay you back."

"I don't. I've a note if that's any help?"

"No, it's okay."

"Stay here as long as you like. Get a rest. If you feel down or you need anything my work number is on the corkboard. Spare keys on the sideboard. But I won't mind a single bit if you're lying on that sofa asleep when I get back." She smiled and nodded and ruffled my straggly hair with her hand, then she goes, "And don't forget Jumpy!" and then she walked out the room in her shiny shoes.

Soon as I heard the front door click closed, I got up and pulled some clothes out of Gunner's carrier bag. I put my big jeans and my Fila jumper straight over Donna's pajamas, then I tied her dressing gown over it all tight, and then I put my parka on. I was like a big Muircross tramp. I got the dry Reeboks off the radiator, then switched the radio off and took her spare key and I left, without washing, without thinking, without worrying who might see.

On the front step there was the usual feeling that I should give up and go back to Gunner and say sorry again for something and try to keep everything sweet. On the road the bike was nowhere to be seen and the fresh snow had covered up everything I'd done last night. I was breathing fast. As soon as I felt all that I stepped down into the thick snow and started walking.

Up by the golf course you smelled that amazing wet freshness. In the distance the mist made the TV transmitter vanish. I was sweating in my parka and pajamas and I didn't want to put my nose inside the collar because I knew I'd be reeking. I kept my head down and walked the edge of the golf course without looking and ignored the pain in my shoulder and my hip.

I waited for a second by the junction and watched all the long shiny grass and the weeds sticking up through the fat layer of perfect snow. I wanted to put my hands in there and wash them in the wetness. I wanted to make a snowball. I wanted to throw myself face-first in the snow and sleep.

I headed onto the Reservoir Road with my heart still pounding. Walking up there let you look back and see the whole of Abbotscraig, see right over the estate, the soft snowy bright square mile that contained all the pain of the past year. Nothing moved but smoke from chimneys. I started to picture Kira's family in there, what her house was like, where her body might be now. Then I turned and walked on. The phone boxes were in view.

Inside was freezing and wet and there was that smell that always made me think of Moira and my mam. I lifted the handset and dialed the operator. "I'd like to make a reverse charge call," I went, and gave the number.

"And who is calling?"

"Cora Mowat. It's a big emergency."

I waited while the operator dialed and then I heard his doofy voice going, *"Hullo? Fulton Gillespie."* I was so glad I wasn't wasting twenty pences on this.

The operator spoke to him. *"I have a Cora Mowat on the line who is looking to reverse the charges. Do you accept the call? It is an emergency."* I heard him say, *"Eh, aye. Aye. Okay."*

I couldn't stop beaming at his voice—the wee bit puzzlement that had come in. The hope. The operator said to me, louder, "I am connecting the call and the charges are reversed. Thank you."

There was a silence and I had to turn my head into my shoulder from the giggles. Fulton goes, "Cora?"

"Hi," I says, straightening myself up, getting into my role, "you not going to ask if I'm all right?"

"You sound all right."

"I am all right."

"What's this about? I'm glad you rang, like. I missed you."

"We're finished, Fulton." There was a silence and on the other end all you could hear was distant sport noises off the telly.

"No."

"Aye."

"Is this about the tracksuit? It's limited edition. I've got you some amazing stuff for actual Christmas Day. Or before. Can I see you, please?"

"The tracksuit's in the bin and we are done." I was tingling.

"But how? I love you, babe."

"Do you really want to know? Fulton, the reason I liked you in the first place was because it felt like you had my back. You were nice to me in your own weird way, and you helped me with money, and you were full of ideas and you were there and I felt protected. We were never going to be perfect but you were good at the wee things, and when your life is as crap as mine the wee things mean the world." I gulped. My mouth was still chocolatey. "Then a crack appeared and when I looked through it there was nothing underneath. Yogi touched me. I could have been raped. The first time I really needed you, you weren't there."

"Don't say that."

"And what you did to Eldo was disgusting. Your granda is a vile old cunt. You, your granda, your granda's pals—scumbags."

"I'm sorry if Yogi hurt you."

"You hurt me more."

"I'm sorry. Cora, I'm getting my flat and I want you to be there."

"Fuck your flat," I went with a wee excitable nod, tiptoeing a bit, keeping it nice and calm in a way that I knew would wind him right up. I was all alone with dazzly white snow at all four sides of the phone box. "I want a real future. Not hiding pornos up a tree. Not scramblers. Not grappa out a water pistol. And whoever it is with, they have to have my back. They have to want what I want." I jumped, once. Just a wee one, maybe an inch off the ground. "Do you really think it's funny to come in to hug me then shout KACHOW and fake karate-chop my neck?"

"I was showing you my skills." There was a pause and I could hear him breathe. "You know what? I've given you so much fucking money. You owe me. You ruined my Helly Hansen, for a start."

"You ruined your own fucking Helly Hansen."

"And where's the bike?"

"The scrambler was a gift from your darling grandfather. I'll be keeping that."

"See you, I'll—I'll kick your cunt in, you cheeky cow."

I did a cute chuckle. "You'll get nowhere near my cunt again." He was screaming now so I pulled the receiver away and looked at it. His voice came out of it all crazy and crackly like a wee electronic talking prawn. I didn't need to think about money. I'd lived most of my life without money. "Cheery-bye, Fulton!" I says, and then I slammed it down.

My breathing was fine. My heart was calm. I couldn't stop smiling.

I thought of how, when I was a wee lassie, I used to have to say difficult things to myself in other people's voices. I was saying them out loud now. I wasn't even seventeen yet. I had to start going easier on myself.

I opened the door and the world was freezing and bright. As I clomped back from the verge onto the pavement the phone started ringing behind me. It was a normal ring, but I could still feel the desperation and anger. I honestly couldn't stop smiling at how free I felt.

Right there up to my ankles in snow in my soaking Reeboks I thought ahead, to warmish school nights when the sunlight lasts and you're sat in circles of crumpled dandelions and bum-flattened grass listening to your pals' problems. Nights when you'll roll home later smelling of kebab grease and strawberry wine thinking that there's nothing so bad that can't be solved.

On the other side of the golf course I walked down by Jackie's house, down past the silent phone box with the smoke-black windows, round into my street. I'd get in and have a bath and I'd heat the pajamas on Donna's radiator then I'd lie on her soft settee under a blanket and watch endless shite on her telly alone.

I used her key, then in the kitchen I took the Reeboks off and put the kettle on. I knelt down to speak to Jumpy. I thought about giving him a handful of dry Coco Pops and then I heard Donna's toilet flush.

The tap went, and handwashing noises, then you heard the living room door and footsteps. I froze. Then he's stood there all long and gangly in the kitchen doorway, with another carrier bag.

"How are you here?"

"Me and Donna have each other's keys. I was looking for you."

I'd never seen him look the way he looked. Still and quiet but raging underneath. "Gunner, can you just leave please? I want some time to think about everything that's happened. Stuff has happened you don't even know about. Donna agreed I could stay here. Please."

He looked like a wreck. He goes, "I'll be gone in a minute. I came to give you this." He held the bag up slightly.

I couldn't move. I didn't want to see what was in that bag. "I crashed my scrambler."

"Donna's filled me in on everything. It's just a few scrapes, like."

"Please, I need to be by myself just now."

He stepped toward me. "What you need's a dose of reality, lass, eh."

I leaned back against the bench. "What's that meant to mean?"

"It means I'm sick of running about after you. Getting no cooperation in return. You've got an attitude problem. You're a nightmare. A jumped-up stupid wee nightmare."

I could hear Jumpy scrabbling. I was hoping he was listening to all this because I'd maybe need him as a witness if Gunner went too far. "You absolute prick," I went.

I looked around—Donna's milk jug, her fruit bowl, her kettle. All of a sudden I needed to throw something at his head, but she'd been kind to me and I couldn't break her nice stuff.

Then I remembered. I reached in the parka pocket. I took out the bottle of White Musk, held it like a hard wee cannonball. I fired it right at his face and he ducked, and it smashed on the door frame behind him, and the lid bounced back over the lino and hit my shin.

"You fucking wee nutter."

"Don't call me that!"

"Wee Cora Gillespie. The nutcase."

"I hate you! You're not my da and I hate you!" I screamed it. One of those throat-ripping screams. Probably the best scream I'd done in at least two years.

Jumpy was scrabbling now like he was running on the spot in his hutch.

"And thankfully you're not my daughter. Does it ever occur to you the life I could have had if you weren't here? Do you realize what I've had to sacrifice for you? And what do I get in return? You won't even turn up to the school."

"What are the dishes then?"

"Oh doing the dishes, big fucking deal. Get her a fucking medal! Anyway"—he held up the carrier bag in his left hand—"I'm not here for excuses and chit-chat, like."

He walked over to the kitchen table and emptied the bag upside down. There was a box, my house keys on the cartoon banana key ring, a load of bank notes loose and landing everywhere. More money than I'd ever seen. "The motorbike's gone, this morning. That's the money off the scrappy. A hundred and fifty. Take it." I moved some of the money to look at the box. A Walkman, a little cute expensive silver metal one, with headphones. "And that there's your Christmas. Or it would have been. Anyway, you've got till lunchtime to come round and get anything else you need. Then the locks are getting changed."

"That's my mam's house."

"It's in my name. And this is for your own good."

There was a feeling right over my skin, like getting rubbed with an electric balloon at a party. Energy was making my blood mental. Everything smelled of White Musk and I started randomly worrying about how Jumpy was going to cope with that. "What am I meant to do?" I says.

"At your age I'd been on the street five years." He folded his arms like he was guarding himself and I saw the muscles twitching under the Tweety Pie tattoo. "It's time you stood on your own two feet, Cora."

Part
Three

GLASGOW,
1998

26

Our manager Graham had printed out the letter and pinned it to the noticeboard. Robyn read it out as I sat stuffing my uniform into my shoulder bag.

"*All Staff Memo, April.* Ooh, serious! *Damage to stock . . . disciplinary action*, yadda, yadda, yadda. *Build trust . . . challenges of a busy environment*, blah, blah, *Warmest regards, Graham.*" She blew a raspberry. "They're definitely onto us!"

Robyn was my best pal out of all my colleagues. She was tall and German and a part-timer like me. She was a uni student and she'd done loads of shite jobs—it was her that taught me the trick with the ready meals and showed me the ropes on our chaotic wee shopfloor.

On Fridays me and Robyn would get a couple of macaronis or cottage pies and play football with them in the changing room—you'd bash the packaging up then put it back out at 60 percent off and buy it yourself. I was barely eating otherwise so I'd got good quite quick.

"Has he not asked you into a meeting yet?" She started grinning. "You know, in the year before last Graham had to be disciplined by the regional manager because he asked a girl on a date?"

I laughed. "Poor Graham."

"It was before my time. He asked the girl for a drink at Mulligans. I think he was taking her for a basket of nachos. She walked round the corner and saw him at the pub door in a tweed jacket with a bunch of carnations. She turned and ran. You are clearly next."

"Well, I couldn't turn down free nachos." I reached on top of my locker and found the curries.

"I think he fancies you!" She walked over to Graham's locker and crouched, trying to look into the vents. "I guarantee he sweeps the hair up and picks yours out. Keeps it in a ball, probably. In here."

Graham's breath smelled like goldfish flakes but apart from that he seemed all right. Our supermarket was called Saver Local. It was an Easyprice rip-off but bigger and with crapper products and everything discounted and two-for-one. It was at the top end of Byres Road and so it was always busy—Graham was too stressed to ever stay on the ball and that's why everyone tolerated him.

I pulled my ponytail out and swung my hair loose. "I can't blame him. Now, one last kickabout?"

"We will get caught, you know."

"I've got three pound seventy-two until next payday and shooting pains where the food's supposed to go." I dropped both meals and punted them at the wall, then picked them up and repriced them with the gun. I always did two at a time so I could take one home for Pauline.

I'd rung her up after Gunner kicked me out. She had quit her new job and gone on the dole so I went through to Glasgow and we sat the days out together. Pauline sensed what I needed—after the summer she told me I could move in properly and make a go of it. She had chosen me. I didn't have the words for what it meant.

She was living in Partick in a bedsit above a burned-out café called Wullie's, on a long row of tenements just off the Dumbarton Road. Wullie owned the café and all the upstairs too. You knew Pauline's building a mile off because of the black smoke stripes that went up the front from Wullie's red shutters.

Pauline's room was tiny and dark, and the halls were noisy from her other pals, and there was at least two dogs. To be honest it was scary, but when the door clicked closed it felt to me like my life was beginning again. I moved in properly on a spitting-rain, slimy-leaf Sunday—18 October, six days before my mam's birthday.

We dragged my two bin bags in, then had gin and Lilt in the road to celebrate while the building shook from happy hardcore off the boys on the third floor. "If I go back to Abbotscraig it'll be in a box!" Pauline goes, cheersing her mug, and even though I did a loud laugh I was thinking to myself under that street light, *Maybe same?*

We lasted three weeks together in her crowded room, living off Pot Noodle sandwiches and *large chips and gravy with two forks please* when her crisis checks came. Glasgow was fun at first—big pishing-rain pajama mornings and pretty overcast afternoons that faded down to night through different booze shops and dance floors, our two damp bodies squeezed into dresses from the Sue Ryder thrift, dancing our futures away, forgetting. No school. No Gunner. No trudging round in an itchy jumper. Nobody that really knew Cora Mowat at all.

At night I'd lie on Pauline's settee making an effort to sleep, but just like when I ran away aged ten there was no big change inside. Pauline had at least two guys on the go so she was gone a lot and when she wasn't gone she was shagging. So I'd eat alone in the top kitchen, or walk by myself at night.

I'd sometimes replay Jo's Glasgow stories. I'd look at the streets and people around me and wonder how it was possible for any magic to happen here. The old diabetic boy with no feet who was in the bedsit below Pauline says to me one day, "Best thing about Partick, doll—it's a three-minute walk to get out the place." I laughed but at the same time I was thinking, *You've no clue where I've come from.*

And the more I thought back the more I realized that my whole life I'd been pathetic—that was the main thing pissing me off. I was sick of help and sick of my own wee fraud routine. One Monday lunchtime I took two big secret swigs of Pauline's backup value vodka and I felt it so much so I just came out with it, *I want to try and find a place of my own.*

She laughed till I saw the roof of her mouth then when I explained more she marched me out across the hall and opened the weird double doors there. It was a room, a room where Wullie had dumped all the salvaged stuff from the downstairs fire—two stacks of chairs, a long table, a deep-fat fryer, a sandwich-bar fridge and a tall glass-door drinks fridge. I flicked the wall switch but no bulb came on. Then Pauline plugged the tall fridge in and the 7UP logo at the top lit everything green.

She explained how a pensioner woman had dossed in there and died a month back and how her haunted stuff was still there too—a telly and a Sanyo boombox and a mirror and pans and towels. Pauline said that nobody had claimed it and all that was mine to use. I did a face at her. She goes, "Wullie's never here and no one's going to grass you. This stuff's been here ages. Your call." I looked down at the floor in the room—kind of public toilet lino. I looked at her again. I knew she wouldn't expect me to say it so I went, "This will be perfect."

That first night, when Pauline pulled the door shut, I put my face against the cold glass door of the tall 7UP fridge and bawled for twenty minutes at how not perfect it was. Even in my most mental hopeless Muircross moment I could never have dreamed up a future for myself in a room that had lino. I wanted to apologize to the fridge for weeping on it but instead I spoke out loud to my mam. I said sorry. That this wasn't forever. And for her just to shush about everything, because I hated Gunner and just like Pauline the only way I'd be going back to Abbotscraig now was in a box.

When all my scrambler money ran out not long after New Year Pauline took me to Hillhead Library and invented my exam results then printed them out as a CV. She thefted me two cashmere turtleneck jumpers from BHS and I picked the beige. I was late for the interview but I did Fiona's skipping rope trick and Graham loved the lies that Pauline told me to tell. It was a crappy temp restocking job and only supposed to be for the store refit, but I got kept on like a miracle. There was no rent on Wullie's storeroom, at least until Wullie found out, so I'd usually skip food and save the money for finding a proper future.

Robyn was slipping into her purple Nikes. "If money's really still a problem you know you can have some of my babysitting shifts?"

"Imagine me looking after children. I live in a hovel."

"Cora, they are cool people. I'll say I've got a good mate you can trust, do you want to meet her? Just don't judge her on her accent." Robyn started her eye shadow in the scuffed wall mirror. "Anyway, are you coming tonight?"

I got my coat out of my locker and put the bashed curries in my bag. "I'm having an early night."

She spoke while admiring herself. "Early night! You know, when you first started I mentioned *Muir-cross* to Susan off checkouts and she said, *Oh god another moon unit scheme lassie*. I had to ask her what a moon unit was. And a scheme. You're not much of a moon unit though!"

I watched her giggling. Robyn did cute probably German things like count on her fingers and look up when she was thinking, like the clouds might know. She moved her eyebrows a lot, like me. But every room and every situation was easy for Robyn.

I says, "My boaking days are over."

"*Boa-king?*"

"It's a word us moon units use for throwing up."

The others started streaming in as I said bye. I never went to work drinks because eventually words came up like *home*, then *pals*, then *parents*, and *oh where are you from, what does yours do?* It was only speaking but words make pictures and then the feelings come.

Outside the pavements were glittery and dampish and it was nearly dark. I got my headphones in and the volume right up. It was a tape Pauline made me, the album *King* by a band called Belly. She copied me the weirdest stuff—Smog, The Delgados, Blake Babies, Jim Carroll, Squirrel Bait, Cocteau Twins, Marine Girls. She said everything she learned about music she got from her da. I put my head down and headed for the bottom of Byres Road.

The Walkman Gunner got me was my best pal. It was my most precious thing because music was predictable and it gave me a wee bit control over my surroundings. You could rewind and replay and I listened to that Belly song "Red" over and over, rewinding the second verse, turning it up and up until I felt the lassie singer in my wisdom teeth.

It had a roughish aluminum body that I loved stroking with my thumb and tiny buttons that clicked all neat and satisfying through your pocket. Fourteen-year-old me would probably have given it a cutesy name like Meg or Julie-Anne. Grown-up me had ruined the blank metal front by scraping in *CMM*.

It was one night sitting at Cowcaddens station, thinking too much, so I got my key out and gouged my initials for something to do. I looked at that big spidery *CMM* nearly every day. Maybe you had to ruin something a bit to make it feel like yours. Folk that are used to ruined things maybe don't feel right when they're given something shiny and special that works.

I turned right, then crossed the road. The street around Wullie's was never quiet because directly opposite there was a blank, weedy square with benches. It was broken glass and dafties with dogs and druggies speaking to the sky—the exact folk you got in Muircross, but more of them, and way less predictable to me. I kept my head down like normal and fiddled my keys out in the dark.

Inside there was the usual sweet, dry smell of gas heaters and never-hoovered carpet, and a weird tangy burning smell too. I went upstair and knocked on Pauline's door. There was no answer so I cracked it open and the room was dark and full of her breath and she was in her bed, asleep. I closed her door and crossed the hall.

My room was a big gloss paint square with the fridges all unshiftable in the middle. The lino was manky so I took the wire shelves out of the 7UP one and kept my clothes in the bottom, like a wardrobe. The other haunted pensioner bits I put in one corner, then I flipped the long table upside down to make a stumpy four-poster. I piled it up with cushions and blankets off Pauline's settee.

I never cleaned the place, and there could never be boys because of how weird it was, but I woke up every day to a beautiful shitscape of crisp packets and knickers and Pauline's unravelly jumpers and cereal bowls of gone-gray milk and that helped me too. There was no lock on the door but it was my space and my mess and it even started smelling of me.

The only bit I organized was my tidy tray, a metal serving thing that Pauline had thefted out of O'Neill's. I kept it on one of the café chairs, laying things out on it daily in neat rows—my hair pins, my keys, my bank card, my Walkman, my *Hi, I'm Cora* badge for work. It was the thing that Kira taught me.

At night I would plug the big sandwich-bar fridge in. It vibrated through the floor and was whinier than me and the hum was soothing, and when I put the 7UP one on too the pair of them helped block the other weird noises from the other weird rooms. And I loved that green light—one night I dreamed I was a brussels sprout.

I was stood lining up my earrings on the tray when it came to me what that tangy burning smell was. I raced out my door and did the steps two at a time toward the top floor kitchen with my bag still on my shoulder.

Up there everything was dark except for the glow of the oven door like a tiny shop front at Christmas, and a diamond of moonlight on the lino coming from the single skylight in the roof. I stood in the doorway feeling the beautiful toasty heat on me. I couldn't help beaming at the stupidity of how everything was exactly like I left it.

"Set wee Minnie if you're making food, Cora," I says, to no one.

I got the ratty old oven gloves and opened the door and felt a blast of heat bloom. I pulled out the tray and slid it onto the bench with my face turned away. The hum stopped as I switched the oven off and there was distant gothy metal and shouting from a room downstairs. I dropped my bag.

There were five black screwed-up faces on the tray, the size of fifty pences. Little rock-hard devil heads made of coal—the potato smileys that I'd stuck on for lunch, before I went to work. Food I'd started heating up about nine hours before. The harder I worked on getting everything right for my job the more I struggled in my own life.

I looked up at the angled skylight. I saw night-clouds lit browny-pink by the street lamps and my reflection hovering over them. My eyes were tired. My hair hadn't been cut in ten months and it was starting to look like I should be riding a unicorn round in the scud. On my angriest days I tried to convince myself that Gunner wouldn't even know me, but it was definitely Cora Mowat up there.

I heard the stairs squeak then the landing floorboards. Pauline, bowl cut licking everywhere, bare-legged in a big baggy T-shirt, floaty like a ghost. "Jesus, it's roasting. Why are you standing in the dark, chick?" She flicked the light on and everything turned weak yellow. She tiptoed over and hugged me tight. "Burned your dinner?"

"My lunch. I can't believe the freaks in here just leave your shit alone. Like, surely you can tell by the seventh hour that this oven being on is a mistake."

"It's pure maliciousness. It's like when they spot something going moldy on your shelf. They probably watch it daily, egging the spores on." She looked down at the five little cremated faces on the tray and burst out in a sleepy laugh. "Bit of ketchup. They'll be fine."

I tipped the charcoal lumps into the bin. "I was thinking. I would like you to cut my hair."

"You wee lunatic."

"Short, maybe. But not short as yours." I took a curry out of my bag and put it in the microwave, then shut the door. I pressed start and it went into a wee trance. "I want to look in the mirror and not see a person I recognize from a load of shitey wee mining town stories."

"Fair enough." She opened one of the cupboards on tiptoes. "Do you want wine? I'm putting *Shawshank Redemption* on again."

Pauline would get a liter of Bulgarian red out the corner shop most weeks. I'd sometimes have a glass with her on the stairs then she'd take the rest to one of her mate's rooms to start an all-nighter. I'd sit on a café chair in front of my inherited telly or look out my window and try and make sense of the street outside.

"I'm going to eat my curry. I got you one too, I'll leave it in the fridge to go moldy."

"Too wildly independent to watch a film with your old pal now?"

"Too exhausted."

"Well, let's do your hair this week. And listen, it's my dad's birthday thing a week tomorrow. Please come?"

"Not into dads."

"This one's cool."

The microwave pinged and I got a fork then carried the curry to the table. The more I thought of Gunner the more I told myself I'd just live the life that Glasgow gave me, however hard it got.

Pauline turned back in the doorway with her wine in her hand. "Cora, he means the world to me. You'll have to meet him at some point."

I ate a forkful of curry and burned my tongue. "Cut my hair for me," I goes, chewing and blowing, "then maybe we can talk."

27

It wasn't just the place and what it did to you that made you feel lonely—the traffic all day, the skintness, the long tummy-ache mornings and the skyline of buildings that trapped you in like a wall. In Partick and all the rest of Glasgow it wasn't just the amount of people that was weird, it was that I could sit and spy on them basically all day and still not know a single thing about who they were.

When I was wee me and my mam always had folk sussed. From their faces, their footsteps, the way they pronounced *jail*. We knew the chain smoker's fingers and the screwdriver scars and how doing the glue gave you a scabby wee goatee. Even when people were on their good weeks or in their court suits their bodies still told you *Muircross*— the *High Flats Cheekbones*, the *Kirk Road Limp*. The clues linked everyone together, including me and her.

I'd heaved my window up and was sat sideways in my joggers and the old plum fleece, watching life round the benches below. You had to wonder about benches. They were magnets for the homeless but councils seemed to love dotting them round. There were three scary grandas sharing Thunderbird, a younger guy sleeping on the ground, one twig-leg lassie in a vest dancing alone by a big planter of dead flowers. In the middle a dog with a face like a scouring pad was licking crisp crumbs off a manhole cover.

Seeing these Glasgow folk you realized you'd spent your whole life learning the small-town ways without ever really having to try. How did you even start that again? Here you saw blazer kids and fake-tan shaggers and men in suits with rectangular specs and students every-where, and you knew their outfits, and you knew their expressions, but not who they were. It was like a whole wee way of moving through the world had gone. I wanted my mam there, just so I could ask, *What's that one there been up to?*

The Kira dreams had started in Glasgow. Her going had made everything more raw and alive but it wasn't until I left Abbotscraig that I ended up going back there in my sleep, having weird dreams full of faces I could read and recognize. Pauline said that Kira dying had brought back all the emotion of my mam, that I was *carrying the weight of them both*. Pauline sounded like counselor Dan sometimes, but then she'd grown up on printouts.

Those dreams always started in the English corridor at St. Therese. It's summer and the ties are off and the carpets are cooking and the air's pure Brut. The bell goes. I spin round and Kira's next to me, and we stand like mannequins while all the second years I recognize rush round us to lunch. Nothing gets said, I just get the same hopeless dread feeling that I'm the living one who should be taking charge of something, without ever knowing exactly what.

In dreams I look at her and she's almost a woman. She moves in a gentler way and her face has changed, and for a wee imaginary minute of pain I feel a bit proud of being pals with a beautiful ghost. Then when our eyes meet my thoughts start sliding softly, like cutlery on a boat, and snowflakes start, and there's breathing and Mariah and a feeling gently rising like I have to intervene. Then I crash awake in Pauline's stale blankets with my breath gone.

Dreams reminded me what going back to Abbotscraig would mean. Being *sensible* and pretending and smiling at all the same faces, but older. Rewinding the rain. Making the trees take their leaves back. Apologizing to Gunner. Some days there were certain wee bits of our life together that I weirdly missed—things he said, faces he made—but I'd rather have chewed lightbulbs than apologize again for anything.

I stood up and got the haunted Sanyo boombox out from next to the telly and plugged it in by the window. It's hard admitting it, but when you're skint and alone and starving to death in a stoory storeroom, the past is sometimes the easiest place to go.

Fulton had written to me back in Abbotscraig—or he'd had a warder write for him—begging me to send him tapes. He'd been done for the Eldo thing. He knew me and him were finished, he only needed some sort of human contact beyond his vile old granda. And he had no telly in there. I wasn't writing back straight away because the boy was a cock but I couldn't just chuck the letter out. It ended up coming through to Glasgow in a bin bag, with my printouts and other important crinkly things.

What I'd started doing was recording tapes for him once a fortnight. Pauline had lifted me an eight-pack of Memorex cassettes from Woolies on Byres Road and I put audio onto them off the old haunted telly, programs like *Friends* or *Roseanne*, with me at the end saying hello so he'd have one small friendly voice at least. I'd leave the label blank because Fulton couldn't read.

I held down the play and record buttons together. "All right! Well I hope you enjoyed that. Keep your chin up and stay out of trouble, please. Cora."

I wrapped the tape then put it in my work bag for next week. I washed and did my teeth in the hallway bathroom then changed into my going-out jeans and one of Pauline's jumpers. I did my eyeliner and put my hair in a bun, then slipped on the semi-rancid Golas I'd found in the Sue Ryder shop at Kelvinbridge. On the way out I knocked on Pauline's door. I'd agreed to go with her to get presents for her da's birthday, thinking maybe if I did that then I'd get spared the actual party.

Outside, April rain was going again. Everyone from before was gone and four tracksuited guys were having a morning wrestle by the benches. I started power walking and Pauline ran up behind me in her bashed red boots and shapeless fake fur coat, the one with all the pockets inside. She didn't have to tell me her plans for the record fair.

She did her crap American accent. "Why you always such a Speedy Gonzalez?"

"Let me guess the budget for your da's present."

She jogged ahead of me and turned back. "Don't get fruity about it! These record fairs are a free-for-all."

We crossed onto Byres Road and headed up. You only needed to go half a mile from Wullie's to find the nice bit where life began. Here and there you saw those student girls in cherry-red DMs and dog-smell coats dodging home in the downpour.

I says, "You never wonder about everyone's stories?"

"They're just students, chick."

"Everyone's got a story. My mam would know. *See that one there!*"

"That's the first time you've mentioned her since you moved here."

"Really?"

She shrugged. "It's not a bad thing. Maybe you're—coping?"

I stopped, and she did too. I looked at her. "Did you find a way to cope?"

"I wouldn't be stood here otherwise."

"Can I ask what your mam's name was?"

She started walking again. "Janey," she goes, over her shoulder.

"Janey Sclater. Pretty." I looked up at where the buildings met the blank sky. No sun, no clouds, no seagulls, no nothing. "So how did you cope?

"Brown."

"You serious?"

"Always." A bus ripped through a big puddle to our right. "In the mood for a story?"

"If you're in it."

"My boyfriend at the time, he was basically an insufferable wee penis but he was a decent kisser, a looker, actually ended up shagging my best mate at the time in an abandoned cash and carry, but anyway! My mam had just died and I couldn't stop bawling. Like, day in, day out crying, like, I'm crying uncontrollably and he's looking at me, arm draped over my shoulders, vacant. Then one night he says, *I've got you something, Polly, to help*. I says, *Oh aye?* He worked as a key cutter in Debenhams and lived off Crispy Pancakes, but still. I was thinking maybe he was going to pay for me to get my hair done? New CD player? Something to cheer me up."

"Did you have your bowl cut then?"

"Aye, exact same. Anyway, he takes this Jacob's Cream Cracker tin out from under his bed and opens it. This was my present. Couple of syringes and wee bits of folded-up paper. Scribbled-on paper. His dealer had a daughter and he tore up her crayon drawings for wraps."

"He gave you heroin to stop you crying?"

"You make it sound more pathetic than it was."

"You didn't have to take it."

She laughed as we crossed the greasy road. "There's no good reason to jag a needle in your arm, Cora. You only try it because you think it won't get you. You dump it and come back, dump it and come back. The thinking doesn't change. *It will never, ever get me.*"

"Did it get you?"

"Well, I nearly died. Does that count?"

I kept my voice down for no reason. "Do people who work in Debenhams really do heroin?"

"You'd be surprised."

We turned up the lane then crossed toward the QMU. "So what's it like?"

"It's like your bones have been crying out for light since the day you were born. Then heroin pulls you inside out."

"Sounds like when you eat white bread but you squeeze it and roll it into wee balls first, between your palms. On a day like this. On the settee. In your cozies, with *Neighbours* going."

"Maybe not quite as good as that."

I looked down, started plucking the white denim threads on my ripped jeans and said it quick. "What happened to your mam?"

"Oh, same as me. Brown. But without the luck. No Saracen to keep her going. Vicki found her."

The last time I went round for Vicki her mam came to the door and told me she was tired. Then suddenly she appeared down the stairs in a long teddy-bear nightshirt and mumbled to me for five minutes like a weakly smiling robot. As we spoke I noticed she was edging the door shut inch by inch. I didn't try and wedge my foot in. Life was changing.

Vicki'd had an abortion. Apparently her mam had been sound about it and took her in a taxi to the clinic and everything. What do you even say? *Oh, sorry*? It was sad though, because things had been so easy for us—blazers round our waists, weekday afternoons doing daisy chains on the grass by the council buildings with three Twixes and a half bottle of Totov. Whenever I mentioned it all to Pauline her face went weird. They'd fallen out. She never said it, but I knew.

I goes, "Will Vicki be at your da's party?"

"Vicki?" She shook her hair. "First, it's only a barbecue. And, I dunno?"

"You pair okay?"

"Her and my da are still best pals." She did her wee Vicki impression. "*Hiya, Uncle Ger.* Wee shite. I guess we'll see. She never forgets his birthday."

The QMU was one of the university union buildings, a big gray Muircrossy thing, but studenty too. It made me wonder. I would walk through crowds of students most days and it all felt as far away as when I was fourteen.

Inside tables were laid out in rows, covered in boxes and stacks of records and CDs and tapes. The folk behind the stalls were mainly split-end ponytail men. All you heard was muttering and crinkling plastic bags.

"What does your da like?"

"All sorts. He's a big sad nerd. Plainsong, zydeco, Ethio-jazz. Pecker Dunne, Margo Guryan. Nic Jones. Indie music. He got me into The Smiths."

"So what you getting him?"

"Whatever's easiest?" She picked up a stack of cassettes from the stall we were at. "I got an original Smiths T-shirt off a washing line once. Probably the highlight of my childhood." She put the tapes back and we turned and walked into the next aisle. "Did you never do the washing lines when you were wee?"

"What's that?"

She was running her fingers over the edges of the cassettes. "*Doing the back gardens!* Jumping hedges and stealing folks' washing? When you're drunk?"

I laughed. "No but when I was wee my knickers always went missing off the line. My mam used to go mental about it. She'd tell me they'd blown into the Firth. My good *Little Mermaid* ones. Muircross was absolutely crawling."

Pauline had a cassette in her hands. "See, my da loves X-Ray Spex but I get the feeling he already has this."

The guy behind the stall was clipping his fingernails into a polystyrene cup. "He's not looking," I whispered.

She ran her hands over the plastic dividers with the different letters of the alphabet on that were stuck in each box. "Fair play to X-Ray Spex for giving these nerds a reason to put out the X, Y, Z boxes."

"*Zavaroni?*"

"Who buys Lena Zavaroni records?"

"My mam did. Her records are all in Gunner's shed. Or maybe chucked now, actually."

Pauline went to the Z box and lifted out the only Lena Zavaroni tape and held it up, reading the back. "This is probably a bootleg of some sort." It was the one my mam had on vinyl, *Lena Zavaroni and Her Music*. Her hair was short like Pauline's on the front. I couldn't keep looking at her. I squeezed past a group of students and kept walking.

Pauline jogged up behind and tapped me on the shoulder. "Sorry. Don't get moody."

"People are watching us wandering round in circles here, Miss Suspicious."

Pauline started stomping toward the door. "Fine, come on."

"What about the present?"

Outside the rain was hurtling down in little blots. We turned and headed up the hill toward the old posh uni buildings and at the corner Pauline opened her coat and lifted out a big chunk of cassettes, six or seven of them together. "Job done." She turned and started walking backward in front of me, her fringe starting to get wetted down. "You'd think working in a supermarket you'd have your wits about you for this sort of stuff?" I was about to reply when she did the face. "Chick. Run!"

She turned and started bolting full-pelt so I followed. We ran together with our feet slapping and plapping in the wet and I followed her red boots right up University Gardens then through the main road traffic, where I stopped and looked both ways like I always did these days. It wasn't long until the pain in my hip was going with every step. I wanted to find a table and lie on it and have five expert people run over and fix me like a race car. Then I'd never think of that fucking scrambler ever again.

I followed her down the front of the main uni building, then she darted right and in through the vehicle entrance, a tunnel that took you into the wee ancient squares of grass in the middle. I'd never seen a lassie run like Pauline did in a chase. She was like a gazelle.

She threw herself down sideways on one of the wet benches and I stood in front of her, panting. It was silent and dead in there and we were surrounded by arches and turrets. All you could hear was my breathing. "Do you not think we should keep moving?"

"Oh, there's nobody coming. I just wanted to liven things up."

I shoved her legs off and chucked myself down next to her. "At least you got what you went for."

"You make it sound simple! If you'd ever shoplifted yourself you'd have a bit more respect." She did her stupid grin. "For the craft!"

I laughed. "*Craft.*"

"Thefting's hard! Or it was. Now I need imaginary security guards just to get a chase." She took the tapes out again and started clacking through them, reading the backs. "You must have known shoplifters in Muicross?"

I just shrugged *maybe* because I just couldn't be arsed explaining.

Pauline stood up and put her hands in the fur coat pockets. "Cheer up for god's sake. Do you fancy the café? My treat. Saved a fortune this morning already."

I stood up and did some scissor movements for my hip. "If we can walk very slowly?"

Pauline started across the wee square of soggy grass. "I got you a present, by the way." She reached into the other side of her coat and brought out a cassette. "Happy however many rainy Glasgow months, Cora Mowat."

She handed me the Lena Zavaroni tape, warm from her pocket. "I hate presents," I goes, in a voice that sounded different. "But cheers."

Lena was as cheesy as she'd been when I was looking down at her on my mam's stoory carpet—the image was burned into my brain from those net-curtain afternoons, but when I saw her now the feelings were fresher. Stood there on the wet grass it was like for the very first time I couldn't go back. Like even if I scrunched my eyes shut those days were locked and sealed and unreachable. It was like at some point along the way a chain had been broken and now I was on my own.

28

If Robyn was with me on lunch we would walk up the hill a bit from the supermarket and sit on the wall to eat. At this end of Byres Road nobody seemed to notice you—not a single half-munched sausage roll chucked, not a single *tits out* shouted.

Speaking to Robyn there were no thoughts tangled in about what school you had been to or those gutties off the market that you wore age eight. Did you get shitey wee mining towns in Germany? Everything we said to each other about our childhoods seemed interesting. Or she made me feel that way, at least.

"You know I have my uni deadlines coming up." She plucked at her tights then sat down. "I am not saying they will agree to it, but why don't I ask about the babysitting for you? They will need to find someone to cover me."

"Trying to force me out?"

"Trying to line your pockets. Save you from Graham."

"I'm holding out for the nachos."

She did a big toothy bite into her boiled egg. "I get that it might feel weird, me asking, but it's a way out of this." She plucked the Saver Local logo on her work polo and pinged it back on her chest.

I did a face into the wind. "What are they like?"

"The Andersons? They are okay, quite normal. It's a very nice house and you can relax there. Just say yes, you awkward person!"

"I want a Lilt first."

"Be quick please."

I left my bag and ran off down the hill toward Barrett's newsagent. It was one of those chilly Tuesday afternoons that surprised you with birds' sudden singing, and the spring-ish wind and the sun flashing on windows. And no rain. It was like certain short rare moments everything around you clicked for a second and let you think things were going to be okay. I paid for the tins and as I ran back even the pain from how freezing they felt in my hands couldn't stop my smile.

Robyn had one eye shut from the sun. "Fulton Gillespie?" she goes.

First it was funny to hear it in a German accent. Then I had that usual gripping feeling that he was out, and near, and watching. Robyn stood up. I grabbed my bag back off the wall. "What about him?" I handed her a can and we started walking.

"Who is he?"

How could I make people understand the way I felt when I moved to Abbotscraig? If I couldn't do that there was no point explaining everything else. "My ex." I took a big glug. "Why were you even looking in there?"

"For a hairband. Fulton! Sounds like a hunk from a novel. A man in a hat who understands horses."

I had to wipe the juice off my bottom lip with the laughter. I goes, "Tiny willy and big round head, actually."

"Oh, how terrible. Anyway. The babysitting?"

I looked both ways down the road as I lifted Fulton's parcel out of my bag. "I don't know."

"What is it about Scottish lassies and not accepting help? Maybe it's you that has a thing for Graham and not the other way round?"

I slapped the back of her head. "It's you that never shuts up about him!"

When there was a break in all the whizzing, we crossed. At the door to the post office I stretched my arms back then said it. "Fulton's from Abbotscraig. Him and his family attacked a boy. Called Eldo. He got jailed for it. Fulton's in Polmont now, a prison for young folk. His so-called mates have all abandoned him."

"Why the hell are you sending him parcels?"

"I hated myself, but he picked me. He's an arsehole. But I owe him."

In the post office I weighed his parcel and filled the form then got my purse out and paid. Outside, the street was quiet and you heard our work shoes scuff for a minute or two. Eventually Robyn goes, "You know, I think a lot of people have someone like this in their lives, from their childhood."

"Sixteen's not a child. Not in my bit of Fife."

Outside the subway station I spun and fired my empty tin into a bin. Then something in my belly made me turn again and when I looked up there was a face I knew, by the entrance.

I pulled Robyn over. "You head in. I'll catch you up?"

"Okey-doke."

Donna stepped out into the sun. "Hello, stranger." She was shielding her eyes. Her hair was curled. She seemed a lot shorter.

"He's not ill, is he?" I glanced up over her shoulder. "Is he here?"

"No. And he's not sick. But he's very miserable!"

"My job's to keep him smiling, is it?" People were moving around us and down into the subway. She didn't speak. I goes, "How's Jumpy?"

She laughed. "Jumpy's doing fine." She scrunched her hair up with her fingers, then flicked it. "How is Cora doing?"

"Well right now I need to get back to work."

She twiddled her handbag strap. "I thought me and you could have a chat?"

"I'm nearly eighteen, Donna. I'm fine."

"You don't look well."

I breathed in slowly. "I'm tired, aye. But my life is all right, actually."

"I don't believe you."

"You don't believe I'm able to move on. I am. I don't need anyone's help."

"Five minutes. Please?"

I walked behind her through the back lane and up across the car park and we sat randomly on the steps of one of the old uni buildings, with the flowers all around.

She brushed her hands together. "Nice bit, this."

"I live way down the road." I started plucking at leaves through the railings. "How did you know I worked round here?"

"Everyone knows the Sclaters. It's Abbotscraig—someone's always got the latest goss on Pauline. And her pals." She chuckled like something was funny. "How are you finding things anyway?"

I looked at the sky. "It's normally raining. And, I dunno. Truthfully some days I wish I was back in school. Timetable days. Daydreaming. Easy."

"It'll take time. It's a big city. This was your dream." She put her eyebrows up. "I bet you've a lovely wee place. It'd be great to see it, so I could tell him you're doing okay."

"Mentions me, does he?"

"I'm sick of listening to him!" She laughed again. "Cora, I'm not saying it's easy but someone has to make the first move. You know, just saying sorry to him would make you the bigger person."

I tore a tiny leaf in two, then tore the halves down more. "Apologize for being myself?" I stood straight up, then she did. "That's what you and him want. So I crashed a scrambler? Got drunk, made some decisions? Big whoop. It's who I am." I folded out my fingers in sequence to stop them doing a fist. "If you knew half of what he'd done you wouldn't be asking me to apologize."

I turned and had started crossing the empty road when I felt her grip my forearm. She birled me round to face her, exact same as Mr. Easthope would when I was singing to myself, cleaning the paintbrushes in art. I shrugged myself away. "Get your fucking hands off me."

"He's worried sick about you and you won't even listen! Please—"
She puffed her cheeks out and looked like she might greet. "Show me
where you're staying. Let me put his mind at ease."

"Who do you think you are, stalking me and groping me?"

"I'm sorry. Please."

I started down the slope. "I'm going back to work."

"He gave me this. For you."

When I turned she was holding a wee bag, the crappy fakey-velvet
pouch I kept my hoops in, about 1995. I took it and tipped it out in my
hand—a warm heap of twenty pences, some of them manky and some
of them glinting silver.

I felt a wee moment of zooming upward hot and dizzy, like my
body was dropping. I bit my bottom lip hard.

"He was adamant about those twenty pences."

"Ah, it's—me and my mam, we used to—" I started gathering the
coins back into the pouch.

"He'd love you to ring him."

I put the pouch in my coat pocket. "And apologize."

"Just speak to him."

"Bye, Donna."

I walked down the hill, saying to myself over and over, *Fuck her,
Cora, don't look back*. Ten steps then fifteen steps and I was nearly
across the car park when I could not help my nosey wee arse and I
turned. She was stood exactly like I left her but with her hands in her
pockets and her head tilted back staring right up.

Seeing her there in her smart peachy thirty-something outfit,
I knew, I could picture so clearly her going back—jogging down
Weavers Row, slicing up sponge cake. Him on the step hearing the
whole lot word for word. About Pauline's wee raging pal. Then one
day soon me coming out on lunch again and it being Gunner stood
there, not her.

"Donna." She lowered her head from the sky. I pointed in the direction of the Saver Local and raised my voice. "I'm finishing at five. Be outside the front door."

Her face went all reasonable. "Thank you."

"You can see it once and tell him about it. Then you can both leave me alone forever."

At five the sky had changed. The walk down Byres Road was mainly in silence then at the benches outside Wullie's we stopped. There was only one old boy asleep under a sheet of card on the far bench, but I still saw her grip her handbag. I pointed at my building then stood and watched her eyes go wide as she traced the black smoke stripes from the shutter up toward my window. "Pauline says there's no real structural damage," I goes. "Wullie explained it all."

Upstair in the noise of the hall I showed her the payphone and the fire extinguisher and the framed letter from the council about Legionnaires' disease. I took her straight up and made her a cup of tea in the top kitchen then when we came back down I led her straight to Pauline's door. I used my spare key and did my bashful lassie face and says, "It's really not that nice," and then opened.

Right away Donna's head was going like an owl on a documentary. It was pure relief that Pauline wasn't there, but she'd left her curtains open and her tulip-pattern bedspread all neatly done and the nice-color sheets were across the cushionless settee and the sun was over everything. There was some underwear and unwashed mugs and a family-sized Wotsits bag spilt in the corner, but it all just added I felt to the unmistakable Cora-ness. Donna's face softened a bit. "Oh. This is not bad at all."

I jumped bum-first back onto Pauline's bed and bounced all fun and natural like it was mine. "That settee's ancient. Was here when I took the room. I had to chuck the cushions because they were reeking."

"You've made it really nice with those sheets."

"Thanks." There was a silence as she kept looking casually round. A dog started yowling upstair.

Then she power walked over to the tall cream wardrobe by the window and swung it open. She grabbed out a cheetah-print fur coat and held it in front of her and did a comedy wiggle at me. "Ooh!" Then she pulled out this mad torn-apart babydoll dress with a joined-on latex bralette and held that up too. "Your tastes have fairly changed!"

"I got that in—"

"No you never!" She was laughing now. She started flicking through the other clothes. "This is Pauline's stuff. Pauline's room. Ha! Look at this." She pulled a faded blue T-shirt out and held it up. There was a logo of a dove wearing a helmet and round that it said *ABBOTSCRAIG SURVIVORS CIRCLE—ABSEILING CHALLENGE 1994*. I thought of Pauline's days on the beach making up poems about hairy rope. "You never said you were in rehab, Cora?" I closed my eyes. "Spoon-burners' Circle. They were in the *Abbotscraig Herald* wearing these. Anyway, up you get. Time for a look at your room."

I shuffled up slowly. "How did you know?"

"From everything Gunner's told me it just seemed way too tidy."

Across the hallway I let her in without saying a thing. On the other side of the room the window showed the reflection of the door going back then the two of us in the wide doorway—I was nearly taller than her now. There was no emotion in me, just the usual feeling of wanting to be alone.

She tiptoed in looking down as if the lino was red hot. It was a minute before she spoke. "Love. I don't—oh, pet—"

The smell was moisturizer and crisps so it wasn't as bad as it could have been but I squeezed between the fridges and pulled the window up anyway. Engine sounds started and the shouts from down on the benches got bigger. I took the twenty pences out of my coat and put them on my tidy tray, then took my coat off.

I threw myself down on my four-poster and leaned sideways on my elbow, grinning. "You can ask Gunner if he ever read *Stig of the Dump*. That's me now."

"Cora." Slamming and screaming started upstair and she looked at the ceiling. "Like, I get it. When you come in here and lock that door behind you it must feel like—"

"There's no lock." I did a wee smug mouth. "I wedge it closed with one of the café chairs."

She looked behind her at the door. "Brilliant. Well, I get it. I know having your own place must feel like independence. But this?" She did a big soap-opera gob. "This building—it's basically a shooting gallery."

I flopped back and laughed. "Fuck sake. Away back to your tea-pots, Donna."

"I'm serious!"

"Do you not think I've got my mam clear in my ear every day? I know exactly how bad it looks. I don't need your moaning."

She stood there, not moving, not speaking. I jumped up. "The fridges are not ideal. But hey—" I bent down and plugged the big wide one in. There was a rumble then the humming started. I hopped twice. "Can you feel that?"

"The floor's trembling."

"See when you're sleeping, that's amazing." I switched the 7UP one on and watched Donna's wee appalled face go Martian green. "I keep my clothes in this one. I put both fridges on at night because the sound's soothing and I don't pay electric anyway. My clothes are cold in the morning. I always said to myself, *Cora, that's going to be amazing in the summer!*" I laughed. She was staring at me like I was a halfwit. I walked next to the 7UP fridge and stood all straight, comparing my height with it. "Tell Gunner I sleep standing up in here." I went to open the door. "Look."

"Cora—"

I laughed. "Kidding."

She looked down and bit her thumbnail and started moody scuffs with her plimsoll. "I'm supposed to tell him you're living in a store-room?"

"Tell him I'm living in a seedy Partick gangster hotbed and if he comes here snooping there will be some big bastard waiting to shank out his other eye."

There were no laughs off her. She was looking traumatized and I hadn't even told her yet that a pensioner had died face down on the section of floor she was standing on. Or that my boombox was haunted. Then she started actually crying.

I rolled my eyes and did a big cheek-puff but deep down I felt boaky right away because how the fuck did you stop an adult bawling? It wasn't like with babies where you could give them a spoon to chew or put them in a cupboard. And she really did look upset. I stood up and put my arms around her and she kept sniveling for ages and didn't say a thing.

When I was wee my mam always said Glasgow was rough and full of criminals—all pishpuddles and kids with blades. I was picturing fancy houses and six-foot women who looked like they'd come alive off the side of a hair-dye packet but who might still be pals with you. In the end it was wet streets and wet bricks and wet slates and me in the middle trying with everything I had to look like I was enjoying it. To believe it was sorting me. Because if Glasgow didn't work, then what?

I says, "Glasgow's not maybe what I thought. I dunno how long all this will last, but it's not forever. I'm saving for my next place. Tell him that. The next place will be better."

She was wiping her face with her anorak sleeve. "I worry about him. He works all hours and when I speak to him he's chirpy but then every conversation turns to you. He's worried he didn't do enough, those years you had together. He's full of questions about you. I don't know what I'm going to tell him."

"Hang on a sec."

I bent down and lifted the settee cushion on my wee upside-down table bed and got the blue card folder out that I kept my crumpled papers in. I opened it and raked through some pay slips then took out the printouts Samantha gave me in 1994.

The sheets were folded into a soft gray grubby rectangle that curved still where it had lived in my jeans pocket against my thigh. On the back you could see my impatient ballpoint scribbles from all the sad years.

I concentrated to stop the trembles and shoved it at her. "Take that back for him."

"A letter?"

"Printouts. About hyperactivity. I got given it years ago and I never showed him, but when he reads it—I dunno. He'll know."

She rubbed her snottery nose. "They thought you were hyperactive?"

"I am." The big fridge started doing its random rattling where the top glass panel was loose, noises that would have done my tits in once but that were now just part of something that was mine.

"Have you seen someone about it?"

"I've got ways of coping."

She nodded, softly. I could tell she had sensed what I wanted her to sense. She put her hand on my shoulder. "You'll probably be hungry for your dinner. Thanks for this."

Out on the landing she raised her voice over the techno pumping down the stair. "Can I say something?"

"Quickly."

"You and him—necessity brought you together and necessity never feels right." She looked at her feet. "After everything, wouldn't it be nice if you could meet up again as older people who had been through things together, and build something brand new? Without the old feelings."

I tugged at my left earlobe a bit then moved past her and down the stair. I spoke over my shoulder. "We're not sharing a house now. There's no law linking me and him. There's nothing linking us at all apart from a few boring stories about my dead mam."

At the front door she turned to me again. Her ruined mascara had printed thundery wee horizons below her eyes. "You can give him a visit without getting stuck there." She stroked my shoulder again. "He's a good man. He cares about you." I lifted her hand off and did my smile. I clacked the big front door open and daylight broke in. I says, "I'm never going back."

29

Gerald came toward me with a beer in his hand. He was wearing a Thin Lizzy T-shirt with jeans and flip-flops. I knew it was Gerald because he had the same lips and nose as Pauline and she always called her da a short-arse and this guy was tiny.

"You must be the Muircross lassie?"

"Cora." I took a drink of my beer and stuck my other hand out.

He shook it. "Nice to finally meet you. Pauline's aye fond of you. She's told me loads. I'm Gerald, by the way."

"I know. Same. I mean, she's told me about you. Happy Birthday!" His hand wasn't sweaty so I gave him a hug. "You're looking great."

Gerald was odd-looking but you could tell he was lovely just from how he spoke—he took a wee smiley second to think before talking and the sides of his eyes went creased but not in the sleekit way. You knew he had slept in a few doorways over the years and it made me like him even more.

"Och, I'm amazed I'm alive!" He took a drink. "You're looking tremendous yourself, darling."

"Pauline was supposed to cut my hair this morning, but she slept in."

"She'll have nagged you to come, no doubt!"

Work had been mental all week but I felt better now I was here. It was the first real warmish day of the year and I was wearing my jelly sandals and a vest and denim shorts with nothing in the pockets but a

ten-pound note and the wee bag of twenty pences that I couldn't not
carry round. I really didn't want to come but I'd says to myself that I
had to do more Glasgow things outside my wee room. *Cora, this was
your dream.*

Gerald lived in Whiteinch, in a tenement above a row of shops, but
without the smoke stripes. At the back there were squared-off gardens
with washing lines and in the middle a wee walled area with vegetables
growing and grass and a shed and hanging things that jingled when the
wind blew. A table had been set up in there with beers on it. Behind
the barbecue someone had painted *HAPPY BIRTHDAY GERONIMO
SCLATER* on a big splintery sheet of wood.

When we'd first arrived Pauline had taken me round introducing
me to loads of her da's pals, mainly dry-skin folk in Jesus shoes. I just
smiled and did my *hiya*s. Pauline had walked off after that—someone
had told her Vicki wasn't coming and I could tell she was upset.

Gerald was looking about. I says to him, "It's a lovely bit you've got."

"I've been here years. There's a right few muesli munchers now
but I still see my old muckers." He pointed at the barbecue, where
Pauline and another man were moving chicken around. "Kenneth runs
the garden, he's our Community Navigator. But everyone chips in. It's
his Cajun drumsticks you're smelling!"

"Nice."

"Listen, did Pauline show you round? Come on, I'll take you."

Gerald's place was a bedsit smaller than Pauline's. He had a big
neatly made double bed, rugs round the floor, a wee fridge in the corner. On top of that was a bowl of bananas and a *Jurassic Park* mug full
of plastic-handled forks and spoons. It wasn't a place women had been
but you couldn't call it creepy.

At one side of his telly was a pile of photo albums with a lamp on
top, then behind it rows of tapes and records and stacks of labeled
VHS tapes. Hung round the walls were framed photos and taped-up
flyers saying stuff about *Jobs* and *Bailiffs* and *Break the Tory Poll Tax*.

"You'll have to not mind the·chaos, darling. I love my guitars." He picked one out of the mess of cables in the corner and did a twang. "I record my songs in here. I've got a portable four-track and a drum machine."

I smiled at him. He was a nice guy but he did remind you of a goblin. You probably weren't going to get wee lassies writing *Gerald* in a heart on the inside of their pencil case.

There was an old photo of a boxer next to some concert tickets. I goes, "Gerald, is that your da? Pauline was telling me about him! Frank?"

"My da?" He smiled and put the guitar down then walked over to the photo. "That's Benny Lynch, love."

"Pauline told me your da was a champion. That he got called the Scorpion, like her tattoo?"

"My da messed about and took a few tankings and that was that. He worked most his life as a driver for Duncan's Lemonade."

"So why did he get called the Scorpion?"

"He didn't!" He screwed his face up and chuckled as he swigged his beer.

I felt my face going pink and I started looking round because I didn't know what to say. Sitting on a doily on top of the brown telly there was a framed photo of Gerald with a lassie and a woman on a beach. I goes, "Is that you on holiday?"

"Lossiemouth." He handed it to me. "1986. The last time we got away the three of us. The bairn was fourteen then." Pauline had big boots and turned-up jeans and an army coat and her hair in a quiff. She looked like a beautiful boy. It made me nearly want to greet when I thought about myself at fourteen, on the Causey, trying to suck up to Jo. "Pauline loves a story. She gets carried away, her thinking gets messed up. Losing a mam will do that to a girl."

I looked back at the photo. Pauline and her mam, Janey, were holding hands and squinting at the wind and they looked almost the same.

I could feel my heart reminding me of things in the silence so I smiled and spoke. "You've got a lot of videos!"

"Music, darling. Concerts. I'm a collector. Here, look at this." He slipped a tape from the middle of a stack and clacked it into his video player, then flicked the telly on. "I was in a band once, The Crystal Clearing. We put out two singles." In a second or two some wobbly old footage started. "That's me on the bass guitar. 1984. This was our biggest gig, an afternoon fundraiser on the drying green up at the Cruzie flats. We were quite popular, you see. Good following, locally."

The band were playing funky music on a wee scaffold stage in front of high-rise buildings. Gerald had a curly mullet and tight white football shorts and a shirt like a retirement home curtain. The sun was bright and permy women in sleeveless T-shirts were twirling toddlers round the grass. Dogs were in the audience too.

"Those flats are all gone now, so they are. Mold. Mice and spiders. Polystyrene tiles. Terrible state they were in." He crouched beside the telly and pointed. "Pauline was born in the stairwell of that one there, Alyth Tower. Four a.m., 29 January 1972. The New Seekers were number one. Janey loved The New Seekers."

The video cut to a close-up of the singer, dancing like an octopus in a fishing net. "Born in a stairwell?" I goes. "That's so cool."

"I never saw so much blood, poor wee thing. We were halfway out but the ambulance couldn't get to us that day, because of the snow. I held her. I was a bundle of nerves. You know, thinking back I wonder if all her problems started with the way she arrived."

The only thing I knew about my own birth was that my head was huge and they needed tongs to pull me out. I could see Gerald's room was like a weird museum of himself and I started to think he might greet. "Will we go and see if those Cajun drumsticks are ready?"

Walking back the path to the barbecue I thought of things I could keep asking because I knew the video had changed Gerald's mood. "Did you do any other jobs then?"

"I ran an ice cream van once, when Pauline was a kid. She loved the broken cones."

"Oh, wow! Did you ever eat the Mr. Whippy straight out the machine?"

He laughed. "Not exactly." As we went through the gate he lifted the Thin Lizzy shirt with both hands. There was a scar like a line of ham-color toothpaste right across his gray furry chest. "Samurai sword. I got moved off my route by one of the gangs. See, there weren't many shops on those estates. The ice cream vans were basically mobile gold mines."

When Pauline saw us she ran over with her beer, all shiny-faced. "You better not be stripping off for my mate." She glugged from her bottle.

He laughed and sat down on one of the plastic chairs. "Those days are over!"

In one movement she sat down on his knee then put her arm around him and did a long childish kiss on his forehead. He smiled and she lay back all over him in that normal loving way you probably saw all girls do with their das.

"So did you like your tapes?"

"I loved my tapes, darling." He ruffled her bowl cut at the front. "But how are you affording all that? There was no need."

"I still get my brew, Da. I applied for the New Deal thing like you said, but it's twenty-four and under. I'm officially not a young person now!"

He goes, "Cora would qualify?"

Hearing my name seemed to wake me out of something I didn't know I was in and there was a sudden horrible exhausted feeling. Gerald had his arms tight round his daughter now with one thumb in the belt loop of her shorts. "I work in a Saver Local," I says, to my sandals.

He spoke to Pauline again like I wasn't there. "Take them for every penny you're entitled to, darling."

Then Pauline goes, "Cora helped pick your tapes, Da!"

I smiled. "I'll get us food."

Over by the table I arranged some salad round the three paper plates, then Kenneth piled the chicken onto each one while I nodded as if I was interested in his story about where the charcoal came from. The relief of getting Pauline and her da out of my sight for just a minute made me want to grab four beers and down them at once, but I cheerily picked up forks and napkins instead. Then I breathed in and smiled more and walked back toward them with my footsteps going in time with my pulse.

Pauline sat up straight. "Cheers, chick." I gave Gerald his plate then got a second white plastic chair for Pauline and made her sit in it.

Gerald bit some chicken. "I'm sorry it's all a bit dead the now, Cora, just us fuddy-duddies! Tam-the-Bam's throwing me a mad one later, up at his place. I hope you'll come?" I smiled like it was okay, like I had never thought there would be young folk here anyway. He finished his beer and smiled like he was back to his old self. "Here, I was reminding Pauline about wee Harold."

Pauline thumped his shoulder. "Daaaa!"

"Now, Cora, she'll not mind me saying this, because well, look at the beautiful, smart specimen she's grown into, but can you believe that my daughter Pauline Sclater never had any pals at school?"

"Actually, Claire Ferg—"

"Broke my heart, so it did. So I bought her a cockatiel."

I could feel my vest itching me at the armpits. I needed the loo. I wriggled a bit and watched Pauline staring into Gerald's crinkly eyes. Her neck was sunburned a bit and the Scorpion looked pinkish—it was weird to be sat smiling away like this, as if the truth about things didn't matter.

"Aye well," Gerald goes, "we fed it all sorts. Seeds and nuts and blocks of paste and Wispa bars. Treated Harold like a tiny yellow prince. He would cheep along to Luke Kelly and dance on her wrist while we watched *Top of the Pops*. Anyway, one day we decided to let him out the window. Wee arsehole flew over the road onto the roof of the warehouse opposite and just sat there. Sat there taunting us!"

Pauline was giggling, trying to keep lettuce in her mouth with her fingers. "He was there for two weeks!"

"Chilling out, cleaning his wings, watching us. Wee dignified head scanning this way and that. Smug-looking chirpy wee shite." I kept smiling. "Then poof! He vanished! Broke my heart, because this one here went back to square one." He turned to her. "School was a nightmare, wasn't it?"

She chucked her plate in the grass then wiped her hands on her skinny legs. "I had you and mam."

"I've loads of photos of Harold and you up in the photo albums. I should get them down and show your pal."

Pauline looked at me. I was trying to tongue some of the dry Cajun spice powder off the roof of my mouth and I wondered if I should stop. She goes, "Cora, he is never out of his fucking photo albums!"

They both started doing big laughs. I downed my beer, then without really thinking I stood up. "I'll be back in a minute or two," I says.

I came out the gate and walked the back path where Pauline and me had come in. More cars were going by on the main street now, and boys were drinking outside a newsagent. I had no clue where I was going but my legs were moving quick and I needed to leave.

Over the road I counted the street-light poles as I walked then ducked into the big park. The sky was wider in there and you could smell the whole sunny day off the grass. I had that urgency and there were boys in groups giving me snake eyes so I turned onto a path that went behind a bowling club then along the back of a DIY center car park, randomly.

Why did you need to know about your own birth anyway? You took it for granted that there would always be someone to ask. You never expected there not to be a person with a few total beamer sentences for you about when you were just tiny.

I walked for maybe ten minutes in a loop telling myself bad things about me and Gunner and just enjoying it. I banged my hand along the flaky railings and karate-chopped the branches poking through and then I crossed back into the park. Minute by minute it seemed to get darker and I got nervous about the amount of boys huddled under the trees. I told myself, *Cora, you're from Muircross for fuck sake*, but I also really needed the toilet so I started walking toward Gerald's row of shops.

In the wee garden, the barbecue was out. The group was thinner and Gerald had gone. A weird, tall dog had arrived and a man in thick specs was fiddling with a speaker, trying to get tunes going. Pauline was sat by the shed in someone else's jumper, drunkenly telling a story to a circle of folk who were stood round chuckling and flapping at flies.

Gunner wasn't my da, but he'd been there. Before Fulton and the cousin-fucker and Dan and the scrambler and that freezing house. Back when my mam was here. He was the link to all that.

I could hardly think straight from how much I needed to go. Kenneth was over at the speaker now, bent down helping the specs man. I interrupted them. "Sorry, is there a loo I can use?"

"Go upstair and beyond Gerald's room, end of the corridor, doll."

In the toilet I sat down and pished with weird tears nearly starting. As I stood up and wiped I heard spec man's muffled techno starting in the garden. I washed my hands then walked back along the corridor looking down at carpet and thinking to myself how much of a good hoover it needed.

Then as I passed I noticed Gerald's door slightly open, like we'd left it. There wasn't even a question in my mind—I would sit down shivery on his big bed and be alone and look through those photo albums in my own time. To see the old Pauline. To see Janey, and Geronimo. And

Harold. To work out how a family linked together and to see what led to what and when. To see if anything Pauline had said to me was true.

I pushed the door just a gentle silent touch and then I stopped my breaths because there was Gerald actually in there.

He was facing away from me, leaning sideways on the neatly made bed, with his leg crossed over, topless in the lamplight. There were small moles smeared round his back like crumbs of sat-on chocolate on a pale clean sheet. The sole of his foot was orangey-yellow. He was breathing hard and he didn't look round because there was a syringe in his hand and he was plunging dark liquid into his shin. My eyes went soft, like they always did when I didn't want to see.

I stepped back without touching the door again and took the stairs with my head down. I couldn't go back to smiling in front of Pauline so out on the dusky path I stood for a minute, alone and apart from almost everything, looking up the back of the tenement at all the lights in the different-size windows, at the colors the curtains made.

Over the roof the sky was deep blue and the moon had put a tiny sheen across everything. I closed my eyes. I could hear a tumble dryer stop and start, plates being stacked, traffic, again, and even through the thump of the techno behind me in the garden I could still pick out the yelp of Pauline's laughter. And then because I felt like I had no other choice, I ran.

pulled out the wee fakey-velvet pouch and emptied it into my palm. The twenty pences were warm from my pocket.

It was good to be out of breath and achy-footed under a street light, alone on a warmish evening. To be in a wee torn-off corner of the world where you've no real idea where you are, to have nobody, to feel things falling apart.

I'd been running for maybe ten minutes when I saw the phone box. I opened the door and smelled that smell then I hobbled in and jangled up the twenty pences and slid five in the slot and dialed before I could stop myself.

After a wee minute the ringing stopped. "Hello?"

His voice was flat but it weakened me right away. It was like the air had changed around me.

"It's Cora."

I squished the earpiece onto my lug so I could nearly hear him breathing. Everything in me stopped. When he spoke his voice hadn't changed. "How you keeping, chief?"

"Oh, fine! How are you keeping? Thanks for the twenty pences!" I closed my eyes because of the beamer adult voice I was trying to do.

"Aye, good. And that's okay."

There was no excitement from him at all and it made me think that Donna was lying. I goes, "Thanks for my Walkman. I finally took it out of the box. When I settled in. Pauline's given me tapes. I use it every day. I should have opened it sooner. It must have cost—I'm sorry."

"That's all right."

I turned my back to the phone and looked out down the road. A peeled-off poster was covering most of the view and someone called *NICOLE* had scraped her name in jaggy skeleton letters through the streaks of white paper.

"Well I'm skint. I am fine, though. I've got a part-time job. Maybe another coming soon! I've got a pal called Robyn. I make your chicken soup spaghetti sometimes, when I can afford the soup and the kitchen doesn't have a party in it. My manager Graham's an arse. What else?"

I could hardly tell him the truth. I trudge the ten-minute walk to work and back. My fingertips go numb from stacking frozen food. I shower. I eat. I see Pauline sometimes, but mainly she's with pals or men. I sit in my room listening to other people's fun through the ceiling. I close my eyes and see my dreams drop apart like a craply made snowball.

What did I really have to tell him? That my pal's da's a dirty junkie, but he's still a da to my pal? I do miss you now and then but I don't want to feel it and I can't admit it? That I used to hate my mam telling all those stupid stories but I realized now that being linked to people who remembered all the old versions of you was what living was actually about?

"Well my hip hurts still. Off the scrambler. That's me an old waddler and I'm not even eighteen yet."

Cars pulled into the petrol station next to the box. He laughed. "You liking it there then? It's nice hearing from you, lass."

I closed my eyes. It was amazing how much angry energy I got from believing that nobody cared. I sometimes loved how hating myself felt, but nothing felt like the rush of excitement and warmness I got from hearing those words. "Glasgow's just a load of buildings next to one another," I goes.

He laughed. I rolled my lips together for a second. Weird moss was growing round the rubber that held the window in the door and I started scraping it up with the corner of one of my coins. Then I went, "I spoke to Donna. You'll know. She talks sense sometimes. I miss you."

"I miss you too. House is like a graveyard."

"My house is a right midden. As my mam would say."

"You coping?"

"I don't know. I still feel like a leech. I'm tired of being stuck to the side of someone else."

"There's nothing wrong with accepting help."

I looked down again. "Well I used the scrambler money to survive before the job. It felt like my rainy-day money." I did a crap laugh. "There's been loads of rainy days."

"You know, I got thirty quid for that bike. I made up the rest of the one-fifty myself. I was raging but I was worried you'd actually get up and go. Disappear forever. And then you did, right enough."

"Not forever."

"All I've ever wanted is to help you." He did a big breathe-in. "You turned me into a softie."

I felt relief rushing over me like just-right bathwater. I says, "That's maybe not how I'd describe you."

He laughed then stopped. "Donna's gave me these papers of yours."

"That's me on there."

"To the letter, lass." There was silence. I could hear our telly in our old living room behind him—a comedian finishing a joke, then clapping. Then he goes, "So Glasgow's treating you well, is it?"

I looked at my feet to try and make the words come. Glasgow was going to be forever. It would be like magic, like a big car wash for my brain and my heart. It was the dream. But I changed my dreams like TV channels and sometimes when I got finished with all the thinking and the crying I wasn't sure what I wanted at all. That was part of the reason I was stood in this phone box. Because things weren't solved like I thought they were.

"Glasgow's Glasgow."

"Look, why don't you come for a visit? I've got news. Donna didn't go through there creeping for the good of her health, eh."

"I don't think so."

"What was it you screamed at me that day, about the house? *A big box of darkness*?" He laughed. "Come on. Come for a night in the big box of darkness, stay over. I want to speak to you face to face. Your room's not changed."

"Have you kept it all perfect like a wee tragic museum to me?"

"Weep most nights in there, like."

"Well I sometimes wear your fleece."

"Ach, hardly the same."

An ambulance flew by with its big waily siren ribboning in and out of all the buildings and lampposts and its light flashing my stubbly bare shins blue. I says, "You remember the fridge?" I put my last coin in. "Our old fridge. You punched it."

"What about it?"

"I used to spell words out for my mam on it, swearwords, with the magnets. High up where she couldn't reach to rearrange them."

He laughed. "Wee ratbag."

"I was remembering, that's all. But I think I've maybe said enough. This soppy shite is making me ill. And I'm down to my last coin."

"Think about coming through. Hey, we could even give her a wee visit? If you're ready."

"What's this news? It's not about my mam?"

"It's a happy thing, it's not—"

And then the money ran out and the line went dead. I clacked the handset back and suddenly the road and the petrol station started up again, like the world had waited on me finishing.

I looked down at the coiling silver cable and wondered if any of my words might be in there—gathered together in tiny tangles, mixed with the things that other people had tried to say.

There was a shooting pain in my hip. I looked down at my feet and did some scissor movements with my legs. Wee plants were sprouting up, at the bit where the back wall of the phone box went into the ground.

Imagine you're a sexy wee delicate plant breaking through for the first time. You could be growing anywhere in the world, and you twiddle your petally head round for a look and realize you're stuck for life growing in a crack in the tarmac in Whiteinch. Peeping out of the bit where the wires off a phone box go underground.

I creaked the door open and walked. Me and him were from the same square mile. Gunner had that normal Muircross voice you'd hear in any chip shop or police station waiting room, one my mam would know anywhere, but there was a softness in it when he spoke to me and that seemed suddenly precious. I'd never noticed it back then but I noticed it now. I couldn't stop trying to replay everything in my head.

I'd got to a big block of dark flats a bit beyond the petrol station when I decided to turn around. I crossed the forecourt and took the little path through the square of park for a shortcut and went back into the phone box.

I dialed the operator. Usually when it was ringing was the time I stood there feeling impatient with my mind wandering. I wondered what would happen to all the wee plants in here if someone shoved a tray of fireworks in and lit them.

The operator picked up and I spoke. "I need to make a reverse charge call."

It was a woman's voice. "Which number please?"

I said the number, then I goes, "Just tell her it's Cora Mowat and there's been an emotional crisis."

There was a silent pause and then the operator goes all serious, "Hold the line."

I heard the other phone ring and a voice going, *"Hello."* Then the lady operator says, "*I have a Cora Mowat on the line. There has been an emotional crisis. Do you accept the charges?*"

I had to hold the handset away because of my giggling. You actually heard some humor in the operator's voice too. Then I heard the wee puzzled voice going, "*Yes, okay.*"

"*I am connecting the call.*"

Then Robyn went, "Cora?"

"I'll pay you back for this. I'll be quick. I'm stood here in some random bit wearing a vest and silly wee shorts and jelly sandals freezing my arse off. It's a clear and genuine emergency."

"What the fuck has got into you?"

"Four and a half warm bottled beers, two ibuprofen, some dry chicken drumsticks, some sunshine. A weird discovery. And a phone call with my stepda!"

"Oh wow. You did it? So sensible. You can't turn your back on everything."

"I'll explain some other time, I'm really just ringing to say *yes*! To the shift. To the job. I'm having a grown-up moment. So I thought I better grab it."

"Brilliant. Look, I'll go with you. It will be easy. Don't worry."

"I'm hanging up now because I don't want to cost you a fortune, Robyn. I just needed to tell you, tonight. Right now. While I was still feeling good about me."

31

Our wee horrendous square of back garden was separated from the lane behind Wullie's by a high stone wall. It was a bright afternoon and the grass was glinting with empties from last night. I'd wetted my hair and it felt like ice in the breeze.

I kicked some bottles to make a space then stabbed the kitchen chair down into the ground. Pauline had her hood up, making her face look paler, and I was wrapped in the big scratchy orange towel Gunner had got me on our third week in Abbotscraig.

Pauline and me had hardly spoken since the barbecue, so I'd knocked on her door and refused to move until she agreed to do my hair. It was Tuesday and Robyn had set up my babysitting trial for later—if the hair was a fuck-up I could tell myself I didn't even want those stupid shifts anyway.

Pauline walked behind me with the big ancient scissors flashing. It was only when I couldn't see her that the nerves kicked in. "You do realize I am about to sit still for ten whole minutes? It's a big deal!"

She flicked her fringe once sideways and laughed. She rolled her sleeves up. "Chin length? You sure?"

"Make it dramatic. Don't be worrying, you should have seen some of the haircuts my mam used to give me." She started running her fingers through my hair. I did my brightest voice. "Hey, you ever have nits when you were wee?"

"'Course."

"There was this girl at my Muircross school, right, Lucy Deas. Everyone called her Lucy Peas. It ground her down. Poor cow. She did this miserable devastating face every time she heard her own name."

I felt gentle little pricking scalp pains as Pauline bunched the hair tight, then a light crispy crumping sound as the scissors snipped. I couldn't wipe my smile off. Haircuts were such an easy way to feel good.

"Oh fuck," she whispers, like she'd made a mistake.

"Shut up. Anyway, Lucy Peas got nits but her mam refused to put chemicals on them. You know when you buy the comb set you also get a wee bottle of acidy stuff that melts them?"

She did another careful snip. "Aye."

"Lucy Peas's mam was a mad hippy. She said she was going to find a humane way to catch the nits then release them somewhere."

She laughed. "Amazing."

"I always wondered where. Into a tree? Onto another head? In the end her mam found a recipe in *Woman's Own* for homemade headlice paste. When I got nits three weeks later I wanted my mam to try the special paste on me."

She was concentrating close to my head. "Did your mam make it?"

"Tea tree oil! Do you think I'm made of money?"

"I think there's still some in here, you know."

I laughed and there was another snip. I looked down at the soggy frayed-out brown clump of hair separating in the grass and wondered which days of my life it had grown in.

"Sit straighter," Pauline went. Then a silence. Normally when you finished telling Pauline a story she'd be straight off on one of her own.

"You okay?"

She moved in front of me, stood with her legs on either side of mine. "I'm just concentrating." I shut my eyes a little but I could still see—her lilac elbows, the blank perfect skin round her biceps. She did two teeny snips and I smelled her biscuit breath.

"I'm sorry I disappeared. At your da's." Out in the lane two kids ran past, singing and shouting. "I had something I needed to do there and then, and when I feel like that there's not much I can do about it."

"It's all right. I stayed over."

"How was he?"

"Fine."

There was nothing in her voice. I was picking my thumb. "I mean, with his present and stuff?"

"Oh, great. He added the tapes to his big pile. Let's hope he actually listens to them, one day." I felt her step back. "Okay, now. I'll even it all up as best I can. You don't mind it a bit choppy?"

She did three confident snips, and I could almost sense a tiny pain in each root as she did. Then two long, slow snips, and I felt the weather on my neck.

"That's you done." She lifted the orange towel and flapped wee bits of hair into the wind. I felt her pull it back at both sides then she wrapped the towel over into a turban. "I wonder what these folk will say when they see their new babysitter has had her head in the lawnmower?"

"Got all my best lies ready."

The couple Robyn babysat for were called Judith and Craig and they lived toward Anniesland on the Botanic Gardens side, in amongst all the big posh trees. I met Robyn by the gates and watched her eyes go wide for a split second when she saw the hair. I shook it a wee bit. I says, "I needed a change."

Their house was a big hefty stand-alone thing set back from the road with two gleamy cars in front. There were no weeds coming through on the drive and the gravel was flat and when you put your footprint in it you wanted not to exist.

Robyn pressed the doorbell while I checked myself in the polished metal around it. Then the huge door opened and a man was there, youngish with nearly black hair, dressed like an expert on telly you'd see walking over a field explaining things.

"Robs! Looking fantastic." He stepped forward and gave her a hug. Then he looked at me. "And you must be Cora."

He was grinning like he'd won me in a raffle. I nodded quick like I was answering yes to an actual question, then stopped and my cheeks went hot. He put his hand out and I shook it. I couldn't stop picturing my own hair.

I goes, "Pleased to meet you, Mr.—"

"—Anderson. But I'm plain old *Craig* round here!"

When I was wee, Fiona always loved using the word *prat*. To me it always seemed weird and fake and English but suddenly stood in front of this *plain old Craig* I realized I probably never understood the word because I'd never met a real actual prat before.

Robyn had given me clothing tips but then gave up and brought a dress into work for me on the Monday—a vintage blue Laura Ashley prairie thing. I wore it bare-legged with my Golas, minimal eyeliner, hair side-parted and pinned up left and right with my mam's hair pins to try and make an actual style.

Craig and Robyn got on really well and he was sickeningly enthusiastic about everything, like it was Christmas, even when he was explaining to me where the stopcock was and how Alice liked her diluting juice. I just nodded and smiled.

The rooms were huge and the ceilings were high, and all the furniture looked solid and flat and shiny. They had paintings and a huge telly and a carpet so thick your feet bounced and sofas that just made you want to build a den.

Craig's wife appeared, in tight leggings and a gym top. Judith had glamorous red hair and big teeth and she was about Fiona's height. She stood the whole time with her hands on her hips and you could tell someone had suggested that to her. I shook her hand and she smiled like she had won me too.

The kids were called Marcus and Alice. They had been kept awake until I arrived so that we could be introduced. Judith goes, "Say hello to Co-ra!"

I tried not to cringe while they stood shoulder to shoulder in front of the big chunky-looking fireplace and said hello to me at the same time, like in a horror film. Then their da started up toward them with the usual kiddie-on stuff that I knew myself from being wee—*now you be good for Co-ra, now Co-ra knows what to watch for, Co-ra will be telling us if you've misbehaved.* I'd been in this house twenty minutes and I never wanted to hear these voices again.

The kids ran off upstair in their matching pajamas and then we ate. It was a bit like a job interview but I had to speak more—explaining myself and pretending to be pals with these very wealthy folk. It wasn't anywhere near as easy as Robyn had been making out, but then Robyn wasn't to know.

The kitchen was bigger than my Muircross house and the dining table was ten-foot and they used slippery-handled cutlery that made eating things hard. Craig had made paella. He wore an apron the whole time and Judith told him the rice was *superb* and then repeated over and over how good he was at cooking. There were things in it I didn't recognize but I forced them down. Through everything I just kept saying to myself, *Think of the money, Cora.*

My Auntie Janine's neighbor Rab once had a ferret called Paella and it had a hormone imbalance so it was mental and it bit folk. My Auntie Janine's neighbor got called Rabies Rab because of it. Rabies Rab and my Auntie Janine were shagging, my mam told me. Rabies Rab had a secondhand waterbed. It wasn't the time to mention all that but it made me smile inside to think it while I sat there chowing forkfuls of Craig's superb rice.

During the meal Robyn made jokes and told her stories. Judith and Craig asked about her parents in Germany and I saw how close they all were. Craig and Judith explained their marriage and their jobs—all about the shopping center Craig's company was building, their holiday in Crete, the easel Marcus won for coming second in an art prize. I wondered if Robyn had already heard it all. I felt grateful for her sitting there with me.

Everyone said their bit, except me, so when the natural gaps in the talking came they had questions—which school, what hobbies, *are you seeing anyone just now?*

What was I going to say? *No, but when I can't sleep my head sometimes cycles through the boys that turned me down at school. I send cassettes to my imprisoned ex. I'm almost an adult and I still have dreams about Gary Grieve. I'd dearly love to be a goddess for a boy but I'm currently sleeping on an upturned table?*

"Not at the moment, no."

Everything they asked was geared toward things I might do in their house. I skirted over most of my past like I'd learned from Pauline, but the more I spoke the more my accent started appearing, until I just stopped caring altogether.

It was during a story about me and Gunner and how he taught me about the birds that I must have said it, and Craig suddenly stopped. He had a half-eaten prawn in his mouth and when he said the name I saw it on his tongue. "You come from *Muircross?*"

"I do!" I says, grinning away with my heart going *uh-oh* under the fabric of Robyn's fancy dress. It would be typical me to fuck up a chance to get real money just because I couldn't stay concentrated and pretend.

Judith tilted her head sideways and did a huge smile. "You really don't seem that—"

Robyn leaned in. "Wait till you get to know her." And everyone laughed.

They knew a bit about it. Judith worked in an art gallery and one of the painters they knew had moved to Muircross to document the place. She spoke quick and did hand movements as she tried to get it through to me how important these paintings were. I just nodded and said *brilliant* and *incredible* and made it look like I found it all amazing too.

Then we ate really icy ice cream with no flavor in it and drank a tiny coffee. They tidied everything up and Judith loaded the dishwasher while telling me how to set the timers on the living room lamps. When Robyn left she hugged Judith and Craig really tightly so I hugged her as well, as if that was something we did every day too.

Judith and Craig put violin music on their space station stereo that came out of the sideboard and broadcast the sound right through the house. They went upstair while I sat on my hands and burped quietly and nervously to myself in front of a muted repeat of *Mr. Bean* on their colossal telly.

They both came back down looking swanky and smelling of hair mousse. Robyn had gone so it felt weirder but I grinned like it was Christmas and breathed deep and just goes, "You both look utterly incredible!" They smiled and flapped their hands and I kind of despised myself but I just kept grinning away.

"The kids are in bed," Judith goes, putting earrings in, fiddling with the remote to turn the violins off. "You won't get any bother from them. But we know Robyn has talked you through everything." They handed me a scrap of paper with a phone number for reaching them, and said it would be a late one, maybe two a.m. "Help yourself to *anything*!"

There was no handshake, no talk about money. They swung the big door closed and when it clicked shut an amazing silence started, a type I'd never felt before, and then the weird feelings came. First, that I was responsible for other humans that weren't my mam. Second, that it felt like I was being taken care of, by a building. Third, that I was getting money for sitting on my arse.

Like always when I was totally alone I started thinking about my mam. As I pulled her hair pins out and lined them up on the kitchen bench I wondered what she'd make of me being in a house like this. Judith and Craig had all sorts of fancy electric gadgets I wanted to try and I really wished my mam was there to see it. It wasn't long until I was feeling sad—I knew my mam would be ashamed that I wasn't already eating their food. I could hear her right in my lug. *Find the biscuits, Cora.*

I couldn't stop smiling as I tore apart Craig and Judith's big walk-in cupboard, looking for sugar. There were jars and boxes and containers with weird floating fruits, all types of pasta, tins from Spain, baskets of onions and potatoes. On one wall there was a huge wine rack with loads of stoory bottles. It was only when I was putting everything back that I spotted some sponge fingers in a cloudy plastic box. I knew them from home ec trifle, and I didn't like how dry they were, but they seemed like the only sweet thing in the entire house.

I climbed the stairs with the box, trying various light switches on each landing, squishing the carpet, stroking the walls, doing that usual silly thing of worrying how my mam would get up the stair if she were here. Then telling her mentally not to worry because I'll make a note of anything worth telling about, and we can talk again when I get back down.

The kids' rooms were on the first floor. You knew because the doors were open like Robyn had explained, and each one had a painted fin-gerprinty sign. I put my head round each door and both of them were already snoring. As I padded up on the bouncy carpet to the second floor I started wondering how much raking Robyn had done. She prob-ably knew every single one of their secrets. Did German people rake through other folks' stuff? It felt so Scottish to be scrabbling through someone else's onions looking for a custard cream.

The second floor was under the eaves and there was a huge bath-room there. I put the lights on, they were sparkly and pure white like lights in a cinema at the Pick n' Mix. On the left was a huge stone basin, with a big mirror behind it on the wall, and a cabinet. On the right was a shower. The shower wasn't in the bath, it had its own separate glass box in the corner. The floor was tiled and it seemed like the water could just splash everywhere. My gob was just open at everything.

"Whatever happens I am having a shower in there," I says, to my mam.

The bath was huge and tiled in on its own little level so you climbed up a few steps, then dropped yourself down into it. It was next to the window and sitting in it you had a view right over Glasgow. I put the sponge fingers down on the side of the bath. Then I heard my mam again. *Cora, squeeze a wee bit out of a tube, pet—nobody will ever tell.*

I went over to the cabinet. There were all sorts of expensive jars and tubes in there that I hardly recognized. I slipped out of Robyn's dress and dimmed the lights, then took the Immac hair removal cream off the shelf.

It was the kind of thing I used to take for granted. Fulton would zoom round Abbotscraig Superdrug and let me fire anything in the basket—stuff I really needed, and then wee expensive luxury bits I thought might make me happy, like bubble bath with glitter in it or face scrub that came with a wee wood spoon. When you were skint you dreamed of days like those.

I stood in front of the mirror looking thin and corpsey-color with my chopped hair in the half-light. I squirted a wee bit Immac then used my finger to rub it all over my moustache, then did my sideburns and my neck and under my ear where you sometimes had those were-wolf bits. I washed my hands then climbed into the empty bath and looked back out the dark window across Glasgow. I hardly knew how I'd got here but I knew I wasn't letting my wee mam down—I counted out eleven sponge fingers and told myself I'd eat every single one.

32

On a warm Wednesday in the first week of May I got on a train at Glasgow Queen Street and headed back to Abbotscraig. The sun slid through the carriage all the way to Stirling and when I got off there I bought myself a roll and sausage.

I went up the hill then walked in an anxious circle round the shopping center, eating my roll and listening to the Jim Carroll album Pauline taped me, telling myself over and over, *You can't turn your back on everything*. Then I wiped my mouth and walked down to the bus station playing with my hair and made myself get on the 56 to Abbotscraig.

Me and Gunner had spoken again, paid for off my own coins, and when I listened to him speaking away in that same warm voice I was just too tired to resist. When I said out loud for the first time *I don't know if I can stay in Glasgow* my whole body went light. When I told another actual human how much the future worried me it felt like getting changed out of cold wet clothes.

I coiled my earphones back in my pocket before the bus moved. I watched the estates fade out and the sheep and trees begin, and the land became wide and bright, but before I knew it I had fallen asleep. Work had been chaotic and there had been the pub with Pauline and on top I'd done two more babysitting shifts so Judith and Craig could check I wasn't an axe murderer and I felt like spat-out Juicy Fruit.

The window got juddery somewhere after Alloa and I blinked awake and there was the Firth. It was silver in the sun and probably quite pretty if you hadn't grown up staring into it. At Abbotscraig I got off at the Reservoir Road, the stop after the phone box where I dumped the Gillespie boy. The bus rumbled off and I looked out over Abbotscraig toward the hills and in the grassy silence the first thing that filled my head was Kira.

I walked down into the Hellmeadow looking at the golf course through the gaps between houses, wondering for a wee minute what boy's bedroom each of those manky pornos might have ended up in. Then picturing them dangling up there still, all weathered and crispy with the hoolets and the wind.

In front of Jackie's house I held my hand up flat in the spring sun and looked at the scars that Yogi's specs made—a slopey pale Y-shape with a wee white comet shooting out. I wondered how long I'd be carrying those reminders. The lassie on the other end of the arm was already very different.

I crossed the empty street and passed the stumps where the Eldo phone box used to stand, then turned down one of the fenced-in alleys between the houses. Men were shirtless in gardens and all the way down to Weavers Row the smell was the almost-summer stuffiness of baked wood fences and hot weeds sweating to themselves.

Our house was maybe not exactly a big box of darkness but it still had that gray ragey face like it was trying to put the shitters up you. Gunner was in the doorway, waiting, grinning. "What the hell have you done to that hair, lass?"

The grass was neat and the metal gate looked glossy and there was a bird feeder full of peanuts. My mam's ramp was gone. I stepped up the step and gulped a wee mouthful of emotion away. "I'm a trendy city girl now!"

"This what passes for trendy?" He put his hand out and ruffled it and I let him.

He was more healthy-looking than I think I'd ever seen him. If you put a whistle round his neck he might even have passed for a creepy one-eyed PE teacher. I goes, "You not even going to give me a hug?"

He leaned and clamped me in his arms. We hadn't done that many hugs but I could still tell we fitted together different now.

In the living room her records were stacked in a neat pile and he'd got other Muircross stuff out the shed and dotted it round all thought-through and respectable. Everything seemed tidier and calmer without me in it and it hit me all over how weird it was that this man had once looked after me.

We stood like two awkward statues, smiling, then he goes, "Do you want a cup of tea?"

He went into the kitchen and I breathed to let the emotion go. It had only been about twenty seconds but I was still saying *so far so good* to myself. I'd come back because hearing his voice I knew I had to—for my mam, for him, for me. For the three of us, if that was even a thing. Now even the smell of the Shake n' Vac was getting me emotional.

I leaned over—my school photo was on the mantelpiece, the bigger version of the one from his wallet. I stared into that lassie's eyes like I wanted to slap some sense into her.

"Two sugars, still?"

I turned away and walked through. "Just milk please." The kitchen was spotless and he'd bought a fancy light-up kettle. He must have had money for all sorts since he stopped funding my fish fingers. "Place is looking nice," I went.

"Fill my days tidying now. Sad old bastard, like."

I did the eyebrows toward the window like a granny. "Weather's decent."

"You fancy doing a walk later? See the sights!"

"That'd be good." I leaned back against the bench in my vest and folded my arms. "So. What's this news?"

He was ploutering with the teabags. "Let's get our teas first?"

The garden was all the same except he'd dug a flower bed down by the shed and shaky purple flowers were starting to say hello. As we sat on the step I took a burny sip from a mug I didn't recognize.

He told me his news from the hospital, explained how he'd got that ancient beetroot stain off our kitchen bench, said that Donna had told him how nice my room was, and I nodded and smiled and *yes-yessed* and felt like shit. He never mentioned 7UP or fridges once.

Vicki had been to the door twice, asking for me. She was looking all right, doing a STEP course in an office, was maybe getting a paid role in eighteen months. He'd told her I'd be in touch. I did my biggest smile, like there was nothing more important than any of this stuff.

I told him more about being a Saver Local lassie. I explained Robyn and my babysitting shifts. How at first it was like being someone else for a day, then how I told myself, *This could be your life, Cora. You're the grown-up, now*. How it felt amazing to be paid for having fun, the way that being with kids reminded me of being wee too. The subway trips with Alice. Marcus and his tantrums. The evening cinema and the size of the Anderson's bath.

When I stopped I must have been staring at the shed because he goes, "I've sorted through the stuff in there. There was one wee thing, well—I've laid it out for you, up in your room."

"One step at a time, eh?"

He nodded, then out the very corner of my eye I saw him pulling the printouts from his back pocket. I stared into the grass for what seemed like ages, waiting on it. Then he goes, "Aye. So I looked at this," like it was a leaflet about wheelie bin collection times.

I picked my thumb, then stopped. "Is that all you're going to say?"

"I dunno—" He tapped the scruffy folded rectangle against his leg. "It's definitely you."

More than any other feeling I was ashamed. For showing him. For keeping quiet for so long. For being me. For everything. "Aye?"

"It's things your mam told me about. And I've seen a lot of it." His voice went sterner. "How long have you had this, lass?"

I tucked my hair behind my ears. "Since 1994. Remember the nurse who let me sit in her office? Through lunch. Samantha. She gave me it."

"I remember." He looked into the neighbor's garden. "You could have spoke to me. Why have you held on to this all that time without saying anything?"

I tucked my arms together under my knees. "It's hard to admit something's wrong. Some weird thing that nobody believes. And it takes a long time to see yourself different, then probably even longer to explain it to people that know you. Being away from here actually helped." He looked at me and I didn't feel like getting up or moving away. "I've not been in control. Everyone else makes choices. I don't. Other folk look at clocks and make plans and I can't do it. It's hard for me to think before I act."

"And is it getting any better?"

"Not really. It's like you're always tired but you can never rest. You're energized by every little thing, but there's nothing you want to do. You can't remember why you went in a room but you still know every word of the theme to *Ramona* off Channel 4 in 1988. One minute you think you can ride a scrambler, the next you can't motivate yourself to clean your own face."

"We could have spoke."

I goes, "When you're not in control of the wee things, doing your teeth, doing your homework, then when you do manage to make yourself do something it ends up, well, it can be a bit dramatic."

He laughed. "A bit?"

"Samantha said it's not just running round when you're five scribbling lipstick on your mam's wallpaper. It's other things. It stops you—reading, listening, washing. It's not that you forget, you just can't make yourself do stuff. I wake up sometimes and there's this pressure right away, like there are things for me to do, that I have to be somewhere doing them, somewhere away from where I am. There doesn't seem to be any time to stop or think." I went back on my elbows. "Then I rush into another room and say to myself, *Why am I here?* But there isn't anything. You can't do one thing because you're already onto the next. It's a cycle. Sometimes it feels like I'm trapped. Like I can't even look after myself. My thoughts are paralyzed."

"Cora, I only wished—"

"Then the decisions I do make, I get that instant feeling, like, *do it, Cora,* like *this is the best fucking idea in the world.* It usually isn't."

"We can go and get help. The two of us."

I plucked up a dandelion and drummed my knee with it. "Remember Kira-Louise? She was probably the same as me. We only spoke a few times but she gave me some tips. I make lists and I have a tray where I lay my things out. It helps, having wee techniques. And the Walkman, that's amazing, because it helps me switch off the world. I don't know why that helps, but it does."

"Why not get it seen to, properly, like?"

"I'm not changing to please other folk. Not until I've lived a bit."

There was a click. Then Donna's head appeared at her back door. "Cora!" She stepped down into the grass. "Lovely to see you. Wow, your hair!" Her eyes were lit up at me and him sat together. "Sorry. Were you two having a chat?"

Our fence was lowish but Donna had a big parachutey skirt on and it was a bit embarrassing trying to see her hop over it. Gunner slipped the printouts back in his pocket and helped her over, then brought a kitchen chair out. Donna sat down, grinning. There was no trace in her expression of our meeting in Glasgow. That we were keeping a secret together. "Have you been up to see your bedroom?"

"Not yet."

Gunner goes, "Donna's tidied it for you. It's looking braw. We'll get a takeaway tonight, the three of us."

Big pearly clouds were racing over, making shadows. "Thanks," I says.

Then Gunner spoke again. "So, this news."

I did one big gulp because it hit me straight away and I already knew. I felt queasy so I put my mug down. I could hear a lawnmower. A dog was barking over in the park. For some reason it was that, more than any smell or voice or other wee thing, that really brought me back to the boredom and pain of my Abbotscraig life.

Gunner looked at Donna. "When you left, well me and Donna always spoke, but we spoke more after that. So I've you to thank, maybe." He laughed. "You being a pain in the arse."

I looked at Donna. She had her hands clasped between her knees and she was grinning at him. "Okay. Wow," I whispered, trying to do my own big grin.

Gunner looked straight at me. "It's easiest if I just come out and say it right away—me and Donna." They looked at each other again. "I'm glad you came. I wanted us all together for when I told you, like. I wanted things sorted. Me and Donna, we're a couple now."

"How long?"

Donna goes, "Ach, a while."

There was a gentleness in her face I hadn't seen before. My eyes were wobbling. I had a feeling inside, the first feeling in ages that I knew I couldn't force back down, and so I started crying. "Sorry," I says, swallowing, and Gunner leaned over and squeezed me tighter than I ever remembered before. "I don't know what I'm crying about here."

In the kitchen I wiped my face with green hospital paper towels and they stood and told me all about how things had been since I left. Gunner had bought me a six-pack of Lilt for coming and I had a tin of that and it didn't help. Then Donna says, "I've made cake for us, if you want some?"

It was tiring me out how much they were grinning, and the more I stood and listened the more I was feeling old feelings. I wanted to get out of the house and away from her and her cake. I looked at Gunner. "We were going to go for a walk?"

"Oh aye." He turned to Donna and goes, "I'll head out for a walk with Cora," in a kind of whispery playschool *let me sort the brat out* voice. I thought they might do a kiss goodbye so I walked into the living room and picked up my bag then I left.

Gunner caught up with me at the bottom of our road and we crossed over toward the Backy Park without speaking, him doing an irritating whistle, me reading all the new Tipp-ex graffiti on the fences and street signs.

We did a right and turned past that concrete car park where me and Vicki once shared two bottles of flat Diamond White. It was the night that a gang took Eric McPhail down the Mill Loan and done his shins in with a hammer. Vicki had got off with Eric McPhail at the primary seven dance. During "November Rain," she told me, weeping into her cider. It was like every square meter here, around the Hellmeadow and the Deathy and the Mill Loan at least, had a story attached to it.

Gunner shuffled next to me on one of benches up by the slope at the back of the park. I really wanted to speak first. "I'm pleased. But it's a bit much, ten minutes after I've come back. I was trying to speak to you."

"Donna said you might react like this."

"Did she?" I looked out across the park. There were more weeds scrounging round the swing park bit and the info board had been kicked down completely now. A group of boys in hoodies and two-stripe boot sale Adidas were gathered round the bench by the gate, smoking fags.

What was I expecting to find, looking round? My old school tie, flapping in a tree? Me and Vicki's ancient empties? The wee parts of myself I'd left here? Everything had moved on but nothing had changed. I felt like running back to the bus stop.

"She wants to get to know you. It was her idea to go to Glasgow, to try and help us get along, eh. I want that. The three of us."

"You can't expect me to act like this is normal."

"I get it. Look, me and Donna have spoken a lot." He started squeezing his knuckles. "I always felt like the big useless arsehole that turned up and bought you a doughnut and a pair of pink trainers. I was never going to be any use to you until I started to think better of myself."

I tilted my head right back and let my mouth fall open. "You never bought those trainers."

"I bought the doughnut! The point is, lass, I spent a long time telling myself I was useless. And Donna's right, the stuff you tell yourself always finds a way of coming true."

I laughed and folded my arms, my leg was going. "Donna's pumped you full of some amount of shite."

"Well she says to me, *It doesn't work to skirt around*. It's what you said before, it's better to have things out, where we can see them. The shoplifting, the Jo thing. Your mam. There's so much stuff we've never really spoke about. And you're old enough now."

The boys were melting a carrier bag onto the bench with their lighter. I said, "Okay?"

"Back then I was helping a lot of different folk around Muircross, you know, with the lifting. With Jo it started with getting food for her family, then I got sucked in. And I was flattered. I mean, look at me."

"What's this Jo stuff all of a sudden?"

He sat forward and leaned on his knees. "Jo was a right weird one, some of the stuff she got up to. A manipulator. But that doesn't excuse what I did, like. It shouldn't have happened in the house. There's more to it, if you let me explain—"

I looked at him. "Jo was a fucking bully."

"Cora, I'm sorry you saw."

"So am I. Believe me."

He laughed. "I caught her stealing food out our freezer one morning."

My eyes went so big it felt like they might fall out of my head, so I closed them. I could feel my fingers digging into my biceps.

He goes, "It was nice stuff that your mam had bought for you. Those potato croquettes you loved. I says to her—"

I suddenly felt like I was having a power cut. I stood up. "I don't know why you think dragging up the past will make things better!" I picked up my bag and started walking toward the far gate.

"Cora." He jumped up and followed. "Why did you bring that bag?"

"Because I might just go back to Glasgow?" As I said the words a panicky outrage feeling rose up.

"Dealing with all this, you've grown up way too fast—"

"Well I feel fourteen inside right now."

"You ended up shouldering too much responsibility. But I didn't know what else to do. Your mam going affected me too. Just let me explain."

"It's the past. And I didn't want this. Me and you, fine, maybe. But not this."

"How about I come and give you a visit then? To speak."

I was nearly running now. "We've spoken!"

"What will I tell Donna?"

I turned back. I shouted, "Tell her Cora's sick of speaking!" and birds went up, and that last squealy word echoed softly right across the park.

33

I was knackered when I got back to Glasgow. I dumped my bag off my shoulder and knocked on Pauline's door to see if she'd be up for doing something together to take my mind off stuff.

I gave her a minute to get herself decent then I knocked again, which I never did. Then I stood for a second wondering why I did that, and then I opened her door. The curtains were closed but her bedside lamp was on, the red office one with the bendy neck. On her silent telly pensioners were clapping a man who was peeling gold stars off a big blue board.

Pauline was laid back flat on the double bed with her arms out, in a vest, crucified-looking on her tulip-pattern bedspread. Her legs were over the edge with her jeans round her ankles and she was wearing ratty elasticated peach satin knickers.

A topless man I knew from the hallway was kneeling between her legs, jabbing a slim syringe into her groin, holding it like a pen. There were cola-color bruises and dots like the stings off a wasp on the slope by her hip where her leg joined her body. My eyes went soft, just like when I'd seen her da.

She craned her head up slightly like it weighed a ton and croaked, "Jeez, Cora, no." The man never looked at me. I wanted to jump in and help somehow but I pulled the door closed gently with a click and went back to my room instead.

I chucked my bag in the corner then spent twenty minutes crying face down on my bed. Then I got up raging and damp and grabbed my Walkman and keys off my tray again. I put four hoop earrings in because I had to do something quietly and carefully with my hands. I wiped my face with my work shirt and left because even through doors and walls I couldn't be anywhere near her.

Outside I felt rain starting on my new bare neck and as I crossed the road I thought of the old happiness—me and her hauling my bin bags up the pavement back when the branches were bare and the idea of living here with an actual life was a stupid teenage fairy story.

Around the benches there were a load of faces looking for a grave-yard to haunt. I had the Belly tape in and "Judas My Heart" started so I sped up. My legs were still stiff from the bus and the train and I couldn't wait to do an epic soaking walk. I had so much pain in me that I would maybe never stop moving.

On Great Western Road I walked alongside the traffic then I crossed and walked up rainy Bank Street over toward the park. I'd went this route because walking under jittery wet trees usually gave you the feeling that the world really liked you. Rain never really changed much—it just came down. The rest was up to you.

I wondered sometimes why people liked me. Then the more I found out about them the easier it got to understand. Gunner was a hero at first—I couldn't believe he liked me or my mam and I couldn't understand why he was here. Then when I got to know him I realized exactly why we deserved him—a one-eyed shoplifter that was rattling the babysitter. Classic Mowat. Classic Muircross.

Why couldn't there be a middle? Where you liked someone and they liked you and everything was equal and easy and there was no big grotty secret to come out and fuck the lot. Like when you realized your pal was still a spoonburner just like her da and probably only liked you because almost everyone else with their head screwed on had already realized the reality and ran a mile? As usual I got left standing like some pathetic wee gullible bastard lassie. The two of them were taking it and I still couldn't see.

To get to Robyn's you walked the length of Kelvin Way to the fancy tennis courts by the big museum on the other side of Kelvingrove Park. I'd never been inside her flat but I'd walked her home once, the night of the two-for-one sambucas at Mulligans when Graham tried the yard of ale and threw up on his leather-effect brogues. Robyn's flat was probably the only place I had to go.

I passed the soggy churches and at the junction went straight over onto Kelvin Way. The trees gave you shelter here but the pavement still looked fuzzy with jumping droplets, where the rain was hosing down mental through gaps, making a sound like sizzling sausages. After a stompy minute I was in the park, soaked through, thinking *fuck it*.

Kira had been right, there does come a point where you have to accept who you are and start living. That big moment, where you think *I'm not ready but let's jump*—everyone has that moment. I walked by the bridge and down around the bandstand with the heads of the flowers bopping like they could hear my music too. It was coming down in threads now, like tiny wee lasers.

My moment was getting the supermarket job. I couldn't have spent another penny of Pauline's dole money. I probably couldn't have eaten any more Space Raiders for breakfast. I either got a job in Glasgow and earned a living or went back to Abbotscraig with my pickled onion fingers to live under a heap of gray rubble made of the past. And that was never happening.

You feel useless through almost every second of school and now you're going out into the adult world with a tomato sauce moustache praying that people won't see the wee fraud you are. Some days you can't remember what's in your own pockets, you can't hold a conversation without interrupting or humming Wet Wet Wet songs to yourself and you've never once been on time. Now the future you want depends on people thinking you're normal.

Most folk have a mam or a sister or a cousin or a teacher at that big moment. I had a wee pal called Pauline. It wouldn't have mattered if she'd been eating heroin toasties the whole time because just like with Fulton before, nothing was going to change the way she'd made me feel about me. Glasgow helped too. Wandering round with headphones in I got to make sense of stuff for the first time.

School taught you the pH scale and "Frère Jacques" on glockenspiel and the dates of the Beer Hall Putsch, but they never mentioned pals or babies or loneliness. You slid a johnny down a stale banana but who was going to tell you how weird boys were? I'd learned more about life off Pauline than I did off St. Therese. That would always stay true, whatever that idiot lassie was jabbing herself with.

The tennis courts were wet and deserted. It was a downpour everywhere, moving the grass, the branches, smearing big damp dribbles down the side of the yellow tenements.

I rang Robyn's bell. After a wee minute she appeared at the door in her bare feet. "Cora, Jesus. You are like a wet rat!"

"Drowned rat."

"That's it! Come in."

The entrance hall smelled of mice and pencils and it had planks and bin bags in it, but you could tell from the banister and the width of the stairs that the building had been special once.

On the second floor she creaked the big polished door open with her shoulder and I followed her in. I stood there like the helpless thing I was and Robyn peeled my heavy parka off. She looked at me with that face. I just says, "Pauline."

"What now?"

"I came back from Abbotscraig and surprised her. Let's not get into it."

"Stay there."

Her inside hallway was roasting and full of other people's shoes. She reappeared with ancient towels and stood there smiling while I took my jumper and jeans and soaking Golas off. She put everything on one of the chunky radiators then wrapped me in the towels and took me through.

Her living room was right on the corner and huge windows looked out each side over the rained-on tennis courts and the park. The room was lit by four or five yellowy lamps and the carpet was deep red and felty and ripped. It was all short-arse furniture that looked so cozy below the high ceiling, with grumpy-looking bean bags and a big heap of blankets in one corner.

Music came softly from somewhere and when I touched the radiator by the fireplace it was red hot. Like all flats around here her stuff was ancient and unmatching, and when I sat down on her settee it felt dry and scratchy and beautiful behind my knees. I loved the feel of other people's things.

I goes, "What's this music?"

"Lesley Gore. These are my flatmate's records. He is in a band, they have all sorts of strange sixties shit." I must have made a face because then she goes, "It's okay. They're all away. It's me and you." She put her hands in the pockets of her baggy cords. "Do you want to chat?"

"No."

"Drink?"

"Yes."

In the kitchen she shouted through, "I am guessing not tea?" She appeared in the doorway through the long hanging beads with two dark blue tins. "Tennent's Super?"

We cheersed our tins and Robyn pointed round the room telling me stories about things that were hers and the things that weren't, and tales of mad parties and how the downstairs neighbor was eighty-four but actually really sound. The Tennent's tasted like envelope glue but I felt happier just for being there.

After the first tin she sensibly suggested some food then microwaved us two of those wee frozen Chicago Town pizzas. I didn't think Robyn's living room could get any better but when it started smelling like oily pepperoni and burned-on cheese I felt like I had gone to heaven.

We sat for maybe at least two hours until my hair was dry and the Super had done its job. I felt totally calm from record after record that Robyn stood up to change and explain, and the endless unimportant stuff that she wanted to speak about. I knew she was making an effort for me and I let her. I didn't want this afternoon to end because I couldn't face going back to my own lino and discounted cottage pie existence.

I sat up away from her. "Are you free, maybe? Tonight? Usually when something bad happens in my life I just disappear into a wee folded-down heap. So I want to do something."

"Taxi to the Strathclyde Union? It's only six."

"I'll not get in the union."

"I'll sign you in. It's Bubbles tonight. Live a little, you miserable cow. Enough of this money anxiety."

I looked out her window. It was gloomier now and you still heard the rain hiss like a crowd was outside clapping us. If I couldn't walk round all night with my music then I really had nowhere else to run. "Okay, what's Bubbles?"

"Foam party. And I'll treat you to Best Kebab after."

In her room we started on her flatmate's vodka while we did our makeup and hair. Robyn had a big varnished wardrobe full of nice clothes, a big rail of her own stories that smelled like old dry wood and Impulse O2. She'd put R.E.M. on the record player and it was echoing through the airy flat.

She leaned in then chucked a wee scrap of fabric at me from behind the door. "It stretches."

I held the dress up in front of me. It was the size of a face cloth. I goes, "I might be skint but I dunno if I'm ready for going on the game."

It was a pink strapless Spice Girl thing that clung very tight, but when I looked in Robyn's long mirror I actually liked myself. I took a swig of the vodka. "What do you think?"

Her smiley head popped round the door. "It's perfect."

"Not too rompy?"

She downed a huge gulp. "Why would you hide? You look amazing."

In the stuffy warmth of the taxi I began to realize how woozy the vodka had made me. Sat in the back I felt a fuck-off anxiety wave about Pauline dying but I breathed it down. Robyn goes, *Union, John Street, please*, and we rolled off and out onto the main road.

On the steamed window I drew an eyeball with wings, and then a heart with flames, then with a squeak I wiped it all clear with the side of my palm. Outside you saw people in huddles. People alone. Bins and blurred shop fronts and watery brake lights rushing along the edge of the rainy glass—the city flashing like a slot machine. I reached across the fleshy leather car seat and I took her hand.

34

A drawn-out beat was going—a big scruffy jaw-rattler, the kind you knew from being wee, coming from the Fiestas and the Astras with the blacked-out windows, up round the Welfare and the roundabout and the long road out.

I climbed the metal stairs out of the crowd and shuffled along the balcony, doing bump-bump *sorry-sorry* as I squeezed by, nodding, glancing up and out over the tangle of dancers. The foam was mainly in fading heaps round the sides now but the machine in the corner was still pumping out wobbly clouds. Every single student in there had seaweedy hair and bloodshot eyes.

Me and Robyn had danced in the middle for about two hours, making each other foam hair and foam beards and foam horns and downing half-price Aftershocks and pinging bubbles in the faces of bright pink approaching boys. I just loved letting myself go, dancing until I forgot that I even had control. Like the Muircross Fridays with my mam at the social and me and Fiona tearing up the living room rug.

Robyn was still right in the middle with the one or two hopeful-looking guys around her, with her hair flashing, her arms pointed straight above her head and her fingers locked like she was stretching, like some sort of starlet from the olden days. I was tiptoeing in the ruined semi-rancid Golas, leaning on the railing and scanning all the little events taking place around the height of the balcony. Then I saw.

The first thing I felt was at least two feelings at once—a big mental need to run away, and a magnetic pull right toward her. I ducked, almost like a reflex. Then I smiled to myself about the stupidity of doing that and stood up straight. I fixed my dress then turned and walked back down the balcony, moving behind one of the pillars so I could stand and have a nosey from a distance.

I'd lost count of the drinks I'd had since I came in the union, but there had been four Aftershocks, at least. The Super and the vodka was still in me too, but I wasn't seeing things. It was Jo.

She was wearing black silky men's football shorts and an olive-green lace bra. She had a fat gold chain round her neck and hair mascara in her fringe. The foam had made rashes all over her chest and belly and she had love bites up her legs. She looked like a pink exclamation mark.

I felt like leaving. I felt like finding Robyn and going to another bar on another level of the building, or getting a taxi home, or running out into the street and jumping on the first bus I saw. But then, stood there feeling damp and itchy and blootered under the big ache of the lights I thought about my wee mam.

I took one step, then another, then before I knew it I was zig-zagging in and out of the squishy bodies, squeezing round the wet walls until I was right at Jo's back. She was speaking to someone, but I knew that whoever it was couldn't possibly be as exciting as me—back from the dead, in front of her, in Glasgow. All grown up, looking fuck all like a seal in a pillowcase.

"Jo!" I shouted, half-punching her shoulder. The blood was shooting round me with total and utter drunken mischief. "Joanne Fucking Buchanan."

She spun round quick on one heel, like something furry getting disturbed while eating out a bin. Her face was frozen with the kind of fear you saw in folk who were constantly having to avoid people. I was eye to eye with her now.

Then right away the big fake grin. She put both arms out toward me, "Wee Cora!" then clamped me in a slippery CK One hug. I smiled as she stood back and looked me up and down with an expression I knew from right in my depths. "What *happened* to you? You are absolutely stunning, babe!"

"So are you!" I shouted, eyebrows right up, grin on, Fiona's skipping rope pulling my chest forward and my shoulders back. She didn't know where I lived, or who my pals were, or where I'd got my dress. She couldn't take anything that mattered from me now—not with words, not with looks, definitely not from my freezer at seven a.m.

She grabbed my forearm and pulled me toward her, shouting in my lug, "Did I not always say you would suit short hair, babe?!"

I did a wee tilted-head pose and made a cute twinkly face at her like I was hanging on her words.

"You've changed so much, Cora! We must catch up!" she goes, as a big meat-chin guy with an eyebrow ring leaned out from behind her. She turned to him and I heard her shout, "An old friend, Barry. Go and have a dance."

"No, no," I shouted, grabbing her arm now, pulling her in, "you and Barry have a dance, I'll grab us some drinks and then we can catch up!"

"Amazing!"

I turned away thinking how he really did look like a Barry and began squeezing my way back to the stair and down, then round the side of the crowd to the hatch where the drink was sold. The plan landed in my head all beautiful and ready like it wasn't a thought at all. I could hear McClair even now—*Cora's a quick thinker but more often than not she channels her energies into activities unbecoming of her.*

I used the last of my money on two Morgan's Spiced and lemonade then crossed the dance floor in the other direction, hugging the wall, avoiding the elbows, tall glass in each hand. As the strobe flashed round the balcony I looked up and saw Jo and Barry getting into some sort of bitter-looking conversation over something—hopefully me.

I leaned in backward on the big swing doors, careful with the drinks so that none of it sloshed, then kept my head down so as not to start up any wee nodding conversations with the lassies at the mirrors. I slipped right by everyone then reversed into a cubicle and bashed the door closed expertly with my foamy bum. I felt laser-focused. Nothing sobered you up like a plan.

I gulped down half of Jo's in one mouthful, then put it on the cistern. I made a loo-roll beer mat for mine and put it down too. I stood for a second smiling, wondering if I needed to drink more to make the magic happen, but I could already feel a wee distant jangling.

I leaned back against the wall of the cubicle and wriggled my knickers down to my ankles, then I hoicked Robyn's dress up and held the glass between my legs, pressing it right to my body. Music from the dance floor rose and fell as lassies swung in and out the main toilet door. I pictured Jo eating my potato croquettes. Running off with food my mam could barely afford. Bouncing all over Gunner on our settee. Then I relaxed and started pishing.

That second when I let go, but before the pee actually started itself, was so naughty and ridiculous-feeling I just burst out with the giggles. I couldn't stop. I was nearly crying. I thought to myself, *You're a smart wee cookie, Cora Mowat.*

When I'd topped it right up I put Jo's glass on the cistern next to mine, then wiped myself and flushed. I stood up and tugged the dress down over my arse while bending toward the glasses, giggling still, watching the two autumny shades of liquid gently billowing together in her glass.

Out on the floor there were storm noises and thunder. Then the slow piano started, doing three notes over and over. The lights went darker. People started cheering and all over the floor the arms went up, the hugs began, little clumps of foam got batted about.

The lassie's voice started—it was "Set You Free" by N-Trance. That's when I really thought *fuck it*. I started power walking through the foam with the glasses because if there ever was an anthem to make your old babysitter guzzle pish to, this was it.

The beat came in and the crowd below was jumping in the bubbles. The bassline was in me. Idiots with raw faces were doing shapes everywhere. Even the womanless goth boys by the door to the fire escape were howling along like foamy werewolves.

Up on the balcony Barry had disappeared. "Morgan's Spiced and lemonade?" I shouted, over that lassie singer's heart-bursting voice.

"Amazing, babe!" She took the glass and right away a countdown got going inside me. She squealed in my ear, "I always fucking loved this song!"

"Memories, Jo!" I raised my glass. "To Muircross, and my mam."

She scrunched her wee face up. "Aw, Cora!"

We clinked glasses then I goes, "Just a sec, actually." The pure molten excitement was throttling me and I had only just managed to croak the words out.

I couldn't think of an excuse but it didn't matter because I'd never see her again. I turned with my glass and walked away, putting one hand up over my shoulder in that way that says *back in a second.*

As I clomped down the first metal step I did a quick glance back. She was leaning on the railing, moving the glass slowly toward her mouth, locking her long legs in and out in time to the song. She wasn't looking but I ducked again anyway, just for the excitement, then downed a big bit of my own drink and left it on the ledge beside the stairs.

I moved into the bodies and scraps of foam again, letting myself get bumped along and hidden by the crowd. I felt like I'd been plugged into a socket. The strobe had stopped and everything was ultraviolet, and through the heads and the hair I caught Robyn's eye with a thumbs-up She had one of those grins on and did a double thumbs-up back, and I knew she was having fun, so I made my way back out through the crowd and left.

There was a half hour until closing and I had that tired ache from dancing that only chips can fix so I went for some. When I'd finished those I walked back and waited at the door of the union, under the canopy with the crowds of wee shivering rave girls that had started streaming down from the fourth floor looking for taxis.

Out in the road two guys were fighting—the bouncers were laughing between themselves about it, elbow-bumping each other with their hands stuffed in their breast pockets. After a minute the pavement was getting rowdy with carry-on and folk were taking sides, so I pulled the parka tight and began shuffling off with my head ducked down, avoiding the big thunder-drops of rain.

Then halfway down the hill, from the middle of the commotion behind me, a voice goes, "Cora." I turned. She was stood there in the downpour all bandy-legged in Barry's shorts, arms folded tight over the bra, face raging, body glistening in a mix of sweat and foam and rain. It reminded me of that bit in *Jurassic Park*.

"Jo!" I smiled. "Did you forget your jacket?" A wave of the most amazing sexy calm started up inside and I had to tighten my mouth to stop an actual sneer from starting.

There was no point pretending there had been a mix-up—I was halfway down the road in my damp coat, smelling of chip vinegar and spiced rum and Fairy liquid. I wasn't heading back in to have a catch-up about Muircross—I was bolting.

Her eyes were lit up with a kind of insane disbelief—there was no doubt at all that she had drank the drink and guessed the mixer.

Then she shoved me hard by the shoulders and I stumbled back, catching myself in a doorway before I slid down and fell right on my arse. I couldn't stop laughing. She stepped up and leaned in with her hands fisted-up at her sides, all angry-looking and cartoonish.

Her shorts were sucked to her legs, shiny like an eel from night rain, and her legs looked raw and mottled gray with cold, like yesterday's mince. There was a kind of electricity in my throat but I knew that the Aftershocks would get me through. I raised myself up the best I could and tugged the dress then went, "Hit me, you fucking rat."

Then I was on the ground, properly this time, seeing all the wee lakes of rainwater reflecting the stars, like every single puddle was dreaming of the night sky. There was grit in my chin and my arse felt suddenly bony. My left eye socket was roasting and thumping and tight.

Rain was curtaining down round her. "It wasn't all me you know. It was him as well! I was lonely. I was in pain!" She leaned down and screamed, "I loved your mam! When Fozzy went there was nothing that would mend my heart!"

I touched my eye and it felt like a squeezed-out teabag. I stood up and tried to steady myself. Jo had turned and she was already running.

She sprinted up the dark, wet street toward the crowds outside the union—twenty-four years old, long as a toothbrush, still stuck in the dramas she'd dreamed up half a decade ago. I watched her dodge through the huggings and headlockings and all the wee rained-on, wasted sing-songs and as she flung the union door open and stomped back inside I couldn't help wishing that lassie every bit of luck in the world.

lived off discounted red grapes and fruit juice for days, trying to make myself feel iller, lying on my sweaty wee bed checking my purple-green eye each morning in the cracked and haunted makeup mirror that the dead pensioner left behind.

The supermarket was short-staffed and mad and folk were calling me names I didn't get like *Cora Calzaghe*. I dressed in my chilled clothes daily and moped between there and my room and the kitchen at the top with a face like thunder.

I heard rumbling and *The Shawshank Redemption* from behind Pauline's door and saw her toothbrush move and the Kinder Eggs she ate for breakfast coming and going from the fridge. It helped a bit to know she wasn't laid out somewhere mulching completely down to a heroiny skeleton, but that didn't mean I wanted me and her speaking again.

Even more than usual I was jamming my door shut with the café chair. I didn't want her round one night knock-knocking all spaniel-eyed with Bulgarian wine, doing the *Cora, please* routine. I was worried I might even say sorry to her. I always needed things to be right. I had to teach myself to sometimes just let stuff be fucked.

It was real May weather now and when the morning sun came in and heated the lino a kind of Mini Cheddar-ish smell came off it. I got out of bed in my jammies to open the window and when I looked over the road at the square of waste ground, there in the middle of all the usual mingling drunken growlers there was a shape.

I knew the shoulders, the big lugs, his bone structure almost, even from the back. I could see those pale scars on his head that stopped the hair from evenly growing. Those benches were a magnet for all sorts. I shouted before I could stop myself, "Baldy Muircross bastard!"

I ducked down a bit as Gunner turned and stood up slowly. He was in jeans I could picture Donna choosing and he had a carrier bag. He made a visor with his hand and looked up and then he shouted, "Can I come up, chief?"

I peeked up over the windowsill. "What for? And don't say *to speak, lass.*"

A car went by between us. My tummy was going seasick. Gunner looked down the street and back and scratched the top of his head. "For a cup of tea, then. And to help you move those fridges out."

I leaned out properly and shouted louder, "What fridges?"

"Donna and me do a bit of speaking, Cora." He was grinning. Folk on the benches were staring at him now. "Did I not say?"

"Promise you won't mention my lino. Or my eye."

"No issues with a bit of honest lino, eh."

I chucked on leggings and a T-shirt and when I opened the front door I turned my back and started right into a wee tour, just to stop him droning on.

"The bulbs on the landings don't work so watch your step." I pointed down over the banister. "There's two big moany psoriasis bastards here at the back, but other than them everyone's fine. Malc-the-Coupon on the first floor helped me when I had an ingrown toenail." At the top of the stairs I nodded down the hall. "And Pauline's neighbor, Mary, with the Stetson, she always saves me caramel wafers and UHT."

"Which door's Pauline's then?"

"Never mind."

The second floor smelled of beef stew and there was Eagle-Eye

Cherry on repeat again from somewhere. I showed Gunner where the third-floor boys let off the fire extinguisher that night and the room where Sandy kept his dogs, then led him up to the kitchen on the top floor.

He ignored the dishes and the clutter and the smell and walked over to the skylight, looking out. "You gonna explain that eye of yours?"

I started filling the kettle. "Let's get some tea. It took me a tragic amount of time to realize that tea means talking! But not in my house, eh?"

"Here, I brought something."

When I turned he was already sat at the table with his carrier bag open in amongst the mess. Then he lifted out my old Muircross diary.

"Fucking hell." I sat down opposite and he passed it over all careful like a wizard in a film. "I spent hours with this."

"I found it clearing out the shed. Thought it might break the ice, like."

The cover was pink and turquoise with *CMM—KEEP OUT!!!* dug across it in scrapey black ballpoint. It was filled with a million pages of tiny insanely squiggled paragraph outbursts that made the paper all crunkled and crisp.

I opened it randomly. "*Tuesday 11th. Terrys got mam a crystal hedgehog whats he buying her that for!!! Checked Argos catalog—29.99!! Mams got it on window says reflections are spelling things. Beans for tea.*" I laughed. "I remember walking through the tall flats in Muircross looking at bikes on balconies wondering how people who lived in houses worse than ours could buy their kids a BMX. I was always so wound up about money."

"It's called being a kid."

Then as I kept flicking, something flapped out of the diary onto the table. An ancient pressed-flat McDonald's napkin, blotchy from faded barbecue sauce. At the top, above the number, it said *DENNIS WONG (CO-OP GUY)*.

I made a beamer wee-lassie squeak before I had a chance to breathe. "Oh my god! I went on a date. You remember Dennis?"

"That Chinese boy with the piercings."

I held the napkin up to the skylight for a second, waiting for the feelings, then as they came I folded it carefully in half and put it away. I weighed the diary in my hand twice and handed it back to Gunner. "I told you to chuck this shite away."

He put it back in the bag and sat staring at it with a torn lip while I made our teas. I handed him my Maltesers mug and he drank a tiny bit then made that noise old people make after sipping hot liquid.

I sat down again and went to take a drink when he quietly goes, "Cora, I'd have gone to war for you, lass. You and your mam."

I could see my nose-breath doing ripples in the top of my tea. It seemed like he meant it and I didn't know where to point my eyes. "Drink up," I says.

"Cora."

I put the mug down then leaned right back and looked at the ceiling. Someone had done a huge blurry cock there with lighter flame that I'd never noticed. "Drink your tea and say your bit, then go."

"I've not seen your room."

"Donna's told you all about it! I don't need you pair inspecting me."

He smiled then downed his mug in one. "How's about show me where you're kipping, and I'll not speak. No more talking, about anything, at all. Just a quick wee look in painful silence. Then I'm gone. Deal?"

I clicked my door open and went in first and he followed. Stoor was moving in the sunlight. I watched Gunner's face because I knew all its tiny movements, but he dodged around the fridges then walked over to the window without flinching. Then he started speaking. "Donna just says to me, *It's opposite some benches.* I thought I'd sit for a bit—"

"You said no more speaking!"

"—maybe try and relax. I was plucking up courage, I suppose."

I laughed. "Scared of a wee bit smoke damage?"

He turned to me. "I'm not meaning the building." He went to the 7UP fridge and put his hand on the side. "She mentioned about your clothes being in here." He scratched at his eyebrow with his finger-nails. "The big one I dunno, but me and you can get this 7UP thing downstair. I can go first, take the weight. Then we'll sort you a proper wardrobe."

"They're Wullie's. And I'm used to them. I like them."

He looked at me. "Cora, you can't live around this stuff. Fridges. Tables and chairs. It's a right shambles."

"It's mine."

"Till they catch you and fling you out."

"Been flung out before."

He laughed, then tugged his sweater up over his head and chucked it on the floor. "At least let me shift this one into the corner." He put his hands on his hips. "It'll save you dancing round it."

He pulled the tall glass door open and nodded down. I bent and scooped the clothes out the bottom, then stepped back toward the window with every bit of clothing I owned bundled like a ginormous stale-smelling baby between my arms and my chin. Bras were dangling out and I was trying to adjust myself and gather it all and stop the beamer.

"If I tip it back I think I can walk it myself over into the corner, like."

I watched him kind of gently shoulder-barge it a few times, feel-ing the weight of it, rocking it a wee bit, being all sensible and da-like and making a real careful respectful effort. I knew his concentration face, but his expression seemed new. There were wrinkles round his good eye I'd never seen before. It almost felt like I'd never properly looked.

"Why did you come out with that shite about going to war?"

He looked round at me, scuffing the stoor off his palms. "I thought we weren't speaking?"

"I need to know." I squeezed my big clothes baby tighter.

"Well, I couldn't ever sit down and just say it, before. But I've wanted you to understand it for a long time."

"I never understood any of it."

"Like what?"

I shrugged the weight of the clothes up to try and make them behave, and a red sock dropped on the floor. "Why are you stood there now? Wrestling a fridge for me. Why Abbotscraig? Why me and my mam? Why everything?"

He straightened himself and went to speak, then stopped. Then when he did it was like he had five things he wanted to say at once. "I owed your mam." He smiled. "She was there for me."

"Aye, for five whole minutes."

He put his arm up on the glass door and rested his head on it. "She made me swear I'd never bring up our past, because it involves your arsehole da."

My left foot had found a lino bump and had started squishing it down to its own wee beat. "A past?"

"Cora, I knew your mam. Since primary. Jesus, I've wanted to tell you the stories, like. It's been killing me."

I dug my chin in my clothes. "Spit it out, then."

"I loved her right back when we were, what, fourteen?"

He looked me right in the eye, maybe checking for a reaction. I stood there remembering faces and words and places and wanted to crumple myself up in a stale ball and get someone to squidge me tight together the way I was squeezing my clothes.

"When I was in the home, the folk there tried to put me through the school but I got bullied so badly, just for who I was. Your mam got the exact same treatment. I was wild. I was totally lost. She looked after me. That school was cunt city but me and her were some wee team together, eh. *Bonnie and Clyde*, that's what Argyll used to say."

I turned away from him. Out the window some tiny clouds were torn round and the sun was making the sky weird. The benches were empty now. I was hugging the clothes so tight random zips and buttons were poking my chest.

"See the Co-op in Muircross, that used to be a fry-up place called the Old Cross Café. That was our spot. We'd spend every minute we could together. In town, or I'd push her up the benches by the pebble-dash flats. Your mam loved looking over the Firth, just thinking."

I faced him. My lip was going. "What happened then?"

"She had a community care thing, away from the school. They'd do excursions on a bus, beaches and that. She met your da on one of those." He folded his arms and did a massive in-breath. "You okay?"

"I'm okay," I goes, but a wee quiet jolt was already flickering through me everywhere, in my flab and bone and earlobes and knee-caps and all across my skin.

"She made me swear I wouldn't ever mention this to you but the years go by and maybe the meaning of your promises changes. If she saw you here now"—he looked at the ceiling—"I dunno. She'd hope-fully not be too mental at me, eh." He tightened his mouth. I blinked to clear the trembles from my eyes.

"Him and your mam wasn't serious. He fucked off but she wouldn't see me again. She knew she'd made a mistake. You know how head-strong she was. Your mam's pal Agnes told me she was addicted to beet-root, when she was expecting you, and for my last shot I bought her a jar from Fusco's and took it up the road, but she wouldn't see me."

"Right," I says, but it barely made a sound.

"Over the years it softened, and we saw each other in town, at the social, said hello. It was only when she couldn't cope anymore that she rang me up. That's when I turned up with your trainers. I came back, as a pal, like. To help her." He took a step toward me like he couldn't help it and I kept a hold of my clothes. "She was a proud woman. It must have taken a lot for her to ask. It was easier for her to let you think I was just another boyfriend."

I watched my chest rise up and down. My heart was going like a basketball. "What do you mean, *couldn't cope*?" There was a heat behind my eyes and all I could think was how a normal lassie would have dropped these clothes by now.

"You were growing up! She was raising a child—a fourteen-year-old child—by herself. Do you think I did those walks for the good of my health?!" He did a huge grin. "Your mam knew how you were struggling. She wanted to get you out of the house, maybe learn something without the pressure of the school. You had so much energy and there was a limit to what she could do. No money. No help. There wasn't much I could teach you, but I tried, you know? And we fair tired ourselves out, like!"

"I could never understand what you were getting out of it."

"They stopped her benefits, over some load of nonsense. We were keeping the lights on."

"But you shared a bed?"

"We were just good pals. I was single. This is what I was trying to explain when you came to Abbotscraig. You know yourself that times were tough back then in Muircross? And I needed a roof myself."

"You never needed a daughter though."

He winked his good eye. "Still don't!"

"And I threw your lamb in the Firth." There were tears threading down my cheeks now. I was getting emotional over a quantity of meat.

Gunner lurched over to the corner of my room and grabbed a towel from the heap of crap there, then chucked it at me, still keeping his distance. It landed on top of the clothes I was holding. I froze. "That's haunted," I goes, all snivelly.

"Eh?"

"Get it off me. It's haunted."

He screwed his eyebrows together like *what's this lassie on* then walked over and lifted the towel off and flung it back in the corner. He stood there watching me blubbing then he put his arms right around me and all my clothes and gave the entire lump a hug. "You can drop the clothes if you need to, like."

I sooked a big string of slavers in. "The lino's filthy."

He stepped back and gently wrestled the clothes from me as I stood like a soggy statue. He dumped it all on my bed then lifted two of the café chairs from the small stack and arranged them by the window.

He sat down and tapped the seat next to him, and I sat, wiping my snottery nose on my arm. He gripped my kneecap. "It's no easy. In a wee small town everything reflects back on you—you get tricked into believing that reflection is who you are. You carry it all round. Happened to me. Your mam. Maybe you. But here"—he pointed out the window—"nobody knows a single thing."

"That's one of the good bits."

"Your mam took a lot of shit from folk, but she never once apologized for who she was. So don't be carrying weight around—not about me, not about your mam. Chances only come once when you're a teenager, so don't be that wee Muircross girl, that no-quite-sure girl, ashamed of who she is. Your mam would hate to see you stuck down by the past. These memories—it's important you know that stuff. But keep moving, eh? Don't get in your own way, Cora."

"I rang Moira once," I went, in a wee voice. "The psychic Amazing Moira, she was Mam's fave."

"I remember."

I crossed my legs and looked out at the sky going blustery. "I was blootered. I rang her up from the phone box at the Backy Park. To see if she remembered my mam. To see if she had stories."

"What did she say?"

"We can't discuss other clients for confidentiality reasons. I started bashing the handset off the door."

He leaned right over gangly and awkward and put his arm around my back. "See in future, come to me. If we can keep speaking, well— I've got all the stories."

"Good ones, though?" He stood up again and went back to the fridge. He held round the sides then did one more wee shoulder-shove to get a feel for it, then he looked at me all beaming. "The best."

36

We all had glasses of diluting juice. So's not to encourage anything, Craig had said. I stood there in their fancy low-lit
kitchen swilling the Cherries and Berries round, waiting for
him to say his bit. My swollen eye had faded down to a kind of chip
shop curry sauce color. Did he really think you ended up with one of
those from being sober?

He was dashing about in a fancy fleece that looked like it was made
out of Bungle off *Rainbow*. Alice and Marcus were sat all slumped at
the kitchen table, arms out of sight, facing away from their parents.

"It's been a busy few weeks. Judith"—Craig stopped and cheersed
his glass at her—"I know the gallery has been mad in the run-up to the
art fair. And obviously with everything happening on-site it's been a
real nightmare for me." I nodded seriously, like they wanted me to. "I
wanted to get everyone together to say thanks for your efforts. To do
a toast to ourselves." All the air went out of Alice, and she tipped her
head back. "And a toast to Cora."

I woke myself. "Oh?"

Judith spoke for the first time. "Cora, it wouldn't have been possible for us to accomplish everything we needed to do these past few
weeks without you keeping the place ticking over. And all at such short
notice. We haven't missed that German girl at all!"

Robyn rolled her eyes on cue and everyone laughed. Craig goes,

"You've really been a godsend, Cora. From the trial shift forward you've felt like, well—part of the furniture."

Some of their furniture probably cost more than a normal house. I got one thumb fiddling in the label of my shirt. I looked at Robyn. As usual she was calm, existing outside the situation.

"Well, thanks!" I went, sipping the watery juice. My scalp was tingling from awkwardness. I really wanted to tell them to shut up.

Then Craig goes, "Now, hang on a sec," and he wandered off into their big walk-in kitchen cupboard. *Not the sponge fingers*, I was thinking.

He came back with a carton of juice. "Now Robyn says you're a bit of a *Lilt aficionado*." He chuckled when he said *Lilt*. "But as you know we don't do carbonated drinks here, so we got you tropical juice as a thank-you. Silly, I know!"

"Aw, amazing. Thanks!"

He walked round the dining table and held out the carton with two outstretched arms, smiling to himself.

"And listen, there is a reason behind all this, eh, *bonkersness*," Judith went. "Robyn's here because she has some news. A surprise!"

"Yes," Robyn goes, suddenly kind of coming to life at the table like I had before. Alice and Marcus turned their heads to her. "Well," she breathed in, looking swamped in her big mohair jumper, "Craig and Judith already know, but they wanted us all together to tell you, Cora—I won't be working for them any longer." There was silence. "They have decided that they'd like you as their regular babysitter. I mean, if you want to."

Judith was showing all her teeth. "Robyn wants you to have those hours, Cora, and we want you, more than anything, to say yes. The kids would be delighted."

The kids looked bored. Craig started up with his supply teacher voice. "Look, we're totally flexible. If you want to stay with the supermarket, fine. We can work around you and you can work around us. And you know you have the use of our place. We'll be a team together!"

"Oh I won't stay at the supermarket." I smiled at him, the way I'd practiced. Then I turned and says, "How come, Robyn?"

Her voice was all bored. "I have extra modules coming up. Classes. I really don't need the hours."

Craig hoisted his chinos up by the pockets. "We all know that Cora's had some ups and downs in—"

"I'm not going to sit around blubbering because I didn't get a Mr. Frosty for Christmas," I went, kind of keen now to stop whatever this was turning into. Alice was killing herself laughing.

"Ha!" he goes, saying the actual word. Judith was grinning. Nobody knew where to look. I realized I'd brought a nice happy event down to an awkward silence in record time. "Cora, we haven't had a toast yet. Glasses everyone."

I picked at my finger. Then Alice goes, "She wants time to think about it, Dad."

"She'll have time, poppet."

Then Judith went, "Sorry, Cora. You know what dads are like!"

I almost wanted to laugh. Everyone held their glasses. Robyn looked at me and did a tiny shrug and I shrugged tinily back.

"So," Craig goes, "regardless of what she decides, to Cora—in Glasgow!"

We did a toast while I wondered inside if it was possible to kill yourself by holding your breath. Then Craig did the usual surprised-looking glance at his watch, and they were off, clunking things into the sink then doing the stairs two at a time with the kids in tow. Another event they should have been ready for an hour ago.

I sat down next to Robyn at the table and we hugged in the silence. "That was bad," she goes.

"Why do they act like this?"

"Can you imagine if I'd actually kept it a secret like she wanted?"

I walked her to the door and outside on the step she goes, "How long will you let them sweat?" I shrugged. She went, "Good luck."

"Thanks," I whispered, and she smiled, and I clicked the door shut behind her.

I lined their umbrellas up for them and got the car keys out on the hall table as usual. I went through to the kitchen and rounded up the plates and glasses and put them in the dishwasher and started it. I wiped down the benches and the dining table. They had flowers everywhere and one of my jobs was to go around and water those so I filled a jug and started in the downstairs hallway.

I liked the downstairs hallway because the carpet was thickest, and there were no windows and it was almost soundproof. Judith hung lots of paintings from her gallery there—landscapes and paintings of people, and some of dogs and horses and still lives too.

I stopped at the big flower display on the table halfway down. Opposite was a huge square mixed-up landscape in a fat golden frame, way taller than me on the wall. There was water and land, but the painter had used colors over everything—red, yellow, green, blue.

I'd never really looked at it but now I could see it was Muircross. The painter had scraped in squiggly lines for roads and railways, and scratched the names of other places around, like a map—Alloa, Tullibody, Kincardine, Culross, Inverkeithing. But Muircross was right in the middle. He'd painted Riggs—the two big clouds joined together to make a big laughable love-heart shape in the sky.

Out the corner of my eye I saw Judith coming down the hall. I picked up the water jug. She stopped and stood beside me. "You've spotted the jewel in the crown? *Fringed with Gold*. The artist is Baxter Dallachy."

"That's Fife."

"Yes!" She flung her hair back. "The title is a quote by James VI, about the Fife coast, *a beggar's mantle, fringed with gold*. Old Baxter loves that part of the world."

I goes, "There's no gold. I lived there."

"He meant the coal." She did a big sigh out. "Between me and you, Cora, like, Baxter's a cross-eyed cunt." I looked at her. She had a wee cheeky smile suddenly on and her voice had gone all Muircrossy. It wasn't fake, or an impression. She sounded like someone from the high flats. "He's got a weakness for young girls, eh, but his work flies out the door so we turn a blind eye."

"Your accent!"

"Why else would you have a painting of that place in a house like this, eh?"

I stared at her. Her eyelashes were very long. Up close her perfume smelled like Malibu but you knew it was probably fancy stuff that cost a bomb.

I looked back at the painting, with its scrabbly wee brush strokes in all different shades. I'd never seen Baxter Dallachy but I could picture him, right away, all demented in the hedges of Muircross, wearing a waistcoat, with his brushes. In me and my mam's back garden, maybe. Stealing my knickers off the washing line.

"It's bright, I suppose."

She did a big cackle. "It is! Artistic license, I think they call that." She walked up toward the frame and leaned in and pointed to a bit in the middle of the maze of streets. Not every detail was painted in but you could see it was near the waste ground by the old Muircross leisure center. That place was shut for four months when I was eleven because there was disease in the vents and me and Cherie Sinclair's wee sister Lesley used to lift planks off that waste ground and drop them off the concrete entrance ramp at the front. "Now, don't you be telling anyone, but I grew up in a house there, Ferryfield Road."

I says, "Where the newsagent went on fire?"

"My mum worked in that newsagent." I looked at her. I used to sometimes get ice lollies out of that shop. Was her mam the one with the sideburns and the Bart Simpson T-shirt off the market? I didn't want to ask. "I never liked Muircross. I felt trapped. Then I got hooked on my studies and that set me on a totally different path. But I've still got my memories."

"Are seagulls in them?"

She burst out cackling. "You know the Sycamore Park? We used to steal those huge blue rolls of scratchy industrial toilet roll out of the loos there and roll them into the water." Her face lit up. "Did you ever go down the Causey?"

I kept my face straight and looked at her. I looked back at the painting. The Causey was there, a wee greeny-brown splodge. Right away my own memories felt like really precious things, in this city. In this house. In this hall. "I didn't, no. I had a pal that sometimes did."

Then she says, "Are you okay?"

I realized I had been staring into the painting. "I'm amazed—that you've come from there."

"Rule one—write your own backstory, babe." She was back to her art gallery voice. She crouched down and slipped her shiny loafers off, then she was stood all tiny in her tights. "Anyway, I better find some heels for tonight."

I was at the front door when they all came rumbling down. Judith was in the same dress and Alice was matching her. Marcus and Craig both had black suits on. The kids looked so cute. I wondered where it was they were going but I'd learned not to ask about it because when you did they never shut up.

I did my nods and my smile and they grabbed their brollies and keys and coats and they left. It must have been hellish having to go out for a fancy meal on Sunday in those stupid clothes right before going back to school. Did they never just watch *Heartbeat* in leggings and a vest?

The kitchen was pure beautiful silence. I pulled a stool from the breakfast bar over to the bench by the sink. In the food cupboard I took the first tin I found, sweetcorn, then went back and sat down. I used the dimmer to turn the light up then opened the tropical juice and slugged some—soapy-tasting crap.

Then I got to work. I carefully fed the tin onto their electric tin opener. It was amazing. You didn't have to press a button, it just sensed when the tin was in its wee mouth and started buzzing. It did it all slow and controlled and at the end the lid popped off dead easy. I'd wanted to try it ever since I spotted the thing. I couldn't stop grinning. I couldn't stop thinking about my mam.

I got shat on so many times by seagulls when I was wee. My mam or Auntie Janine would wipe it off with the antibac baby wipes then tell me again about how it was supposed to be good luck. The amount of shite I'd had splatted on me I should have been the luckiest girl in at least Fife if not the whole of fucking Scotland.

I always used to think, *Imagine calling me lucky.* For a long time it seemed like the world just wanted to fill me with grime and guilt and plughole gunk. Like I was the center of the universe and everything bad that happened radiated back to a tiny target somewhere under my ribs. But I'd had a mam who loved me and when you got up and got the crisp crumbs off yourself and thought about things properly, life didn't seem so shite.

I was stood there nearly crying soppy tears when the doorbell went. I grabbed the open tin to hide it like a criminal, then I realized the Andersons wouldn't be ringing their own bell. It would be their laundry—Craig's shirts for the week were always brought over on a Sunday afternoon.

I tucked my hair behind my ears and stood up straight so I wouldn't get mistaken for a housebreaker, then I wiped my nose and opened the door.

It was Pauline stood there on the sunlit gravel. She had that cheetah-print coat on with the front open, and her white bony chest showing above the neck of her torn T-shirt. "Hello!" She made a nervous face and looked at her boots then back again. "I waited till they went. You got a minute?"

I glanced up and down the road. "What are you doing here?"

She was tired, but also more beautiful than I'd probably ever seen. Her makeup was perfect. Her hair was shorter. I could see and feel every bit of effort she'd made to be standing there and that was pulling my heart apart but I kept on smiling casually.

"Cora, first off I'm sorry for coming round here. I went to your work. Then I went to Robyn's. Then I came here. Don't be angry. I won't be long. Robyn's lovely, by the way."

"She is."

"We chatted! I showed her Frank. She loved him."

I smiled. "I'll bet."

"I proved I was your good pal when I told her you love the Lilt. And that your middle name's Marie. She didn't even know that herself. I says, *Me and wee Cora go right back to Abbotscraig.* Then she gave me this address." There was a pause and a moped went by, behind her. "Listen, chick, I'm not going over it all. I've been staying with my da for a bit, and we've decided I'm going back to Abbotscraig."

"I thought you came here to get away from Abbotscraig?"

"I did. It's funny how what you need just, like"—she wobbled her head—"flips sometimes? I've got a program, a course. I'm going to stay with my cousin Ken up the Deathy and he's going to help me see it through. And I'm going to speak to Vicki. Sort things out. This time will be different, with support."

"Good." There was a pause and then I says, "I never knew you did abseiling?"

"Aye! See the things you sign up for when you're high?" She burst into giggles and I did too but then I bit my tongue. She looked up at me through her eyelashes. "Will you be back through in Abbotscraig ever? We could meet up, maybe. Like the White Musk days."

"Vicki's coming through here, to see me. She's been round pestering Gunner and all of a sudden he thinks he's the big matchmaker, agreeing to all sorts on my behalf. *You need to keep in touch with folk, lass.* So she's through next Saturday."

"That's sweet of him. Say hi to her."

"I will."

"What's your plan?"

"Put my notice in at the supermarket." I nodded back toward the house. "Make a go of it with these freaks. I dunno, maybe all the things we ever spoke about. Find a proper room to live in and have a wee life that my mam would be proud of."

"She'd be proud right now."

I laughed. "You never knew her."

"Well, I'm proud of you." There was a smile then it died quick. She breathed in and looked down again at her bashed red boots. "Cora, it'll be out my system in no time."

Stood there, I had mainly questions. How long and who she was and what was real and what wasn't. But words off her couldn't really make a difference now. I stepped off the step and I hugged her. She smelled like ointment and sleep. "Good luck, Pauline." She was gripping me. "I need to go back in. I'll see you soon."

She smiled as she let me go. "Not if I see you first, chick," and as I stepped back and nodded and shut the huge door the last thing I saw was the brightness of her boots in the gravel.

I'd learned in moments when you got sucker-punched it was best just to sit down and let it wash over. I put the telly on and curled up into the huge armchair. I was wishing it was a month ago. I'd have had Pauline in here—we'd have been up dancing on the kitchen bench and guzzling Judith's wine.

Then I thought. I went back to the front porch and got my bag. I clacked through the few tapes I had and then I found it, at the bottom. I clicked the living room telly off and put the Lena tape in their big spaceship stereo and when I pressed play her beautiful voice filled up the building top to bottom.

It was "Somebody Should Have Told Me." Probably my mam's favorite. The thing about wee Lena is that it was emotional and embarrassing right at the same time, so it made you feel weird and amazing just listening to it. It was old dancey beamer music, like something off a crappy Sunday Disney film, but my mam had really loved it.

I couldn't sit back down with the drama coming out the stereo. I went back through the kitchen, grabbed my spare key off the hall table so's not to lock myself out, then went out onto the drive. I checked and when the coast was clear I closed the door behind me and carried the tin of sweetcorn over to the park across the road.

My mam had died and her story had stopped unfolding and that was something you never thought about for a minute—that life is a thing, a story that unfolds and you are somehow in charge of it. I was supposed to be in charge of mine right now. Without my mam. Without anyone, really.

By the gate I emptied the tin so there was a wee yellow mound for the pigeons to eat, just inside the wrought-iron fence of the park. I crossed back over and sat on the wall and waited. I touched around my eye and the pain had gone and as I sat there doing a few casual wee hip exercises a squirrel appeared.

He did that squirrelly thing of moving in stages along the railing toward the sweetcorn like a wee paranoid thief, maybe knowing someone was watching. His wee heart must have been pounding with pure ecstasy when he got to the pile. He started picking the bits up one by one and having a munch. He'd probably never seen so much grub in his life.

When I was nine I did actually want to be a squirrel—racing round railings all mental, styling my tail, eating pinecones and cheeseburger gherkins off the pavement. Speed and free food and freedom. I dreamed of being small and beautiful and perfectly groomed with cool hair and cute teeth and loads of branches to sleep on. And there was fuck all wrong with that.

The shame I used to feel about things still made me angry. Shame was just a cheap badly fitting neon ski jacket with a broken zip that you had to go round wearing forever, making you a flat-chested hunch-back, reminding you of the past. Reminding you of the person that other people thought you were. It felt like day by day I was finally managing to grind that shitey rusted zip down a bit at a time and that maybe soon I'd wriggle out completely. I stood up and watched my wee mate nibbling for one more minute, then I waved him bye and crossed the road. I made a game of following my own prints back over the Anderson's gravel and went back to the music inside.

37

It was probably only a year since I'd last spoke to Vicki Conroy but it felt like a lifetime. Gunner had told me she was nearly in tears one time coming to the door, so I gave in and rang her. These days it was like I had a big red flashing Batphone to the past.

Vicki was a different person now, but I was never going to say that to her face. It was the same lassie—the tiara of half-curls, the tumble-dryer smell when you got up close—but she'd been taken apart and put back together different by everything that happened. You saw the seams now.

"You got a corkscrew?" she went, looking up from faffing with the first bottle.

Our eyes met and even in the dark I noticed the weirdness of her new lip liner. The way she knew that I'd been staring. "Corkscrew?"

The Andersons had a big store of wine in their laundry room that they got given by clients. It was Judith that called it *the swill heap* and told me I could help myself whenever I wanted.

I'd never drank much wine before but I'd estimated three bottles for Vicki and me's reunion. I'd met her off the subway and we'd walked round weirdly trying to make it feel like school blazer days, looking at the park benches, thinking about maybe a pub. Eventually I just says maybe there's a rooftop?

We'd had to scout around but that was good because it let the sky go dark and it gave me time to explain about my work and Jo and Robyn and my eye and my hair and my room and my haunted Sanyo boombox, and she explained all her things too. We never mentioned Pauline but I knew that would change when the wine came out.

We ended up down a cobbled lane that came off the bridge, opposite the Kelvinbridge Subway station. It was a wee extension bit at the back of a big brick warehouse and from up there you could look over the Kelvin as it came out under the bridge, all frothy and brown like Coke. Once we were up it felt amazing. It was like before, almost—our own wee private room of sky.

I was laughing. "I laid a corkscrew out but I've forgot to bring it."

She squatted in her jeans and boots, holding the bottle from its base like a club. "I'll knock the top off." She swung the bottle down on the brick ledge behind us and there was a hollow splitting sound as it broke in two, and all the wine splashed out, leaving the spiky base of the bottle in her hand with about a mouthful in it.

She emptied the wine dregs into her mouth. "Job done," she goes, amongst the giggles. When we laughed together it was like rewinding time.

I pulled the second bottle out. "Let's try again." My own voice still sounded strange but I knew we'd get comfy eventually, in the old way, like we were back lying about our dates of birth and pacing ourselves. She took the top of the neck off second time and passed me the cold bottle.

I thought of the perfect blue-gray afternoons in underpasses, up on the steps of clanking metal fire escapes. The nights on rooftops. Some of the shite we drank. Sat there I couldn't work out why I'd been so scared to look back at everything.

I took a swig, pouring it in my mouth without my lips touching the broken neck. I goes, "To making do, as usual!"

I passed her it and she drank some. "Making do." She sat down and wiggled back against the wall and I followed.

"We can't really do a cheers, but cheers," I went, and did a crap thumbs-up.

When she smiled I saw the little marks around the curve of her chin, from the plooks she had two summers ago. She says, "I'm pleased for you. Escaping."

"Drinking wine like a grown-up."

"It tastes like cider." She held the shardy bottle up. "Vee-og-nerr? So what these posh folk like?"

"They do a lot of grinning."

She handed me the wine. "How's wee moany arse fitting into that?"

"I'm taking their money off them, Vicki. I'm not turning into one."

"Bet your wee flatmate's jealous?"

I looked at my reflection all slanted in the greenish bottle. "Never see her really. Her and me had some mental times, though. And she's told me loads. Weird stuff, awful stuff." I took a glug of wine. "Like, I never knew you found her mam!"

She took the bottle. "I never found Auntie Janey. That's not true. Pauline came back from school and found her on the pavement." She sighed and took a drink. "Cora, it was her that told me, years back, *Vicks, don't go becoming a wee cog in drama created by men.* I never forgot that, because that was the life of my gran and my mam and her mam and her. Then when I got the termination she never even picked up the phone. There's up and downs with her, but she's no a bad lassie."

The sky was browny-black with no stars and there was a nice wind as if we were out somewhere grassy with trees. I nodded and did the eyebrows but I wasn't going to keep on about it. I says, "Gunner came through."

"I met Donna when I went to your door."

"They're speaking about moving." I heaved my legs up, put my chin on my knees. "She can get a transfer to a hospital down south. Her brother lives there, in some town."

"How you feeling about that?"

I thought for a second then I goes, "It'll probably never happen. What else?" I tipped wine into my mouth like it might make words come. "Gunner says you're applying to the Muircross Heritage Center."

"Four-forty an hour! All you do is put an anorak on and roar at tourists. Amanda McNicol's already working there. Says it's a piece of pish. There's a travel scheme for the bus fare."

"Fucking hell, remember Amanda McNicol?"

There was awkward silence again. Vicki put the bottle down next to her and folded her arms. "The way things ended up at school. It wasn't your fault. You know, after the dancing, with Kira."

My mind spun slowly trying to dredge it all up, but I'd forgotten half the names. I scratched my forehead and squidged my eyes but I had to just say it. "Me and Kira—it's probably going to be easier if I say all this at once. When I say it all at once—well, you'll know why I say things all at once." I listened to the river and the traffic then I goes, "I've been affected by this thing. Like, I'm hyperactive."

"Eh? Fuck off."

"It's been years. Forever."

"You don't seem—"

"I didn't believe it myself for a long time. But I realize now. When I look back over everything"—I laughed, to stop my voice wobbling—"it's not been easy."

"Kira-Louise was a right weirdo." She took an awkward sip.

"Ach. I don't regret me and her dancing, but I never thought it through. The impulse was so big there was nothing I could do but act. Same as when I got down off the roof to speak to Fulton. Same as loads of times. Sometimes it looks like bravery, sometimes it's just stupidity. No control either way."

"Sounds terrible."

I looked at her and let myself smile and in a blink the thought appeared that maybe I'd lived with myself long enough now to not hate the things I said and did so much. "I wouldn't say terrible." I sipped the wine. "At first you just grow up thinking everyone's the same as you."

"And they're not."

"No."

"Well, you don't seem hyper but you're defo mental."

I laughed and looked down at my leggings, plucking at the bobbles. "I'm sure Kira was too. I've actually spoken to someone about it, I started last week. A clinical psychologist. Me and Gunner only properly made up about three weeks ago. He wore me down, so I went."

She laughed. "Sounds pricey."

"I've been saving. Gunner's helped. And see when someone hands you a fifty-pound note and tells you *take the kids to the pictures and keep the rest*? You know you've found your dream job." I took a drink. "Anyway. I never knew a place as full of cunts as Abbotscraig."

"And are you still sending stuff to Fulton? No doubt that's because you're hyper?"

I looked at her. "You and Gunner must have had some cozy wee chats."

"He said you went all pink when you admitted it." She crawled over to my bag and got the third bottle. She started hitting it on the ledge the same way. "Sending him telly programs on tape?" The bottle broke near the top again and she put it down between us then spread out on her back with her knees bent and the Filas flat.

I lifted the bottle and drank. "A lassie like me was never going to be able to sit and speak into a tape machine and keep herself sounding cheery, like. So I thought I'd tape the telly. But he's had his last parcel off me."

Then over the river suddenly sirens started, and a police car came out between two buildings there. We both got down, on autopilot, lying sideways on the damp gritty roof. There was blue light over everything.

She goes, "Is that for us? We're not doing anything wrong."

"I think we probably are." Two police jumped out of the car and went into one of the blocks of flats to the side of the station. "We're like a pair of fugitives here." When the door to the flat shut I shuffled up and sat cross-legged. Vicki moved on her back.

We sat there in silence watching the blue light bleeding through the trees like we were waiting for a sign—to be rained on, to be caught, to be split apart by lightning. To be given the answer to something, from somewhere.

"Fulton's out in a fortnight," I went. I scratched at my forehead again even though there was no itch. I took another gulp. Tapped the Golas together.

She went up on her elbows. I couldn't look but I knew she was freezing me with the Conroy eyes. "Serious?"

"He's a silly wee laddie, Vicki."

"He'll want to see you!" she goes, all pained. She waited for my words, then when there was none she looked away. "Your life, I suppose."

"It is."

Over the river two men were being led to the car by the policemen, shouting bastarding this and that. Then she spoke. "Just don't go in any phone boxes with him." I stared straight out over the water, at the policeman writing something in his book as he leaned on the roof of his car. There was silence, then she goes, "What you thinking about?"

"Praying for rain. We need some drama drizzle up here." I watched her laughing, with the bottle at her mouth. I wondered if the rain came now in tiny pecks, would Vicki want to move? Would she still be up for getting drenched out here beside me, like when we were young?

I took a swig and when I gulped it I knew I was nearly wasted. I goes, "I'm going to visit my mam." It felt so easy to say on a dampish roof in the dark, a million miles from reality, but that was the whole point of climbing up in places like this with your pals.

"She'll be pleased."

"Then I'm going to enjoy myself. Maybe think about college or something."

"What about the supermarket?"

"Putting my notice in. I've never written a serious letter before."

"Record it on your haunted boombox!"

My eyes went so big I hiccupped. "Vicki Conroy, you fucking genius!"

"What's the pervy manager called again?"

"Graham."

"Like this, *Right, Graham, you fucking rotter.*" She fixed her collar and pressed an imaginary record button and leaned down low like there was a stereo there in front of her. "Graham, Mr. Graham, wee Cora has had enough of your nonsense. She's single aye, but look, we both know she's way too good for a dafty like you. She's saving herself. So you can do one."

"He's not actually done anything."

"So?"

I leaned in. "Dear Graham! I'll keep it short. It's ten o'clock, and"—I went into a little whisper—"I think the police might be after me!" I burped.

"Wee wonky-eyed Muircross fugitive on the loose."

I held the bottle straight above my head and watched the police light turning the green glass blue. My head was spinning. "Just getting our fresh air, Chief Inspector."

"An evening picnic, Chief Inspector."

There was a crackle from the roof as I shunted myself across the grit, hauling at my waistband to keep me decent in the dark, eventually feeling the shiver of her shoulder right against mine. "Cora's been having a think," I went, and burped. "Actually, first I want to thank you for so many dented dinners. For saving me from starvation."

"But she's got no need for you now, Graham."

"Growing up my mam told me Santa couldn't find Muircross. I'm a bit of a noodles and bus exhaust kind of girl—but that's just me."

Vicki whispered, "It's not *This Is Your Life.*"

"I wanted to give you a big explanation but I should sign off now

because my wee best Abbotscraig pal will be away for her train soon."
The bleary blue light kept swooping. All you could smell was leaves
and spilled wine and air off the river. "Lots of love? Best regards? Off
you fuck? Anyway, this is my notice. Signed—"

I paused, practicing my name inside over and over again, loving the
sound, feeling all the beautiful weight of the flat wine on my fizzy brain.

"Signed, but with her drunken voice!" I leaned right down. "With
my own wee voice—" I went, and when my words died off you heard
the water again, the traffic, the buzz of all the lives separate to mine—
"signed, with my own wee voice—*Cora Mowat*."

MUIRCROSS, JULY 1998

We walked together up to the new safety fencing that stopped you going near the water. All the bin bags and rubble and heaps of crap had
disappeared and yellow signs had been stuck in the ground along the
bit where the lamb went over. They said *Danger of Death*.

For a wee minute we just stood there under the seagull sounds. I
looked him up and down as he tried with his palms to make his fringe
stop floating in the wind. The piercings and eyeliner were gone and he
was taller and I couldn't get over how handsome he looked in a suit.

I goes, "Dennis, remember you swore to me you'd never stop being a goth?"

He flicked his head and turned. "Remember you said you'd never
come back to Muircross?"

I looked out at the Firth. "Where do you think that water's been?
Has it just sat there waiting on me while I've been away? Going all out
of date? This place smells exactly like it did in ninety-four."

"Well, the Firth's an estuary, so technically there will be convection
currents and wind-driven currents, which both—"

"I'm just meaning is it the same water, Dennis?"

"Going round and round?"

"Aye."

"It would explain the smell!"

We crossed back over the churned-up Causey, past the sleeping diggers and brick stacks and the big sign, to where he'd parked his car. It was amazing that he'd come on his lunch break at such short notice to give me a lift. He worked at a fancy estate agent's, but it was cute how he still lived at home with his mam. I didn't ask him what had happened to all his dreams.

I took one last look at the sign while he started the engine. The writing was swirly, like on decent biscuits—*COLLIERS GROVE. A NEW HISTORY AWAITS.*

There was a big computer graphic on it, of a kind of cleaner, make-believe Muircross, with real blue water and Riggs gone and no trolleys or tramps anywhere. The Causey was all covered in big digital rectangly cream-color houses with orange tile roofs and patios.

Underneath it said, *1 & 2 Bedroom Bungalows, artificial pitches and a community hub. Only a short drive from the A985 and the Forth Bridge, Colliers Grove presents a rare opportunity to combine local identity and industrial tradition, with stunning views across the Firth and outstanding transport links to the whole of the Central Belt.*

At the bottom there was a photo of a grinning councillor and a big quote from him about hardworking people. The bottom half of his face was enormous, like a mumps-face. Did adults get mumps? Maybe he was the first.

We drove up through the town and onto the back roundabout, nice and sensible, then along the new road to the heritage center.

The four glass pyramids were huge close up, and greenish already with old grimy rain streaks. The queue outside snaked right back and the car park was hoaching. Heaps of ancient Americans rolled out of coaches in their chinos and caps while seagulls shat on them from above.

"If I wasn't on lunch we could have gone in for a look."

"Queue up to learn about rust and rubble?"

"Ah, but did you know there was actually a coal mine in the water here, circa 1610? They've done a brilliant scale model."

I screwed my eyes up and pointed my finger on the car window toward the Americans. "Aye, but will they learn about the floating lamb, circa 1994? *Darleen, this is incredible!*"

"They'll need wee waxworks of you and me."

I laughed. "Can we keep moving? I think you can drop me at the cemetery now."

We went round the big roundabout again, then out past the high flats. When we stopped at the traffic lights with the windows down I could hear the gulls arguing, bus horns, boys playing football—sounds of another Muircross day that would have had me in it if things had been different. It made me think for a minute, of when I was wee. When the world spun slower and my blood type was Lilt and all I needed from life was a love bite. All that was out there still, but different, and for someone else.

We went out beyond the brand-new Asda market and onto the coastal road. Fences and pylons flicked past. A sun-faded bus stop with a melted bench and crushed cans flashing in the grass around it.

"It's a braw day for it," he goes.

"It is!" I took the old napkin out of my bag and held it up in the sun. "I'm too old to believe in signs, but I did get a wee shiver when this turned up. Took me right back."

"I can't believe you finished all those fries."

I looked out the window as chunks of gray housing smudged by. "You were so brave that night."

We did a right and traveled down a track between yellow fields for a minute or two, and then I recognized the road. We dipped under the old railway bridge and pulled in by the noticeboard at the far side of the car park.

"You sure you don't want me to wait?"

"You'll be late. And I'm going to walk back into the town. I've got my headphones."

I stepped out and saw the empty red-ash car park, the crackly path that took you up the hill to the tiny wee walled-off cemetery.

"Well, Dennis Wong. It's been lovely catching up."

"Thanks for the coffee."

"I owed you. For three large fries, at least."

"Well, any time you're back."

I leaned in and hugged him. I says, "I'll ring you, I will," and when I stood up again I felt a real wee bit of emotion. We'd only known each other back then for a few weeks but everything counted for more when you came from the same place.

He nodded and pulled the door closed. The wheels crunched and the car went and then everything was suddenly quiet. I crossed the car park and started up the long path, listening to the sound of my Golas.

Her grave was three along from the wall in the far corner, right where Gunner said. It was a small shiny marbly-peach heart with *Margaret Catherine Mowat* and her dates in gold. I says, "Hello, Mam. I'm here." Then I laughed at my own stupidity and got myself comfy in the grass.

When I was four I wet myself in the Muircross Somerfields—the creep off the fish counter with the cauliflower ear had to help my mam wipe up the puddle I made. I was wearing my new Snoopy boots that day. My mam put baking soda in them to try and make the smell go but they were ruined and had to be binned. It was hilarious to her. She told that story all the time.

Years later me and my mam were in that same supermarket. It had turned into a Kwik Save but it still had that same creep working in it. I always recognized him because he had screamed at me once for trying to shake hands with a crab, but he didn't know me at all. Then that day he hands my mam her haddock in a bag and I remember, he turns and he says to me, "No wee accidents today then, Cora?"

I was nearly a teenager! My ears were pierced! I was about two foot taller with longer hair and I had my brand-new slouch socks on. I looked at my mam with my face burning hot because I couldn't believe he remembered me. And how did he even know my name? It was classic Muircross, and my mam just laughed along. *Pee-the-bed, pee-the-floor, pee-the-whatever.* I was a total joke to her.

Out in the car park I just says it. "Do you know why I really hate Muircross? Because round here I'll always be that lassie with the mam in the chair."

She never went mental. The main reason I remember that day is because she never went mental. She was smiling, she wheels herself round and goes, "Cora, one day you'll stop blaming this place for everything. Then maybe you'll stop blaming me too."

I brushed the dried grass off her wee marker then I lay back flat. The summer sky looked silvery and massive and just about cloudless. I goes, "You were right, Mam."

Down the slope, beyond the other stones, the sun was turning tiny diamonds all over the Firth. I lay for a wee minute finger-snipping the grass, feeling stupid for speaking again, but feeling calm.

Then I laughed. "Do you know, Mam, when someone dies all anyone tells you is to speak?" I cleared my throat. "Gunner and me—we're going to be all right. And he told me all about you pair! So those days don't seem so weird to me now."

A plane went slowly over, then a bee came, and I watched his fuzzy bum bounce round the grass.

And before I said another thing there was a feeling that I had no need for words. That she knew I couldn't come before. That she could see me here, now.

A NOTE ON ADHD IN THE UK

In 1990, there were forty children in the UK receiving medical treatment for the condition known today as ADHD. By the end of that decade, the number had risen to three in every one thousand children. Persistent skepticism surrounding the condition meant that ADHD was not recognized by the National Institute of Clinical Excellence until the year 2000.

ACKNOWLEDGMENTS

Love and thanks to my mum, dad, and sister—for your support down the years, and for so many laughs. I owe you everything.

As a teenager I was fortunate to encounter a wonderful English teacher—thank you to Margaret Lee, in whose class I discovered how writing felt.

My thanks to Anna Jean Hughes and Eleanor Penny for feedback on the manuscript, to Annie who leant me her flat for a week of writing, and to all at Creative Future, New Writing North, Curtis Brown Creative, and Spread the Word for support during the writing process. I am very grateful to David Peace for his advice and encouragement and to Michael Sheen for his commitment to the written word.

An enormous thank you to my agent, Sophie Lambert, for understanding this story from day one and being the best guide an author could wish for. Huge gratitude to Gráinne Fox at United Talent Agency for her magic, and to Alice Hoskyns for her assistance and input. Francesca Main helped shape this manuscript with skill, wisdom, and generosity and I owe her a great debt.

Tara Parsons—thank you for your faith in me as a writer, and for opening my eyes to the power of storytelling all over again; you have made my dream a reality. At HarperVia I would also like to thank Alexa Frank, Ashley Yepsen, Laura Gonzalez, Emily Strode, Mary Calvez, Stacy Silnik, Stephen Brayda, and Yvonne Chan.

Above all, my thanks to WMC—for before, during, and after, and without whom there would be no book. I love you.

ABOUT THE AUTHOR

Tom Newlands is a multiply neurodivergent Scottish writer. He is a recipient of a London Writers Award and a Creative Future Writers' Award. In 2021 he was selected for New Writing North's "A Writing Chance," which aims to showcase the most talented British writers from underrepresented backgrounds. He lives in London.